THE BULAWAYO BOYS' CLUB

L. T. KAY

MJB

To Maggie
With my love and thanks for your continued support and
encouragement that enabled me to write this book

Acknowledgments

I am indebted to all those who helped me in writing this book. These include my beta readers who comment on grammatical and structural errors that have slipped through the net.

Also, my thanks go to Melody and Russell for their line edits, picking up several small omissions and typos.

I especially want to thank Maggie, my editor-in-chief, who read and re-read the manuscript several times, pointing out typos and other errors affecting the flow of the narrative.

Any remaining errors are entirely my responsibility.

Finally, I wish to thank you, the reader, for taking the time to read this book. If you notice any typos or errors of fact, no matter how small, please let me know through my website or my email address ltkay@ltkay.com, so I can improve the reading experience for those that follow.

L.T. Kay

Find out more at my website https://ltkay.com

The quickest way to help someone stop worrying about a problem is to give them a much bigger one.

L. T. Kay

PROLOGUE

Zimbabwe – Summary of Events to July 2013 Elections

For most of Zimbabwe's citizens, the Mugabe regime was a disaster. For a few, it proved an opportunity. In Zimbabwe, the government bigwigs and the corrupt saw an easy path to riches. For others, like George Drake, who moved to Australia, the international business world opened opportunities beyond anything Zimbabwe could have supported. He and a few of his associates took the road to significant wealth.

The Ndebele were first to feel the sting of the Mugabe regime. In early 1983 Mugabe sent the North Korean trained 5th Brigade into Matabeleland on a five-year genocidal campaign labelled the Gukurahundi. The pretext of dealing with criminal dissidents was a cover for a blatant attempt to create a one-party state. Various observers estimate the brutal rampage by the members of the Shona brigade led to the massacre of twenty thousand Ndebele civilians. The remaining sections of Zimbabwe society continued their daily lives in blithe indifference.

Next, the white commercial farmers experienced the true nature of Mugabe's regime when the dictator encouraged their forced and violent eviction from the land. White farmers and their black farm workers were beaten or killed if they resisted the land grab. The mindless farm invasions displaced seven hundred thousand black farm workers and saw the economic ruination of the country.

A land reform programme, aimed at transferring white-owned land to black ownership, began in 1980 when the interested parties signed the Lancaster House Agreement. The UK government agreed to pay half the cost of land sold by willing sellers to willing buyers. The United States also offered financial support for the programme.

In the late 1990s, Tony Blair's Labour government reneged on the deal, and the Mugabe regime responded by encouraging the eviction of white farmers, without compensation. The rot set in from February 2000 when the Zimbabwe National Liberation War Veterans Association (ZNLWVA) organised people to march onto white-owned farms and seize them by force. This became known as the Fast-Track Land Reform Programme (FTLRP).

While far from ideal, Zimbabwe progressed in its first two decades of independence from Britain. Before the FTLRP, the white commercial farm sector employed 30% of the paid workforce and accounted for 40% of the country's exports. Over the next nine years, the farm invasions crippled the country. Zimbabwe, a former maize exporter, needed to rely on food aid, which it distributed to supporters of the governing party. Export crops such as tobacco, coffee and tea were the worst hit, resulting in a shortage of foreign exchange. The dire consequences saw the slide of the country's currency into hyperinflation and the later abandonment of the Zimbabwe dollar in April 2009.

Many of the displaced black farm workers were never resettled and ended up in slums on the fringes of Harare and other centres. Unsurprisingly, they became supporters of the opposition MDC party led by Morgan Tsvangirai. In early winter in May 2005, Mugabe ordered the Murambatsvina, a campaign to bulldoze the houses of the slum dwellers. Once again, many thousands were homeless.

Election violence started in 2000 and reached a peak in 2008. It followed the loss of Mugabe's year 2000 referendum which aimed to give him two more terms in office, grant government officials immunity from prosecution, and authorise the seizure of white-owned land.

Now, thousands of Shona also suffered, opposition and government supporters alike. The population exploded from seven million in 1980 to almost twelve million by 1996. Then, because of the large numbers fleeing the economic disaster, it plateaued until 2008-09 when the Zimbabwe Government of National Unity came into being. Young people knew no different regime to Mugabe's dictatorship. For them it was a normal situation.

In March 2008, Mugabe signed into law the Indigenisation and Economic Empowerment Act. It required foreign-owned companies to offer at least fifty-one percent of their shares to indigenous Zimbabweans. Foreign capital fled the country as did the remaining business expertise.

In the short period from the turn of the century to February 2009, Robert Mugabe and his Zimbabwe African National Union - Patriotic Front (ZANU-PF) regime oversaw the disastrous decline of Zimbabwe.

The country was violent and politically unstable, and the currency worthless. The politicised army and police force couldn't be trusted, and incompetent and corrupt officials ran government departments and authorities. There was no tap water in Harare, and the city suffered constant power cuts. A cholera epidemic raged, caused by poor sanitation and the lack of garbage collection. To make matters worse, there was a shortage of chlorine to treat the water. The country's health system was in a state of collapse with essential medicines scarce or unavailable. Zimbabwe was in economic meltdown, and Zimbabweans fled to neighbouring countries and overseas to escape the crisis at home.

Mugabe refused to accept the results of the July 2008 elections, and months of violence and unrest ensued. In February 2009, pressure from neighbouring countries and other members of the Southern African Development Community (SADC) forced Mugabe into an uneasy coalition called the Zimbabwe Government of National Unity. Morgan Tsvangirai, leader of the opposition Movement for Democratic Change (MDC), became the prime minister, while Mugabe hung on to the presidency. The real power stayed with Mugabe, but the opposition improved Zimbabwe's image overseas and with it, the economy.

The Zimbabwe Government of National Unity lasted from 15th February 2009 to 31st July 2013. During this time the country went through a period of relative stability. Conditions in the country improved, though still well short of the circumstances that prevailed in the first two decades of its existence.

In the July 2013 elections, Mugabe and his party won a two-thirds majority in parliament. Mugabe was back in complete control, unhampered by Tsvangirai and his MDC opposition. Once again, there were accusations of electoral fraud and manipulation. Many people feared the country would return to the dire circumstances that preceded the Government of National Unity. Even more Zimbabweans fled the country, but others stayed and resisted the decay.

The Northern Ndebele people of Zimbabwe's south-west saw how the regime treated its own Shona opposition and held little hope there would ever be a Zimbabwe government they could accept.

The Ndebele, a proud offshoot of South Africa's Zulus, could not forget the atrocities of Mugabe's genocidal Gukurahundi campaign. Some Ndebele, or the Matabele as the whites preferred to call them, considered the prospect of Mthwakazi, the kingdom ruled over by Lobengula, their last tribal king. Mthwakazi covered the areas known today as Matabeleland and the Midlands and splits Zimbabwe down the middle from north to south. It would have made sense at the end of white rule in Rhodesia to create two new countries, Zimbabwe and Mthwakazi. Britain's failure to take that opportunity would inevitably lead to dispute and conflict.

CHAPTER 1

GEORGE Drake was in a rage. Once again, his son, Alan, embarrassed him. Since the death of the boy's mother, it happened more and more often. George glared over the edge of his glasses at his son. The boy was too damned handsome for his own good. He was tall and blond, and many a time, George caught his business associates' wives staring appreciatively at Alan. It was no surprise the daughters of his associates also found the boy irresistible.

'For God's sake, Alan, you're fifteen years old; don't you have any common sense? Mrs Frost almost burned my ear off over the phone. She doesn't want you going near Gina again. I haven't brought you up to go around pinching young girl's bottoms.'

'Gina doesn't mind, Dad.'

'That's not the point. Any mother would be upset with you harassing their daughter.'

'It's only because Mrs Frost saw me pinch Gina and got jealous.'

'Stop talking rubbish, Alan.'

'Well, Mrs Frost doesn't mind me pinching her bottom, under water in the swimming pool.'

'What are you saying, Alan?'

'I've pinched Mrs Frost's bottom in the swimming pool lots of times. She always just laughs and gives me that look. If you saw her bikini, Dad, you'd also want to pinch her bottom.'

'Enough, Alan! Enough of this nonsense.'

'If I promise not to pinch Gina again, she might let me go back.'

'No, Alan. I forbid you to visit there again. Swim here in your own pool. Do you hear me?'

'Yes, Dad.'

'How on earth did you have the nerve to pinch Mrs Frost's bottom?'

'She started it, so I pinched her back.'

'Well, that's the end of it. I'm sick of all the mothers in the neighbourhood phoning up to complain about you. At your age, you're too young to be chasing girls.'

'Yes, Dad.'

Alan meant to keep his promise to his father, but temptation is a powerful force, particularly for one so young. When he was at a loose end in the blistering Melbourne heat of the January school holidays and received a call on his cell phone, his resistance was low.

'Hello, Alan. We haven't seen you for a long time. We wondered if you were OK?'

'Mrs Frost!'

'I hope I didn't get you into too much trouble with your Dad?'

'Well, maybe just a little.'

'The swimming pool is beautiful and sparkling if you'd like to come around for a swim.'

'Dad says I mustn't go to your place anymore.'

'Well, if you want to come, I won't tell him.'

Alan grabbed his swimming costume and towel and stuffed them into his backpack. He hopped on his mountain bike and raced down the road to the Frosts' house.

As he'd done many times before, Alan let himself in through the side gate into the pool area behind the house. Mrs Frost lay face down on a towel by the pool. Alan's eyes at once set upon her tiny bikini bottom, the briefest yet, and he noticed her bikini top's strings lay undone. She was almost naked.

'Ah! there you are, Alan. I've been waiting for you to rub sunscreen on my back.'

'Oh! where's Gina, Mrs Frost?'

'Gina's with her father, visiting her grandmother in Brisbane for the week.'

Suddenly, Alan's mouth went dry.

CHAPTER 2

IT was a long time since George Drake last saw his old friend, Andrew Dube. They kept in touch by email and social media but had not seen each other in over ten years. George remembered their conversation the last time they met.

'I tell you Andrew, this boy will age me fast. I don't know what's got into him, but he's gone wild since his mother died.'

'Wild? In what way?'

'He spends his time chasing girls, but not satisfied with that, he also goes after their mothers. Alan is big for his age and is a good-looking bugger. The trouble is he knows that and takes advantage of it.'

'Don't forget, George, he's entered his teens now, and his hormones are raging. Do you remember how you were at that age?'

'No, I was never like that. My father encouraged me to take an interest in business, and that was my passion. Dinner conversation at home was always about business. I've tried the same thing with Alan. It should be an educational opportunity for him, but he's shown no interest at all. The boy spent too much time with his mother; that's the problem. With hindsight, I see my mistake, but he's a stubborn so-and-so, and now, it's impossible to change him.'

'Give him time. He'll grow out of it.'

'You reckon? I'm not so sure about that.'

'Well, at least he's not taking drugs, stealing or getting into fights.'

'If you spend your time chasing girls and their mothers, you can't help getting into fights. There's always a jealous boyfriend or angry husband to navigate. And for Heaven's sake, he's only fifteen. But you're right, he doesn't do drugs or anything criminal.'

* * *

Andrew Dube and George Drake went back a long way. Dube, now a prominent Zimbabwean businessman, got his start with a loan from Drake. He tapped into the large African market, and his electronics business grew faster than even he expected. In less than two years he paid back the loan, and the pair established a close friendship with each recognising a kindred spirit.

Following the 2013 elections, the Mthwakazi Freedom Front (MFF) elected Andrew Dube as their new president. His enthusiastic leadership brought a new energy to the movement. Soon, he got in touch with George Drake to discuss the plan they'd tossed around many times over the years. The idea started with a light-hearted brain-storming session and developed from there. With each round of drinks, the plan became more ambitious and seemed more achievable.

On the occasions they got together, George would start by playing the Devil's advocate. As their evening warmed up with each glass of Scotch on the rocks, their views would align, and they would convince each other Mthwakazi was a realistic prospect. Over time, their support for the cause grew, and now, Andrew felt confident enough to take their plan to the MFF committee.

He addressed the committee at its next monthly meeting where they agreed a wider group known as the inner circle should contribute their views on the idea. Everyone in the MFF would support the concept of Mthwakazi as a separate state, for that was the organisation's raison d'être. But the method of achieving an independent Mthwakazi might not be so readily agreed.

Andrew's main rival for the leadership of the organisation, Senior Kholose, led a faction of the MFF. An ambitious man, Kholose gained a reputation for ruthlessness, so the membership voted for the safer choice and selected Andrew. They viewed Kholose as a dictatorial hothead whose leadership might create unnecessary problems for the organisation. Andrew was regarded as a consultative leader who considered all options before embarking on any course of action. Ironic, then, he now put forward an idea more suited to Kholose.

Andrew Dube was a stirring speaker, and the inner circle of the MFF listened to his words with growing enthusiasm. Senior Kholose raised several objections and counter proposals, but the leaders saw this as being just his way. They remembered many earlier instances where he objected to anything, he did not himself propose.

The inner circle voted unanimously in favour of giving Andrew the green light to meet with his old friend, George Drake, to consider the possibilities. Soon, Andrew and his deputy, Peter Nkala, arranged to meet George and his like-minded business associates to see what actions might be open to them. The MFF did not want the meeting held under the scrutiny of the Zimbabwe authorities. After a few phone calls to George, Andrew reluctantly agreed to meet in Chiang Mai.

Aside from the Mthwakazi project, Andrew looked forward to seeing his old friend again. It was over twenty years since George migrated to Australia and made his fortune. His business dealings gave him no cause to visit Zimbabwe, and Andrew, who feared flying, only travelled by land-based transport within Southern Africa. But now, for the sake of privacy, he would have to fly to make their secret rendezvous in Thailand.

Senior Kholose was secretly pleased with Andrew's proposal. He'd run with it if he assumed leadership of the MFF. And it would also give him something to hold over the organisation should he need it to get his own way down the line.

Andrew knew the risk Senior Kholose and his faction presented, and he reflected on how the Kholose hotheads got into the MFF. It was not obvious at first, but over time the group grew and gravitated towards Kholose's populist, intransigent stance. If caught earlier, the problem could have been eradicated through expulsions from the organisation, but now it was much too late for Andrew and his supporters to try that approach.

CHAPTER 3

Doctor Abel Sibanda closed his eyes and listened to the hum of the engines. He battled to keep his eyelids open. Every three or four minutes his head jerked towards his chest, waking him with a start. An early rise to catch the ten-forty flight to Livingstone in Zambia was bad enough, but the nervous tension brought on by his first air flight added to his exhaustion. Abel worried the South African Airways Airbus A319 was missing two engines. Most of the other planes he'd seen at Johannesburg's OR Tambo International Airport boasted four. Somehow, he felt short-changed. The hint of aviation fuel, as he boarded the plane, and the plastic smell of the interior made him nauseous. Worse still his head ached, and his tummy churned.

His flat-mate, Professor Gideon Ncube, refused to go with him on the trip. Abel shook his head and smiled. That Gideon was a crusty old bugger, and he trusted no one he hadn't known for at least thirty years. He especially didn't trust Abel's new friend, Hilton Nyoka. 'Go with him if you wish,' he'd said, 'but I won't.'

* * *

From Abel's point of view, his chance meeting with Hilton in the local bar was a godsend. He was intelligent and polite; a nice guy who empathised with Abel's situation.

Abel hadn't seen his wife and children for over a year. As an Ndebele activist and critic of the Zimbabwe government, he needed to skip the country at short notice. The journey to cross into South Africa and on to Johannesburg was difficult. His wife, Mary, would never have managed it, and since then, all her attempts to get a passport for herself and the children failed. Abel convinced himself it was a punishment for his opposition to the regime in Harare.

One evening, when Abel drank alone in the bar near his flat, he bumped into Hilton Nyoka. After a few too many beers, Abel related his life story to the younger man, whom he found friendly and charming. Hilton was a Matabele, and Abel saw no risk in being open with him. The young man said he had his own business and often travelled to Zambia to sell a range of his products. Unlike crusty old Gideon, Hilton seemed happy to listen to Abel's long list of complaints and his tale of woe.

Soon, Abel viewed Hilton as a good friend. After the third or fourth time they met in the bar, Abel invited Hilton back to the flat for a drink. Gideon was unimpressed. 'That young man is too friendly for my liking. Never trust people like that.' Abel laughed off Gideon's concerns. Circumstances also forced Gideon to flee Zimbabwe, and he distrusted, even disliked, everybody since then.

On a cool and blustery autumn Saturday afternoon the gusts of wind swept up the dust in the canyons between the high-rise apartment blocks in Berea, the densely populated inner-city suburb of Johannesburg where Abel lived. Hilton helped Abel drain a bottle of Scotch as they discussed the ills of their homeland. Gideon joined them but not because he now accepted Hilton. Rather it was because he did not want to miss his share in the fast-dwindling supply of Scotch, and he was not shy in letting the others know it.

'Don't worry,' said Hilton, 'I'm going to Zambia next week and I'll bring back duty-free Scotch for you.'

'You're a lucky man,' said Abel.

'Well, come with me. I'm going to Livingstone. You can visit your family while I'm attending to my business. Lupane is only four-and-a-half hours by car from Victoria Falls.'

'Four-and-a-half hours is quite a long time.'

'In a luxury vehicle it won't seem long. My contacts have a BMW; you'll love it.'

'The authorities won't let me back into Zimbabwe, or if they do, I'll go straight into one of Mugabe's prisons.'

'Don't worry, I can get you across the Zambezi and organise a lift for you to Lupane. How about you, Gideon? Would you like to visit your family in Bulawayo? We can all go to Livingstone together.'

Gideon grunted. 'No, not for me thank you.'

'Well, maybe next time,' said Hilton.

* * *

Abel chastised Gideon with his harsh though well-meant parting words. 'You're a grumpy old fool my friend. You should've agreed to come. Now you've missed this opportunity to visit your family.'

The plane was full, so he sat apart from Hilton, and it gave him plenty of time to reflect. He wasn't flush with money, but Hilton lent him half the airfare. The man was a blessing. Abel didn't yet have a return ticket, but Hilton assured him it would be cheaper to buy it in Zambia.

Abel rested his head in the corner between his headrest and the window and closed his eyes. At first, he hoped for an aisle seat as the prospect of looking out the window scared him. Now, he recognised the advantage in having a corner to make himself comfortable. Mary, his dear wife, and the children would be so excited to see him, and she'd love the gold bracelet he'd bought her. It wasn't real gold, but it looked as beautiful as anything he'd seen other women wearing. Abel scanned his memory for pictures of his happy family life, and soon he slept.

The air hostess shook Abel, 'Please fasten your seatbelt, Sir, we're landing in five minutes.' Abel's beautiful dream seemed so real with the aromas and tastes of his wife's cooking. He could almost touch his lovely wife and kids. Even the bumpy landing did not detract from his excitement. After the inevitable delay, standing in the queue to disembark, Abel stepped out of the plane into the warm tropical air of the Zambezi valley. No chilling autumn gusts here. He felt alive. Someone tugged at his elbow; it was Hilton. 'As soon as we get out of the airport, I'm taking you for a slap-up lunch at the Royal Livingstone Hotel. It's on me, so you can order whatever you want.'

'You're a good friend, Hilton. I won't forget this.'

'Oh, it's nothing, and it's all tax deductible. I can't get you across the river until dark, so we might as well act like tourists in the meantime.'

'Don't you have to attend to your business?'

'That can wait until tomorrow.'

* * *

Abel grew up in Lupane, but he'd never seen the Victoria Falls. Following high school, he studied medicine in the UK. After a long ten years working in London, Abel returned to Zimbabwe and settled in Bulawayo. He found the Ndebele people boiling with rage. They'd suffered at the hands of the North Korean trained 5th Brigade, which reported to the prime minister's office, Mugabe's office. The Gukurahundi was a five-year genocidal assault by the brigade on the Ndebele people. Before too long, Abel got involved with the MFF, a clandestine group demanding independence for the country's western provinces. Abel's activism led to his flight to South Africa. His wife and family gave up their nice home in Bulawayo and returned to their traditional village outside Lupane. Now, Abel forever struggled with guilt for the downturn in his family's fortunes.

* * *

The Victoria Falls were a sight to behold, and Abel stared in awe. The spectacular site and the thrill of soon seeing his wife again made him tingle. What a wonderful life!

The afternoon raced by in a dream and time lost its meaning. Soon, dusk fell, and Hilton suggested an early meal before the river crossing. Three Scotches later, Abel struggled to contain his excitement. 'Come my friend,' said Hilton, 'it's time for you to go home.'

Hilton took Abel in the hire car to a quiet spot on the river. 'Now listen my friend, here's where I leave you. The boat will take you to where Phineas and his two cousins are waiting. They will drive you to your wife's home and pick you up again in precisely seventy-two hours from the time they drop you. Then, you will cross back here where I will wait for you. Good luck.'

'I don't know how I can ever repay you for your kindness, Hilton. Thank you.'

'Think nothing of it my friend.'

The small boat with its tiny outboard motor made its way across the Zambezi. Abel worried the gentle putt-putt of the motor might not be up to the task. The boatman didn't say a word as he concentrated on the dark river surface and small islands.

Phineas and his cousins waited beside their car as the boat reached the Zimbabwe side of the river. They were in a big hurry to leave the area. 'We can't hang around here,' said Phineas. 'The police sometimes patrol. We'll take the back roads and go through the national park to avoid the roadblocks, but you must stay in the boot in case we're stopped. Your face is too well known. There is a cushion for your head and a blanket to keep you warm.'

It wasn't the home-coming Abel expected, but the discomfort of the boot was a small price to pay for seeing his wife and kids again. Would his oldest boy still live at home or have already left to make his way in the bright lights of Bulawayo? Young boys became young men early these days. Corresponding with his wife in their traditional village was a slow and uncertain process, and he was always behind with the family news.

The car bounced along while Abel did his best to make himself comfortable. He now regretted those three Scotches. His head swam, and the black claustrophobic boot gave him no point of focus, and soon an irresistible drowsiness came over him.

Abel woke with a start. The car stood still with the motor idling, and he heard voices, but he couldn't make out what they said. Perhaps a roadblock? He held his breath, not daring to breathe. The car advanced a few feet, and then, the squeal of metal and the sound of a bouncing boom gate dropped against its wooden rest. Now the car set off again, and Abel breathed normally. He'd no idea how long he'd been asleep and what distance they'd travelled. His watch didn't have luminous hands. What was the time? We must be close. It couldn't be much further.

The car bounced along, as did Abel; his joints stiff and his bones aching. He wasn't a young man anymore. There was much to tell his wife. She would be proud of him. He'd become the secretary of the Joburg branch of the MFF.

'Stop, stop, here's the spot,' a voice shouted, and the car slowed to a halt. Abel heard the handbrake applied and the car doors opening followed by the muffled voices of the men at the boot. He grabbed the handle of his travel bag and waited. The boot lid swung up and a brilliant flash of light from a strong torch stung Abel's eyes.

'Here we are my friend. We've arrived.'

'I can't see. Your torch is too bright.'

'I'm sorry. Your eyes will clear as soon as they get used to the dark. Walk up to the corner of the road about one hundred metres, and you will recognise where you are. Your wife's village is close. We'll be waiting for you here at nine o'clock, three nights from now.'

'Yes, yes, but I can't see. My eyes are watering too much.'

'Just wait a few minutes for your eyes to clear. We must go now before we attract too much attention.' The men jumped into the car and slammed the doors.

Abel stood by as Phineas turned the car around and sped back the way they'd come. Why such a hurry? The headlights weren't even switched on as they raced away. Abel, blinded and with his eyes watering, was impatient to see his wife. He picked up his case and stood looking in the opposite direction to which the car drove. A hundred metres to the corner shouldn't be too difficult. If he took care, he could edge his way on the dirt road even though flashes of brilliant light still danced in his eyes. With small steps, if he wandered off the road, he'd know. Abel shuffled in the direction Phineas indicated. In the isolated spot, the silence was pervasive.

A snap of a twig brought Abel to a halt. Not a loud noise, but the silence on the dark, lonely road amplified the sound. Abel waited, but all was quiet. His vision was still blurred, and he cursed Phineas' careless cousin for shining the torch in his face. After a short pause, Abel took a few tentative steps. There it was again, a strange rustling sound. Each time he moved, he sensed something keeping pace with him. Someone was following him! Now he strained his ears, and he was sure he could hear soft footsteps and heavy breathing. There was more than one! 'Who's there?' Abel shouted. No reply. 'I know you're following me. Stop playing games!' A cold chill ran down his spine and Abel quickened his pace. But as he stumbled along, his pursuers gave up all attempts at stealth. Abel now panicked. With his eyes gradually clearing, he turned to face his tormentors.

CHAPTER 4

Every mouthful, a delight. The tender flesh fell off the bone. Aged, it would melt in the mouth and be even better, but she'd grown up eating much tougher meat than this. Even the little ones found no difficulty chewing their succulent portions.

Sometimes lean but often fatty like rib-eye steak, either way, she loved it. Without exception, the family enjoyed their meat rare and bloody, when the flavoursome salty taste was the strongest.

If alone, she might have savoured each mouthful. But never alone, and with the whole family tucking in, she needed to get her share before it was all gone. With all snatching for the best bits, the family didn't give table manners a high priority. They prized the tender meat and liked to suck on the bones to get at the marrow.

She remembered the time before this distinctive smelling meat was so readily available. Once they'd tried it, no other meat compared. It only took one large, fresh, juicy meal, and the family was hooked. Their diet became more varied and interesting, and they coped with the live deliveries better than they first expected.

But supply was unpredictable. The deliveries often arrived after the weekend, and then the family enjoyed the treat. For the rest of the week, they'd no choice but to revert to their more traditional meals. Those who'd not sampled the tasty delicacy carried on in blissful ignorance.

In the African bush everyone competed for food, humans and wildlife alike. What you did not catch for yourself, you could always try to steal from others. People fled the cities to escape the excesses of the regime. After dark, the family would sometimes approach the huts that sprang up like mushrooms on the edge of the park. Dangerous, yes, but if they were lucky, they'd find something good to eat.

The family was not above scavenging, but they mostly hunted. Often, they would have to fight for the food. They would even take on the great cape buffalo if they caught one alone. Young elephants also formed part of their diet if they could separate them from their mothers. Few stood up against the family.

No, they would never go hungry, now they'd changed their methods. Most important, was the need to carry out their raids in silence. They took care the villagers did not notice their presence. Persisting with the old ways did not lead to success.

CHAPTER 5

A loud knock at the door aroused Gideon Ncube from his Sunday afternoon nap on the sofa. Aha! That would be Abel back from his trip to Zimbabwe. Gideon yawned, stretched and eased himself up from the sofa and padded across the room in his socks. But when he opened the door and saw who it was, he gave a derisive grunt. 'Where's Abel?' he demanded.

'Good afternoon, Professor,' said Hilton Nyoka. 'Abel wanted to stay on another week, and he asked me to let you know. And here's the Scotch I promised; two bottles.'

'I suppose you'd better come in then,' said Gideon, with little enthusiasm.

'Why don't we open a bottle now and celebrate Abel enjoying his time with his family?'

'If you say so,' said Gideon, eyeing the bottle of Johnnie Walker Black Label. 'Wait, I'll get the glasses.'

Hilton made himself at home and admired the view over the Johannesburg apartment-block suburb of Berea. 'The thirteenth floor; isn't that unlucky?'

Gideon cracked open the screw cap of the bottle and poured generous tots into the two glasses. 'Well, it hasn't been unlucky for Abel and me; it suits us. How is Abel getting back to Joburg?'

'I'll be back in Livingstone next week, and I'll pick him up then.'

'So, he got to his wife safely?' said Gideon, watching Hilton's eyes for any flicker.

'Yes, and he's having a wonderful time and doesn't want to leave.'

'He can't stay there; it's too dangerous for him.'

'Yes, he knows, but one more week won't harm. Come, Professor, how about another tot? Can I interest you in joining me on my trip next week? You could spend a week or two with your family in Bulawayo.'

'No thank you, I'll wait until it's safe for me to return.'

'That's a pity. You could be in for a long wait my friend. Mugabe and ZANU-PF aren't going anywhere soon.'

'Mugabe's an old man. He can't last much longer.'

'You're not that young, yourself. Can you afford to wait years to see your wife and family?'

'I'll wait as long as necessary. The authorities there would love to get their hands on me, but I won't give them the opportunity.'

Gideon didn't trust Hilton, but the Scotch relaxed him as the level of the amber coloured liquid in the bottle lowered. Hilton poured him another glass as their small talk continued. 'The authorities in Zimbabwe will have forgotten you by now.'

'As long as they're in power, they'll not forget me. They see me as a Matabele dissident and activist, and they'll want to silence me.'

'Well, it's not just because you're a Matabele. You're an active member of the MFF, seeking independence for Mthwakazi.'

'It's the only way our people will find justice. We are Mthwakazians, not Zimbabweans. When Matabeleland and the Midlands separate from Zimbabwe, we will rename them, Mthwakazi.'

'But we are disunited, aren't we? Apart from the MFF, there's the old Mthwakazi Liberation Front, the Matabeleland Liberation Organisation and the Mthwakazi National Party. How can we succeed when all these movements can't agree and accuse each other of being spies for the CIO (Zimbabwe's Central Intelligence Organisation)?'

'The government has destroyed industry and infrastructure in Matabeleland and moved businesses from Bulawayo to Harare. They have stolen land and property in the towns, and in the country, they have confiscated farms from the whites and black Matabeles. In the schools they use Shona teachers and try to destroy our culture and language, and in the workplace, they discriminate against us. Every year they celebrate the Gukurahundi, the massacre of at least twenty thousand innocent civilians.'

'Yes, Professor, it's sad, but what can we do?'

'We can fight. That's what we can do.'

'It's not just the black Matabele farmers who've lost their land, you know. The war veterans also evicted black Shona farmers. A few white farmers tried to avoid the farm invasions by giving land or part ownership to their loyal black workers or friends, but that hasn't worked. Are you sure I can't persuade you to come with me on my trip next week?'

'I told you already, I'm not interested.'

'That's a pity.'

Dusk was descending, and the bottle was almost empty. The Scotch and Gideon's anger were a heady mix. He'd drunk almost two-thirds, while Hilton was more careful with his intake. For Gideon the room swayed and then slowly started to spin. 'It's time for my bed, so you'd better go now,' said Gideon, trying to stand. He wobbled and sat down again on the edge of the sofa. Two more attempts to stand both failed. Gideon closed his eyes to concentrate, but his lids were heavy, and he struggled to stay awake.

'Come on, Old Man, I'll help you to your bed.' Hilton picked up the slight-framed, half-conscious Gideon and carried him like a groom carrying his bride across the threshold. With one hand he opened the door and stepped out onto the balcony.

CHAPTER 6

THE four-wheel drive pulled up outside the weathered old house. Big shady trees studded the large property, and smooth, compacted earth, almost like concrete, covered the area. The soil remained untouched by any form of garden tool for years, and nothing apart from the large trees grew in it. It was the ultimate easy-care garden. Hilton Nyoka switched off the engine and stepped out of the vehicle and slammed the door. He was sure he'd found the right place, but it was his first visit to the property, and in his line of work he learnt never to assume.

A low veranda wall fronted the old house, and a lowered bamboo blind offered protection from the afternoon heat. As he walked towards the house, Hilton could make out a figure standing behind the blind. They made no move to come out and greet him until Hilton reached the front steps.

'These are troubled times,' said Hilton.

'Troubled times indeed,' came the response. Yes, this was the right place. 'Come in, I've been waiting for you. Is this your first visit to Gaborone?'

'My first visit to Botswana.'

Hilton stepped onto the veranda and followed the middle-aged woman into the house. Heavy old-fashioned armchairs furnished the cool, dark front room. A long package wrapped in waxy, brown paper tied with string leant against the wall. The woman picked up the package and handed it to Hilton. 'It's best we don't meet again,' she said. 'Tomorrow morning, before you leave town, put it behind the veranda wall, and I'll take it from there.'

'And the bullets?'

'It's loaded and ready. Flick the safety catch and you're good to go.'

'How many rounds?'

'Three. Any more than that and you'll have the police swarming all over you. Gaborone is a quiet town, and gunshots will attract attention. Do you know where to go?'

'Yeah, I checked it out last night. It shouldn't be difficult; it's a quiet street and the houses are well apart.'

'Yes, but it's a good area and people are pretty security conscious there. The police and private security firms patrol it often.'

'So, I noticed, but they have no imagination; they come past every thirty minutes. I'll make my move five minutes after one of their patrols have passed. There are plenty of trees in the street and a drainage ditch for storm water. I'll hide somewhere there until they pass.'

'OK, good luck and goodbye. Remember, we've never met.'

Hilton hid the package in the concealed luggage section of the four-wheel drive. He got into the vehicle, turned on the engine, eased the gear shift into place and drove slowly onto the quiet road. He glanced back to wave, but the woman was gone. Hmm! An interesting contact. What was her connection to the COU (Covert Operations Unit)?

* * *

A moonless night; perfect for the job. Hilton Nyoka parked the four-wheel drive in the street behind the one in which his target lived. He'd noted on his earlier visit the large vacant block that would allow him to move unobserved from one street to the other. It was ideal for his purpose and right next door to his intended target's home. He waited in a secluded spot for the regular security patrol to pass. Soon, he heard a vehicle in the distance, and then headlights appeared around the corner.

The vehicle drove slowly down the empty street. Emblazoned on the side, the sign, Botswana Security Systems. When it was well past him, Hilton grunted in satisfaction and stepped out onto the verge and moved towards the large wrought-iron gate that fronted the property. A twelve-foot wall surrounded the property, but it had a weak point. The wrought-iron gate stood only twenty-five metres from the front door which was wide open. An easy shot for a marksman like Hilton. Now, he only needed to wait for his target to appear. Hilton rested the rifle in a convenient loop in the decorative wrought-iron gate and focused his attention on the open front door.

A white man walked into view and stood in the doorway. Hilton tensed, but he held his fire; it was the woman he wanted in his sights. She was the primary target. The man, a mere bonus if the opportunity arose, but letting the woman escape would mean failure. The woman who gave him the rifle was a real professional. She'd painted the rifle sights white with liquid ink. That was essential for taking aim in the dark.

Time passed, and Hilton looked at his watch. The private security patrol would come around again soon. He withdrew the rifle and retreated around the corner to wait for the security vehicle to pass.

Sure enough, within five minutes the Botswana Security Systems' four-wheel drive drove past at a pedestrian pace. Another five minutes passed, and Hilton returned to the wrought-iron gate. Ten minutes later, the man in the house came into view twice more. On the second occasion, he stopped and stood in the doorway. Still no sign of the woman. Hilton thought it too dark for anyone to see him at the gate. Then suddenly, like magic, an African woman approached the man, and they embraced. What luck! Her back faced Hilton, and with one shot, the bullet from the powerful rifle might pass right through them both.

Hilton breathed in, exhaled and gently squeezed the trigger. The two figures instantly vanished, and the house plunged into darkness. Bingo! An easy shot, and impossible for anyone to survive. But did the shot also knock out the master switch on the electrical switchboard? Once again, he withdrew the rifle from its wrought-iron resting place and casually strolled across the vacant block of land to his vehicle.

As far as Hilton could tell no one from the neighbouring properties emerged to investigate the noise. It was only a single shot, and they may have thought a car backfired, or they might have been too frightened to investigate.

CHAPTER 7

HILTON Nyoka walked into the long, low, single storey building. He waved to the security guard in the first office and smiled at the receptionist in the second. He'd every reason to be pleased. On one trip, he disposed of Abel Sibanda, Gideon Ncube and Captain John's female nemesis and her partner. Sibanda and Ncube were senior MFF activists, and the two in Gaborone were his boss' old enemies. If Captain John held any doubts about Hilton's value to the COU, they would soon evaporate. He looked forward to presenting his report to Captain John and receiving his well-deserved praise.

Getting rid of Sibanda and Ncube was part of Hilton's job. The COU would earn a rich reward for carrying out the contract on the activists. But he dealt with the captain's enemies in Gaborone on his own initiative, as a gift for the captain. The woman wiped out the former COU's number one team and got Captain John fired when his anonymous masters ended COU operations. For a time, Captain John returned to military service in a boring administration role as assistant quartermaster in the army stores. He stewed at his perceived demotion and dreamt of getting out at the first opportunity. As head of the COU he eliminated several of the most senior government opponents, but in the stores his most exciting duty was trying to explain the discrepancies in the quarterly stock-takes.

Captain John resigned from the army soon after he came into money when his father-in-law died. He resurrected the COU, but this time he owned the business, though he ran it along military lines, much as he'd done in earlier times. He bought the building and set up the business and was no longer beholden to an anonymous voice, passing instructions from the other end of the phone line. John hired a personal bodyguard and a secretary with disparate duties, and he rebuilt his operational teams to carry out the darkest deeds for the highest bidders. Most of the COU's clients and their targets were ambitious politicians or senior party officials, competing for a role in the party or government. Incurring the displeasure of a rival or bigwig in the party could be a deadly mistake.

Sometimes, clients put out contracts on one another. If the fee the clients agreed was similar, John would select the easier of the two hits to complete. When confident of carrying out a contract, John would ask for a fifty percent deposit. In these instances, he would collect the full fee from one party and keep the deposit he received from the unfortunate other. If nothing else, Captain John was a savvy businessman. The COU was a profitable assassination business, but even greater funds rolled in from his other interests.

When Hilton walked into Captain John's office, his boss sat, relaxed, behind his big desk. 'Well, Nyoka, let's hear about your trip. You incurred a month's worth of costs, but I suppose, getting Sibanda and Ncube was worth it. Now, tell me about your meeting with my friend in Gaborone. Why did you need the rifle? I don't like to expose the lady to an unnecessary risk of discovery for any trivial purpose. Next time, get my approval before you use one of my assets.'

'Yes, Sir. Sorry, Sir. But I'm sure you will like my news.'

A gleeful Hilton related his hit on the captain's old enemies. 'They both dropped like stones.'

'That's funny! There's no report of any murders in Gaborone that coincide with your visit. My friend tells me that the people in that house are all alive and well. They have covered the wrought-iron gate in sheet metal, and now, two large dogs patrol the property. I understand they have installed a new mirror in the entrance hall of that house. Some idiot shot out the old mirror. I can't imagine why.'

'I'm sorry, Sir, I was certain the shot did the job, but it looks like I made a mistake.'

'Mistakes in the COU are dangerous, Nyoka. Anyway, I want no further distractions from our core business. Money is rolling in, so forget those two in Gaborone. It gives me a headache, thinking about them, and no one is paying me to get rid of them. Do you understand, Nyoka?'

'Yes, Sir. I'm sorry, Sir.'

'That's all, Nyoka.'

'Sir, your friend in Gaborone seemed most professional. What is her background?'

Captain John drew himself up in his seat. 'You need not know her background, Nyoka. Once, she was a beautiful woman. Sadly, age has caught up with her. When she worked for me, she was beautiful, but you can't expect someone in my position to stick with a woman who now looks like that.'

'No Sir. I understand, Sir, thank you.' Hilton Nyoka left Captain John's office relieved his misjudgement did not seem to count against him too badly in his boss' eyes. Those two in Gaborone wriggled out of every trap Captain John set for them, and now, he'd also failed. He would let things lie for now. Maybe one day he might get a different result, but it wouldn't be on Captain John's watch. Still, he'd accounted for Sibanda and Ncube; that must count for something.

After saying hello to his fellow operatives in the open plan office, Hilton headed for home. He'd been away for over a month, and the girls in the nightclub would have missed him. He'd certainly missed them. Hilton was confident Captain John appreciated his work. He was intelligent and got the results his boss wanted. If he played his cards right, he might even end up as Captain John's 2IC, his second in command.

Hilton's only rival was that fellow in Bulawayo. But there was little chance of anyone from Matabeleland reaching the top of the largely Shona-based organisation. Hilton's Shona father and Ndebele mother gave him an effective dual identity. He used his mother's maiden name as a cover for his Ndebele identity, but he switched between his Ndebele and Shona identities at will. No one knew any different, and both sides accepted him as one of their own. It was his great advantage over that Ndebele fellow in Bulawayo.

* * *

The transformation in Hilton's life, from his early village upbringing, couldn't be starker. Each day, he walked barefoot to the church-run school, several kilometres from home. Under other circumstances, his tattered clothes might have made him a target for teasing by the other kids, but in Hilton's school tattered was normal.

The old, white headmaster was a disciplinarian who wielded a bamboo cane with practised ease. Hilton didn't mind the stinging backside but resented the humiliation. The old-fashioned approach paid dividends when the young Hilton won a small scholarship to attend high school in Harare. There, in his new uniform and village ways, the other boys teased him. 'How come you have such a fancy name, Hilton? Does your Dad own the Hilton Hotel?' His father always claimed he named Hilton after the hotel that once employed him. It was a boast Hilton could never corroborate. His father was a simple country villager given to exaggeration and ludicrous, ambitious schemes. None more so than his stated but often postponed goal of standing in the next presidential election.

Hilton achieved top grades in his school exams. His sporting prowess earned him a place in the cricket and soccer teams. In the holidays at the end of his penultimate year at school, things took a turn for the worse; an episode that affected his character rather than his academic achievements.

As Hilton walked along the dirt road to his village on a warm August day during his school holidays, his old junior school principal drove by in his dilapidated car. It was well into the dry season, and the old man remained oblivious to the choking dust stirred up by his vehicle. It settled on Hilton's hair and clothes and enraged the young man beyond reason.

Later that night, when everyone slept, Hilton crept out of the hut and headed for his old junior school. The principal's neat, well-cared for residence sat on one edge of the school grounds. A tall, scrubby rubber hedge (Euphorbia tirrucalli) afforded it privacy and a little protection from the dust storms whipped up by the dry, late-winter winds.

Hilton found a traditional Zimbabwean grass-cutter leaning against a wall near the back door of the house. It was only a piece of flat iron with the cutting toe twisted to an angle of ninety degrees from the shaft, giving it the overall appearance of a hockey stick. A piece of cotton cloth wound around the other end formed a comfortable handle. The cutting edges of the toe, sharpened on both sides, enabled a user to swing it forwards and backwards with equal effect.

Hilton picked up the grass-cutter and tested the back door. Locked! He inspected the other windows and doors. All locked! Only one thing for it! Hilton banged on the front door. After the third round of knocking, a dull light flickered on in the front passage, and a voice called out. 'Who is it? Don't you know it's past ten o'clock?'

'It's me, Sir. Hilton, one of your former students.'

'Hilton? What do you want, boy?'

The door opened, and the old man stood there in his pyjamas and dressing gown, blinking in the passage light. He never saw the blade of the grass-cutter that hit him. One blow was enough.

'That, my friend, is for all the canings and the dust you made me eat.'

Hilton often listened on the radio or television to the president's racist rants and soaked up the message as he saw it. He walked away from his dreadful deed without the slightest sense of guilt or compassion.

* * *

The police made no progress in their investigation. They considered it a robbery gone wrong. No one would have imagined clever, young Hilton to be a killer. Even though his parents knew he ventured out late on the night of the murder, they didn't believe, or want to believe, he'd anything to do with it. Hilton returned for his final year at school in Harare, confident he'd got away with murder. A cold-blooded, ruthless killer was born, and that would lead him straight into the arms of Captain John.

* * *

Captain John sat in his chair with his elbows on his desk and the tips of his fingers together. He contemplated the way things turned out since his relaunch of the COU. The new building was more to his liking than his former premises. Roomier than the old building, his office sat further from the open plan office his operatives shared. Next to his office was the storeroom and then Hilton Nyoka's office.

He hired his own security guards, and a young, compliant secretary, generous with both her time and attention. She didn't mind working back late for the boss. John always dreamed of an arrangement like this, as opposed to his old office, where he'd worked within budgetary constraints forced upon him by the anonymous, disembodied voice at the end of the phone. Now, he lorded it over his own little empire.

Hilton Nyoka looked after the Eastern half of Zimbabwe, including the Gonarezhou National Park. He preferred to use independent agents in his dealings with the Mozambicans in the poaching operation, and the arrangement worked well.

The Bulawayo fellow, as the COU people knew him, used his own team for poaching and a team of COU operatives for dealing with the sales of ivory and rhino horn. The North Korean buyers in Bulawayo eagerly accepted the harvest from the Hwange National Park.

John used his A team, under the watchful eye of the ruthless Hilton Nyoka, to conduct the bulk of his core business. Thanks to them, a good many dissidents and other miscellaneous individuals met an unhappy end, often disappearing without a trace. Captain John was cunning, patient, unseen and deadly. His unsuspecting victims only recognised the danger and their desperate situation when they walked into one of his ambushes. John's exploits were legendary in higher circles and earned him his nickname, *The Leopard*. But his exploits remained unsubstantiated rumours thanks to his excessive attention to secrecy.

John didn't discriminate. He accepted contracts on government supporters and government opponents alike. Either group might buy his services or suffer their sting. It wasn't personal, just business. John had long since given up the 'romantic' idea of assisting the regime. He'd benefited under it but also held a grudge for the arbitrary closure of his first semi-official COU.

Diversification ensured continuity of income and contributed to John's growing wealth. He didn't have to answer to any board; that was the key to his newfound success.

CHAPTER 8

Andrew Dube held on to the armrest of his seat, his black knuckles turning almost white. His stomach turned over as the plane banked for its final approach to the runway. The plane left the cool of Johannesburg a little after lunch for the overnight flight to Singapore. Soon, they'd be landing in the early morning dawn to face the tropical heat of the island city state. Andrew's head buzzed, and his mouth tasted bitter. As he'd feared, flying was not for him.

Tyson, Andrew's oldest son enjoyed every minute of the flight. The pair endured an uncomfortable bus trip from Bulawayo to Johannesburg, and now, his father planned to travel to Chiang Mai by train. Tyson argued it added an unnecessary night or two to the journey when they could have instead been visiting the shops in Singapore or Chiang Mai. Still, the thrill of accompanying his father, as his secretary, to the meeting in Chiang Mai, far outweighed that small disappointment.

Andrew and Tyson passed through immigration and customs without undue delay and stood staring around them in the arrivals' hall. The spectacular airport in Singapore left them speechless. They couldn't believe the display of wealth and abundance that greeted them. The crowd and the bustle overwhelmed them, but to their relief they saw a man with a placard with the name Dube written in large letters. The man saw them and smiled.

'Mr Dube, my name is Wong. I am Mr Drake's manager in Singapore. He asked me to take you to catch the train for Bangkok. Unfortunately, I couldn't get you on the mainline train through Kuala Lumpur and Butterworth, so I've booked you on the Jungle Railway through Khota

Bharu. It's a slower journey but much more beautiful. But don't forget, you must change trains at Gemas.'

Mr Wong prattled on, and Old Andrew closed his eyes and put his hands to his head. 'I can't remember all this. We'll get lost.'

'Don't worry, Dad, Mr Wong has written instructions for us to follow.'

From then on, all was a whirl. Mr Wong took care of everything, and Andrew and Tyson sat back as Wong sped them to the railway station in Johor Bahru. He delighted in his new role as a tourist guide, keeping up a running commentary about the city, of which he was so proud. But Andrew and Tyson took in little as they stared out the window of the air-conditioned car making its way through the busy streets. Both struggled to concentrate on Wong's instructions. 'Remember, when you get to Pasir Mas, you must go by road to Rantau Panjang. It's a short drive by bus or taxi. Only thirty minutes. From there you can cross over the border to Sungai Kolok in Thailand and catch the train to Bangkok. Just ask if you get lost. When you get to Bangkok, tell them you want the train to Chiang Mai. Here, I have written it all down for you on this piece of paper.'

Wong saw Andrew and Tyson through customs and drove them to the station. He was full of last-minute advice. His over-zealous enthusiasm and helpfulness made even young Tyson's mind swim. When at last the train pulled out of the station and they waved goodbye, they were glad to leave behind the over-helpful Mr Wong with his endless chatter.

The four-hour train journey from Johor Bahru to Gemas was pleasant enough with patches of good scenery between the endless stretches of palm oil and rubber tree plantations. Andrew complained about the air conditioning being turned up way too high, and he and Tyson scratched around in their bags to find something warm to wear. They travelled with jackets but never thought to bring warm jumpers to such a hot part of the world.

By the time they reached Gemas, travel-fatigue was catching up with Andrew and Tyson. They booked a first-class sleeper on the overnight train to Pasir Mas. Before embarking on the next leg of their journey, they bought something to eat at the station even though they were too tired to feel hungry. The man in the ticket office recognised them as tourists and assured them they wouldn't miss much as the overnight section of the journey passed through yet more palm oil and rubber tree plantations. 'But be up early so you don't miss the scenery from Kuala Lipis. The best part of the journey starts from there.'

Andrew and Tyson dumped their cases on the floor of the compartment and slumped onto the bench seats that doubled as their beds.

Waking up in time for Kuala Lipis was not a problem for Andrew and Tyson. Their body clocks ensured a restless night for the pair. They marvelled at the huge muddy rivers and the limestone cliffs near Gua Musang, and the rice fields and kampungs (traditional villages) further down the line. It was a restful part of the trip, but they were eager to move on and more than happy to leave the train and its icy air conditioning at Pasir Mas.

The timing was perfect, and they only waited a few minutes for the bus leaving for Rantau Panjang, where they passed quickly through Malaysian immigration. Andrew was thankful for the opportunity to stretch his legs and walk the one kilometre over no man's land and cross the bridge over the river to the Thailand immigration post. From there they walked a further kilometre to the Sungai Kolok railway station. By now, in the afternoon heat, old Andrew looked forward to boarding the train for Hat Yai and on to Bangkok. But he hoped and prayed the Thai trains were not as cold as those in Malaysia.

CHAPTER 9

AUGUST 2013

The big, black Mercedes with tinted, dark windows looked out of place in the narrow lanes of Chiang Mai. It glided down Tha Phae Road and turned into Soi Four before stopping in front of the boutique hotel. The back doors opened, and a tall silver-haired white man dressed in a camel-coloured suit and shiny brown shoes stepped out. On the other side a tall, thin black man in a loose-fitting charcoal suit emerged. The black man looked both ways down the lane and into the dark recesses formed after sundown. 'You need not worry here Mr Nkala,' said the white man. 'This place is private.'

'We can't be too careful Mr Drake. Their agents pop up in the most unexpected places.'

'Please call me George, and I'll call you Peter if I may?'

The two entered the foyer and walked to the small table which functioned as a reception desk. The young Thai woman looked up and smiled. 'Good evening Mr Drake. Your meeting is in room fifty-six on the fifth floor. The gentlemen are waiting for you there.'

Drake and Nkala walked across to the lift, and Drake pressed the up button, and the doors opened in response. They entered the lift, and Drake pressed the button for the fifth floor. As they ascended in silence, Drake examined the colourful posters that covered the lift walls. One poster advertised the hotel's restaurant, showing pictures of delicious Thai lunch and dinner dishes and traditional English breakfasts. Another showed images of serene clients enjoying the pleasures of the basement spa. Nkala stared straight ahead with his hands folded in front of him. For the first time, Drake noticed the sprinkling of grey in Nkala's otherwise short, black, tight spring-like hair.

At room fifty-six, Drake rapped on the locked door. A smiling face appeared. 'George! We thought you missed the flight.'

'Can you see me missing a flight, Solly?'

'No, you wouldn't miss a flight, George. You always were a stickler for timeliness and organisation.'

The others crowded round, shaking hands and slapping Drake on the back.

'Gentleman, let me introduce Peter Nkala from Bulawayo.' One by one the men shook Nkala's hand, welcoming him to the group. 'The closest to you, Peter, is Solly Bernstein from Johannesburg. Kevin lives in London, Mike in New York, Vince in Zurich, Noel in Hong Kong and Barry in Cape Town. And the best part is we are all from Matabeleland, except Noel who came from *Bamba Zonke* (Harare).'

'Yeah,' said Noel, 'but now I'm a member of The Bulawayo Boys' Club.'

'OK folks,' said Drake, 'we better get started. Andrew Dube is coming up from Singapore by train, but he'll be late. We can bring him up to speed when he gets here.'

Solly opened the bottle of Scotch and poured two glasses: Scotch on the rocks for Drake and a Scotch and soda for Nkala. 'So, George, we're going ahead with what we've been dreaming of for years?'

'Matabeleland is being raped and destroyed. If we don't act soon, there'll be nothing to save and nobody to rescue. The Matabeleland separatist groups are disunited. They talk but do nothing. We in the MFF have the resources and ability to act. We all agree that Matabeleland and Midlands would make a wonderful independent country if it had a sane government in place. Many of the whites and blacks who left when ZANU-PF looted the country will return to Matabeleland. Together we will build a vibrant, multiracial democracy, going by the name of Mthwakazi.'

'The disunity in the separatist groups is not the only problem,' said Solly. 'The ZANU government has a policy of inserting Shona people and culture into Matabeleland. Shona teachers are in the schools, teaching classes in Shona. There are quite a lot of Shona living in Matabeleland now. Also, aside from the Shona, the other tribal groups in Matabeleland have reservations about the Ndebele controlling the province. There's the Tonga up north, the Venda and Kalanga down south, and the Shangaan in the south-east. They haven't forgotten the brutal sway the Ndebele held in Mzilikazi and Lobengula's time before the whites arrived. So it's more than just an Ndebele issue.'

'There'll always be minorities,' said Drake. 'Our job will be to make sure Mthwakazi is a peaceful and prosperous country. People don't make trouble when they've got something to lose. The people aren't stupid. If we can give them a better life, they'll be happy. Now they've seen the other side of the coin with Mugabe, they'll be pleased with any government that's not corrupt and works for the benefit of the people.'

'Is there any such government in the world?' said Barry. 'How can we overcome China's support for Zimbabwe, the financial support from the diamond mines, intimidation by the security forces and vote rigging?'

'Well, with the current unrest and the indigenisation laws which require all foreign-owned companies to sell a controlling share to locals, the Chinese might not be as supportive next time.'

'Yes, said Noel, but what about ZANU's arrangement with that Israeli company, Nikuv International Projects? They specialise in population registration and elections.'

'Well, I suppose someone has to organise the elections.'

'Yes, but I read somewhere, Nikuv's brief was to work with the CIO and armed youth. We've all heard about the intimidation and forced relocation of voters and the delays and obstruction of voter registration in areas that favour the opposition. Do you think they help manipulate the election results?'

'Who knows? But we're not talking about winning the election here. We're talking about making Matabeleland independent. ZANU-PF can cheat their way to another rigged election victory in the Shona areas of the country, but we'll be separating Matabeleland from that mess.'

'So, are we talking about going to war with Zimbabwe?' said Vince.

'No, we're talking about helping the people of Matabeleland defend themselves against an abusive government. Many Ndebele have had enough, and they're ready to retaliate against police brutality and intimidation by ZANU-PF. But without weapons and training, they have no chance.'

'It's a bold plan,' said Kevin. 'What if they bring the 5th Brigade in again?'

'We'll be ready for them this time. Mugabe and his cronies will be too busy, running from their own people, to worry about us. Peter here can fill us in about what's happening in Matabeleland.'

'A lot of our leaders have come to an untimely end or disappeared,' said Peter, 'and not just in Matabeleland. Recently, in Johannesburg, our secretary in the northern division of the MFF disappeared without a trace. And then his flatmate, Professor Gideon Ncube, supposedly committed suicide by jumping from his thirteenth-floor balcony. He was a loyal supporter of the MFF, and we're suspicious about the circumstances of his death. These are recent examples of what's happening. We all must be very careful. There is a clear and concerted effort to destroy our organisation. If we are to secede from Zimbabwe, we need help and equipment.'

'Who would have thought a small, bankrupt country like Zimbabwe could have its CIO agents active in the Zimbabwean diaspora?' said Solly. 'It's like the KGB. Remember what happened to Heidi Holland? They claimed she committed suicide by hanging herself, but others think the CIO might have had something to do with it. Grace Mugabe claimed to have put a curse on her for writing a book critical of her husband, Robert Mugabe.'

'I expect that's where all their money goes,' said Vince, 'to the politicians and the CIO. The people go hungry while the politicians and their supporters lead a grand life.'

'If it's so dangerous,' said Mike, 'how are we going to separate Matabeleland from Zimbabwe?'

'Well,' said Drake, 'there's lots of support for the secession of Matabeleland. But there's a reason we're the ones here tonight. All of us have done well in our business ventures outside Zimbabwe. Sitting around this table is more wealth than the Zimbabwe government can muster. Even without contributions from other supporters, we can finance the secession of Matabeleland. No doubt we will get contributions from other supporters, but I propose as a first step we each put in ten million US dollars to get things moving.'

Barry whistled through his teeth. 'That's a lot of money, but as you said, we're here because we can afford it.'

The air was heavy with cigar smoke, and a second bottle of Scotch was doing the rounds. Nkala coughed.

'But,' said Noel, 'with the CIO so active, there's no way we can organise, train and communicate without drawing attention to ourselves.'

'Ah,' said Drake. 'My suggestion is we train near the area where Zimbabwe, Botswana and South Africa meet, so we can jump the border if things get hot. My guess is, we could set up a clandestine training camp without drawing too much attention to ourselves. But training without combat experience isn't much good. I propose we send our trained recruits into areas where there's poaching. Our recruits will need to avoid Zimbabwe Parks and Wildlife rangers while engaging with the poachers, who will undoubtedly give us tough opposition. It'll be good training, and we'll be helping the wildlife and the people of Matabeleland.'

'Well, that's good enough for me,' said Barry. 'I'm in, what about the rest of you guys?' One after another, each of those present raised their hand.

'Who will run this operation?' said Vince.

'If no one has any objections, I'd like to volunteer my son, Alan,' said Drake. 'He's a lieutenant in the Australian special forces, and he's had combat experience in Afghanistan with the SAS (Special Air Service). They are expert in all the skills we need for our Mthwakazi operation, and

Alan has been involved in training inexperienced recruits for the Afghan army. He's keen to get involved with our plans.'

* * *

After the meeting broke up and everyone retired to their rooms, George Drake and Solly Bernstein had a quiet drink together. 'Will Alan be able to get leave from the SAS?' said Solly.

'I omitted to mention he's not with the SAS anymore. He resigned after his last tour of duty when they sent him home early.'

'Oh, why was that?'

'They assigned him and one other to go with a captain on a special mission to Cyprus. Just before their departure, something delayed the captain, and he missed the flight. So, Alan and the other fellow travelled ahead, leaving the captain to follow the next day.'

'And they got into trouble in Cyprus?'

'Unknown to anyone else, the captain arranged for his wife to meet him there. He planned to spend a few days relaxing after the mission. On Alan's first night in Limassol he met an Australian woman, and typical of Alan, he gave her a service and oil change. Unfortunately, it was the wrong brand of oil; she turned out to be the captain's wife.'

'I see!'

'After the mission, Alan returned to Afghanistan, but the captain and the other chap stayed on in Cyprus. Somehow the captain discovered what went on before his arrival. Alan's commanding officer sent him back to Australia before the captain got back from his trip. Alan missed all the excitement and action in Afghanistan, and soon after returning to Australia, he resigned from the army. He's wasting his time in Sydney going to night clubs and chasing women. Music and girls are all he's ever been interested in since his mother died when he was thirteen.'

'And now he's keen to get involved in our African adventure?'

'I also lied about that. Alan knows nothing about it yet. To be honest, I'd rather he worked for me in my business in Melbourne. The sad truth is he's not ready, and I fear he may never be. With prayers and a little nudging from me he might mature and realise there're worse ways to spend your life than running a large business empire.'

Drake looked at his watch. 'Where the devil is Andrew Dube? He should have arrived by now.'

CHAPTER 10

GEORGE Drake came down to breakfast late. The others were already there, enjoying their eggs and bacon and cups of tea and coffee. Solly looked up from his plate. 'Something wrong George? Didn't sleep well?'

'Andrew Dube didn't arrive last night. Mr Wong, my man in Singapore is investigating what happened to him. Apparently, he and his son Tyson travelled on the Jungle Railway, which means they would have crossed the border at Sungai Kolok. Wong says he gave them clear written instructions, but somewhere along the way they've got lost or disappeared.' The spirited chatter of the group came to an abrupt halt. 'That's all the information I have at present.'

Nkala's face turned grey. 'CIO! It must be them.'

'Surely not here in Thailand,' said Mike.

'I tell you, they're watching us, watching everything we do.'

'Well, let's not jump to conclusions,' said Drake. 'We must wait for more news.'

'Have you spoken to Alan yet?' said Solly.

'No, he must have switched off his phone. As soon as I get hold of him, I'll tell him to get over to Joburg and get in touch with you.'

The news of Dube came with the effect of a cold, damp washer on the back of the neck on a winter's morning. By lunchtime, all the group left for home apart from Nkala, Solly and Drake. Nkala would stick close to Solly, at least as far as Joburg. Drake waited for news of Dube. If he heard nothing, he'd head to Singapore to help in the search for his old friend.

* * *

Alan Drake ignored the vibration of the mobile phone in his pocket. The attractive young woman standing next to him at the bar took all his attention. Dark, shoulder length hair framed a pale flawless skin, and the short mini skirt revealed shapely legs. Other guys in the bar tried to break into their conversation from time to time, but Alan made it clear they weren't welcome. The phone vibrated again, but Alan ignored it. Long ago, he learnt the dangers of distraction in a competitive situation.

The barman slid two more Coronas with lime wedges across the counter, and Alan handed one to the young woman.

'So,' she said, 'you were with the SAS in Afghanistan?'

'That's right.'

'Did you get any medals?'

'Yes, would you like to see them?'

'You've got them on you?'

'No, they're in my apartment. It's within close walking distance.'

'We've only just met. Do you really expect me to go with you to your apartment to look at your medals?'

'Well, you might also like to see my war wounds.'

'Show me your war wounds here.'

'You don't expect me to strip off in public, do you? I'd be arrested for public indecency.'

'Hah! And next you'll be expecting me to strip off in your apartment.'

'Gail!' Alan turned to scowl at the man who'd interrupted them, sizing him up quickly, peroxide hair, ritzy looks and a bit of a prick.

'I've got the Porsche tonight, Gail. Coming for a spin?'

'Not tonight, thanks Donald.' Gail turned to Alan. 'Well, I suppose we might as well see those medals.'

The mobile buzzed in his pocket. This time, Alan answered it. 'Alan, don't you ever sleep? Do you know it's two in the morning, your time? Where the hell have you been? I've been trying to call you all evening.'

'I'm having a quiet drink in a bar, Dad. What's up?'

'A quiet drink! What's all that shouting and loud music I can hear in the background?'

'It's just some guys celebrating. Nothing to do with me. Why are you calling me this late at night?'

'Alan, I want you to get over to Joburg ASAP. When you get there, contact your Uncle Solly. He's got an important job for you.'

'What job is that?'

'He'll tell you when you get there. All I can say is, it's in Zimbabwe.'

'Can't you tell me now?' Experience told Alan when his father was evasive, it was best to stay clear.

'How long will this job take?'

'I don't know; a year or two, perhaps more.'

'Are you kidding? Dad, I've just got out of the army. I need a break.'

'Just got out! You've been out of the army for three months. Now you're wasting your time, loafing around in Melbourne. Your Uncle Solly is expecting you, so get moving.'

'I'll check if I can get on a flight to Joburg, but it may not be easy at such short notice.'

'Don't bother checking! My office has already made the bookings for you. Go to the office in the morning and talk to my secretary. Alice will give you all the details, plus your ticket to Perth and your connecting flight to Joburg. And don't try any funny stuff with her. She's new, and I don't want you scaring her away. It's hard to find good secretaries these days. You've got a little over twenty-four hours before your flight, so start packing.'

The phone went dead. 'Bugger!' Alan muttered under his breath, 'He still treats me like a child.' He was silent as they walked to his apartment, three blocks from the bar. Alan opened the front door and switched on the light. The dimmer control was turned down suitably low, giving his studio apartment an immediate romantic ambiance. Alan always took care to set the dimmer control before going out for the evening, in the expectation he'd bring a young lady back to the apartment later.

'Is there a problem?' Gail asked.

'Nah, it's just my Dad. He likes to give orders. He wants me to go to South Africa tomorrow.'

'Well, we've got no time to waste,' she said, reaching for Alan's belt.'

'Hell, I thought I was fast. Hey, why don't you come with me?' said Alan, running his hands up the back of her legs under her short skirt.

'No, I have to work tomorrow.'

'Bugger work! It'll be a great trip.' Alan slipped his hands inside her pants and squeezed her firm backside.

'No, I can't. I've got commitments.'

'What commitments?'

'Well, my husband for a start,' she said, sliding down the zip of Alan's trousers.

'You're married?'

'Yes, you saw my husband, Donald, in the bar. He works in a luxury car dealership.'

'Oh! The way you dismissed him, I thought he was just some random pest.'

'Hey! That's a good description for him. He is a random pest.'

* * *

In the three months since Alan left the army, he'd spent his time leading the life he'd always imagined for himself. He was drinking more and exercising less, and his fitness suffered, though it didn't yet show on his tall, athletic frame. He reasoned, if he chased after enough women, it would compensate for the active military life that kept him in great shape. Alan viewed his womanising as a keep fit programme. As he would in the gym, he stuck to a rigid schedule of at least three times a week, each time with a different partner, living up to his motto, So Many Women, So Little Time.

Often, his carousing would put him on the wrong side of a woman's escort. Unarmed combat was an area in which Alan excelled, which meant he usually walked away with his female prize and a boosted ego.

Alan still smarted from the way he left the military. It was his decision to leave the service, but his posting away from the action in Afghanistan gave him little choice.

Alan was enjoying life. The only dark cloud on the horizon was his father's insistence that Alan join his company. 'When I've gone,' George would say, 'who will run my business empire? You need to think about that, boy. Start at the bottom and learn the business. See how the organisation operates, work hard, and in ten years you'll be on the board. I know you don't like to study, but you don't need a business degree. Hands-on experience is far more valuable. This company will need another Drake at the helm, and like it or not, you're the only one available.'

The flight boarding announcement interrupted Alan's thoughts. He often travelled with his father or the SAS, but he'd never been to Zimbabwe. At least it was somewhere different, a new experience. Although he'd accompanied his father on trips to Johannesburg, he'd not seen anything of the country. It was always a case of racing to the hotel and then dinner with his father's business associates. They were a boring bunch who spent all their time yakking about the stock market and exchange rates. The only ones he was familiar with was his Aunt Ruth and Uncle Solly. They were old friends of the family and stayed with Alan and his parents whenever they visited Melbourne. After Alan's mother died when he was thirteen, they visited once more, but that was years ago.

One consolation for Alan was his belief Uncle Solly would stay away from any crazy scheme. Alan considered him to be a moderating influence even on his father. His father was the troubling side of the equation. George Drake was a very persuasive man, and Alan hoped that his father's persuasiveness did not outweigh Uncle Solly's moderation. Why was his father so evasive about what the mission involved? Two years, maybe more, sounded like forever. Surely, whatever it was wouldn't take that long. Another troubling thought crossed Alan's mind. His father often told him that neither he nor Solly, nor any other of his associates maintained any business interest in Zimbabwe. 'It's no place for business,' his father would say. 'Perhaps one day, but not now.' So why the hell was he headed for Zimbabwe?

The engines roared, reaching a crescendo, and the plane vibrated until the pilot released the brakes. Slowly at first the plane moved forward before picking up speed as it hurtled down the runway. Alan took a deep breath. Oh well! The sooner I'm there, the sooner I'll be back.

CHAPTER 11

ALAN sat in the back seat of the taxi taking him from Johannesburg's OR Tambo International Airport to the city. On the left, in Isando and Meadowdale, large commercial warehouses sprung up like mushrooms. They drove past Bedford View and the old residential suburbs before climbing up onto the raised freeway that edged the city centre. An involuntary shudder ran through Alan as Ponte City loomed on the Johannesburg skyline.

The nightmarish Ponte City tower stood prominent on the right. With its dark inner core and turbulent history, the building always reminded Alan of the gateway to hell. The structure looked like a tube standing on its end. The public balconies surrounding its hollow core rose fifty-five-storeys to the distant view of the sky. Daylight seldom reached ground level inside the massive building. When it opened in 1975, the café at its base required constant floodlighting, adding to the sense of foreboding.

Ponte was the tallest and one of the most luxurious residential apartment blocks in South Africa. When the authorities found it impossible to enforce the segregation laws in the neighbourhood, they declared it a grey area and cut off the entire suburb's power. The police withdrew, and gangsters hijacked the building along with several other apartment blocks. As the whites moved out, the blacks replaced them, and property prices plummeted.

People feared entering Ponte or the surrounding area, and with the lifts not operating, residents threw their rubbish into its hollow core. The rubbish dump grew to a height of fourteen floors, and the building held three times its nominal capacity of three and a half thousand residents. Ponte became a symbol of the inner city's lawlessness. It housed an illegal brothel, and for a price, people could get drugs, guns and false passports.

With the coming of the 2010 Soccer World Cup, the owners began to clean up the property. They evicted the residents and removed the rubbish, and in the process, they discovered dead bodies and huge rats. They also renovated the apartments, but despite stringent security measures, the building never regained its elevated status.

Each time Alan visited, Joburg looked older and more tired. Africa was taking its toll on the once dynamic South African city. The taxi turned off the elevated Francois Oberholzer Freeway onto the De Villiers Graaff Motorway, drove past the railway station and Wits University, and turned left onto Jan Smuts Avenue and headed to the Crowne Plaza Hotel in Rosebank.

After a shower, Alan took the lift to the ground floor bar lounge where he downed a beer and ate a decent meal in the restaurant before turning in for the night. He needed to recover from the long flight from Australia. Tomorrow night he was due for dinner at the Bernstein's house. Breakfast was not a priority, so after dinner, Alan placed the do not disturb sign on his door and took out a Castle Lager from the minibar and slumped into the armchair. What the hell could be so important that he needed to rush to meet with Solly Bernstein? Ah well! He'd find out soon enough.

* * *

After a light lunch in the Rosebank shopping complex, Alan passed the afternoon wandering through the shops. He liked the unique character of the place. Shopping centres in Australia seemed to be clones of one another. The trees and fountains in the open-air walking malls divided the shops, giving the centre a village atmosphere.

At six-thirty that evening, Alan waited at the front of the hotel. Soon a silver-grey Volkswagen Passat pulled up and Solly Bernstein jumped out. 'Welcome to Joburg Alan. It's been a long time.'

'Yes, a long time. I was only fifteen when I last saw you. A lot has happened since then.' Solly looked aged and a lot greyer than when they last met. If they weren't expecting to meet up, Alan doubted they'd recognise one another in the street.

'Has your father explained to you what this project is all about?' Solly asked.

'No, he said you would explain it all.'

After Solly outlined the plan, Alan remained silent. Why does Dad have to foist this crazy project on to me? Independence for Matabeleland was his mad dream, not mine. Alan often suffered through his father's monologues about Bulawayo and Matabeleland, or Mthwakazi, as he liked to call it.

The crunch of the car tyres on gravel brought Alan back to the present. No sooner was he out of the car when the front door of the grand double story mansion burst open. Solly's wife, Ruth, stopped for a second to admire the tall, blond, athletic figure. Then, she rushed to wrap her arms around him. 'My, Alan, how you've grown! What a handsome young man you've become!'

'Hi, Aunt Ruth. Yes, it's been at least ten years, maybe more.'

'You were a handsome young boy, but now! I can't get over it!'

'Stop embarrassing him, Ruth. Let's go in and introduce him to the others.'

Peter Nkala shook Alan's hand. 'I'm pleased to meet you, Mr Drake. Your father told me about your enthusiasm for our project.'

'Hmm, yes,' said Alan.

Next, Solly introduced him to Barry and Marsha Wolf from Cape Town. So, they too supported the mad scheme. A smart-looking African maid poured Alan a cold Castle Lager in a tall glass.

'How many people are privy to this ma—erm, er, project? As few as possible, I would hope.'

'Well, there's seven of us funding it,' said Solly, 'and I presume also their wives.'

'And the MMF leaders,' said Peter. 'At this stage, few know our plans, but when we recruit our forces, it will be a lot more.'

'Hmm, that might be tricky to handle,' said Alan. 'How long do you think you can keep your plans hidden from the Zimbabwe authorities?'

'We'll only recruit the most dedicated,' said Peter. 'One hundred good men will be more than a handful for the authorities.'

'Uh-huh,' said Alan, sounding doubtful.

'When you come to Bulawayo, I will introduce you to the MFF leaders,' said Peter. 'Solly has booked you into the Bulawayo Rainbow Hotel. When you arrive, I will get a message to you, telling you where and when we can meet.'

'Dinner is served,' said the maid. Ruth led the party through to the dining room.

* * *

After dinner, the maid served port and Solly and Barry smoked cigars. Peter Nkala and health-conscious Alan declined the cigars, but the port was too good to refuse. The conversation turned to lighter topics with Solly and Barry regaling the others with tales of their youth back in Bulawayo. Peter could relate to their stories to a degree, but although Alan visited South Africa with his parents twice before, he'd never been to Zimbabwe.

At half-past eleven, Barry and Marsha retired to bed, and Peter Nkala excused himself and went up to his room. 'Do you mind if Ruth sees you home,' said Solly. 'After all those drinks, I don't think I should drive.'

In the car, Ruth said, 'You're going up to Bulawayo day after tomorrow. I know of a wonderful restaurant if you'd like dinner tomorrow night. Peter is travelling to Bulawayo tomorrow morning, and Solly is flying down to Cape Town with Barry and Marsha. It will be just you and me.'

'Thank you, Aunt Ruth, that will be nice.'

'You're too old to call me Aunt Ruth, Alan. Now you're all grown up, just Ruth will do.'

Alan laughed. 'OK, I'll try, but breaking the habit of a lifetime won't be easy.'

'I'm sure we'll find a way to make it work,' said Ruth.

Alan worried people might think he was out with his mother. He'd noticed Ruth's smooth, fresh looking skin and her tight, shapely figure earlier in the evening, but now her attractiveness hit home. She might be double his age, but any man would be proud to escort her.

'OK then, seven o'clock tomorrow,' said Ruth, as she dropped him off at the Crown Plaza.

The concierge saluted Alan as he walked into the hotel's reception area.

* * *

The Bottega Restaurant in 4th Avenue, Parkhurst, lived up to Ruth's promise. Intimate, candlelit tables and the dimmed chandelier provided a romantic atmosphere, with the floor to ceiling windows giving a nice outdoor feel. Excellent table service and a huge choice of alcoholic drinks completed the picture. Ruth's recommendation to try the spare ribs worked a treat. They weren't on the menu, but word-of-mouth spread their reputation far and wide.

After dinner, Ruth drove Alan back to the hotel. 'How is your room?' asked Ruth.

'Very comfortable, thanks, and good views.'

'A lot of our business visitors stay at the house, but I've suggested to Solly that perhaps we should put people up in a hotel. I've never seen the rooms at the Crowne Plaza. May I see your room?'

'Yes, of course you can.'

* * *

Alan pressed the button for the seventh floor. He and Ruth shuffled towards the back of the lift as another couple squeezed though the closing doors and stood in silence in front. Alan felt a little awkward as Ruth glanced across at him and smiled. He'd taken many women back to his room in the past but never anyone he considered an aunt. For as long as he could remember she'd been Aunt Ruth. But she only wanted to see his room to judge its suitability for Solly's business guests. It was unthinkable he'd dare to try anything on her, and she'd be aghast if she could read his mind. Perhaps it would be easier if he continued to call her Aunt Ruth.

The other couple got out at the sixth floor and Alan and Ruth progressed to the seventh. They walked down the carpeted corridor to Alan's room. He held open the door for Ruth to enter first. She at once moved to the window. 'What a beautiful view at night! Those twinkling lights in the distance! Don't put the light on yet. This is so lovely.'

Alan walked up to the window. 'At daytime, it's a sea of green jacarandas with building dropped in here and there, peeping through the canopy. It would be a wonderful sight in October or November when the jacarandas bloom. My favourite time is when the blossoms fall, and the ground looks like it's covered with purple snow. Oh, look! Is that a satellite or a plane?'

'Where, where is it?'

Alan moved behind Ruth and put his left hand on her waist and pointed with his right. 'Oh yes, I see it now,' said Ruth, covering Alan's left hand with her right and leaning back into him. She seemed comfortable with his physical proximity, and in any other circumstance, Alan would interpret such a move as a signal to leave his hand where it lay.

The distant, flying object forgotten, they stood, looking out the window, with Alan unsure what to do next. He was uncertain, even nervous; a sensation he'd not experienced in years. Could he? Should he? Dare he? Alan closed his eyes and took a deep breath; only one way to find out. Alan put his right arm around Ruth and slid his hand into the loose top of her dress and cupped her left breast through the soft bra she wore. He held his breath, waiting for her reaction. There was none.

Then, Ruth leant her head to one side, exposing a delicate neck. Alan kissed it softly as he ran his left hand down Ruth's stomach to her thigh and slipped his right hand under her bra. A delicate three-pronged attack designed to confuse any resistance. Again, there was none. Her nipple swelled as he stroked it gently between his forefinger and thumb. Little by little he raised the loose skirt of her dress and moved his left hand around to her inner thigh. Still no sign of resistance from Ruth. Alan slipped his hand inside the top of her brief panties down to her neat bush. 'Not here,' she whispered. 'Let's go to the bed.'

* * *

The mid-morning flight to Bulawayo meant an early start. Ruth looked fresh considering she'd not come to Alan's hotel with a change of clothes. She always carried a small travelling toothbrush and a lipstick in her handbag. No one would have guessed she'd spent almost the entire night making love. The adrenalin kept Alan going, and he felt bright and energetic. After breakfast in the hotel, Ruth drove Alan to the airport.

'Your father would be appalled if he knew we'd slept together.'

'He's not going to know.'

'Did you plan to sleep with me?'

'Not until the hotel lift. That's when I suspected something might happen. What about you? When did you decide it was OK for us to have sex?'

'I first thought of it when your father complained about you chasing all the girls and their mothers. I was jealous you never tried anything with me.'

'That's because, as far back as when my mother was alive, I always knew you as Aunt Ruth. I never thought of my girlfriends' mothers as my aunts.'

'Yes, but I'm not really your aunt, am I? To answer your question, when you were at our house, night before last, I couldn't take my eyes off you. I knew then, we'd make love. That's why I suggested we have dinner together.'

'So, you weren't just thinking about my nourishment?'

'Good Heavens, no! Well, not in the usually accepted way.'

The drive to the airport passed much too quickly.

At the entrance to immigration, they kissed goodbye. 'Don't leave it too long before you visit us,' said Ruth. 'I need to see you again, soon.' One last wave from Alan, and he disappeared around the corner and was gone.

* * *

Alan passed through immigration and customs without difficulty and walked straight to the departure lounge. His timing was perfect as a few minutes later the air hostess at the gate announced the boarding of his flight. He found his seat and stowed his hand luggage in the overhead locker. The plane was not full, and the flight was smooth and comfortable. Alan's thoughts were still with Ruth. Their lovemaking was tireless and all-consuming. That's what he wanted; that's what he needed, but she belonged to someone else. It was clear old Solly was not meeting her needs.

Alan looked down on the countryside. It was dry and brown. Someone mentioned the last rainy season was a good one. There was no sign of that now. The hot African sun and four rainless months parched the land.

The plane flew directly over Bulawayo, giving Alan his first look at the city that would be his home for at least the next year. It looked pleasant enough from that height. Past the city, the airport loomed in the distance, an isolated cluster of buildings in the middle of flat, open, undulating, yellow grassland.

A banked approach and a smooth landing didn't seem dramatic enough for this new chapter in Alan's life. On the left, the terminal building of the Joshua Mqabuko Nkomo International Airport—formerly Bulawayo Airport—was undergoing building work that appeared near completion. The first thing Alan noticed when descending the steps to the tarmac was the fresh air. A gentle breeze blew across the open countryside surrounding the airport.

It was his first visit to Zimbabwe, and somehow, the stories of 'darkest Africa' did not fit with Alan's first impressions of the city.

CHAPTER 12

CIGARETTE smoke filled the meeting room on the first floor of the old sandstone building in the Bulawayo CBD. For a non-smoker the hazy atmosphere was choking, but no one present seemed to mind. A dozen leaders of the MFF gathered for Peter Nkala's debrief about his trip to Chiang Mai. Hushed, excited chatter and an air of anticipation filled the room. The news, Andrew Dube and his son were missing in Thailand, put a chill through those present. Everyone suspected foul play. How would anyone know what Andrew Dube was doing in that part of the world, and how on earth could they arrange for his abduction? He was the leading light in the MFF, and his disappearance a serious blow. The leaders voiced several suggestions.

'The president visits Singapore often. Perhaps his bodyguards saw Dube and arranged for his abduction.'

'No, it must be the CIO. Don't they also go there?'

'We must be very careful,' said Nkala. 'If the CIO are watching us, the next step we take will be dangerous.'

'What is the next step?' someone asked.

'Our wealthy, white business friends are keen to support our movement, but they believe we need professional help. I'm sure many of you remember George Drake, who once lived in Bulawayo?'

'Yes,' someone called out, 'he was an important person in this town. My brother worked in one of his factories. After he left, the factory closed, and the workers are still unemployed.'

'Yes, well,' said Nkala, 'he and his friends have agreed to fund our struggle and give military training to our leading young men. We can't afford a repeat of the Gukurahundi, so we need the ability to defend our people.'

'How can they give military training?' someone asked. 'Who will train our people?'

'George Drake has volunteered his son, Alan Drake. He's an officer in the Australian special forces and a very experienced soldier. If nothing else that proves their commitment to our cause.'

'Isn't it dangerous for us to be working with someone like that? If they could abduct Andrew Dube in Thailand, we might all be at risk.'

'That is true, and that is why I propose we have only one point of contact with him. Someone who can pass messages to him and receive reports on progress and then report back to our group.'

'They'll know you've just returned from Thailand and might have you under surveillance. How will you explain all the meetings with Alan Drake?'

'It doesn't have to be me who keeps in touch with him. If one of us has a suitable daughter living at home who would pretend to be his girlfriend, he could pass messages through regular visits to her house. That shouldn't look too suspicious.'

'Does anyone here have a suitable daughter?'

Horace Gumede put his hand up to speak. 'I have three daughters. Perhaps one of them—.'

Leonard Donda, the comedic loudmouth of the group called out, 'Oh, come on Gumede! Your daughters have the backsides of elephants. Can you imagine them attracting a white man?' Everyone, including Gumede, laughed. 'We might say they're beautiful, but the whites have different tastes.'

'What about you, Ndlovu, don't you have thin, pretty daughters?'

Luke Ndlovu, a tall, slim, dignified-looking man, listened more than he spoke. 'My two older daughters are married, and my fourth daughter is still at school. I can ask my third daughter if she will help us.'

'What do you mean, "ask her", just tell her.'

'It doesn't work like that in our house, Donda. My daughters are strong-willed and independent. I will ask her and let Nkala know if she agrees.'

'OK then, let's move on,' said Nkala. 'I've invited Alan Drake to come here tonight and meet you all. He might have ideas of his own. He should be here soon.'

* * *

Alan arrived in Bulawayo, early afternoon on the South African Airways flight from Johannesburg. On the horizon he noted the distant skyline of the city. The warm, late winter day gave no hint of the evening chill that would follow. Solly forewarned Alan about the surly officials and endless queues and delays at the Beit Bridge border crossing from South Africa. Alan expected the same at Bulawayo Airport, but going through immigration and customs was quick and easy, a novelty for Zimbabwe. The immigration officers proved friendly, and even the customs officers smiled and waved him through after one or two cursory questions.

Out front of the airport terminal he boarded a small, near-empty minibus for the city. The only other passengers, a middle-aged Chinese man sitting at the back, and a young Indian woman sitting at the front, behind the driver. Alan chose a seat on the right, halfway down the aisle. When Alan greeted the occupants as he entered the minibus, the young Indian woman smiled and nodded, and the Chinese man ignored him. They all sat in silence as the driver got in and started the motor and drove down the road. The minibus vibrated and shook, sounding more like a tractor as it picked up speed. That was the Zimbabwe Alan expected.

Yellow, sunburnt grass waved as the bus trundled past, and soon they were on the edge of the city which was much closer than it looked when viewed from the airport. The accommodating driver dropped off the Chinese man at the Grey's Inn and Alan at the Bulawayo Rainbow Hotel. The young Indian woman remained on the minibus as it rumbled off to its final stop.

George Drake's secretary in Melbourne made Alan's hotel booking when she booked his flights. The friendly hotel staff gave him an enthusiastic welcome. 'There's a message for you, Sir,' said the receptionist, handing Alan a sealed envelope.

In his hotel room, Alan opened the envelope and read the message. It requested his presence at a welcome drink at seven p.m. that evening. The invitation stated he should walk to the corner of 10th Avenue and Main Street where a guide would wait to take him to the gathering. The message, signed Peter, didn't mention dinner, so Alan showered before a quick walk to get his bearings, and after an early meal downstairs, he headed for the rendezvous.

Darkness fell soon after six o'clock, and Alan strolled through the empty streets to the meeting place. When he arrived at the specified meeting point, he noticed an African man standing on the diagonally opposite corner. Alan waited to see any sign of recognition from the man, but suddenly a voice behind him said, 'Mr Drake, please follow me.' Alan turned to see a scruffy, young man in grey trousers, an old khaki felt jacket and dirty white runners. Before Alan could say anything, the young man walked off down Main Street, with his hands in his pockets. It was clear the young African wanted no one to see them walking together, so Alan followed at a discreet distance. The young man walked in circles, back-tracked and zig-zagged for about fifteen minutes. By then, Alan was sure no one followed them. Without signalling his intent, the young man suddenly turned into a doorway which Alan was sure they'd passed twice before in their circuitous walk. 'First floor, they're expecting you,' the young man said, and walked off without looking back.

Alan ascended the long, wide, wooden staircase of the old colonial-style building with its high ceilings. Near the top of the stairs he saw a heavily built African man standing guard at a single door on the landing. He opened the door and motioned Alan to enter. Peter Nkala stepped forward to greet Alan with a warm handshake. 'Welcome to Bulawayo. My colleagues are keen to meet you.' Nkala led Alan to a desk on a raised platform at the end of the room. 'Gentlemen, may I present Mr Alan

Drake, who has come all the way from Australia to help us achieve our goals.' The people present gave Alan a murmured, if cautious, greeting. 'Alan, let me tell you what our thoughts are, and then you can tell us if you have any more ideas.'

After Peter filled him in, the room waited to hear what Alan might say. 'It's a good idea I have only one point of contact. The fewer people who know of our plans and operations the better for our security. My only thought at this point is that if questioned, I should say I am a security contractor hired to look after someone's business or residential property. But again, the fewer of you involved the better, and that leads me to the biggest question I have. How can you keep the secrecy needed to train a small army for such an ambitious project? What if someone drinks too much in a bar somewhere and talks about our plans? I know you take great care with your security; I saw that this evening. But if someone abducted Andrew Dube and his son in Thailand, doesn't that mean state intelligence, the CIO or someone else is on to you?'

'Yes, we are careful with our security,' said Nkala. 'Almost everyone in this room has lost relatives or friends during the Gukurahundi. All the young people we recruit to our cause are in the same situation. None of them are looking for money or a job. They are all unpaid volunteers who want justice for their lost loved ones. Loyalty to the cause will ensure the secrecy we need.'

'OK,' said Alan, 'but I had to ask.'

One of the MFF leaders raised his hand, and Peter Nkala nodded, giving him permission to speak. 'I would like to ask our new friend,' said a timid-looking elderly man, 'if this visit is your first to Zimbabwe and you don't speak our language, how will you manage with training our recruits?'

'That's a good question,' said Alan. 'I'll try to learn your language as fast as possible. As a soldier, I'm used to adapting to unfamiliar environments. That is part of my training and my speciality. In Afghanistan, I trained recruits who spoke little or no English. The language barrier there was far worse than here.'

The questioner seemed satisfied with Alan's answer, nodded and sat down on his chair.

Nine o'clock, and most of the attendees made their apologies and drifted away. Three or four, including Peter Nkala and Luke Ndlovu, remained. Only then, Alan noticed an attractive young woman, standing near the door. She wore a brown, suede miniskirt and jacket. 'Who is she?' Alan asked. 'She's not one of the MFF leaders, is she?'

'That's Molly Dlamini,' said Peter Nkala. 'No, she's not a leader, but she supports our cause. She is fluent in English, Ndebele and Shona, more so than any of us. She is a real asset. The 5th Brigade murdered her parents in the Gukurahundi, and she wants retribution, though she's never said as much. I understand she is also a first-class tracker.'

It was time for them to go their separate ways. 'Someone will contact you in the next couple of days,' said Nkala. Luke here will see if his daughter will cooperate with us, but if not, we'll find someone else. Alan looked for Molly Dlamini, but she'd left, melted into the night along with the others. Alan walked back to the hotel with a lot on his mind. How would this operation play out? His father suggested it was a one-year project, but from the tone of the meeting, it looked to be a much longer campaign. And then there were all those MFF leaders, looking to him to help achieve their goal. How realistic was it? How could a small band of dedicated Africans split a country down the middle?

The quiet dignity and determination of the leaders gave Alan a little more confidence, but were they being naïve? They took the project most seriously, and Alan considered it might be time he did too. While he waited for contact about the arrangements, he would relax and if possible, enjoy himself. Near the hotel a loud noise and bass music attracted his attention. A nightclub? Time to check the local scene. As he entered, the excited chatter and loud music hit him like a wave on a king tide. It was deafening. Alan bought a beer and stood at the bar to survey the scene. The men outnumbered the women by a large margin, but the few women present flitted amongst the men like butterflies in a flower garden. If those girls visited the night club on their own, what was their purpose? Perhaps they were not the company he sought.

The dress of several of the male patrons fascinated Alan. True peacocks, displaying their wealth or trying to attract a partner. They would have to compete for the few women present, or could they be planning to attract someone else? He'd heard gays were not welcome in black Africa, so perhaps it was just a matter of dress sense. In Johannesburg he'd seen men's clothing shops display fashions that would stand up well in the Rio de Janeiro Mardi Gras.

No, he'd have to look elsewhere for his entertainment, but where? Maybe back at the hotel? When Alan walked into the hotel, everything was quiet. The bar was open, but it was empty. Oh well! There's always tomorrow.

CHAPTER 13

THE visit to Luke Ndlovu's family village would prove an unforget-table experience for Alan. Before, he'd only seen Luke in the city where he always dressed in a smart navy-blue pin-striped suit, white shirt, light blue tie and shiny black shoes. He appeared every bit the successful African businessman. But now in his rural village, dressed in the traditional regalia of an Ndebele headman, Luke presented a different image. Alan looked twice and blinked a few times before he recognised him. He wore an animal skin skirt and cloak, and a ring made of serval fur around his head.

Luke lived in a comfortable five-bedroom house in The Suburbs, one of Bulawayo's smarter addresses close to the city centre. He also maintained a rondavel in his home village in the bush, about sixty kilometres out on the Plumtree Road to Botswana.

This evening, Alan was the guest of honour at the village. He was there to meet Luke's relatives. The men, bare above the waist, wore a short skirt-like garment made from fabric and animal skins. Luke told them Alan was an agronomist from Australia, there to help the village increase the productivity of the land on which they all depended. In fact, Alan was there to help assess the men for suitability for recruitment into the top-secret project the MFF planned.

The men sat in a large circle, some on low stools and others on the ground. Counting Alan and Luke, there were twenty men in all.

'We seldom wear our traditional dress,' said Luke, 'but tonight you are our special guest, so we thought we'd give you an experience of the old Africa. For us it's like a fancy-dress party. All these people are my family. Here we have my girls, and my nephews from my brother and two sisters.'

'I am honoured,' said Alan, 'They are fine-looking young men with clear eyes. Many of them could make good recruits.'

'Ah! Here are the women with the beer,' said Luke. 'We will drink and eat first and then we will talk; just you and I.'

Two young women, wearing short skirts and multi-coloured boob tubes, stood behind Alan and Luke. Each held a large, rounded, hollowed-out, calabash gourd made from the mature, dried fruit of the Lagenaria Siceraria vine. Lightly carved, traditional Ndebele decoration covered the hard, brown, shiny outer surface of the gourds. The villagers sometimes ate the young fruit of the vine as a vegetable, but the original purpose of cultivating the plant was to use the mature fruit as vessels for carrying water and food.

On this occasion the gourds contained the home brewed African beer that the women of the village made from sorghum and millet, and sometimes maize. The young woman behind Alan gave him a gourd, and the other young woman passed the second gourd to his host. 'Drink and pass it on,' said Luke. The gourd was almost full and heavy, and Alan hesitated, wondering how he would drink from the gourd without it running down either side of his mouth and onto his shirt.

The beer's strong smell pre-warned Alan of the sour, lemony flavoured sip he was about to take. Careful not to spill any of the beer, after one sip, Alan handed the gourd to the man on his right and watched as he hungrily gulped down the thick, milky white liquid. The gourd worked its way anti-clockwise round the circle, while Luke's gourd moved in the opposite direction. When the two gourds met in the circle's middle, opposite Alan and Luke, they worked their way back towards them. Alan breathed a sigh of relief when halfway back, one man held the gourd aloft, showing it was empty. But then the young woman behind Alan gave him a shy smile and curtsey and handed him another gourd full of the home brewed African beer. This time Alan took a big gulp and ended up chewing and swallowing the sediment that floated in the liquid.

The young women delivered several more gourds, and Alan soon moderated the volume of beer he drank from each new gourd handed to him. The men around the circle were soon merry, with some drinking twice from the gourd before it ran empty. Luke leant across to Alan and said, 'The men sit in a particular order. Those who are less suited for our purpose are the ones who can drink twice from each gourd. The others are more mature and responsible; they're the ones who I believe would most help our cause.'

'I notice the men show particular respect to those two men on the stools opposite us, where the gourds meet,' said Alan.

'Yes, they are my nephews. In time, one will succeed me as the headman, and he can continue the work we have started. The girls who brought us the beer are my daughters. My third daughter is the one who served you, and the other, my fourth daughter, is still at school.'

'You are a lucky man Luke, to have such a fine family.'

'Come, it's time to eat. Later I will introduce you to my children, and then afterwards we can talk in private.'

The women brought Alan and Luke tin plates containing sadza, or isitshwala as the Ndebele preferred to call it. It was a sticky, maize-meal, savoury porridge, served with boiled, wild vegetables and a stew in rich gravy. Alan found it more appealing than the beer though he thought a little salt might improve the sadza's flavour. The rest of the men helped themselves from large communal pots near the cooking fires burning on one side of the circle. Alan appreciated this was a special treat for them as they all chatted excitedly between mouthfuls of food.

When they'd eaten, Luke introduced his two daughters to Alan. Dalubuhle is my third daughter. The one who will be your girlfriend. Dalubuhle smiled shyly and gave a little curtsey. Sibusiso is my fourth daughter and is still at school.

To Alan, the two girls looked similar though Sibusiso was a little fuller-faced. They both wore their hair short-cropped, looking something like crew cuts. It was the most common hairstyle for African women, and it accentuated the girl's smooth skin and pretty faces. As he looked at the girls, Alan had reservations about Dalubuhle playing the part of his girlfriend. He couldn't imagine himself in a relationship with someone who wore their hair shorter than him.

Next, Luke introduced his two nephews. Their bearing impressed Alan. They were young but mature beyond their years. If they were an example of the raw material he was to train, there'd be no difficulty in developing a small, effective armed force that would be more than a handful for any central government in most parts of Africa.

The evening was catching up with Alan, and he found it difficult to keep his eyes open. This didn't escape Luke's attention. 'A little too much African beer I suspect,' he said. 'Come, I will show you to your hut.' Alan paid little notice to his surroundings which included a reed mat on the ground, a cushion for his head and two blankets; one to lie on and one to cover himself. In no time he was fast asleep.

In the morning, Alan heard the door creek, and someone put down a mug of tea next to him. He muttered a vague 'thank you' but was too sleepy to notice who woke him. Damn! Aside from his shoes, he'd slept all night in his clothes. Luke never mentioned the visit to the village would be an overnight affair. Without his shaver and toothbrush and wearing his crumpled clothing, Alan emerged from his hut looking and feeling like a mess. It reminded him of the army patrols in his time with the SAS. A simple breakfast of porridge, fruit and more tea awaited him. Luke and the girls looked neat and fresh, as did the few other early risers.

As Luke drove Alan back to the city after breakfast, Alan was a little more confident of fulfilling the mission the Chiang Mai Group gave him. In his Mercedes, Luke was dressed once more in his city clothes. 'Where are the girls?' Alan asked.

'They'll come back to town later this evening after they help the villagers get everything back to normal. We haven't held a party like that for years. I'm pleased you gave us the excuse to do it.'

'Thank you, but I hope I didn't put you all to too much trouble.'

'That was no trouble, Alan. It was a pleasure. But many Ndebele feel everyday life is trouble, and that's why we have you over here.'

Luke's words reminded Alan of the seriousness of his task in Zimbabwe.

CHAPTER 14

ALAN walked along the pavement of the broad street in Bulawayo's city centre. Angle parking on both sides of the road, and angled centre parking, meant it was easy to find a parking spot in the city. Drivers could thank the city's founders for the wide streets that allowed a span of sixteen oxen to make a comfortable full turn.

The message slipped under his room door during the night gave Alan instructions on how to find Luke Ndlovu's supermarket. He scanned the shop fronts until he saw the sign halfway down the block. The store was bigger than he expected, with several rows of shelving holding a variety of dry goods and cans and jars of all description. A refrigerated section for milk, butter and other cool goods stood against the back wall. How did the section fare with the notorious power blackouts? Perhaps Luke used a generator though petrol and diesel were often in short supply. The supermarket looked better stocked than Alan expected after hearing the horror stories of the shortages in Zimbabwe.

Alan walked up to an idle cashier. 'I would like to see Mr Ndlovu. Could you please tell me where I can find him?'

The cashier called in Ndebele to a man working at the vegetable section. He looked at Alan and pointed to a flight of wooden steps running up one of the side walls of the shop. The steps led to a mezzanine level built into the back third of the supermarket. As Alan ascended the steps, a young woman appeared on the landing at the top. 'Good afternoon Mr Drake, Mr Ndlovu will see you now.' The young woman wore a tight black skirt and a white long-sleeved blouse. Her curly, long, black, shoulder-length hair set off the black-rimmed spectacles she wore. As

Alan followed the young woman, he noticed her shapely legs and figure. The perfect picture of a secretary, and pretty with it too.

Luke Ndlovu rose from his chair and walked across the room to shake Alan's hand. 'Please bring us tea, my dear,' he said, smiling at his secretary. 'If I recall correctly, you take your tea black and no sugar.'

'That's right,' said Alan.

'Yes, me too.'

Luke noted Alan's appreciative look follow the secretary as she left the room, and added, 'There goes my business brain. She looks after our accounts and stock control. I only have to decide what to order from our suppliers, but she also helps me there.'

'Very impressive,' said Alan.

'Yes, she's my accountant. She studied at Wits University in South Africa.'

The secretary brought two cups of tea on a tray and placed them in front of Alan and Luke.

'Well,' said Luke, 'the good news is my daughter has agreed to take part in our little charade. Only she and my wife know of our plan. None of my other family members have any idea about it. They will think you two are in a genuine relationship.'

'Good, and what about my suggestion I act in the role of manager of the security company that looks after your properties?'

'Yes, the MFF leadership likes that idea. It will give you two reasons for your regular visits to my house or office: first as my daughter's boyfriend, and second as my contracted security consultant. Will you need a vehicle and equipment?'

'My father and his friends will take care of all that. What I will need are good employees to act as security guards.'

'That won't be a problem, and when you need them, they can also be your soldiers.'

'In fact, I'll cycle all the trainees through the security guard duties. It will be good for discipline and help me decide the role suited to each man.'

'Come to my house tonight and meet my wife. Have dinner with us and we can talk further. Now, come out the back with me. I want to show you something.' Alan followed Luke through a discreet door leading to the storerooms and an enclosed courtyard that led to the alleyway. Back alleys segmented all of Bulawayo's city blocks. In the enclosed area stood four vehicles. 'Until you make your own arrangements, you can use this Land Rover. It's old, but it's never let me down in all the years I've driven it.'

CHAPTER 15

Beautiful houses and gardens lined Park Road in the inner-city residential area named Suburbs. It was Bulawayo's first suburb and through all the years held on to its 'imaginative' name. The old, well-maintained house nestled in an area bordered by the Bulawayo Athletic Club (BAC) and the Bulawayo Golf Club. The large trees bore witness to the age of the area. As Alan turned into the property, the gravel driveway scrunched under the tyres of the Land Rover.

A beaming Luke emerged from the house to welcome Alan. Inside, Luke introduced him. 'This is my wife, Enid and my daughters, June and Rita, who you've already met.'

The girls were new to Alan. Luke must have got it wrong. June was an attractive young woman dressed in blue jeans and a silky, multi-coloured, short-sleeved blouse. Rita looked like a plumper, teenage version of June. Enid, a mature, dignified-looking woman, kept herself in good shape despite bearing four daughters.

A servant brought Alan and Luke Zambezi beers in tall glasses and beer shandies in tumblers for the women. After a short time, the women left Alan and Luke to talk.

'Luke, there's one thing that worries me a little. I hope you don't think I'm rude, but I'm not sure about your daughter, Dalubuhle, who I met at the village night before last. People might doubt she really is my girlfriend. Perhaps a more sophisticated woman like your secretary or even your daughter, June, might be more suitable.'

Luke looked serious, rubbing his chin. 'Hmm! let me give it some thought.'

Alan worried he might have offended Luke, but for their plan to work, they needed to pay attention to the details.

At dinner, the family chatted about Alan's life back in Australia and his first impressions of Zimbabwe. Luke seemed cheerful and Alan relaxed. It seemed his earlier comments did not offend Luke, but suddenly, Luke changed the conversation. 'Alan has expressed concerns. I promised I would give them serious consideration, and now he deserves an answer.' Alan squirmed with embarrassment when Luke repeated the comments he made when they were alone in the living room. 'June, please ask Dalubuhle to come in here.'

A few minutes later, Luke's third daughter walked in barefoot in the traditional dress she wore at the village beer drink. She smiled at Alan, and for once, he couldn't find the right words. He stood up out of politeness, trying to stammer out a mumbled greeting. Luke said, 'My darling, ask my secretary to come in for a moment.'

Alan's jaw dropped when Luke's secretary walked into the room a short time later. She smiled at Alan and sat down in June's chair. 'Good evening Mr Drake.' Before Alan could reply, everyone burst out laughing. Alan smiled weakly while they laughed and laughed.

'I'd like to ask all three girls to join us at the table, but we didn't prepare enough food for all,' said Luke.

'So, these are your other daughters?' Luke.

'No, my two oldest are married and live elsewhere.'

'But you said you had four daughters, and now I count six.'

'Luke smiled. Have you ever seen a chameleon, Alan? Isn't it amazing what a change of clothes, a hairpiece and a pair of glasses can do? June, Dalubuhle and my secretary are all the same person.'

'But, but...'

'Yes, I know we blacks all look alike to you whites, especially if you haven't grown up in Africa, but I can assure you, there's only one third daughter.'

Now, Alan saw the funny side. The family were having a joke at his expense. This time, everybody, including Alan, laughed until their tears flowed and their sides hurt. 'And I presume Sibusiso is Rita,' said Alan.

'Yes, she is,' Luke responded.

'So, when you say we whites think all blacks look the same, it's because sometimes they are the same; not so?'

Luke chuckled. 'Yes, that is true.'

To Alan's relief, the evening wasn't a disaster, and better still, now he'd paid more attention to the girls, he saw Luke's third daughter was a real beauty. Her smooth milk chocolate skin complimented her full lips and even white teeth. Intelligent eyes and arching eyebrows gave her an alluring appearance while her high cheekbones and relatively narrow nose set off her features to form a lovely face. How did he miss noticing her good looks before now? Perhaps he'd been preoccupied with his mission. He paid her scant attention at the village beer drink.

'It was hard to recognise June as the secretary with glasses,' said Alan. 'She's not wearing them tonight nor at the village night before last.'

'Those are plain glass, not lenses,' said Luke. 'June believes our suppliers and other business connections take her more seriously when she wears them.'

'Well, it's an excellent disguise.'

* * *

After dinner Luke took Alan into his home office. Set out with classic Chesterfield wing back chairs, a sofa and a huge oak desk, it was most impressive. The wood-panelled walls gave the room the dark, cosy atmosphere of an exclusive London club. Alan sat on the plush three-seater while Luke took out a paper from his draw.

'Here is a list of the recruits,' said Luke, as he handed Alan a Scotch with ice from the built-in bar-fridge behind one of the wood panels. 'The MFF leadership has selected the first team for training. There are twelve recruits and a tracker. These are our most loyal and committed volunteers. You will probably need a couple of experienced men to assist you with the training. I am thinking that you can find them when we select the security guards. Only brave men will apply for that work. Often they are former soldiers or policemen.'

Alan was a little annoyed. He would have liked to take part in the choice of recruits. With his military experience, he could almost always tell in advance the ones likely to make good candidates. 'I wish the MFF asked me to help select the recruits. We can't afford the time or effort to train people who aren't suitable.'

'Ah, Alan my friend, you must remember there's politics involved in this process. Each leader in the MFF wanted at least one of their people selected, and nothing you said would have influenced their choice.'

'And who's your choice, Luke?'

'The committee felt it too risky for one of my nephews and my daughter's "boyfriend" to both take part in this exercise, so you are my choice.'

'That's a good idea. You don't want too many participants in the training programme linked back to you. In that circumstance, you'd stand out like a beacon and your whole family could be at risk. I'm still worried about Andrew Dube and Tyson and the implications for the rest of the MFF leadership.'

'Andrew Dube was a high-profile individual. The CIO or someone must have watched him for a long time, even before he assumed the presidency of our organisation. The rest of us in the MFF have much lower profiles.'

'What if Andrew and his son disclosed under torture the MFF's plans and the purpose of the Chiang Mai meeting?'

'That is a problem, Alan, so we must make sure you stay one step ahead of the authorities.'

Alan drove back to the hotel with a lot on his mind. This project would be much trickier than his father and the Chiang Mai Group imagined. He didn't fancy the prospect of a spell in one of Zimbabwe's notorious prisons. The cause wasn't his cause. He'd not even heard of Mthwakazi before his father's summons.

The nightclub near the Bulawayo Rainbow was again in full swing, but this time, Alan gave it a miss. He checked out the hotel bar, but that was too quiet, so he went straight up to his room. He sat in an armchair by the window to plan the way forward. The deep thump, thump of the rhythmic bass from the music in the nightclub did little to clear his mind.

CHAPTER 16

AFTER a week at the Bulawayo Rainbow Hotel, Alan found a first-floor apartment above shops in Fife Street. His was the only apartment in the building, with no floors above him and no neighbours. The only access to the flat was the metal fire escape, which led from the open courtyard facing the back alley to the landing at his front door. He could access the street in front of his apartment through a narrow open corridor at one edge of the courtyard. Alan liked the privacy, a perfect bachelor pad.

* * *

Apart from the supermarket in the CBD, Luke owned three other little shops: two in small shopping centres in the more affluent suburbs and one in a poorer suburb, which Luke explained was once referred to as an African location.

Alan's first task was to recruit security guards for all Luke's properties, including his residence. Soon, Luke presented Alan with several older candidates for the security guard positions. 'These are suitable men for the purpose,' Luke explained, 'but you will need younger men to train for our greater cause. These older ones are former soldiers from the Rhodesian African Rifles (RAR). Perhaps too old for your main purpose. There might be one or two young enough to join your team, but I will leave that decision to you.'

'Good, I'll need experienced men.'

Soon Alan was a familiar face around Luke's properties, checking on the men working the different shifts, morning, afternoon and night. That gave Alan the freedom and flexibility to be out at all hours without raising suspicion. Alan thought many of the disciplined former RAR soldiers might be valuable recruits to the cause down the line. He singled out two, Alexander and Daniel, as potential Instructors for his training programme.

Alan organised the security guards on a military structure. They wore uniforms, courtesy of the Chiang Mai Group, as George Drake's associates came to be known among the MFF leadership. The senior men organised military style inspections before each shift. Guards needed to turn out smartly dressed, complete with their equipment, which included a torch, knobkerrie, whistle and prepaid cell phone. A select few had a German shepherd dog to support them in their guard duties.

The former soldiers seemed to enjoy the inspections and occasional parades. They were accustomed to the discipline, and it reminded them of their youthful past in the army. Alexander and Daniel took to their roles with enthusiastic relish. They were not Instructors in the RAR, but they fulfilled a similar role now and talked of whipping the men into shape. When Alan looked at some of the older men, he doubted that would ever happen, but others proved surprisingly fit and energetic despite their years.

Alexander and Daniel were full of helpful ideas for training the men. Alan couldn't tell whether the proposed ideas originated from the two Instructors or the other old soldiers. Either way, the Instructors were quick to claim credit for the suggestions.

Alan soon sorted out which guards were reliable and an asset to the cause. Aside from physical ability, he looked for loyalty and honesty. He dispensed with the few that liked to drink or gamble, and soon he boasted a core of dependable men. Already he envisioned his guards as the nucleus of a future defence force for Mthwakazi. They would lead and guide the young recruits when the time came.

* * *

When alone in his apartment, Alan would often stand on his balcony with a beer and watch the prostitutes gathered under the pavement canopy of the shops across the road. Eight or ten would congregate there each night waiting for prospective clients. Often, a car would crawl past and then go around the block and return for a second viewing. Alan presumed there must be a pecking order as there were few disputes between the ladies. When a car stopped, one woman would cross the road and chat to the driver. If they struck a deal, the woman would get into the car and drive to an apartment or alley nearby. If the woman walked away, seldom would another step forward to replace her. Most of the cars were luxury vehicles, which suggested important or well-off clients doing a little overtime after a hard day's work.

The women soon noticed Alan, and once they understood he was not a potential client, they teased him, offering their services in return for one favour or another. They possessed a great sense of humour and laughed at each other's vain efforts to tempt him. 'I love you,' one woman called. 'If you ask me to marry you, I will accept.'

'I love you too, but I don't deserve you. You will find better than me.'

The women shrieked with laughter. 'If you show me, I will tell you if I can find better than you.' More hoots of laughter.

'No, you must believe me.'

'Are you shy?' The women waited in silence for Alan's reply.

'No, but you are too much woman for me.' Shrieks of laughter.

A police car cruised past, and the women melted into the shop doorways. When it moved on, Alan called out. 'Why are you hiding? Are you shy of the police?'

'Agh! Those police always want favours. If we don't give favours, sometimes if we have money, they give us fines for loitering.'

'I can give you a favour,' one woman called out, 'then you can pay me next time. You'll be very happy.' The women all laughed at each competing invitation with the ribald offers continuing while Alan remained on the balcony. Time would pass unnoticed and often Alan went to bed much later than he intended.

Alan always politely declined their offers but kept fruit and cigarettes handy though he wasn't a smoker. Sometimes he tossed down a piece of fruit or cigarettes to the last two or three women who'd not been fortunate enough to earn any money that evening.

The women enjoyed light-hearted banter, and he found them much more entertaining than the television, which he seldom turned on. They were also useful in providing local gossip and information. Although most of it did not pertain to his mission, it was interesting to hear what the poor unemployed people on the streets were saying. Alan soon realised there lay a world of difference between his privileged colleagues in the MFF and the less educated masses in Zimbabwe.

CHAPTER 17

FINDING a secluded spot to run the training operations would be more difficult than Alan expected. The suggestion he could train recruits in the area where the borders of Zimbabwe, Botswana and South Africa meet was impractical. National parks and game reserves in the three countries merged at this point to form the Greater Mapungubwe Transfrontier Conservation Area (GMTFCA). Camp staff and tourists did not sit well with a clandestine military training base.

The other problem Alan faced was the large increase in the rural population. Many urban dwellers moved to the country, hoping to escape the hassles of city life under the Mugabe regime. In most third-world or developing countries, people moved to the city in search of work and an improved lifestyle. Given Zimbabwe's economic circumstances, this avenue was not open to its citizens.

Alan soon decided on three strategies. First, his recruits must train in small groups to avoid detection. Second, in the early stages at least, there would be no base camp. Training in the bush provided the essential and most authentic conditions they would face in action. Every morning they would bury their rubbish, and as far as possible, erase all signs that anyone camped there. Third was the need to find an isolated area for firearms training. Accurate shooting took a lot of practice.

In Zimbabwe the police roadblocks presented a problem for unhindered movement. Alan planned to use them as part of the training. He and his men would walk to their destination in the south-west area of the country. They would get fit in the process and gain experience in avoiding detection by the authorities or nosy villagers. They needed to find an isolated area to practise shooting. At this stage, they would not carry weapons or equipment that might cause suspicion as to their motives. When they found a suitable location, Alan would call Solly Bernstein's contact in Francistown to arrange an airdrop.

Now, Alan needed to carry out the plan.

* * *

Luke Ndlovu met Alan at the same meeting room where he first met the MFF leaders. The young men present were eager to meet Alan and begin their new adventure. The two mature former soldiers, Daniel and Alexander, pleased Alan. He found their professional manner reassuring. They would be valuable backup for training the raw recruits.

Suddenly, Alan noticed Molly Dlamini at the back of the room. 'What is she doing here? We need to keep this operation top secret. We can't have all sorts listening to our plans.'

'She's your tracker,' said Luke. 'You'll be glad to have her, I promise you.'

'One woman amongst the men will lead to trouble.'

'You'll change your mind when you get to know her. Her instructions are to stick to you like glue. We can't have anything happen to our overseas star.'

Alan was unconvinced, but he saw there was no use arguing about it.

Luke also suggested a suitable area where they might conduct their shooting practice, and Alan worked out the structure of the training team. The participants would break into groups of two and make their own way to a point on the northern edge of Mpopoma Dam in the Matopos National Park. Daniel and Alexander would each take overall responsibility for three pairings.

Alan cleared his throat to address the team. 'Aim to be there by six o'clock, Friday evening. We have backpacks here for you. Inside you will find a light sleeping bag and food for four days. Make the food last. Don't be greedy and eat it all at once. Fill your canteens with water before you set off on your hike. In your backpack, you will also find a straining cloth and iodine pills to help purify any water you collect from the rivers. But if you can, boil the water you collect.

'You are camping out, so supplies are an issue. Try to make everything last. And remember, this training isn't a fashion parade. Don't wear colourful clothing; no whites, yellows or reds. Try to wear dull colours like green, brown or khaki.

'There's also a sheet of plastic in your backpack. When we receive our rifles, there may be a need to bury them to prevent their discovery. They must stay dry and clean. Only use your plastic sheet for wrapping your rifles and ammunition when we bury them. Do not use your plastic sheet for any other purpose. Do you understand?'

'Yes, Sah,' the team replied in chorus.

Alexander and Daniel smiled at one another. It reminded them of the old days in the RAR.

* * *

Ethan, one of Luke's trusted drivers, ostensibly on a trip to pick up fruit and vegetables, took Alan and Molly by van to within a kilometre of the meeting point. From there they walked, arriving mid-afternoon. By six o'clock, everyone arrived bar one pair. 'Daniel, where the hell is your third team?' said an impatient Alan. 'I hope the police didn't stop and question them.' Alan didn't relish the thought of the police turning up and him having to explain how and why these separate groups came together carrying backpacks with identical contents.

'Don't worry, Sah,' said Daniel. 'I saw them this morning, and they were on the right track to get here.'

'We can't risk continuing with the mission without knowing what's happened to them.'

The group ate while they waited. At least, the area seemed deserted, and as far as they were aware, no one knew of their presence. At around midnight, they heard a low whistle, and upon investigating, they discovered the exhausted pair.

'Sorry, Sah. We got lost.'

Alan shook his head. 'You better get rest. We're moving out first thing in the morning.'

* * *

The day dawned bright with everyone eager to get started. They would first have to walk north west to circumvent a cluster of cultivated properties and then thread their way west and south-west through more farming areas. Alan calculated their destination to be as far away as a hundred kilometres or more.

At one point a dog barked at them as they passed. They saw no one, but the dog's owners would be somewhere in the area. Alan estimated it would take three days for his group to reach an isolated area suitable for target practice.

It was risky to travel through the bush at night without weapons. Daniel and Alexander fashioned knobkerries from fallen branches they found along the way. The others copied their example. If they needed to defend themselves against a wild animal, knobkerries were better than nothing. A convenient tree to climb might be the best protection.

Another problem travelling at night was the difficulty in getting a feel for the lie of the land. Was there a village they missed seeing? Was there a nearby road or path that might be busy during daylight? But with luck, they might find an isolated area a lot nearer than they expected.

Three days out, civilisation was far behind them. Their first task was to reconnoitre the area and make sure it was deserted. Daniel and Alexander each took out one of their teams while Alan accompanied Molly on a similar quest.

Back in camp by five in the evening, they all agreed this was the spot for them. While the others made tea and prepared something to eat, Alan called his Francistown contact on the satellite phone.

The camp was in easy range of the Botswana border, and only six hours after the call they heard the dull throb of a helicopter. Earlier, Alan picked out a suitable clearing in which to stand and pulse the beam of his military grade torch to guide in the chopper.

The helicopter landed in a swirl of dust. It was mid-September, the height of the dry season. There'd been no rain since April, and the winter sun parched the ground.

'Hi, I'm Jim,' said the cheery helicopter pilot in a strong Australian accent. 'Time is tight mate. Let's get this lot unloaded.'

The dozen wooden crates took Alan's team five minutes to unload and carry into the camp. 'I'll be back to pick up this lot when you're finished with your exercise. Just phone and say ready.'

'OK, thanks. Take care. Cheers.'

Alan was keen to inspect the contents of the crates. Long nails held the lids in place and prising them open took time. When at last, they removed the lids and took stock, they discovered sixteen AK47s, a thousand rounds of ammunition which seemed to weigh a ton, and enough food supplies to last a week.

'Tomorrow morning, we start weapon training,' said Alan. When you are familiar with your weapons and can safely handle them, we'll begin shooting practice. There are only sixty rounds per person, so make each one count.

The Instructors helped the recruits select suitable sleeping spots. They spread out, so if any intruder discovered one of the team, the others could stay undetected. But they were close enough to each other to give support if someone needed it. Daniel chose a spot on one edge of the group and Alexander chose the middle. Alan took his place on the other edge, but Molly insisted that was her role. She wouldn't risk any harm befalling the MFF's imported trainer.

Still three months before the rainy season, the cloudless, moonless night blanketed the scene in a blackness only country folk would understand. Alan enjoyed camping out in such conditions. He lay, looking up into the heavens, and gradually the milky way seemed to increase in intensity. The night sky filled with millions of stars. They were everywhere, but in the city only the brightest were visible. Then a shooting star raced across the sky. A satellite made its steady way from west to east, followed by another on a different trajectory. The stars twinkled red, white, yellow and blue, while the planets remained fixed in their assortment of colours. It was a light show beyond anything mankind could produce. It seemed incongruous to Alan such beauty covered a divided world where a few men with self-serving agendas created so much trouble for so many others.

CHAPTER 18

THE training teams were quick on the uptake, and Alan sensed he trained a capable group of young men. Their progress pleased him. The trainees practised stripping, cleaning and reassembling their rifles several times a day. Within three days, they could all strip and reassemble the AK47s in under ninety seconds. They took great pride in maintaining their rifles in a spotless condition and were disappointed to learn they would hand them back at the end of the week. 'Don't worry,' said Alan, 'we'll make a note of the serial number above the magazine on your rifle, and you'll get the same one back next time.'

As a precaution, each morning and early afternoon, the teams did a sweep of the neighbourhood before shooting practice. Daniel and his team of six would be out checking the surrounding bush while Alexander's team was shooting, and then they would swop places. When a team was out on reconnoitre, their leader taught them bushcraft and ambush techniques. The two former RAR soldiers made all the difference to the speed with which the recruits picked up the essential soldiering skills. Daniel and Alexander were the best shots. This was no surprise, but Molly impressed everyone by almost matching their accuracy.

Day five started out like any other and followed the usual routine. Alan watched Alexander's team at shooting practice with a certain amount of pride. These young men were developing into soldiers much quicker than he envisaged. Their shooting improved, and bushcraft seemed to come naturally to them. They grew in confidence and loved the ambush practice, turning it into a game. All the recruits appeared dedicated to the cause, and soon they would train groups of their own.

During a lull in the late afternoon's shooting practice Daniel spoke to his men about the differences between shooting during daytime and at night. Suddenly, there was the sound of sporadic gunfire about a kilometre away. Alan sprang to his feet. 'Daniel and Molly come with me! The rest of you men stay here and guard the camp! Spread out! now!'

Grabbing their rifles, the trio ran into the bush towards the firing. They hadn't gone far when they found Alexander and his team, hurrying in their direction. 'What's going on?' Alan shouted.

'Soldiers, Sah,' said Alexander. 'They were heading towards our camp. They saw us and opened fire. We fired back, and they ran away.'

'Did you hit any of them?'

'I don't think so, Sah, but they dropped two rifles. We've brought them with us.'

'Hmm, FNs. They might come in handy. We'll keep those. Let's get back to camp before they return with reinforcements. Our cover is blown here. We must move out ASAP.'

Back in the camp, Alan phoned his Botswana contact. 'It's urgent. We need to move out fast.'

'Roger, copied that.' The voice wasn't Jim's, the friendly Aussie helicopter pilot. How many people did the project involve? If his father organised it, it would be too many. George Drake did everything on a grand scale.

While they waited for the helicopter the training group scrambled to pack everything away and obliterate any signs of their presence. Alan looked at his watch. It was over an hour since the contact with the soldiers, and depending on where their base was, they could soon turn up in numbers. 'C'mon, c'mon,' said Alan, straining his ears for the sound of the approaching chopper or the returning soldiers. With everything packed away, ready for the helicopter, the group only had the two FN rifles with their loaded magazines. 'I hope these things are in good condition,' said Alan. 'Not every soldier looks after their weapon the way we do.' The Instructors had cleaned the FNs, but without test firing them, their overall condition was uncertain.

Everybody jumped at the sound of heavy steps in the nearby bush. The whole group rushed for cover. Daniel and Alexander held the FNs at the ready. They strained their eyes to see in the gathering gloom. Suddenly, a donkey stepped into the clearing where they waited. 'Bloody hell!' said Alan. 'Everything is happening here this evening.'

At last! The faint sound of a helicopter in the distance. Alan raced forward to chase the donkey away from the landing site. Just then, he heard someone call out a name. 'Pancho, Pancho, where are you?' The last thing they needed was a villager and his lost donkey. Alan pulsed his torch towards the sound of the helicopter, and a moment later, it dropped out of the sky like an eagle attacking its prey.

'Hi mate. Put everything flat on the chopper's floor and I'll be out of here before you know it.' How could Jim sound so cheerful and relaxed? 'I had to wait until dark you know. We can't risk flying across the border in daylight.'

In less than five minutes they'd loaded the chopper, and in another minute, it took off and disappeared into the darkness. Where was the donkey? If the owner saw everything, he might report it to the soldiers.

The group moved out of camp, retracing their steps from the inward journey, but this time at night. As they surmounted a rise four hundred metres from their camp, they heard firing and shouting. The loud braying of a frightened donkey cut through the darkness.

'Those soldiers came back to find us,' said Alan. 'That means they've got the numbers. We'd better be extra careful when we pass those farms and settlements. They might already look for us there.'

Nobody thought about supper or taking a break. They wanted to put as much distance as possible between themselves and the soldiers. A bright, rising moon and the cooler night temperatures helped the group to travel faster than they managed on their inward journey. Sometimes, farm or village dogs barked as they passed, but they saw no sign of any villagers. Perhaps they'd learnt from the Gukurahundi to melt away when strangers moved through the area.

The group walked throughout the night and up to mid-morning when they found a wooded area to shelter. 'Get some sleep,' said Alan. 'We'll set off again at four o'clock. That's four o'clock this evening.'

They repeated the process the next day, and on the second night, Alexander and his team broke away to follow a separate route back to Bulawayo. Alan, Molly and Daniel's team continued towards their original meeting point at the northern end of Mpopoma Dam. They arrived in the early hours of the third day. Before breaking up the group, Alan and Daniel walked into an area of bush they'd be able to find again later and buried the two FN rifles wrapped in the plastic sheeting they carried in their backpacks.

Daniel and his team left to make their way back to Bulawayo. The night before, Alan phoned to arrange for Luke's driver to meet him and Molly at the point he dropped them almost two weeks earlier.

Alan was pleased to be back in the city, and the realisation hit him that his army days were well behind him. It was only a two-week training camp, including the long walk there and back, but he was tired after the last two sleepless nights. He'd been out of the Australian special forces only a few months, and already his fitness level showed a significant decline. Perhaps he should take a more gradual approach and ease himself into the questionable fun of roughing it in the bush? But if he hoped to be back in Australia within a year, gradual was not an option.

CHAPTER 19

OCTOBER 2013

Over the next few weeks, Alan took the team out for another two short camps in an isolated area the Instructors identified near Bulawayo. The first of the camps focussed on bushcraft, but the second was on setting up ambushes and defensive positions. On the second of these camps, Jim, the friendly Australian helicopter pilot dropped off arms and ammunition. From now on the trainees would keep their weapons. This pleased Jim, who was a lot less friendly about the distance he needed to fly over hostile territory.

Alan decided it was time for phase two of the training programme. The first obstacle he faced was getting the trainees and equipment to Gonarezhou National Park in the south-east of the country. His team totalled sixteen members, including himself. How would he get the trainees with their arms and equipment to Gonarezhou? He made it a training exercise. He and his female African tracker, Molly, would go by car, pretending to be tourists, and the rest would follow in a minibus.

Alan and Molly would go on ahead and note the police roadblocks or any other obstacles and phone back the details to the group. The team would disembark with the equipment before each roadblock, bypass the obstacle on foot and board the minibus on the far side. Two of the team would stay on the minibus with papers showing they bought the vehicle for their tour-guide business in the national park. It was a slow and exhausting process despite the men's fitness gained at their three basic training camps in the bush south-west of Bulawayo.

On the morning of the third day, after two uncomfortable nights on the road, the group approached the edge of the park, halfway between the South Entrance Gate and the North Entrance Gate. At either end of the park there were several campsites, and even an airstrip on the southern end, but the map showed the middle to be empty. That, Alan reasoned, would be the best area of the park to base themselves in their search for poachers.

The party intended to walk into the park unseen, but they needed a secluded spot to hide their vehicles. A lengthy search rewarded them with a rocky area covered in trees and thick bushes. An ideal location for the vehicles, which disappeared in the undergrowth within two or three metres. It would be difficult for anyone to notice them parked there.

'OK guys, we are heading straight for the Mozambique border. It's about forty-five kilometres from here. We'll stick to the bush which means it'll be slow going. About six hours from now, at five o'clock, we'll stop for the night. We might break for a rest around two o'clock, but it will be short, so we must eat on the move. Does anyone have questions? If not, let's move.'

* * *

The oppressive, early afternoon heat closed in on Alan like a smothering blanket. He felt dizzy and weak. He'd not eaten since breakfast, other than the peanut bar he gulped down mid-morning. Alan searched the pouch on his belt for the tiny packet of salt crackers he'd brought with him. With thoughts about their next move swirling in his head, he'd not slept well in his first night in the park. This, despite their long, tiring walk through the bush the previous day.

The sweat trickled down his temples, and more ran down his arms and chest. Two metres to Alan's right, stood Joao, a picture of tense concentration, his face a shiny black mask of beaded perspiration.

'You better bring a towel next time,' said Alan. 'Your face is like a mirror reflecting the sun.'

To Alan's left, Molly fared little better. With the top two buttons of her shirt undone, droplets of sweat ran down her cleavage, staining her khaki shirt with an expanding patch of damp.

Joao, a raw recruit, was not Alan's first choice for the reconnoitre of the area. But he spoke Portuguese, a valuable skill for their venture into the Gonarezhou National Park on Zimbabwe's south-east border with Mozambique.

While the bulk of Alan's team rested up in their temporary camp, where they'd slept the night before, he and his two companions set out after breakfast to familiarise themselves with the surrounding area. With luck, they might find an even more secluded spot to base themselves, though the one they found the previous evening wasn't too bad. Either way, he didn't plan for them to spend more than two nights in any one location.

After only five kilometres, trekking through the bush, they stumbled across fresh tracks of a gang of men. 'Four with boots, and the others barefoot,' said Molly. 'I'm not sure how many, but at least eight.'.

'Let's follow and find out what they're up to,' said Alan. 'They must be poachers; who else would walk in a national park? Be quiet and careful; we don't want to walk into an ambush.'

The fresh early morning turned stifling well before noon, and the leaves on the trees hung motionless in the still air. The silence in the midday heat amplified the slightest sound, and the buzzing flies sounded like a chorus of distant chainsaws. No birds and animals were visible as they sheltered in the deep shade of the bush.

Molly, with her eagle eye and tracking skills, led the way, with Alan three metres back and Joao a similar distance behind him. Their rifles at the ready, they picked their way forward, taking care not to step on any twigs, dried leaves or tussocks of dried grass.

Mid-afternoon, and Alan struggled to concentrate. Suddenly, Molly raised her arm, and the three stopped and crouched in the brush. At first, Alan couldn't hear anything, but then, the faintest murmuring of voices and occasional bursts of laughter. Once again, Molly proved her worth to the team.

'Let's try to count them,' said Alan. 'Joao, you wait here for us.' The young black man nodded, relieved to keep his distance from the poachers. One wrong move and they would react with deadly force. Many park rangers could attest to that.

Hidden behind a low rise covered with thick bushes, Alan and Molly counted three soldiers in Zimbabwe army uniforms. A fourth man wore a park ranger's uniform, and six others wore tatty shirts and shorts. An assortment of rifles and AK47s leant against the surrounding trees. On the ground lay four large elephant tusks. The men sat on the bare earth, smoking and chatting loudly. Their relaxed demeanour suggested they must have carried out many other poaching expeditions before now. The tatty-clothed civilians spoke Portuguese, and Alan turned to beckon the anxious-looking Joao.

After ten minutes the poachers prepared to leave, and the trio silently withdrew before their luck ran out and their presence discovered.

When they'd retreated a safe distance, Alan spoke, 'Well, what did they say?'

'The Mozambicans are bearers to carry the tusks,' said Joao. 'They are taking them to a contact over the border. One week from now, they'll meet at this spot and bring the money for payment. If the soldiers get more tusks, they'll do it all again.'

'Yes,' said Molly, 'the soldiers spoke Shona. Next week, they will try to get bigger tusks.'

'OK,' said Alan, 'We'll be ready for them when—' A large shadow fell across the ground near him. He turned and looked up, startled by the sudden intrusion.

A massive bull elephant towered over them. None of them noticed its silent approach while they all stood looking in the direction in which the poachers had gone.

'Don't move and don't show fear,' Molly whispered. 'He's just curious and will leave in a minute.'

The shock prevented Alan from any reaction, but Molly's words helped to calm him. Joao stood with his legs shaking and his eyes wide as saucers that seemed to grow by the second. The elephant extended its trunk towards Alan as if sniffing him. When it moved its trunk towards Joao, the young man recoiled and then bolted. There was no prospect of him outrunning the elephant, and in a few strides, the great beast was on to him and sent him sprawling. In an instant it knelt on him and crushed the life out of the unfortunate African.

Alan raised his rifle, but Molly put her hand on his arm. 'It's too late. You'll only warn the poachers if you fire now.' A quick and graceful withdrawal was their only recourse as the enraged beast tossed Joao's body in the air, again and again.

'Let's get the hell out of here before he turns his attention to us,' said Alan. Well, so much for the jumbo's cute and friendly reputation. 'I hope he doesn't associate us with those poachers.' Alan was learning about Africa fast.

A sombre mood pervaded the camp with the men now aware their training in the bush wasn't a game. Alan cursed the unfortunate encounter with the elephant. Their first full day in the national park and he'd already lost one man. Now, it was clear to Alan, he and his team needed a greater familiarity with animals and the bush. Many of the trainees were just young city men keen to help the cause. He could train them to fight, but Molly and more experienced men would need to train them in the ways of the African bush. Alan recognised he survived the elephant because he heeded Molly's advice.

* * *

The next morning Alan, Molly and a team of six men went to find Joao's body. At first glance it looked like it was missing. 'Maybe the hyenas found it,' Daniel suggested. 'They leave nothing.'

'See that pile of broken branches,' said Molly. 'Let's check there.' Sure enough, the branches covered the remains of Joao's battered body. 'I've seen this before, Sir. When elephants kill someone or another animal, they often cover them with branches.'

'None of us know anything about Joao's family,' said Alan, 'so we might as well bury him here.'

'It will have to be deep, otherwise the animals will dig him up,' said Molly. 'Hyenas are bad like that.'

The men worked hard in the late morning sun. Alan saw it as part of their training and insisted Joao's grave be six feet deep. Joao was a Christian, so Alan spoke a few words, followed by Alexander, the most religious of the group.

After the brief ceremony, the team moved on to inspect the site of the poachers' planned rendezvous. Alan selected concealed vantage points for each member of his team where they could watch the rendezvous without the risk of being caught in any crossfire if shooting started. He allotted each member a specific arc of fire in the expected rendezvous zone. The men at either end of the line faced outwards in case someone approached from a different direction.

By the time they headed back to camp, each member of Alan's team knew their place and was familiar with the layout of the area. Further training would occupy the team in the remaining five days before the rendezvous.

Alan's leadership team comprised Molly and his Instructors, Daniel and Alexander. The Instructors, trained soldiers, learnt their skills in the RAR, the Rhodesian African Rifles. After independence there was no room for the Ndebele in Mugabe's army, and one by one, they all returned to civilian life. They were young recruits in the RAR, but now, hardened men in their early fifties. In addition, Alan's team now comprised eleven raw recruits he needed to bring up to speed. It would have been twelve if not for Joao's untimely end.

* * *

The day of the rendezvous arrived bright and sunny. The weather in October was reliable; always hot, hot, hot. The rainy season didn't arrive until late November or early December. That suited Alan because the sun-hardened ground concealed the tracks of his men from all but the most expert of trackers.

Breakfast was at four a.m. By seven o'clock, Alan, Molly, Daniel and six recruits were in position and well-hidden. The five other recruits, under the command of Alexander, were in back-up positions seven hundred metres to the rear. The back-up team faced the opposite direction to the forward group to counter any approach from the rear.

It was hot and uncomfortable even in their shaded hiding places. The wait was longer than expected. Did they have the wrong day? Had the poachers cancelled the rendezvous? If anyone needed to pee, they would have to do it where they lay.

At last, at one in the afternoon, the six Mozambicans in their tatty shirts and shorts appeared out of the bushes only twenty metres ahead. They laid their weapons against the trees and sat around smoking cigarettes and chatting. Without Joao, Alan didn't understand what they said, but he presumed they waited for the soldiers to arrive.

One of the Mozambicans stood up, gathered his rifle and walked towards Alan and his men. The ambush team was spread well apart, so with luck the Mozambican wouldn't see any of them. The man searched for a private spot to answer the call of nature and headed for an area where the bushes were thickest. He walked straight into the hiding place of one recruit. Two shots from the recruit's rifle, a double tap, cut short his cry of alarm. The other Mozambicans scrambled for their rifles under the withering fire of the forward team.

In the silence that followed the shooting, the unmistakable, pungent smell of gunpowder hung in the air. The trainees fired a lot more rounds than necessary. It was not the most disciplined firefight, but at least Alan's men were unharmed. He conducted a quick check. Four dead Mozambican poachers. Two got away. He puzzled how they'd escaped. Bullets riddled the bodies of the four dead men and shredded the surrounding foliage.

'Look, Sir,' said Molly, 'blood trails here. Lots of blood. Those two are badly wounded. I don't think they'll get far.'

'Well spotted, Molly. Now let's see what these poachers brought with them. We know they promised to pay for the tusks we saw them carry off the last time.'

One dead Mozambicans carried an old backpack which lay on the ground next to his body. Alan opened it and saw small bundles wrapped in sheets of newspaper held in place with elastic bands. He unwrapped one bundle to find it contained US one-hundred-dollar notes. The excited trainees gathered round to see the contents of the backpack, but just then, the sound of firing from the back-up team's position interrupted their chatter.

'OK, now let's check what's happening with our back-up team. Move it!'

Alan grabbed the backpack and hurried with his team to support Alexander's men seven hundred metres to their rear. The gunfire ended well before the breathless forward team reached their back-up comrades. To his relief, Alan found all his men safe. In the bushes lay the bodies of the park ranger and one soldier. Four elephants' tusks lay scattered on the ground. 'I'm sorry, Sah,' said Alexander, two soldiers got away. They saw us first and fired, but we were lucky. Two other men helping to carry the tusks also escaped.'

'The main thing is we all survived,' said Alan. 'Now let's bury these tusks and get going before those soldiers return with reinforcements.'

Later that night, Alan and the leadership group discussed their options. 'Maybe we should leave the area as soon as possible,' said Daniel.

'No,' said Alexander, 'they'll be expecting us to make a run. The roads will crawl with soldiers and police.'

'Perhaps we could go over the border to Mozambique,' said Molly.

'Relax, folks. I'll tell you what we'll do. We'll wait here a couple of days and see what happens. Then, we can decide our best course of action. That wooded koppie we passed earlier has a good view of the surrounding area. Tomorrow, Molly and I will climb the koppie and watch for any activity. You two must stay down here and keep the recruits calm and out of site. If we see any movement, we'll call you with instructions. We must keep an eye out for any army trucks or helicopters. The choppers would be our greatest threat.'

Alan called the whole team together for a few words. 'I want to congratulate you on the way you all operated today. We did not intend to get into a firefight, but to watch the poachers and follow unseen. Remember, our role is to be the ghosts of the bush and work undetected by the enemy. Today, the events were beyond our control, and we were forced into a contact, but we've learnt a lot from what happened.'

Later that night, Alan checked the contents of the poacher's backpack. A few items of food and sixty thousand US dollars. Someone would be furious. He was sure there would be consequences.

* * *

After a nervous night with everyone listening out for any sound of approaching vehicles, dawn crept across the horizon. Alan and Molly ate breakfast at five a.m. and took their position on the peak by six. The thick cover would make it almost impossible to see them from the air.

Another hot day, and the hours dragged. Alan chatted with Molly, making small talk. She was a lot more intelligent than he first imagined. With everything going on, he'd not given her much thought. Everyone knew her as the young woman whose parents the 5th Brigade murdered in the Gukurahundi. But then most of the recruits were young men who'd suffered a similar experience when they lost family members in the genocide. Most were babies or unborn when the atrocities were committed.

'Molly, most young women your age are out and about with friends, enjoying life. Don't you ever feel you'd like to join them going to parties, dancing and eating at restaurants?'

'I like it here, Sir.'

'Are you going to spend the rest of your life working with the MFF?'

'Do you know what happened to my family, Sir?'

'I know your parents died in the Gukurahundi.'

'The Fifth Brigade forced my father and the other men of the village to dig their own graves before they shot them. They locked my mother and older sisters with other village women in a hut and burned them alive. I can't sing and dance while those men go unpunished.'

'I'm sorry your family faced such a terrible fate, but will you ever know who the perpetrators were? You must live your own life. If you dwell in the past, you will waste it.'

'I honour my family by educating myself and helping our cause. It is enough for me to work against the regime that murdered our families.'

'You don't want to be the end of your family line, do you? An intelligent and pretty girl like you could find a husband and start a family of your own.'

'Perhaps one day, Sir.'

Time spent sitting on the koppie all day gave Alan the opportunity to observe Molly more closely. Widespread, hooded eyes gave her a smouldering look. Her shoulder-length dreadlocks, broadish nose and full lips complimented her features to perfection. She was muscular and shapely with a body that could become matronly in her later years if she didn't take care. But as he watched her, she looked tight and delicious. Alan found his thoughts wandering to how she might be in bed. He tried to shake the idea, but to no avail. If he gave in to temptation, it would shred the team's discipline, so that was not an option. His mission was to train a team of fighters to free Mthwakazi from the prison that was Zimbabwe.

The day was uneventful. Tomorrow, they would repeat the process.

* * *

The next day was also quiet, but Alan decided they would continue the watch for the rest of the week. Remaining out of sight was tedious but good training, for they would need to draw on their patience in the struggle that lay ahead. Alan found Molly more and more attractive, and try as he might, he couldn't get rid of his carnal thoughts. In the bush, men's urgings are greater than in the city. It was the old story; a thing beyond reach is more desired.

By the end of the week an idea crystallised in Alan's head. The total lack of response by the military meant the soldiers and the park ranger were not acting with official sanction. Their poaching must make them a small fortune, and they were just as keen as Alan's team to keep quiet about the whole business.

That evening, Alan gathered his men around him to announce their withdrawal the next day. 'We will retrace our steps and exit the way we entered.' All the men received the news with a collective sigh of relief.

CHAPTER 20

November 2013

A summons to Johannesburg; that's how Alan viewed it. George Drake was in town and he instructed Alan to attend a meeting for a debrief on how the project was going. Alan wasn't entirely against the idea as it might afford him the opportunity for another dinner date with Aunt Ruth. He'd been in Zimbabwe for almost four months and he needed meaningful social time. There'd not been much in Bulawayo. Yes, there were the late-night chats with June, but they couldn't make up for the close physical attention he craved.

Alan's strike rate in his pursuit of various women would satisfy the most insatiable of men, but they all amounted to meaningless one-night stands. Until his dinner with Ruth, he'd experienced no intimacy with a woman he'd known for any length of time. Somehow, the familiarity that emanated from knowing Solly and Ruth as his parent's friends over many years made his evening with Ruth deliciously different.

Customs and immigration did not take too long, and as Alan walked out into the arrival hall, he saw Ruth waiting for him. She looked fresh and smiled when he caught her eye. It was the start he hoped for to the Joburg visit.

Ruth gave Alan a kiss and held his hand as she led him through the arrival hall to the airport parking where she'd left her Volkswagen Golf. 'Any chance of stopping off at the hotel?' said Alan.

'They're all impatient for your latest report. Maybe there'll be time later.'

Ruth drove in the busy traffic along Albertina Sisulu Freeway, the Eastern Bypass and onto Francois Oberholzer, past the ominous looking Ponte City Apartments and the CBD. Along De Villiers Graaff Freeway they passed the notorious Johannesburg Park Station and the University of the Witwatersrand (Wits) and drove onto Jan Smuts Avenue and past the zoo.

Soon they turned in the driveway of Solly and Ruth's luxurious home. After recent rains washed away the dust of the dry winter months, the property looked even more glorious than Alan remembered it. A maid opened the front door, and Ruth and Alan walked through the spacious entrance hall into the front room that looked onto the magnificent atrium. 'Ah, there you are at last,' said George Drake, getting up from his armchair to welcome Alan. Solly Bernstein, Peter Nkala and Barry from Cape Town were also there and greeted Alan warmly.

'Let's go into the study,' said Solly, 'it's more private in there.' The study, which led off the lounge, boasted tall, quarter-pained windows overlooking the back garden. It was a huge room with a large desk to one side, and on the other, furnished with plush, burgundy-coloured, soft leather lounge chairs set around a coffee table. The room was the equal of the lounge they'd just vacated. The main difference was the dark furnishings as opposed to the light creamy pink of the lounge area. An imposing executive chair took pride of place behind the huge walnut desk.

'So, Alan,' George Drake began, 'Peter tells us things are going well from his point of view. How do you see it from your end?'

'The training is coming along well, but the trainees are city boys with little knowledge of the bush. It was unfortunate we ran into those poachers and their Mozambican collaborators. Yes, it blooded the recruits, but our aim was to keep an unseen watch on the poachers in the national park. The first training mission failed because the poachers discovered our presence and we had to fight our way out of the situation. But having seen action prepares our recruits for the real thing.'

'Well, I've no sympathy for those poaching bastards. They're stealing the country's heritage and resources for their own greedy ends.'

'Isn't that what many people accused the white colonists of doing?'

'We weren't colonists, Alan. Many of us were second or third generation. The whites may have started out as colonists, seeing Britain as home, but for us, Rhodesia was our only home. Anyway,' said George turning to the others present, 'what do you chaps say?'

Solly and Barry supported George's view. 'And you, Peter, any qualms about what happened?'

'None, Mr Drake … er … George. Alan is doing a splendid job. If we lose a few poachers along the way, so be it.'

Typical, thought Alan. His father controlled his colleagues in the same way he controlled him. He backs them into a corner so it's almost impossible to be a dissenting voice. 'The problem is more shootouts will attract undesirable attention. The authorities or the poachers might worry we are a rival gang breaking into their market. That would be dangerous. We might even end up having to postpone the project until things settle.'

'Oh, come, come, Alan,' said George, 'that's not likely. You said yourself there was no response to the death of the soldier and the national parks ranger.'

'We saw no response! That doesn't mean someone somewhere isn't planning to investigate the incident. News of the dead Mozambicans will have reached their ears, and someone will want back their sixty thousand US dollars.'

* * *

The discussion continued through lunch and most of the afternoon. 'OK,' said George, 'Barry will drop you back at your hotel. He's hired a car and is also staying there.'

Damn! Time alone with Ruth looked less and less likely.

'We've booked a table at Level Four in Bath Avenue in Rosebank,' said George. 'Do you know it?'

'Yes, I do,' said Barry.

'Good! Be there at seven sharp.'

No doubt George would dominate the conversation all evening. It was not what Alan planned for his night in Johannesburg.

Alan enjoyed his meal. The duck cooked to perfection and well matched with the pinot noir the waiter recommended. The service was excellent and the atmosphere cosy. It would have been a great choice for a romantic dinner with Ruth, but there she was, wedged between his father and Peter Nkala. Other than the drive from the airport, he'd no opportunity to be alone with her. He imagined they would have plenty of time together, but he'd barely spoken to her since arriving at the house.

'Poor old Andrew Dube and Tyson,' said George. 'It's odd, despite my many connections in Malaysia and Thailand, my people have found no trace of them. It's as if they vanished. The police believe it was a paid hit and checked out the usual suspects but found nothing.'

'Yes,' said Peter, 'Andrew would have been a great leader for the MFF, but he disappeared before he could achieve his goals. He only just beat Senior Kholose in the leadership vote, so when the MFF voted for a replacement, I expected Kholose to get the position. I was surprised when they chose me.'

The conversation and the evening dragged on with Alan hoping for a sign from Ruth they might somehow escape from the boring company.

'Now, Alan,' said George, 'when are you going to give us a full list of your requirements? With the contributions from the Chiang Mai Group we're flush with funds. Do you need a helicopter, motor vehicles, more arms? Just tell us what you want, and we'll organise it.'

'Too early for that, Dad. I'm still training the leadership team who'll help train the foot soldiers. And we must also decide where we'll store everything.'

'You met Jim, the Aussie helicopter pilot. He and two others established a store on the Botswana side of the border. That's how he responded so fast to your call to extract the weapons and equipment when you were in a hurry to vacate your training camp. I reckon we might store everything we need over there.'

'Should we be talking about this in a public restaurant,' said Alan.

'You worry too much,' said George. 'I'll take you to the airport tomorrow morning. There's more to cover.' Alan glanced across at Ruth and imagined he detected a slight raise of her right eyebrow, but he wasn't sure.

As the evening ended, Alan watched Ruth leave with Solly, Peter Nkala and his father. Barry said, 'Let's get a beer at the hotel.' Some company was better than none, but a cold beer was no substitute for a warm Ruth.

* * *

On the drive to the airport, George made small talk with Alan. Why did his father insist on taking him to the airport that morning? 'What's this Luke Ndlovu fellow like?' asked George.

'He's a pleasant chap. Nice family.'

'With a wife and four daughters, I understand.'

'Yes, the two older ones are married, and the two younger daughters live at home.'

'You need to keep focussed on the mission, My Boy. I don't want to hear about any entanglements with those girls.'

'Of course not! Why would I?'

'I know you too well. If you put Luke Ndlovu offside, it could wreck the whole mission. The Chiang Mai Group have invested too much in this project to have it ruined by you running after girls.'

'I won't get involved with those girls. We've nothing in common.'

George dropped Alan at the departures hall and drove off without a backward glance. Alan watched his father disappear into the distance, and he could breathe freely again. It seemed, his father still treated him as a boy rather than a man.

Alan was early, which gave him time to look through the shops. He bought a bottle of Royal Salute Scotch for Luke, a huge box of hand-made Belgian chocolates for Enid, and costume jewellery bracelets for June and Rita. He put the Scotch in his suitcase and checked in for his flight. Alan kept the chocolates and bracelets with him in the large plastic bag he got from the shop where he bought the chocolates. He boarded the plane feeling frustrated by his short, tightly controlled visit to Johannesburg. What did Ruth think about it? When could he visit Joburg again? Whenever it was, he hoped his father would not be in town.

CHAPTER 21

DECEMBER 2013

Soon, it would be Christmas. Alan groaned. He regretted his rash agreement to spend Christmas with Luke and his family. But in August, Christmas seemed far away, and he didn't know if he'd still be in the country by December. He'd forgotten all about it until Luke reminded him. Now, Christmas was under a month away. Alan would rather fly home to Australia for a quick break or even down to Joburg to spend it with the Bernsteins. Ruth and Solly, his father's close associates, would have given him a good time. Although Jews, they celebrated Christmas with carols and presents and parties spread across the ten days to New Year. That's the Christmas Alan enjoyed.

But Christmas with Luke's family; how would that go? As owner of a supermarket and liquor store, Luke should manage a good spread. He lived with his charming wife, Enid, and two younger daughters in one of the nicer houses in the Suburbs in Bulawayo. That sounded OK, but now Luke said his whole immediate family would be there. Alan worried he'd stand out like a beacon in Luke's black family. Were they being polite, or did they really want him to join them? Maybe they were also having second thoughts. Bugger! Too late to pull out. He'd have to go along with it and spend Christmas with them.

Alan's idea of a good time revolved around making a move on an attractive young woman at a party. Luke had four daughters, but Alan was not free from prejudice and didn't think of African women in that way. Even if so inclined, it wouldn't be possible for him. Luke's two older daughters were married, and his youngest daughter only fifteen or six-teen. That left June, the second youngest. Yes, he found her attractive, but Alan respected old Luke too much to make a play for his favourite daughter. Alan's tastes ran to blondes with golden tans or redheads with pale skin, and June fell short on both counts.

The charade of being June's white boyfriend worked well, and it gave Luke and Alan the cover they needed for their frequent meetings. The ruse allowed them to avoid raising the suspicions of the authorities or nosey neighbours. Enid and June shared in the subterfuge, but other members of Luke's family did not. They would assume Alan and June were in a genuine relationship, and he worried how that might play out.

Alan's father, George, was a disciplinarian. He demanded of Alan a sense of duty and responsibility, hoping one day he would take over running the family business in Australia. But the more George pushed, the more his son pushed back. Alan's idea of life was to live it while it lasted. He focussed on parties, cars and girls, especially the girls, and he made the most of his natural charm, old-fashioned manners and good looks. The girls loved him and so did their mothers.

George railed against his young son's habit of chasing the daughters of his business associates. He dubbed him the scourge of the neighbour-hood. Ruth Bernstein called him Prince Charming. Alan didn't like it, but the nickname stuck, and even George used it when at his sarcastic best.

When Alan applied to enter the Royal Military College, Duntroon, near Canberra, George could barely hide his delight. The army would knock discipline into his son. It never occurred to George that Alan might be trying to escape the stifling atmosphere at home. Alan enjoyed active service, but the spells back in Australia bored him. Army discipline was a drag on his social life. In the SAS, he'd gained valuable skills which his father now needed for the MFF mission in Zimbabwe. Would he never escape the controlling grasp of his old man?

* * *

Christmas Day dawned bright and fresh. The overnight rain washed the air clean, and the early morning sun sparkled. Alan bounced out of bed and walked out onto the balcony and drew in a lungful of air, heavy with the smell of summer rain. After a bath and a light breakfast, Alan checked the time; only eight o'clock. Luke told him to be at his place around eleven. Alan got ready early because he didn't want to be the last to arrive with the whole family assembled.

At a quarter to eleven, Alan jumped into the old Land Rover to make the short drive from his inner-city flat to Luke's house in Park Road. Muddy puddles edged the road, shining in the sun like black pearls on a grey ribbon. The large jacarandas and silver oaks lining the road looked greener, washed of their coating of dust.

Alan turned into Luke's property, and the tyres of the Land Rover scrunched on the hard, gravel drive. He'd planned to be the first to arrive and noted with satisfaction no other visitors' cars were there. He grabbed the large bag from the passenger seat as a smiling June emerged from the house. She wore a white cotton blouse and bottle-green flared skirt. Alan looked passed her, searching for a sign of Luke.

'Happy Christmas, June! Where are your mum and dad?'

June took Alan's hand in a friendly gesture. 'They're inside, supervising the maids.'

It was the first physical touch between them, and Alan felt like a little boy led by the hand to Santa. He exhaled as Luke appeared at the front door.

'Ah, Alan, there you are, nice and early. Happy Christmas! Can I get you a beer? June, fetch Alan a nice cold beer.'

June released Alan's hand, and he breathed easier. Enid came out to greet Alan with a peck on the cheek.

'Come inside and make yourself comfortable. The others should be here soon.'

'I have presents here for all of you,' said Alan. 'Can I give them to you now?'

'Yes, I'll get the girls together,' said Luke.

Alan spent more money on the presents than he'd intended. Still, the family entertained him, and he'd eaten at Luke's house so often, he considered himself indebted.

'Just act like part of the family,' Luke said. But for Alan it was difficult. He liked Luke but found it awkward being the only white in the group.

The gifts delighted them, and Alan relaxed. 'We'll share this, Alan,' said Luke, holding up the velvet bag containing the bottle of Royal Salute Scotch. Enid put her box of Belgian chocolates aside for later, while June and Rita put on their gold bracelets straight away.

The scrunch of car tyres on the drive signalled the arrival of Luke's second daughter and her family. Two six-year-olds rushed into the house, followed by their parents. Mae was polite but reserved, and after she walked over to talk to Enid, Alan caught her inspecting him out of the corner of her eye. She looked like a heavier, more matronly version of June. Her unsmiling husband, Ted, shook Alan's hand and then moved away to talk to Luke on the far side of the room. Alan glanced at him and suppressed a smile; reliable and boring he concluded. Ted was clean-shaven, balding and of average height and build. His unremarkable appearance and dour manner suited his job as an accountant, working in an insurance brokerage.

A loud hooting out front announced Avril, Luke's oldest daughter. Three small children of assorted ages and sizes ran through the room to the backyard to join Mae's kids, playing in the garden. A loud excitable male voice came from the driveway.

'That'll be Don, Avril's husband. Come and meet them,' said June, taking Alan's hand. June made the introductions on the front drive. Don, a large, chubby man with a moustache and a receding hairline pumped Alan's hand and slapped him on the back.

'So, you're the lucky bugger who wins the best sister?' he said, grinning all over his face. June beamed as Alan responded with a weak smile.

'And here is my sister, Avril.' June's oldest sister was tall and slim with pretty, penetrating eyes set in an intelligent looking face.

Alan shook her hand, sensing that Avril and Don were more accepting of him than Mae and Ted. Avril seemed to assess Alan, looking straight into his eyes. Her gaze and handshake were both a little longer than necessary. Alan shifted his weight to his other foot. Avril released his hand and turned to June. 'My, you are the lucky one!'

All Alan's witty quips and comebacks seemed to have deserted him, and he just stood there, grinning like an idiot.

'Stop teasing him; he's shy. You're embarrassing him,' said June, laughing.

It surprised Alan, to hear June describe him in those terms. He'd always thought of her as the shy one, at least with him. But now, June was with her family, while he was out of his comfort zone, and perhaps it showed. Everything about Don was loud and jolly. Between Don and Luke, Christmas might be a little better than he'd expected. It soon seemed obvious to Alan that Avril and June shared a close bond. Mae stuck close to Ted, and Rita maintained the remoteness teenagers affect.

Luke and the maids served drinks, topping them up often. There'd be no standing around with empty glasses here. The servants served lunch at one o'clock. It was an eye-opener for Alan as it reminded him of Christmas dinner at home in Australia, when his mother was still alive. After the turkey, ham, stuffing and all the usual accompaniments, came a traditional Christmas pudding with brandy sauce and cream. Luke made a Christmas speech which ended with a special welcome for Alan, who could have done without the last bit. A maid served coffee in the lounge where everyone relaxed in armchairs with traditional Christmas cake.

'Let's put on dance music,' said Avril, looking through a rack of CDs. 'Ah, here we are, Donna Summer and Diana Ross.' It was all romantic, late night, disco music. Avril crossed the floor to Alan and held out her hand. 'Come Alan, dance with me.'

'Well, uhm.'

'C'mon, don't be shy.'

Alan couldn't get out of it. He looked across to June who smiled; no sanctuary there. Alan stood up, and Avril took hold of his left hand and placed her own left hand on his shoulder. So, it would be ballroom dancing, not jigging around in the modern style. Don grabbed hold of Rita to dance, and the others, including the servants, stood around watching the show. Luke and Enid beamed with pride. The hint of a smile played at the corners of Mae's mouth, as Ted looked on, grim-faced.

Alan tried to keep a polite, formal distance between himself and Avril, but the more he pulled away, the closer she snuggled into his chest. He tried to hold out his left hand in a more formal dance pose, but Avril manoeuvred their clasped hands into the intimate space between them near his heart. Her left hand slipped from Alan's shoulder and now rested on his chest. Alan could feel his heart pounding and hoped to hell she didn't notice it.

Avril's thighs pressed close to Alan's as they moved in unison around the room. She was a good dancer, but with every step, her thighs pressed against his. It shocked him to realise he was stirring. He tried to think of something else, anything else, but he was losing the battle. Did she know her effect on him? Was it deliberate?

Alan couldn't keep any distance between them now, for fear of others seeing his predicament. A sense of panic rose in his throat. What to do? Everyone focused on the two couples, dancing round the room. June's smile broader than ever now.

With the aid of the alcohol he'd drunk, and his suspicion that Avril knew what she was doing, Alan acted. On the next twirl on the dance floor, he pulled Avril tight against him. Her eyes widened in surprise and he looked deep into them to get a sense of her response. They paused for a moment, and he held her gaze as her eyes slowly returned to normal. Avril smiled, and they resumed dancing even closer together. Though it seemed longer, it was only a moment, and they'd not missed a beat. He was grateful that Avril wore a flared dress that disguised the situation. It would be their little secret.

Now, Alan enjoyed himself. This was more like it. He never imagined Christmas at Luke's would be so much fun. Avril also appeared to be enjoying herself, but after two more dances, it came to a sudden halt. 'June, it's your turn to dance with Alan,' said Avril, passing him over to her younger sister standing nearby. Alan had no time to protest, and panic at once replaced his relaxed sense of enjoyment. Avril was a tease, and it amused her to put Alan on the spot. Now, he'd have the problem again. He tried to keep just the right distance between himself and June, so she wouldn't know, and the others wouldn't see.

June was not as bold as Avril, and that, together with his fear of discovery, helped Alan resolve his problem. Soon everything was back to normal, and he breathed a sigh of relief. He'd got away with it.

It was getting dark when Mae, Ted and the twins left to go home. Soon after, Avril, Don and the children prepared to leave. Don shook Alan's hand. 'You know, you and I should stick together. We were the only white bloods at this gathering of blacks.' Don saw the disbelief in Alan's face. Don looked as African as any of the others at Luke's party. 'My great-grandfather on my mother's side was white. That's why I understand whites more than most. But being black is OK these days. If you marry into the family, I'll give you tips. On second thoughts, that may be too late, so I'll give you tips before you join the family.'

Just before getting into the car, Avril smiled and said to Alan, 'Thank you for the dance, I enjoyed it. We must do it again sometime.' Her eyes twinkled, and she leant forward and gave him a kiss on the cheek. She whispered, 'June may have noticed.'

'How?' he murmured. 'I was careful.'

Avril winked. 'Not careful enough.' And with that, she hopped in the car and they drove away.

Don hooted and waved until they were out of sight.

June took Alan's hand. 'Don't worry about them. They love to tease and make mischief. You can stay longer, can't you? The maids have gone home, and Mum's making tea.'

'Well Alan, how did you enjoy your first black Christmas?' said Luke.

'Better than I expected if I'm to be honest. It's the first traditional Christmas I've had since my mother died. Since then, we always celebrated Christmas at my father's club. They were nice enough Christmas dinners, but not family occasions like today.'

After tea, and two ports with Luke, Alan made his apologies and stood to leave. He thanked Luke and Enid again for a wonderful Christmas.

'I'll see you off,' said June, walking Alan to the door. Once outside, she said, 'I hope Avril didn't embarrass you? She's always been the femme fatale of the family, and in the past, it has caused a little misunderstanding with Mae and Ted. But she must have liked you to tease you like that.'

'Oh?'

'I realised what was happening when I took you from her.'

'Oh, yes?'

'Yes, I noticed because I took you straight from her. Otherwise I wouldn't have known. You were discreet.'

'Did anyone else notice?'

'I don't think so.'

'And what about Don; wouldn't he have guessed at something?'

'Don's also a big flirt, and he knows it's just harmless fun. At my high school dances, the girls kept score of how many boys they could arouse. It was like a competition.'

'Did you do that?'

'No, I was always too shy.'

'Don is a good-looking guy. Is he Ndebele?'

'Yes, but as you heard, he claims to have white blood in him from his maternal great-grandfather. That would make Don twelve-and-a-half percent white. The thing is, with Don, you never know whether he's joking or telling the truth.'

June leant forward and gave Alan a kiss on the cheek. He climbed into the old Land Rover and started the engine. The tyres scrunched on the drive before he turned onto the tarmac and drove for home. The moon was high, and Alan felt euphoric. What a Christmas! One of the best he could remember.

Alan lay in bed looking at the ceiling. He couldn't sleep, thinking of Avril and her bold behaviour. She oozed sex-appeal, but its effect on him and the way he responded, surprised him. It must have been the champagne.

And then there was June. For her to talk to him about such an intimate matter was the mother of all ice-breakers. Till now, there'd always been a formal shyness between them, but now, they'd crossed a line. What line, he wasn't sure?

His father once told him, in the army, after weeks in the bush, the black women looked whiter with each passing day. Now he understood what his father meant. He'd been in Zimbabwe since August, and given the sensitivity and pressure of his mission, there'd been little time for socialising. Where were the suitable, unattached white women in Bulawayo? Eager males, like flies at a braaivleis, always surrounded the few available. He never bothered to compete for any woman, but then, before now, he'd never experienced rationing. Bugger the mission; he'd have to do something about getting his social life back to normal. If he was Prince Charming, where was his Cinderella?

CHAPTER 22

Luke and Enid met at the University of Rhodesia, towards the end of the old Ian Smith regime. Luke studied for his science degree and Enid studied arts. Soon after leaving university, Luke borrowed money from an uncle, and with Enid's help established a tiny retail business selling dry goods, including tinned foods and other packets. A little later they added fresh fruit and vegetables. They expanded into new lines as and when they could afford it, and within two years the business grew to a size that provided the couple a middle-class lifestyle in the new Zimbabwe.

The couple bought an old house in the inner city in Josiah Tongogara Street (formerly Wilson Street). They planned their life and family with care, considering the state of their finances. Avril and Mae, the two oldest, completed their schooling with *A Level* certificates and started work in Luke's supermarket. Both married young before their twenty-first birthdays. Soon after the two older girls left home, Luke bought and renovated the house in which he, Enid and his two younger daughters now lived.

Avril and Don led a busy social life of parties, dinners and other engagements with Don's business acquaintances. The couple remained childless, and their social whirl provided a constant distraction. Don focussed on money and business dealings while Avril ran a home worthy of the wife of a successful commercial lawyer. Avril's motherly instincts were more than satisfied by Mae's children and those of her cousins.

June, the ambitious third daughter, attended the University of the

Witwatersrand (Wits) in Johannesburg to study for an accounting degree, which she put to good use in her father's supermarket.

* * *

Ironic then, that Luke chose not to involve himself in politics in the hotbed of revolt and dissension that the University of Rhodesia provided. He and Enid focussed on the life they planned together. Luke considered politics to be an interest for the disaffected. He and Enid knew what was happening in the country as the African nationalists planned and plotted the downfall of the white regime. The couple believed they could live a successful life whatever the outcome of the Bush War. If a black government and independence from Britain eventuated, they hoped their future children would live in a land of great opportunity for young black people. If this didn't come about, they were still confident their own success would enable their children to lead a full and rewarding life.

It didn't take long for the Mugabe regime to launch a genocidal attack on the Ndebele people of Matabeleland. In 1983, a little over two years after independence, Mugabe unleashed the North Korean trained 5th Brigade on the unsuspecting Ndebele. The onslaught mainly targeted the rural population where the authorities hoped it would be easier to conceal the atrocities. Twenty thousand civilians perished under the unspeakable cruelty of the Shona rampage that came to be known as the Gukurahundi.

Some of Luke and Enid's family members lived in the affected areas, though none of them faced torture or death. Reports of the atrocities soon spread. Luke saw no future for his children under the Mugabe regime. He along with many others decided the only way to free themselves from the repression, was to revive Mthwakazi, the kingdom ruled over by Lobengula, the last Ndebele king.

Not even Joshua Nkomo, the first leader of the African Nationalist movement, proposed this ambitious idea. Nkomo identified as an Ndebele and expected to be the first prime minister of an independent Zimbabwe. By the time he realised this would not happen, it was too late to raise the prospect of Mthwakazi. Britain, the colonial power responsible for the artificial creation that was Rhodesia, should have foreseen Mthwakazi as one way forward. Unfortunately, the British politicians charged with overseeing the independence process were too ignorant of local conditions and too unimaginative to think about the country's best interests. It was an epic historical failure, reflecting the tragedy of Kashmir in the separation of India.

Most whites in Rhodesia lived in Salisbury—now Harare—, and they too fell for Mugabe's fine words and threw in their lot with the regime. Mugabe the statesman was a short-lived illusion, a myth. He first gave the Ndebele, followed later by the whites, and later still by many Shona, good reason to debunk the myth. The MFF and other similar groups would have a mountain to climb to convince the outside world of the legitimacy of Mthwakazi. If thirteen-and-a-half million Biafrans couldn't overcome the outside world's indifference, what chance two-and-a-quarter million Ndebele? One or two members of the Chiang Mai Group privately thought the MFF and the ambitious George Drake were attempting the impossible.

CHAPTER 23

To add authenticity to his cover, Alan visited Luke's home most days, even if there was nothing to report. Each evening, Luke and Enid would chat with Alan and their daughters, June and Rita. As the family got accustomed to his presence, Alan found himself alone with June more and more often, and he sensed a relationship of sorts developing between them. Later in the evening, when the others retired to their rooms, they'd sit in the darkened lounge listening to music and chatting.

To his surprise, Alan found more in common with June than he'd expected. Little by little they became closer and their conversations more intimate. He loved those after dinner discussions and looked forward to them as the highlight of his day.

Alan promised himself he'd let nothing distract him from the task at hand, but he appreciated it wouldn't be easy. He felt the electricity the first time he ran the back of his fingers down June's smooth upper arm. The hair on his own arm stood up as a current seemed to tingle through his fingers and forearm. Neither he nor June seemed to want to end their chats, and when she saw him off at the front door, she sometimes gave him a hesitant goodnight kiss on the cheek.

He lay in bed at night, thinking about June and trying to work out the difference between the occasions she pecked him on the cheek and the times she didn't. Did his actions somehow trigger the kiss, or was it down to June's mood on the night?

Then one evening, with no warning, a light kiss on the lips replaced the kiss on the cheek. Alan instinctively put his arms around June and tried to draw her close, but she slipped from his grasp and wished him goodnight. Alan worried he might have overstepped the mark, but the next evening all seemed fine. Thereafter, an occasional brush of the lips was in the mix, but on those occasions, June's tactical withdrawal always followed the light kiss.

Now, Alan often drifted off to sleep trying to imagine what form of goodnight the next day might bring. Would it be a peck on the cheek, a brush of the lips or neither? The guessing game and anticipation added a little spice to his dreams as he lay in bed wondering what went on in June's head.

CHAPTER 24

Enid sat in bed, propped up with pillows, watching Luke lay out clothes for the next morning. He selected a light blue-grey suit with a matching blue silk tie and as usual, a white shirt and black leather shoes and belt.

'I'm a little concerned about June,' said Enid.

Luke stopped and looked at his wife. 'Oh, why is that?'

'There're signs she's getting a little too fond of your young colleague.'

'Alan?'

'Yes, the way she looks at him. When Alan's finished here, he'll go back to Australia, and I'm worried June might get hurt by all this business.'

'Both of them appreciate the relationship is a convenience for the benefit of the MFF. June is too level-headed to imagine it's a real relationship. She knows Alan's only here for a year or two.'

'Let's hope you're right, but it's the first time June's shown any interest in a man. If it's all just an act, it's rather too convincing. Perhaps you should remind them it's a charade. Remember, Peter Nkala's warning about Alan's reputation with women.'

'OK, I'll remind them if that makes you happy, but you're worrying about nothing.' Luke got into bed and turned off the bedside lamp.

'Alan is a nice young man though, don't you think?'

'Yes, everyone likes him. You spend so much time with him these days. You're ignoring old friends. If they drift away, what will you do when Alan returns to Australia?'

'I'm not ignoring old friends. We are all working towards the same goal, and they knew when they selected me as the sole contact with Alan it would take up my free time.'

'Well, it looks like he's fast becoming your best friend and June's centre of attention.'

'What about you? You're always encouraging Alan to stay for dinner, and you love receiving his compliments about your cooking.'

'True, I'll also miss him when he goes. We are mature enough to recognise a temporary situation, but will June see it the same way. That's why I want you to talk to her.'

'I'll talk to her, but you can also have a word when you two next speak.'

'Is the alarm set for tomorrow morning?'

'Yes, it's set for seven.'

Luke leant over and gave Enid a goodnight kiss before turning on his side and falling asleep. Enid lay there staring at the ceiling for several minutes, thinking about the discussion. Tomorrow, she'd speak to June.

CHAPTER 25

January 2014

Alan drove to Luke's house to pick up June for their dinner date. Luke encouraged the pair to go out together in public to add authenticity to their supposed relationship.

June walked into the room looking radiant in a short, burnt-orange dress. Alan whistled under his breath. It was the first time they would be out in public as a couple, and with June's looks, they wouldn't go unnoticed. One look at June and no one would question the motives behind Alan's frequent visits to Luke's house. Under other circumstances Alan's motives might be less than honourable, but with June it was different. There was not only her but her whole family to consider. It felt like they all stood over his shoulder to make sure he did his duty. No, he was on a mission; a twelve-month mission according to his father, and he wouldn't be buggering it up with any distractions. He liked Luke too much to abuse his hospitality.

The Indaba Book Cafe was one of the best restaurants in Bulawayo with simple furnishings and a cosy atmosphere. A waiter showed them to a window table and lit the candle. Alan enjoyed the meal, though later, he struggled to remember what they'd eaten. His companion preoccupied him with her good looks and her sparkling conversation. He saw her in a new light and toyed with breaking his no distractions rule, but no, this one was too close to home.

While drinking coffee after dinner, June leant across the table and took Alan's hand. His heart skipped a beat. Was she trying to tell him something, or was she acting out her role in the charade? Alan wasn't sure, and for once, his confidence left him. He didn't have the nerve to ask her what she was thinking. It frustrated him. Here he was, the master of handling women, tongue tied on a first date in Bulawayo.

'How is your new apartment?' June asked.

'It's comfortable. It's in Fife Street.'

'Yes, I know.'

'Would you like to see it?' Alan held his breath. To hell with the no distractions rule.

'Perhaps next time.' June smiled and Alan almost melted.

'I'm not sure when I'll be back in Bulawayo.' Alan annoyed himself with his weak plea for June to change her mind.

'Perhaps next time,' June said, more firmly.

Back at Luke's front door, June pecked Alan on the cheek. 'Thank you for a wonderful evening.' Then she gave Alan a kiss on the lips that lingered a moment longer than the quick brush of the lips she'd given him before now. Without thinking, he brought his hand up to her breast. For an instant, she didn't react. Alan held his breath, but in the next second, she pulled away and disappeared into the house. In the evening's quiet, Luke's voice carried. 'Why didn't you invite him in for a drink?' Yes, why didn't she? The question troubled Alan all the way back to his apartment. Perhaps he'd overstepped the mark.

Alan lay awake, dreaming about June. This is crazy, I've never been like this about any woman since Mary Lou LeBauer in kindergarten. The problem is, I've been here almost five months without a woman, and I'm not thinking straight. Five months! Hell! I can't do this for a whole year. Perhaps in the bush with the heat and heavy training, the feeling will pass. But then, maybe not.

At least, one of Alan's questions might be closer to finding an answer. If June ever accepted his invitation to visit his flat, it would be a green light for him. What about Luke though? Alan promised himself, and his father, he would never make a play for any of Luke's daughters. Oh God, save me from making impossible promises no red-blooded man could keep.

Alan drifted off to sleep after what seemed like ages. He'd almost forgotten about his scheduled rendezvous the next evening with his men in the training team.

* * *

An aimless day passed as Alan struggled to focus on his plans for the training team. Day after next, they'd head to the Hwange National Park to see the situation there. On this first reconnoitre, Alan would only take his two Instructors, Daniel and Alexander, Molly his tracker, and two recruits, Henry and David. The other recruits would join them once Alan and the advance team checked out the national park and satisfied themselves the larger group could operate in the area without attracting undue attention. Hwange, bigger than Gonarezhou but not as remote, presented its own set of problems. The proximity of Victoria Falls might cause tourists to add to the complexity of the training they planned to undertake.

Alan's thoughts kept drifting back to June. The day before, everything was normal. Now, everything seemed different. His father said the project might take a year or two, perhaps longer. Suddenly, that didn't seem like such a bad idea. Focus, Alan, focus. Get the hell out of this crazy project as soon as possible. Back to normality and civilisation in Australia where everything was in plentiful supply and no power blackouts, well, fewer blackouts. Back to the coffee lattes in Melbourne. Mind you, the latte at the Indaba Book Cafe wasn't at all bad; better than the ones in Joburg.

Alan looked at his watch. Half-past six. Damn! Time to rendezvous with the team.

When Alan arrived at the meeting room, he found the Hwange team already there, waiting for him. They packed their backpacks together checking each other's, making sure nothing was forgotten. This time, each person carried a short-handle shovel or short-handle mattock. There was a buzz of excitement amongst the members of the small group as they looked forward with anticipation to the operation.

Alan addressed the group. 'Now remember, four and a half kilometres south of Lupane, on the left-hand side, is Maloba Road. Molly and I will drop off five hundred metres further north. We will then walk due west for five hundred metres. That is our meeting point. It is the quietest spot we could find on the map. Molly and I will carry our backpacks and the six rifles and ammunition and two pangas, so make sure you are there to meet us. We'll aim to be there at four o'clock in the evening, two days from now. That's day after tomorrow. It should take us a further two days to get into the national park. Questions? None? OK, see you there.'

* * *

Luke's van headed to Victoria Falls on a trip to pick up vegetables, eggs and live chickens along the way. Alan played his usual role of tourist backpacker with Molly as his guide. The internal side walls of the panel van were expertly modified, and it would be difficult for anyone to notice the alteration. In the van's false wall panels were the six rifles and ammunition, wrapped in cotton fabric to prevent them rattling on the drive. Alan knew about the police roadblocks and how difficult the policemen manning them could be. He also knew if there was nothing wrong with a motor vehicle, they focussed on little things like dirty windscreens or headlamps. Alan took with him a few US one-dollar notes and bottles of cool drinks to ease the way through the roadblocks. Despite their well-concealed hiding place, the rifles and ammunition did nothing to boost Alan's confidence. The rifles seemed to shout out their presence to anyone who might be interested.

At one roadblock the policeman made Ethan, the driver, unload the empty crates in the back of the van before taking a cursory look. The extra work annoyed Ethan, and he made his displeasure known to the policeman. Alan wished Ethan would shut up and not goad the policeman into a second search of the van. Perhaps the behaviour was normal. After several angry, shouted threats by the policeman he waved them on their way. Alan exhaled as Ethan accelerated the car through the road-block and headed towards Lupane. Ethan appeared not to notice the tension as he laughed about the incident.

After another twenty minutes of driving, Ethan slowed the van and stopped at an intersection. 'Maloba Road,' he said pointing to the left at a road that ran back at a forty-five-degree angle from the main road.

'OK,' said Alan, 'exactly half a kilometre more.' He and Ethan watched the odometer as it clicked up the tenths of a kilometre and stopped on the five.

'We are here,' said Ethan. Just then they noticed the police van parked only twenty metres ahead of them.

'Damn!' said Alan. 'Perhaps we should drive into Lupane and come back later.'

'There are police roadblocks on both sides of Lupane,' said Ethan. 'Here they are particular about their searches. Do you want to risk another roadblock?'

'No, let's wait. Maybe they'll move off in a few minutes. Let's get out and look like we're stretching our legs and have a cool drink while we wait.'

The three got out of the panel van and Alan made a show of opening the drinks with his bottle opener. He and Molly stood opposite Ethan who leant against the side of the van. The passenger side door of the police van opened and a policeman in khaki shorts and hat and a grey/blue shirt walked towards them. 'Here he comes,' warned Alan.

'Where're you going?' said the policeman, in English.

'I'm going to Victoria Falls to pick up supplies for my boss' supermarket, and these two wanted a lift.'

The policeman questioned Alan where he was from, how long he'd been in Zimbabwe and how much longer he planned to stay. Then he asked, 'Do you have any cool drinks to spare?'

'Sure,' said Alan taking out two bottles from the van. 'One for you and one for your driver.'

He opened the bottles and handed them to the policeman who thanked him and returned to the police car. The policemen took a sip from their bottles and started their van before U-turning and driving off in the direction of Bulawayo. Alan used the panel van's wing mirror to watch the police van into the distance.

'Phew! Thank goodness for that,' said Alan. He and Molly took out their backpacks and the rifles and ammunition wrapped in cloth. The bundles were heavy. Alan helped Molly load one on her shoulder and picked up the other bundle. They were both fit but thankful they only needed to walk five hundred metres with their loads. Ethan waved good-bye and headed into Lupane, while Alan and Molly hurried into the bush, counting their steps as they went.

Alan estimated he would need six hundred and forty steps and Molly seven hundred and twenty, to cover five hundred metres. 'If we both count our steps, between us we should be close to five hundred metres from the road.' Ahead, there was no sign of anyone in the distance. 'Let's hope they are all here, Molly. I don't fancy standing in the middle of this empty area, waiting for them.'

'They will be here, Sir. They might hide in the bushes. Perhaps they are lying down or sitting.'

As Alan and Molly neared their estimated five hundred metres, like magic, their four companions fell in behind them. 'That's excellent cam-ouflage,' said Alan. 'We walked right past you.' Their response was four rows of gleaming white teeth, stretching from ear to ear.

'OK, you guys. Grab your rifles and let's go. Keep your eyes open for people or animals. We don't want anyone to see us, and we need to cover some distance before it gets too dark.'

The team moved at a fast pace and covered over eight kilometres when at six o'clock, Alan called a halt. 'We'll stop here for tonight and make an early start tomorrow morning.' Although fit, they all flopped down on the ground after their two-hour ordeal.

Nothing distinguished the area. In all directions as far as they could see there were low scrubby trees and sparse tufted grass. The team set about selecting a spot for their sleeping bags and took out their ration packs for the evening meal. Alan organised the team for guard duty through the night, starting from ten o'clock. Each person would take a ninety-minute shift. Alan rostered himself from two-thirty to four in the morning.

The group sat around chatting until ten o'clock. There was no campfire for fear of attracting unwelcome attention. They were not yet in the national park, but wild animals did not always pay attention to the park boundaries. Alan reminded the team to keep a lookout for people, who could prove just as dangerous as any wild creature. They might report the team's presence to the authorities or, worse still, the poachers.

Everyone used a different method to make themselves comfortable in their sleeping bag. Alan put the neck of one of his boots inside the neck of the other and placed them behind his head, with both toes pointing towards his feet. It made for a comfortable pillow when camping out in the army. He noticed Molly followed his example. As in Gonarezhou, she slept close at hand. The MFF charged her with the responsibility of keeping their foreign asset safe in the African bush, and she took the duty most seriously.

Alan loved sleeping under the stars on a clear moonless night. He knew from experience if he watched them long enough, they seemed to get closer and closer. Suddenly, the stars turned into Molly's eyes. Was it already his turn for guard duty? Molly was on guard before him, and now, she gently shook him awake. Ah well, there could be worse ways to be woken for guard duty.

By seven o'clock, everyone was ready to move. They'd eaten breakfast, drunk a mug of tea and erased all signs anybody camped there. Today would be one of the most difficult of this training exercise. They had a long way to go, and from the map it looked like they'd be walking through the sparsely wooded countryside with few trees to offer shade. 'Make sure you ration your water,' said Alan 'We have to cross the Sikumbi Forest Reserve before we reach the park. I can't see anywhere on the map where we can replenish our supply.' Every member of the team carried two water bottles, but between the night before and the morning's breakfast they'd already drunk two shallow mugs of tea.

Any chatter between the team members soon dried up as the mid-morning sun burned down on them. Daniel and Alexander, the two Instructors, walked in stoic silence, their faces shiny with sweat. The trainees, city boys David and Henry, struggled to keep up, stumbling from time to time. Alan pressed the pace. He'd often hiked in arid heat, but he was yet to reach peak fitness. Molly kept pace with Alan, determined not to be the one who slowed the group.

They were all grateful for a ten-minute break at eleven o'clock and a twenty-minute stop at one o'clock. They ate an army biscuit or two and drank a sip of water. Soon they pressed on to their third stop of the day at three-thirty. As tired as they were, they felt stronger as the sun lost its bite around half past four. The early evening in Zimbabwe was a most pleasant time of the day with beautiful sunsets and a cooling, gentle breeze. By the time Alan called a stop to their march he estimated they'd covered over twenty-five kilometres through rough bush.

'We're about ten kilometres from the boundary, so we should cross into the park by lunchtime tomorrow,' said Alan. 'The closer we get the more alert we need to be.' He was happy with the progress they'd made. Their guard duty roster would stay the same for the rest of the trip, but from now on they would need to move with more caution in daylight hours. Once in the park, the team would need to avoid the possibility of running into tourists, park rangers or poachers. To make matters worse, everyone in the park is on the lookout for wildlife. That would increase the chances of someone spotting them.

While the others set up camp, Alan, Molly and Alexander scouted the area. They walked only a short distance when Alexander pointed out a small buck standing on a rise about seventy metres ahead of them. Alan took careful aim and brought the animal down with a clean shot. 'We can eat this tonight and save our ration packs,' said Alexander.

'I hope no one heard the shot,' said Alan.

'We're near the park,' said Alexander. 'People won't walk here in the evening.'

There was much excitement in the camp when the party brought back their prize. It was the first time on this trip Alan permitted a fire to be lit. 'Eat well tonight,' he said. 'Tomorrow it's back to cold bully beef.' The two Instructors set about skinning the buck and preparing the evening meal.

One by one the members of the party left their place by the campfire to go find their sleeping bags and get some sleep. A lion roared in the distance, sending a shiver down Alan's spine and reminding the party how close they were to the predators' territory. Hearing a lion roar from the safety of a hut or a boma was one thing, but when sleeping out in the open, it was a chilling experience. Tonight, the person on guard would keep the fire going but what about their security in the park? How feasible would it be to get the team to cut thorn bushes and build a small boma around their campsite each night? Would that be enough to protect them?

CHAPTER 26

THE blistering sun was a little past its peak, and Alan was grateful for the floppy hat, long-sleeved shirt and long trousers he wore. He envied his sleeveless, bare legged, black companions, but his fair skin would not tolerate the sun's direct rays. Rivulets of sweat trickled down his chest and his soaked shirt clung to his back and stuck to his armpits. Even his black companions' faces and arms shone in the heat. Alan brushed his neck in response to the sharp sting of a sand fly attracted to the sweaty bodies. Two pairs of socks and a worn-in pair of boots didn't prevent the early signs of blisters.

Alan knew his focus was on his discomfort, and he was not paying enough attention to his surroundings. A second or two could mean the difference between life and death, and the silence of the bush gave an eerie feel to the bright day. In this heat, lions rest in the shade of a tree, but a more dangerous predator might still be active. Only the crunch of their boots on the dry grass interrupted the silence. Alan needed his wits about him if he was to survive in this dangerous place. His quarry might lie in wait, but it would be just as dangerous to stumble across them by chance.

An hour before, the group walked past a pride of eight lions resting in the shade of a tree. As they passed, one of the two big males got up and walked into the sparse bushes and somehow vanished from view. The other male watched them but did not bother to rise. The six females seemed disinterested. 'Just stay calm, and walk normally,' said Molly. 'Keep an eye out for the one that walked into the bushes. That's the dangerous one.'

Acting calm was one thing but stopping the stomach from churning was something else. Every member of the group was tense and watchful, their nerves coiled for action. After twenty minutes the team relaxed, but Molly warned them against complacency. 'Lions sense when you're not on guard. It is the time of greatest danger. If this was late afternoon or early morning, they would be very interested in us. They were not hungry, so they rest while it's hot. Now they have seen us, they might still follow.'

Alan noticed the buzzing of flies growing louder and disturbing the silence of the bush. He raised his right hand and the little spread-out group stopped. He wrinkled his nose and then covered it with the handkerchief he always carried. The others used their T-shirts or cupped their noses in their hands.

There it was, only twenty metres ahead. The partially eaten body was a bloody mess, and someone had cut out the tusks. Scattered around were the lifeless forms of a dozen vultures. 'Cyanide,' whispered Molly. 'They poison the waterhole and lace the elephant's body with cyanide, so the vultures don't give away their location. If those lions come here and eat from this elephant, they might also die.'

'You three stay here and cover us,' said Alan. 'Molly and Alexander, come with me.' They approached the waterhole with caution. The trampled ground around it was clear, but who knew what the surrounding bush might conceal. Two dead jackals lay by the waterhole. 'Poisoning is the worst form of poaching, it's indiscriminate. Those bastards! How many were there Alexander?'

'Six, Sah. I think six.'

'Yes,' Molly agreed, 'six.'

'How long ago were they here?'

'About two hours,' Alexander and Molly spoke in unison.

'Six of them and six of us,' said Alan. 'That sounds fair. OK, let's follow them.'

An hour later and Alan's team was closing in on the poacher's fast.

'They must have stopped to rest in this heat,' said Alan.

'Yes,' Molly agreed, 'but they are also carrying the elephant tusks.'

The group slowed to a crawl as they sensed the poachers were nearby. They crouched in the grass and then crept forward to peer over a low rise. Another waterhole, and there were the poachers. Alan signalled to Daniel and his two comrades to move around the waterhole to the right where there was thick cover. There, they'd get a side view of the poachers.

Laughter and loud chatter carried on the gentlest breeze. The poachers sat on a rise on the far side of the waterhole and smoked cigarettes. Finished smoking, one poacher stood up, stretched, picked up a large white container and walked towards the waterhole.

'What's he doing?' said Alexander.

'I think he will pour it into the waterhole. It must be the cyanide,' said Molly.

Alan raised his rifle and fired a warning shot before the man released the deadly poison. He fell on his back on the ground, spilling a little cyanide. The other poachers scattered with their rifles into the long grass behind the ridge. The fallen man jumped up, leaving the container, and raced after his companions.

Alan couldn't see beyond the ridge where the poachers retreated. Were they still there or were they making their escape? The cyanide container sat on the ground as a witness to the evil deed the warning shot prevented. Also, on the ground, where the poachers rested moments earlier, lay two large elephant tusks and three smaller items wrapped in cotton cloth.

Even if the poachers abandoned the cyanide which was cheap and easy to replace, would they leave the elephant tusks? Alan didn't need to wait long for an answer. As he scanned the ridge opposite, a shot sounding like an angry hornet buzzed passed his head. He fancied he felt the wind of the bullet, centimetres from his right cheek. Alan and his companions flattened themselves into the dry dirt behind the rise that protected them.

While their colleagues kept up a heavy fire on the rise where Alan, Alexander and Molly lay, two of the poachers ran towards the heavy cover to outflank Alan. They didn't see Daniel and his men already hidden there. A sudden burst of fire erupted and the two poachers fell. The other poachers behind the ridge turned their attention to the firing on their left. As they tried to get a better view, they raised their heads for a second. It was the opportunity Alan, Molly and Alexander needed. They fired as one, and two more poachers collapsed in a heap. One poacher raised his hands in surrender, and Alan shouted for his men to cease fire.

'Don't shoot,' shouted the poacher. 'I surrender.'

'Where's your other man?' Alan shouted.

'He's gone, Sah.'

'Come out! Hands above your head! If you try any tricks, my men will shoot you.'

The poacher stood up slowly with his hands resting on his head and walked down from the ridge, keeping his eyes on the thick cover to his left. Sure enough, the sixth man had fled. 'Has he got a rifle?' Alan asked.

'No, he was just carrying the poison.'

'The cyanide?'

'Yes, Sah.'

'We might have to shoot you,' said Alan. 'We can't have you going around poisoning waterholes.'

'No, please, no shooting. I can give you much information. I was the leader of this group.'

'What information?'

'The men are coming from Bulawayo to pick up the tusks and rhino horns. In half an hour they will be here in their truck.'

'Rhino horns, so that's what is wrapped in those pieces of cloth. Who are these men who are coming? Who's their boss?'

'They work with someone in Bulawayo. I don't know who they are.'

'What is your name?'

'Michael Duze, Sah.'

'OK, Michael, my men will meet them when they arrive.'

'If they don't see me, they'll get suspicious. These are dangerous men with guns.'

'OK, when they come you can talk to them, but my men will be with you. One wrong word and you'll get it.'

'No wrong words, Sah.'

'How much do they pay you for the tusks and rhino horns?'

'Two tusks and three rhino horns, maybe five thousand dollars, Sah.'

'Five thousand dollars? They're cheating you. When they arrive, tell them the price is now ten thousand dollars.'

'No, Sah, they will kill me.'

'We're here to protect you or kill you. You choose.'

'OK, Sah, ten thousand dollars.'

'If you play your cards right, Michael, we may even let you join us in the service of the National Parks. Molly, can you keep Michael company when they arrive.'

'Yes, Sir.'

'Daniel and Henry, I want you to stay here with Michael and Molly. Keep your rifles handy. Fortunately, the poachers also use AK47s, so that shouldn't create any suspicion. Alexander, David and I will hide separately in the bush so we can cover them from all angles.'

Alan selected the positions from which each of them might observe the proceedings when the visitors arrived. At three points of the triangle, they could open fire on the visitors without hitting each other. 'But remember everyone, despite what happened this afternoon, we don't want shooting unless we have no choice. OK, now let's get these bodies hidden away before the truck arrives.'

As everyone waited in place, the tension rose. The silence of the bush and the buzzing flies were reminiscent of Gonarezhou. No one spoke and Alan questioned the wisdom of his plan. What if the poacher who escaped reached the road and warned the visitors of the events at the waterhole? Was he putting Molly and the others in too much danger? Could they trust Michael Duze to play along with their charade?

It was too late for second thoughts now as the sound of a motor vehicle steadily grew louder.

In a cloud of dust, the dual cab Toyota bakkie slid to a halt on the sandy surface of the sun-hardened ground.

The doors opened and three men wearing sunglasses, polo shirts and beige chinos, stepped out. They wore watches and good shoes. Their look and swagger told Alan these were no ordinary folk. Military officers or secret police, Alan guessed. Two men stood by the vehicle, and one who looked like the leader walked across to the group sitting with Michael Duze. There were no pleasantries. 'Well, Duze, let's see what you've got for us?'

'Two good tusks, Sah, and three rhino horns.'

'Show me!'

After a brief inspection, the man called to one of his colleagues standing by the bakkie. 'Matthew, bring the Money!' As they waited, he eyed Molly. 'Is this your wife or your whore, Duze?'

'Just one of the team, Sah.'

'It's a pity we are in a hurry, otherwise we might have entertained her.'

'No, Sah, this one has a sting.'

'Don't worry, Duze, we'd soon remove that sting. Bring her with you next time. Me and my men need fun.'

Matthew handed over a sealed envelope. Duze opened it to check the contents.

'What's the matter, Duze? Don't you trust us now? There's five thousand dollars there.'

'I'm sorry, Sah, but the price has risen. The market tells us it should be ten thousand dollars.'

'Don't be greedy, Duze. Your stupidity will cost you. Dr Kim won't be happy about this.'

'Sorry, Sah, the market fixes the price.'

'We don't have that much money with us.'

The leader looked at Molly and the other two, sitting on the ground, holding their rifles. He smiled. 'Oh! Wait a minute, two of the teams didn't turn up at our meeting points. Perhaps we can pay you from their envelopes, but next time, I must clear the higher price with Dr Kim.' He turned to his companion and spoke in Shona. 'Go to the truck, Matthew, and pretend you are looking for money. When you and Justin have your rifles ready call me over to help you search. Stay behind the open doors of our truck, so they can't see what you are doing. As soon as I get level with you, kill them all, except maybe the bitch if she doesn't join in the shooting. We can have fun with her later and kill her afterwards.' The leader glared at Duze, 'Let no one say Ace Mapfumo is not generous.'

Matthew returned to the bakkie and made a show of looking for the money while readying his semi-automatic. Justin, his colleague, also readied his weapon. They called Ace, asking him to come show them where the money was.

Ace Mapfumo didn't know someone in the Ndebele group, Molly, could speak Shona. As he walked away, Molly warned her two companions. 'Be ready, they will shoot as soon as he reaches the truck.'

Alan, hidden amongst rocks in the brush behind the vehicle, saw the two men readying their weapons. Their intentions were obvious. He watched the leader walk towards the man he'd sent back to the truck, so he picked out the other and took aim. Alan waited for the leader to cover over half the distance back to the vehicle before he squeezed the trigger. The shot rang out, and Justin pitched forward. Matthew raised his semi-automatic, confused, not knowing where the shot came from, and as he did so, Molly and her two companions opened fire. Meanwhile, Alan flattened himself behind the rocks as the shots whistled overhead.

The firing lasted only a few seconds though it seemed longer. When the shooting stopped, Alan stood up and walked to the where the bodies lay. Bullet holes riddled Ace Mapfumo's body, front and back. It seemed unlikely they all came from Molly and her two companions. In the panic, Matthew may also have unintentionally shot him with his semi-automatic. There was no accident with the swathe of bullet holes that cut into Matthew. Justin's body displayed only the single, neat wound from Alan's shot that started the firefight.

'Three more bodies,' said Alan. 'It's not what we planned.'

Molly reported what Ace Mapfumo said.

'Who is Dr Kim, Michael?' Alan asked.

'He's a doctor in Bulawayo. That's all I know.'

'Have you met him?'

'He came once with Ace Mapfumo.'

'Where can we find him?'

'I don't know, Sah, but one time I heard Ace tell his men they'd be late delivering the tusks to Hillside.'

'OK, guys, bury all the bodies. And bury the tusks and rhino horns. Put the lid on the cyanide nice and tight, cover it with plastic and bury it deep. Make sure you keep it upright. Wrap your rifles and ammo tight in plastic before you bury them. Molly and I will drive the bakkie back to Bulawayo and try to find Dr Kim. We'll meet up in the usual place at seven o'clock, one week from now.'

'What do we do with this one, Sah?' said Alexander, pointing to Michael Duze.

'I said he should join National Parks, so drop him there.'

'Michael, when you get to National Parks, tell them you were poisoning waterholes with cyanide. Say National Parks rangers caught you, and they persuaded you to surrender and work for National Parks against the poachers. I'll clear the way for you, so you'll have no trouble.'

Alan and Molly jumped into the bakkie and set off down the dirt road.

'Do you think National Parks will believe him, Sir?'

'I doubt it, Molly. They'll probably send him to prison. But if they believe him and give him a job working against the poachers that's not a bad result, is it?'

Chapter 27

Alan always enjoyed being alone with Molly. Ever since their days together as lookouts on the kopje in Gonarezhou, they'd become closer. She was not afraid to express her opinion on any topic of conversation. Her broad knowledge of day-to-day affairs, both domestic and international, surprised Alan, and her sense of humour kept them both amused. In the company of others, they adopted a more formal working relationship. Both knew of the potential for trouble if the men imagined Alan showed anyone favouritism.

The MFF gave Molly the role of tracker and guide for Alan and tasked her to keep him safe. As a result, no one questioned why she stuck by his side. The arrangement worked well. They were the odd ones out, Alan a white outsider and Molly the only woman.

Though no physical relationship existed between them Alan often considered the prospect. Somehow, this strange, intelligent woman, with no formal education, attracted him. Molly was self-taught. She'd spent endless hours learning to read and then used it to her advantage in the library and the internet whenever she could get access. Her connection with the MFF brought her enough money to get by, and let her engage in her consuming passion, an independent Mthwakazi.

* * *

The time was close to five in the evening when Alan noticed the temperature gauge on the dashboard showing high. He jumped out of the vehicle and opened the bonnet. The engine steamed, and the radiator hissed. There'd been no sign of damage to the car from the firefight, but now, on closer inspection, Alan found a hole in the radiator. 'Damn! It might have been a stray shot. We won't get far with this. We need water.'

'See those huts,' said Molly. 'We're near the edge of the park. They can tell us where the closest water is.'

Alan grabbed an empty jerry can from the back of the bakkie. He opened the lid and smelt it. 'There's no petrol smell. They must have used this to carry water, but it's empty now. Perhaps the radiator leaked before now.'

Alan and Molly grabbed their hats and rifles and set off with the jerry can across the open bush, leaving their vehicle on the edge of the lonely dirt road.

'It's lucky we have our rifles, Molly. Someone told me about an elderly couple who took a wrong turn and got lost in the park. To make matters worse, their car broke down when it over-heated. They couldn't get it started again. They were on a quiet road and waited for hours with no sign of another vehicle.

'In the afternoon, the husband walked back to where they turned off the busier road. His wife pleaded with him not to go, but he argued it was their best chance of rescue. It was mid-afternoon and blistering hot when he left, but soon early evening arrived and then the shadows lengthened. He hadn't returned by sunset, and his wife panicked, but she'd no choice but to wait.

'The rangers discovered the elderly couple had not left the park when the lodge at which they stayed reported them missing. The authorities began a search by road and air, checking all the quiet unused roads and bush tracks. By mid-morning they found the wife waiting in the missing car. There was no sign of her husband anywhere, and she never saw him again. Perhaps a predator got hold of him, but they found no evidence.'

'I'm glad we have our rifles, Sir.'

* * *

Distances can be hard to judge in the flat open bush. The longer they walked, the further away the huts seemed to be. At last, the perspective changed, and the huts seemed closer. Both Alan and Molly were fit, thanks to all the hard, physical training. Despite this, the heat of the day drained them. It was dusk by the time they arrived at the village. It was eerily quiet with no sign of life. Alan knocked on the door of a hut on the village edge. It creaked open a few inches, and a woman peeked out. Molly spoke to her in Ndebele and explained their predicament.

'Come, come in,' the woman said.

'We only want water,' said Alan.

'Tomorrow, tomorrow you can get water. Tonight, it's dangerous.'

'You want us to come back tomorrow?'

'No, you stay here. Too dangerous at night.'

'What is your name?'

'Nancy, Sah.'

'Where are the other villagers?' said Alan.

The woman spoke to Molly in Ndebele. 'She says the Devil's Children come out at night. People stay in huts. Too scared after dark. People disappear.'

'It's just superstition. Who are these Devil's Children? Are they evil spirits?'

Molly spoke again to the woman. 'Nancy says no one knows. They are silent, like ghosts, and people disappear. She wants us to stay with her. We can use a mat and a blanket and sleep here.'

'Wouldn't we be more comfortable in the bakkie?'

'No, she says, it's too dangerous for us to leave. We must sleep here tonight.'

In the gloomy interior of the hut, Alan saw four children sitting against the wall. 'Well that sounds like fun, but it'll be crowded'

Nancy raided her meagre supplies and prepared a meal of sadza and thin strips of cooked meat, which she now stretched to include Alan and Molly. Alan responded by handing out the peanut bars he kept in the pouch on his belt. The children were excited to receive the strange gifts wrapped in transparent paper.

After a little polite conversation following the meal, Nancy laid out a reed mat on one side of the room and handed Molly a blanket. Nancy and her four children all piled onto another mat on the other side of the room and covered themselves with a single blanket. She leaned over to turn off the battered paraffin lamp that glowed near her.

'This'll be interesting,' said Alan. 'The mat is only wide enough for one. If Nancy and her four children can manage on one mat, I suppose we also can. We'll have to sleep on our sides. If one of us turns, we'll both have to turn. Which side do you want to sleep?'

'On my right side, Sir.'

'In that case, I'll sleep against the wall and hold on to you to prevent you falling out of bed. If we turn to face the wall, you must hold on to me to stop yourself from falling out.' Alan took off his boots and got onto the mat, moving over close to the wall. 'Come on then!'

'Wait, I need a pee.'

'Shall I come with you?'

'No!'

'OK then but take my pocket torch and your rifle.'

'I'm going behind the hut. I'll be back in a minute.'

Alan stirred at the tantalising prospect of cuddling up to Molly. Hell! I hope she won't notice, but then, perhaps I won't need to break my promise about messing with one of Luke's daughters.

* * *

Alan stretched out. It was a most comfortable night. Exhausted from the excitement and activity of the day, he slept well. He stretched his arms out to the side and… Where was Molly? No wonder he could stretch out; she wasn't there. Damn! He'd fallen asleep before she returned last night and missed the fun of sharing the single mat with her. With the door ajar, the early dawn light woke him. She'd probably gone out for an early morning pee. He'd go when she got back. In the meantime, he'd enjoy a few more minutes of relaxation.

Minutes passed. Alan sat up and looked around the dim interior of the hut. Nancy, on the other mat, raised herself on one elbow. 'Have you seen Molly,' he asked. Nancy shrugged. Alan put on his boots and opened the door wide and walked out with Nancy close behind him. They walked around the hut. No Molly, but there, leaning against the wall was her rifle, and on the ground, Alan's pocket torch.

Nancy raised her hands to her face, which held a look of horror. 'The Devil's Children she whispered.'

An icy cold hand seemed to twist at Alan's insides. 'Perhaps she's gone for a walk.' But he knew it wasn't likely. His throat suddenly dry as a hollow sensation drifted down to his stomach. He felt sick. Alan took out his satellite phone and dialled the number.

'Alexander, where are you?'

'Two kilometres from the waterhole, Sah.'

'Why are you still in the area? You should be far away by now. What if someone else comes looking for those men we met yesterday?'

'By the time we buried all seven, Sah, it was almost dark, so we walked a little way and camped.'

'Now listen, does anyone in the group speak Shona?'

'Wait, Sah, I'll check.'

Alan cursed himself. He should have known the capabilities of all his men. Away from the Australian special forces, he was getting sloppy.

'Henry can speak Shona, Sah.'

'Good! I need him here, now. If he walks down the road about five kilometres, he'll find our truck. If he looks to the right, he'll see a village. That's where I am. Tell him to keep an eye out for Molly. She is missing. While I wait for him, I will search for her. Take Michael Duze back to Bulawayo as fast as you can.'

Silence on the end of the line told Alan something was wrong. 'What is it, Alexander? What the problem?'

'Michael Duze ran off during the night, Sah. The guard fell asleep.'

'Don't tell me. David, right?'

'Yes Sah. Sorry, Sah.'

'We'll deal with that when we get back to Bulawayo. Now, tell Henry to hurry.'

'Yes Sah, bye.'

* * *

The villagers all helped Alan in the search for Molly. They feared the Devil's Children took her, but prayed it wasn't the case. They all spread out in a long line and walked through the open grassland towards the stranded bakkie.

Alan spotted a blood-soaked area of soil behind the hut, but Nancy said it was where they killed the chickens and goats. The rock-hard, bare earth around the village gave up no clue to what happened. One woman claimed she saw hyena tracks on the edge of the village. Alan looked at the area she showed him, but he couldn't make out any sign of animal tracks on the hard, dry ground.

'Might hyenas have taken her, said Alan.'

'No, Sah, hyenas make a lot of noise. We would have heard them. It must have been the Devil's Children.'

'Who do you think the Devil's Children are?'

'I don't know, Sah. One Sunday, my husband cycled to the beer hall. Later, other people saw him coming home, very near here, but he never arrived. He disappeared. It was almost dark, the time for the Devil's Children.'

'Yes,' said Nancy, 'since the Devil's Children came, many people have disappeared. Another woman woke up one morning and her eldest son was gone. Her children would never go outside alone once darkness fell. Her door was ajar, and she believed it might not have been properly shut that night. One month ago, it was a hot night, and the men sat outside drinking beer and talking. They all drank too much and fell asleep. In the morning, one man was missing. No one heard anything.'

'Why do you say it's the Devil's Children who are responsible? Might it have been a leopard? They are silent killers and strong enough to carry a man away, leaving no drag marks.'

'No, Sah,' said the woman, 'we don't think it's a leopard. The people usually disappear on a Sunday. Yesterday was also Sunday. God rests on Sundays, so it's safe for the Devil's Children to come out.'

'If it always happens on a Sunday, perhaps it's a man who doesn't work on Sundays. Perhaps it's a serial killer.' The women looked at Alan as if he'd made a ridiculous suggestion.

They searched for over an hour when one villager shouted and waved. Alan and the other villagers ran to the spot and saw the green bandanna on the ground; the one Molly always wore. Alan picked it up and examined it. Could those dark stains be blood? Possibly, but it was hard to tell. Molly's likely fate suddenly ratcheted up a notch, and Alan brought up on the spot while the sympathetic Nancy and other villagers patted him on the back. They searched another two hours, without success.

Just then Henry arrived. 'No sign of Molly, Sah.' Alan managed a thin, rueful smile. In his entire life, he'd never felt so empty. He'd seen comrades die in Afghanistan and he was with his mother when she passed, but somehow, this was different. Being torn apart by a savage beast was something more than Alan wanted to contemplate.

CHAPTER 28

THERE was nothing more Alan could do. Molly was gone, and he felt crushed. She'd been his closest companion since the basic training camp two months back. Now, he prepared to leave the village but found it hard to tear himself away. This was Molly's land. It was where she died, and he found it hard to leave her.

Henry fancied himself as a mechanic and he worked to plug the hole in the bakkie's radiator. Alan didn't care how Henry did it. One villager walked to a nearby stream and filled the jerry can with water. Now, it was time to go.

As Alan said goodbye to Nancy, she handed him an old faded passport damaged by the elements. 'A villager found this, Sah. This person might have met the Devil's Children.'

Alan opened the passport and read the name. 'Dr Abel Sibanda. He noticed the immigration stamps from South Africa and Zambia. OK, Nancy, I'll give it to the right people. Did the villager find anything else?'

'Just this, Sah.' Nancy held a gold bracelet in her palm. 'I don't need it, Sah. In the bush, I can never wear it. Can you take it to his family?'

'A women's bracelet! Perhaps it was a gift for someone, his wife or daughter. Thank you, Nancy, for giving us shelter last night. Goodbye.'

As Alan pulled away in the bakkie, the villagers all waved and shouted their goodbyes. His unexpected visit interrupted their simple lives, but they couldn't have been more welcoming and supportive.

Henry looked at Alan and said, 'I'm sorry, Sah.'

'What are you sorry about, Henry?' said Alan, sounding less gracious than he intended.

'Because you lost your girlfriend, Sah.'

'Molly wasn't my girlfriend, Henry, she was my colleague, just like you are my colleague.'

'All the men say she's your girlfriend, Sah.'

Alan lapsed into silence and tried to take his mind off Molly by thinking about the poaching in the country's national parks. The extent of the poaching dawned on him. They picked up the trail of the poachers in Gonarezhou on their first patrol. The same happened in Hwange when they stumbled upon the horror of poisoning at the waterhole. The threat to the country's wildlife was greater than he imagined. Alan read about it, but seeing it first-hand brought the severity of the crisis home to him. Someone in authority must do something. But what chance was there under the present regime when so many government bigwigs reaped the rewards of poaching? Might the MFF and other like-minded groups bring an end to the carnage? If so, he could commit to the cause of Mthwakazi.

Henry remained quiet for as long as possible. But remaining quiet wasn't in Henry's nature, and soon he chatted away again, trying to cheer up his forlorn leader.

'It's a miracle,' said Alan.

'What, Sah.'

'Whatever you've done to the radiator seems to be working. The temperature gauge is staying on cool.'

'Oh, yes, Sah. I didn't know how to fix the radiator, so I disconnected the temperature gauge.'

They both laughed at Henry's little joke. At least, Alan hoped it was a joke. Henry didn't seem concerned, so Alan took comfort from that.

'We need to bury our rifles in a quiet spot. Keep a lookout for an unused bush track and we'll drive down it a short way.'

'There's a lot of bushes there, Sah.'

'No, it's too close to the road. We'd have to walk to that spot and leave our car parked here on the side of the road. We don't want tourists driving past and reporting to the rangers they saw two men burying guns in the bush.'

Alan worried they were getting too close to the park entrance when Henry shouted out, 'There, Sah, a bush track.'

A track veered off to the left. It was little used and in danger of being overgrown.

Alan drove about two hundred yards into the bush before he was satisfied they would not be seen from the road. He pulled up next to a sandy spot they'd recognise when they needed their rifles again.

'Wrap your rifle nice and tight in your plastic sheet, Henry. I'll wrap Molly's rifle together with mine.' Alan rummaged amongst the items in the bakkie's tray, looking for anything with which to dig. Under a tarpaulin he found several pieces of wood and assorted junk. Perhaps they planned to hide the ivory amongst this lot. 'There is a god!' Alan exclaimed, holding up a pick and a spade.

Alan's discovery was fortuitous because even with those implements, digging a suitable hole was hard work. The patch of ground looked sandy but was rock hard inches below the surface. Even with his work-hardened hands, Alan felt blisters forming before they'd finished digging a long, rectangular hole deep enough for the three rifles. 'Let's hope the white ants don't get to these rifles,' said Alan, as he smoothed the sand over the hole to disguise any signs the ground had been disturbed.

Henry smiled with his perfect white teeth. 'We have hidden them well, Sah. Even from the white ants.'

'If Michael Duze got out of the park last night,' said Alan, 'he might have contacted his connections. They might search for us right now. He doesn't know we're still in the park, so they may watch for this vehicle all the way from Vic Falls to Bulawayo. If he reported to the police his vehicle was stolen, how are we going to get through the roadblocks?'

'New number plates, Sah.'

'Yes, but where?'

'A hotel or store or pub.'

They drove along, looking for a spot where multiple vehicles parked.

'We need to find somewhere before we hit the main road,' said Alan.

A tour vehicle passed with several people on board. 'Those tourists must have parked their cars somewhere, said Alan.'

'Perhaps that hotel, Sah.'

'OK, let's see.'

A few cars sat unattended in the car park.

'We need a screwdriver to change number plates,' said Alan.

They searched in the glove box and other compartments but found nothing suitable. 'What's in the toolkit, Henry.'

'Just spanners and a jack, Sah.' Henry spotted a gardener walking by and called out to him in Ndebele. 'That man will bring me a screwdriver from the workshop. I told him I needed it to fix my engine.'

'Henry, I'll go into the hotel and distract them while you find a car with Zimbabwe number plates in a similar condition to ours. Put our number plates on their car first and then put their number plates on ours. People know their cars and don't look at their number plates too often. It may be days before they even notice. Make sure no one sees what you're doing.'

Alan walked into the hotel lobby. No one was at the front desk though he heard someone moving around in the office behind it. Alan took a brochure from the rack and flipped through it. An African man walked out of the office and Alan coughed to attract his attention.

'Can I help you, Sir?'

'Yes please, can you tell me about your room rates?'

Alan positioned himself to one side of reception, so he could see the car park over the receptionist's shoulder. He peppered the unsuspecting man with several more questions: the best time of the year to visit, whether the restaurant was open to the public, their cancellation policy, how far from the national park and how far to Victoria Falls?

'It's all in the brochure, Sir, and you'll also find us on the internet.'

Alan was running out of questions to ask when he saw Henry give him a thumbs up from the car park. 'Oh, can you please exchange my twenty-dollar note for one-dollar notes for the roadblocks? Thank you very much. I must consider staying here on my next visit. Goodbye.'

Henry stood by the bakkie, smiling. Everything went well, and he'd even returned the screwdriver to the gardener. While he had the bonnet up, he also filled the radiator. 'All done, Sah.'

'Good work, Henry. You're a champion.'

This time, Henry drove.

As expected, soon after they turned on to the main road, they hit the first police roadblock. There was no difficulty getting through with a polite 'good afternoon' and a dollar paid. The same applied to the next two, near Gwayi River Farms and Jotsholo. But outside Lupane it was different. The policeman walked around to Henry's window. 'Where have you come from?'

'We've come down from Victoria Falls and are going to Bulawayo.'

The policeman glared at Alan. 'And your passenger?'

'A tourist hitchhiker.'

The policeman checked the number plate. 'Have you seen a vehicle like yours on the road?'

'No, sorry.'

The policeman walked around the truck, examining it with care. He looked under the tarpaulin. He waved his hand over the bakkie's tray. 'Where are you taking all this?'

Henry smiled his most genial smile. 'It's for my brother-in-law in Bulawayo.'

The policeman waved them on their way.

'Well, someone knows their bakkie is missing,' said Alan. 'Either Michael Duze reported it, or perhaps his contacts are wondering why he didn't turn up with the tusks and rhino horn. If he got out of the park, we'd better be careful he doesn't recognise us back in Bulawayo. That's a complication we don't need.'

'It will be better when we shave,' said Henry.

Alan always ensured he and his men did not shave when out in the bush. It was not a question of convenience or recognition, but one of detection and sunburn. Shaving cream, aftershave or sunscreen could give away their presence to a sensitive nose, and in Alan's view the best protection from the blistering sun was a bush hat and a few days growth.

The other police roadblocks presented no difficulty. At Kenmaur, the policeman waved them through without stopping, and a one-dollar note took care of the rest. Outside Bulawayo they were once again asked similar questions to those at the Lupane roadblock. 'Have you seen a vehicle similar in appearance to your one?' said the policeman.

'No, we've seen nothing like ours,' said Henry.

'Let me see your driving licence.'

Alan forgot all about the small matter of a driving licence, but to his great relief, Henry dug in his shirt pocket and produced it.

'Lucky you had the foresight to bring your driving licence with you on this operation, Henry.'

'Oh no, Sah, I don't have a licence. The police took it away from me for drinking and driving. I can get it back if I pay the bribe.'

'Well, what licence did you show the policeman?'

'That was Michael Duze's licence. The police never check properly. I will change the photo and use his one. That way I won't have to pay the bribe.'

Alan shook his head. 'Only in Africa!'

They drove on into the city. 'We've got to dump the bakkie and walk,' said Alan. 'How about here.'

'Yes, Sah.'

'First, wipe the door handles and the number plates. I'll wipe the steering wheel and dashboard. Just in case.'

Alan put the car keys on the front right tyre. As they walked off down the road, Henry said, 'Why did you choose that place to leave the car, Sah?'

'That spot is quiet now, but I've noticed lots of cars park there during business hours, so it might be days before anyone notices it.'

'But why opposite the police station, Sah?'

'Police station? I didn't know it was the police station. Why didn't you tell me?'

'Because I thought you did it on purpose, Sah, to show the police they don't scare us.'

'I'm not Zorro, you know, Henry. I don't deliberately want to provoke the authorities.'

CHAPTER 29

'NYOKA,' said Captain John, 'Dr Kim phoned to say Michael Duze didn't turn up last night as scheduled.'

'Perhaps the poachers were late,' Hilton Nyoka responded.

'No, in the past when they've been late, but Duze delivered the goods even at two in the morning.'

'I'm sure he'll get in touch soon. There could be a hundred reasons he didn't show. Perhaps his car broke down or he ran out of petrol.'

'Yes, and maybe he's run off with the goods. I've never trusted that bastard with his smarmy ways.'

'OK, I'll get in touch with our police contacts in the area and on the Bulawayo road from Hwange.'

'That's what I like about you, Nyoka. You've got initiative, and I don't need to lead you by the hand. You're not like the other idiots. Mind you, you have your faults.'

'What faults, Sir.'

'Standing there, making idle chatter, for example. Now get on with it! Get in touch with our contacts and tell them to keep a lookout for Michael Duze's bakkie. There'll be a bottle of Black Label for the man who finds Duze and the bakkie.'

'Black Label, Sir!'

'No, you idiot! Do you really think I'd waste a bottle of my good Scotch on those buffoons? No, it'll be more like a carton of Chibuku, but they won't know the difference.'

'All right, Sir.'

'But don't talk to the Bulawayo cop. That guy is Duze's cousin.'

'OK, Sir.'

'Off you go then.' Captain John took out his cell phone and punched a number on the screen's dial pad.

'Khumalo, where the hell are you? What's going on down your way?'

'There's no sign of Michael Duze and his team, Sir, and Dr Kim is threatening to take his business elsewhere. He says he has high connections, willing to supply him with all the ivory and rhino horn he needs.'

'Yes, I'm also sick of his threats, but he's the only significant buyer down your way. Perhaps you should look for a substitute in case that North Korean bastard carries out his threat. Keep me up to date on what's happening. Bye.'

Hilton Nyoka returned and stood in Captain John's doorway. 'Any news, Sir.'

'Khumalo says there's no news from the Hwange poachers. They've either gone to ground or also disappeared. They might all be in this together. Perhaps Dr Kim is dealing directly with them and doesn't need us anymore.'

'Dr Kim couldn't do that, Sir. It's your operation, and he wouldn't know how to handle those boys.'

'You'd be surprised what those inscrutable North Koreans can handle, Nyoka. They're no fools, unlike most of our team.'

'You judge our men too harshly, Sir.'

'Now listen. Let's think about this. Your Gonarezhou soldiers claim another poaching gang shot a park ranger and one of their team. Our Mozambican friend says his six men all disappeared on the same day. Now, Khumalo's six-man team has not contacted him, and our three men are also missing. I smell a rat, Nyoka. Someone is trying to muscle in on our territory. Either, they've somehow persuaded our men to move across to them, or they've done away with them.'

'Well, I never trusted Ace Mapfumo and his two cronies. All three were sleazy hoods. There'd be no problem if we'd used Phineas' team.'

'I'm not risking our best team on something like that. Their anonymity is their strength. They've dealt with heaps of people for us, including that nuisance Dr Abel Sibanda. Phineas and his team, work in the COU's core business. If the poaching business gets too difficult, we can always fall back on that.'

'Yes Sir, I suppose you're right.'

'Yes, I am right. You must have heard the rumours the first lady is selling ivory. If that's true, and she sees us as competition, things could get very awkward. No, let's keep things in perspective.'

'So, what do we do now?'

'First, we try to find out who's working against us. And if it's another gang, we'll deal with them, starting with the top. Find that bakkie. It might give us a useful lead. This is war, Nyoka. Do you understand that?'

CHAPTER 30

February 2014

Alan was pleased to be back in the relative comfort of Bulawayo. The Hwange operation turned out to be a traumatic affair he'd rather forget, but it preoccupied his mind. But now, his thoughts turned to June. The last time they were together he sensed a growing intimacy between them, but he worried he might have overstepped the mark and pushed a little too hard on that occasion.

The secret in any relationship was pace; not too fast and not too slow. He'd always considered himself the master of timing in his dealings with women. He even got the timing just right with his Aunt Ruth. Although he didn't pre-plan the night with her, he still needed to judge how far he could go.

With June, Alan was all at sea. Perhaps because she was Luke's daughter, or because of her colour? Was she a novelty? Before now, he'd never associated with a black woman. Weren't all women the same? Might it be, he maintained professional standards and needed to avoid distractions when in the middle of a serious mission. No, he doubted that reason; his brief encounter with the captain's wife in Cyprus came in the middle of a serious operation. The real reason might be he cared for her more than he would admit, even to himself.

How would she react to him? He'd find out soon enough. Perhaps too soon. Alan turned into the drive and heard the familiar crunch of gravel under the wheels of his old Land Rover. He climbed out of the old vehicle and walked along the drive. Halfway to the front door it opened, and a smiling June stood there. Relief flowed through Alan's body; everything looked fine.

June kissed Alan on the cheek and moments later Luke came out and shook his hand and slapped him on the back. 'Welcome back Alan. Come, tell me about your trip. Enid's preparing one of her special dinners. You'll stay, won't you?'

Alan didn't need a second invitation. Luke's wife prided herself on her European cooking, as she liked to call it, typical of the food whites ate and of a high standard. From time to time, Enid would cook traditional African meals, but mostly she prepared Western dishes that Alan relished. Many men claimed nothing surpassed their mother's or their wife's cooking. Alan's mother died in his early teens. He barely remembered her cooking now, and for him, Enid's cooking was the gold standard.

Luke sent June to help her mother in the kitchen and poured two Scotches for Alan and himself. They settled down on the comfy Chesterfield sofa in Luke's study, and Alan related the events of the past several days. 'As much as I hate to leave the wildlife to the mercies of those greedy bastards, we must look after the welfare of our recruits. I don't mind facing the poachers with their modern weapons, but if the authorities get on to us, our efforts might backfire and bring the whole project undone.'

Luke nodded in agreement as Alan continued. 'Dr Kim is the main marketing contact. We can disrupt his operations. If we can't stop the poaching in the national parks, at least we could reduce it by disrupting the supply chain. Perhaps that will save a few of the animals, although it may only be a temporary relief.'

June came into Luke's office to call him and Alan for dinner. Enid waited in the dining room and gave Alan a welcoming peck on the cheek. When the maid brought in the dishes, Alan couldn't hide his pleasure. 'Ah! Roast beef and vegetables, my favourite meal.'

Alan's sincere compliment made Enid beam with pride. 'It's wonderful to cook for someone who appreciates my efforts. You are always welcome here, Alan. The whole family enjoys my cooking, but to get compliments from someone outside the family boosts my ego.'

'I see Alan as part of the family,' said Luke.

'Thank you all. You make me feel like part of the family because you're all so welcoming.'

June's wide smile at the comments warmed Alan with a sense of well-being. This cosy family home, so much more inviting than the sterile luxury of his father's Toorak mansion back in Melbourne.

After dinner, the family moved to the lounge for coffee and more chatter, while the maid cleared the dinner table and washed the dishes in the kitchen. Later, she came into the lounge to offer more coffee. 'You can go now, Bella'; 'I will wash the coffee cups,' said Enid. The maid curtsied and said goodnight.

'Where is Rita?' Alan asked.

'Where she always is these days,' June responded. 'She has an overnighter at a class-mate's house. They say they want to study together. I'm not sure how much studying gets done when they have music playing all the time.'

Around ten o'clock, Luke and Enid excused themselves and retired to bed. 'Us old folk need our sleep,' said Luke. Were they just being discreet? June's parents liked Alan, but even more important, it seemed she did too.

June turned on the music system and switched off the lounge lights. She sat down next to Alan on the sofa by the windows. A brilliant full moon flooded the lounge, interrupted by frequent rain clouds, scurrying across its face. The steady drip of water from the leaves of the large trees in the garden, soaked from the earlier downpour, contributed to the romantic atmosphere. The gentle breeze through the open windows on the warm January night was heady with the smell of summer rain.

Alan laid his hand on June's upper arm and ran his fingers down to her wrist. This time she did not pull back but leant into him and gave him a light kiss on his lips. Her reaction surprised him. Her lips lingered, and her breath was fresh. Alan moved nearer to June and put his arm around her waist and held her close. Through his thin shirt, he felt her firm breasts pressed against his chest.

No awkward holding back now. June kissed Alan full on the lips, and soon the two melted into each other with long tender kisses. Alan was aroused and saw no need to hide it. June broke away and walked over to the music player to replace the dulcet tones of Frank Sinatra with the sexual songs of Barry White. Between their intimate moments, the two chatted late into the night. Alan wasn't in a hurry. There was plenty of time; no need to rush things. He enjoyed their intimacy and was content to let things take their course. Delicious anticipation would make things sweeter down the line.

At midnight, Alan kissed June goodnight and eased the Land Rover out of the drive and onto the road. He was exhilarated. He suffered from a bad case of lover's balls, but he didn't care. What a wonderful evening! What would Luke think of this development? He wouldn't say anything to him about it; that was up to June. In his excitement, Alan struggled to sleep. He would have liked to stay with June longer, but they both worked the next day. What thoughts might run through her head? Would she find it easy to sleep? Eventually, he dozed off with her face imprinted on his mind.

* * *

The next morning, Luke was in a most cheerful mood. Did he guess at something? Did he know something? Probably not, Alan concluded.

Over the next few evenings, Alan and June's relationship deepened. Although their physical connection did not advance beyond their passionate kisses on the sofa by the open window, each occasion seemed more intimate than the last.

Content to let things develop over time, Alan relished the slow-burning fuse to the physical side of their blossoming romance. On their dinner date at the Indaba Book Cafe, June said she might visit his apartment on the next occasion. They'd not been out alone together since that evening, and Alan still worried about Luke and what he might say about their relationship. An even bigger concern was Alan's own feelings for June. Before now, he'd experienced nothing like this, and it scared him. If they made love, he wanted it to be perfect and not a guilty secret.

One evening, June asked Alan, 'Why do you come and see me every day? Is it a novelty for you to be with a black girl?'

Alan sat up, straight. The question surprised him. It was almost as if she'd read his thoughts. 'No,' he protested. But even to him, his denial sounded a little too defensive. The best form of defence? Attack. 'Why do you sit with me on the sofa and kiss me each night? Is it a novelty for you because I'm white?'

June's eyes twinkled. 'Yes, possibly.'

Alan's eyes widened. He frowned. 'To be honest, I think I'm falling in love with you.' It was the first time he'd ever admitted a deep affection for anyone, and his face flushed.

June laughed. 'If you keep telling me nice things like that, I may fall in love with you too.'

Alan now saw she was joking, and his face relaxed, betraying his sense of relief. He'd been caught out by June because he hadn't read her correctly. That didn't happen too often to Alan in his dealings with women. Later, he realised the exchange was just another sign of their growing intimacy, where they could tease and test each other.

Alan couldn't remember a happier time. The Mthwakazi project was the furthest thing from his mind.

CHAPTER 31

THE cell phone on Alan's hip vibrated. It was his father, George. 'Now listen here, Alan, the CMG (Chiang Mai Group) is getting impatient. The group met in New York yesterday, and members are wondering what value they are getting for their money.'

'When we met in Joburg, I told you we weren't yet ready for any major investment in equipment. I'm training the future leaders for the project. When they're ready, they'll train others, and it will build in that way. What's the hurry, anyway? Is the CMG trying to launder money or what?'

'Don't be facetious, Alan. Some members are thinking they should put their money to better use than earning a paltry interest in a bank account. One or two of them are getting cold feet. The members don't want any trouble in Zimbabwe linked back to them. It might be bad for business.'

'Did they imagine I'd walk into the country and be greeted by a population itching for revolution? The Gukurahundi traumatised the people. A few young firebrands are raring to go, but they're in the minority. A movement builds like a volcano before an incident or event causes an eruption that releases the pressure. The people need to trust that those who are pushing for change won't desert them at the eleventh hour and leave them to the mercies of another 5th Brigade. Our people here are aiming to build a defence force, not an invading army.'

'The CMG needs to see movement, Alan. I don't want our funders to withdraw their money.'

'When you first mentioned this crazy project, you said it would be a year or two, maybe more, but that's an optimistic view. Well, it won't be one year; more likely over two.'

'Do I get the impression you're now happy to stay and commit to the cause?'

'No, I'm just stating the facts as I see them.'

'Alan, make a list of the equipment you're likely to need. A list will satisfy the CMG that things are progressing.'

George rang off, and Alan paced around his apartment, frustrated by the expectations of a group of wealthy men sitting in their plush offices around the world. His father and the CMG were treating the cause as a business venture. Alan understood their underlying motivation was ultimately business, and even wars are run on budgets, but this venture was more like a start-up than a mature business operation.

The problem was George Drake was too persuasive. He could talk anyone into anything. In one meeting, he'd talked his business associates into the Mthwakazi project. They all agreed to support it and only thought more about it later. Alan found it surprising that mature businessmen who were multi-millionaires, and accustomed to weighing up the pros and cons of any investment, were so easily led by one man. But that was his father's skill. He could make anyone who didn't go along with his ideas feel left out or excluded, missing a great opportunity. No one would ever say George Drake didn't have a record of making everything he touched a success.

CHAPTER 32

ALAN needed to find out about Dr Kim. His surgery in the CBD was easy enough to locate, but where did he live? Molly said it was somewhere in Hillside. His home address seemed to be a secret. Although Bulawayo was not a large city, Alan and his contacts made little headway with their enquiries.

There was nothing else for it. Someone would have to tail Dr Kim from his surgery to his residence. Alan did not want to raise his profile and risk the whole project. The same applied to Luke, so the task fell to Henry, who was fast becoming one of the more important members of Alan's team.

Dr Kim was not the only Korean working in his practice in Bulawayo, so Henry needed to be sure he tailed the right person. By convenient chance, he'd picked up a cold on his last night in the bush, so he went to the surgery and asked to see Dr Kim.

'Dr Kim is very busy,' said the receptionist. 'Dr Chen is available.'

'Thank you, no. My friends all recommend Dr Kim.'

'Very well,' said the receptionist, put out by the curt dismissal of her suggested alternative.

A thin Asian man came out of a consulting room, walked behind the reception counter and put papers into the receptionist's in-tray.

'This gentleman insists on seeing you, Dr Kim.'

Henry missed the emphasis on the *Dr Kim*.

'Right, come in, young man.'

After the consultation, Henry paid the receptionist. As he opened the door to leave the surgery, the doctor came out of his office, put papers in the receptionist's in-tray and turned to walk back into his office when the receptionist called out, 'Oh! Dr Chen, your wife wants you to call her urgently.' Henry caught the receptionist's eye, and she flushed with embarrassment. She'd been caught out. Henry opened his mouth to comment when a portly, balding Asian man came out of another consulting room and put more papers in the receptionist's in-tray. Henry shook his head. If the other one was Dr Chen, this must be Dr Kim.

The doctors often worked long hours, and darkness fell before Henry saw Dr Kim drive out of the surgery parking area in his large Mercedes. The dark meant Henry and his car would not be recognised, though the quiet streets made it difficult for Henry to follow Doctor Kim, unnoticed. He held back a good distance but closed the gap each time the doctor made a turn. Henry needed to be close enough to be sure which driveway the doctor entered.

As the doctor turned into an unassuming, red-brick, corner property, Henry sped by, confident the doctor remained unaware he'd followed him.

CHAPTER 33

Henry and Daniel sat with Alan in the deep night shadows of large Jacaranda trees, observing the red brick house from a discreet distance. A curtained window to the left of the front door glowed a deep red. The rest of the house remained in darkness. Dr Kim's Mercedes sat in the driveway. 'I wonder what he keeps in the garage,' said Alan. 'With that bare garden, he won't be storing much in the way of gardening tools.'

'Maybe it's a workshop,' Henry suggested.

'We should have a closer look. Daniel, stay in the car, and hoot if you need to warn us of any sign of danger.'

Alan and Henry ran across the road and on to the gravel drive, which crackled underfoot. They jumped off the drive onto the softer earth on the right. Heavy wooden, padlocked double doors stood in their way. 'We won't get through there without making a noise,' said Alan. Set into one of the big wooden doors was a standard door to allow access without the need to open the large garage doors. 'That may be a weak point, Henry. See if the wheel brace in our Land Rover has a tyre lever on it. If it has, bring it back here.'

Henry soon returned, grinning and holding up the wheel brace with its tyre lever. He placed the lever in the gap between the door and the door frame near the old Yale lock. Henry tested the door with the lever, and it groaned under the pressure. 'Slowly,' said Alan. 'We must be as quiet as possible.' With a little added gentle pressure, the door gave way with a soft splintering sound. 'That's a weathered door, to give way so soon with barely a creek. Well done, Henry.'

They entered the dark garage, and Alan took out his pocket torch. The garage was empty except for a tarpaulin, covering something on the concrete floor. The pair eased back the tarpaulin cover. 'Got them!' said Alan. 'At least a dozen tusks, and those little pieces wrapped in cotton must be rhino horn.'

'What are we going to do,' said Henry. 'Should we steal them? If we call the police, they may do nothing, and then we will have warned the poaching gang.'

'No, we won't steal them. It would take us all night to move this lot. And we won't call the police, but we will teach these bastards a lesson. Fetch the jerry can of petrol and the box of matches from the glove box.'

'Remember the jerry can's only half full. Will that be enough petrol?'

'It'll be plenty.'

Henry returned with the jerry can and the matches. Alan and Henry rolled up the tarpaulin and placed it between themselves and the tusks to form a makeshift dam to contain or slow the flow of the petrol they poured over the tusks. 'Right, stand back Henry.' Alan struck a match and tossed it onto the tusks. With a loud 'whoosh' the flames leapt to the roofing timbers, setting alight the cobwebs accumulated over the months or years. In an instant, Alan's face felt as if sunburned.

As Alan and Henry turned to run to the Land Rover waiting in the street, a door at the back of the garage opened and shooting started. Henry was halfway out of the door when a row of dark spots ran across his shirt. He lurched face forward onto the ground. Alan, crouched in the corner of the garage, unseen until he pulled out his Glock 22 and returned fire. The figure in the back door disappeared. Because of the flames, Alan couldn't be sure if his bullets struck their target, but where was Henry?

Alan raced outside and almost tripped over the prone body of Henry. He dropped to one knee; his heart full of dread when he saw the blood-stained shirt. 'No, no Henry, no,' Alan groaned. He turned Henry over, hoping for a miracle, but he knew it was hopeless. Daniel came running. 'Fetch the blanket,' Alan shouted. 'We're not leaving him here.' As

Daniel hurried back with the blanket, he saw a car with two figures inside drive out the side gate of the property.

Alan and Daniel lifted Henry onto the blanket and hurried to the car and lay him on the back seat. They drove off down the road at a leisurely pace. No sign of any police car or fire engine with sirens blaring, and as far as they could tell, no curious neighbours emerged to check on the commotion in their quiet suburb. People learnt from bitter experience, responding to any signs of trouble was not worth the risk. A phone call to the emergency services was the best course of action.

'Where should we take Henry?' Daniel asked.

'We'll ask our friends.' Alan drove down Cecil Avenue towards Esigodini Road and turned left towards the Suburbs.

Luke answered the door. 'It's late. Is there trouble?' Alan explained their predicament. 'Wait here. I must make a call.' Luke returned a few minutes later with instructions. 'It's a quiet dark street, not far from here. Park next to the big hedge on the right. You can't miss it. In fifteen or twenty minutes an ambulance will arrive and collect Henry. They will notify his family and deliver his body to their village.'

Alan drove with Daniel to the nominated spot and waited by the tall hedge for the ambulance to arrive.

'Your eyebrows are funny,' said Daniel 'They've gone curly.'

Alan realised his face was still hot from the explosive fire in Dr. Kim's garage. As he ran his fingers over his eyebrows, the brittle hair crumbled in a small cloud of ash. His eyelashes were the same. 'I'll look funny for a few days, but it's nothing compared to the price poor Henry paid.'

CHAPTER 34

A NOTHER sleepless night for Alan. The fate of three of his team weighed on him. Joao was the first, when the elephant trampled him. Then a wild creature or creatures took Molly. His team operated in dangerous country, and Alan reasoned he was not to blame for the first two deaths. With Henry, it was different. Alan blamed himself for exposing Henry to a dangerous and illegal operation, and he felt bad about it.

As a former soldier with experience of active service, Alan was accustomed to being on guard for his personal safety. His brave young recruits, with their burning desire to help their people find freedom from a rapacious regime, did not yet have the experience and skill to protect themselves in the dangerous working environment they faced. Perhaps he asked too much of them. The approach to the training honed the recruits fighting skills, but there was a cost. If Alan found the cost too much to bear, what must their families be suffering. Molly seemed to have no family, though Alan grieved for her. Joao and Henry's family would grieve unseen, somewhere out in the expanse of the Zimbabwean bush.

Alan resolved to change his approach to the training. Nothing could substitute for experience gained under operational conditions, but the attrition rate was too high. Three of the original fifteen members of Alan's team died; that was twenty percent. No, something had to change. In the same period, at least fifteen poachers died, and the two who ran off in the Hwange National Park might have met their end in the jaws of a predator. A ratio of five to one in Alan's favour was little comfort.

The exercises aimed to develop the skills to stay hidden and observe, to be unseen, yet haunt the poachers in their evil work. There was no plan to get involved in firefights and draw unwanted attention. Circumstances forced their hand, and the killings were unavoidable. The poachers had too much to lose and stood their ground. Perhaps his plan for training raw recruits was naïve and flawed from the start. No, he would have to change his approach.

The one silver lining was the team now boasted ten hardened recruits to help with training newcomers. Daniel and Alexander, Alan's two senior Instructors, would supervise them. It was a start, with the project well underway.

* * *

'When are you coming to see me?' It was June's voice on the phone. In all the excitement, Alan missed seeing or calling her over the past two days. Today she sounded distant and cool. Might she resent he'd not contacted her since their last romantic evening on the sofa? It was only three days ago. That last evening held so much promise.

Alan arrived at Luke's house and knocked on the front door. Rita opened it and stood there, unsmiling. 'Dad wants you to go straight through to the study.'

'Where's June?'

'She said she needed to go out.'

'When will she be back?'

'She didn't say.'

In the study, Luke sat behind his big desk. 'Come in Alan. The MFF committee want an urgent meeting with us at eleven o'clock this morning.'

'In daytime? Isn't that risky?'

'It's when all the interested parties can attend.'

'June's not here?'

'No, Alan, I asked her to phone you to come here, so I could talk to you. But I should warn you, Henry's death has upset her. He was a friend of hers since kindergarten. It's affected her badly.'

'Oh dear! I knew nothing about that.'

'No, it's not your fault. How would you know?'

'Are we going to the meeting together?'

'No, I'll see you at the meeting room. When you get there, just go upstairs.'

* * *

Smoke filled the crowded room. Luke and Peter Nkala sat at a table at the far end away from the door. As Alan entered, they motioned for him to join them at the table. There were many more people present than at the first meeting of senior members Alan attended, and this concerned him. He also worried about the apparent lack of concern for security at this meeting. He contrasted it with his arrival at the first meeting after dark and how it involved subterfuge and a cloak and dagger zig-zag path to make sure no one followed. Alan sensed a tense atmosphere in the room, and some of those present seemed to eye him with hostility.

Alan felt Molly's absence deeply. For him, it left a massive hole in the project. Peter Nkala called the meeting to order. The older committee members, most of whom Alan recognised from the first meeting, sat in the front two rows. The noisy, younger men present sat in the back two rows. Peter Nkala spoke. 'Simon Kholose wishes to raise issues related to our project. His concerns could affect how we move forward, so I will now ask Simon to make his points.'

A slim young man wearing a thin moustache stood up, cleared his throat, and spoke in Ndebele. As he continued, he got more agitated, and his voice grew louder and louder. Peter Nkala asked him several times to stay calm. 'I must remind the meeting we are a minority movement, and the authorities watch us. We do not want to draw their attention and give them an excuse to close us down or arrest us.'

Alan noticed the two burly bouncers at the door and presumed no one from the authorities would be present, but the tone of the meeting worried him. Almost everyone in Zimbabwe spoke English, especially the city dwellers, so why was most of the proceedings conducted in Ndebele. Only Peter Nkala spoke in English while those who spoke from the floor stuck to their African language. It was a sure sign they were excluding Alan from taking part in the meeting. Every time Peter Nkala tried to get the angry young men to speak English, they would say a few words that Alan understood and then revert to Ndebele.

Alan made a mental note to redouble his efforts to learn the local language, but like most English speakers, he struggled with any foreign tongue. It embarrassed him when he remembered his pledge at the first MFF meeting to learn Ndebele as soon as possible. Alan made a good start in his effort to learn the language, but following Molly's disappearance in the national park, he made no progress and slipped back. Daniel and Alexander always spoke English, so they'd been no help at all.

An hour later, Peter Nkala declared the meeting closed. 'We will consider Simon's concerns and the committee will vote on them.' The angry young men filed out of the meeting room in a sullen silence. Alan did not miss the implied threat in the scowls directed at him.

'What was that all about?' Alan asked. 'Was it something to do with Henry's death?'

'No, not at all,' said Luke. 'The poachers your people shot in the Hwange National Park included some of Simon Kholose's men.'

'You mean Michael Duze and his team?'

'Not Michael Duze, and not the cyanide carrier who ran away. Duze works for someone else and he arranged for the carrier and one other, but three of the four killed worked for Simon Kholose. He denies any involvement with the poaching and claims he hired out his men to a hunter going to one of the hunting concessions. A lot of hunters use bearers to carry camping equipment and skinners to skin the carcasses. He believes his men did not knowingly involve themselves in poaching and wouldn't have realised they were in the national park.'

'Oh yes, and how does he explain away the cyanide? Those men poisoned the dead elephant and scavengers we found. And do bearers and skinners carry AK47 rifles instead of camping equipment? They carried elephant tusks and rhino horn, not skins.'

'It's true his story is not convincing, but the committee don't want to offend.'

'If they were so innocent, why did they shoot at us? One bullet just missed my face by centimetres. When they saw us, instead of running away, they attacked. They tried to kill us: Molly, Alexander and me.'

'We understand,' said Peter Nkala, 'but Simon's family has a lot of influence in the MFF. Simon wants you to stop using the poachers for training your men. The committee will discuss the matter and take a vote. When they have decided, Luke will let you know.'

* * *

Luke saw the disbelief in Alan's face and invited him to dinner that night to discuss the situation further.

Following Henry's death, Alan resolved he would change his approach to training, but now he seethed. 'I don't understand these people,' he said. 'They want to separate from Zimbabwe because of the corrupt government in Harare and the leaders enriching themselves at the expense of the people. Now I find influential leaders in Bulawayo doing the same thing.'

'There's good and bad in every society,' said Luke. 'Don't judge Mthwakazi by one or two corrupt families.'

'But that was the start of Zimbabwe's problems. One or two corrupt families led the way and then others followed their example. I have often read about people saying Mugabe and his regime have made Zimbabwe a nation of thieves. The corrupt and powerful in Zimbabwe silence the voices of the majority. What's stopping the same thing happening in Mthwakazi?'

'Let's see what the MFF committee decides.'

'As I've told you, Luke, I've already decided to change the training methods to save the lives of my team members. I have no objection to the committee requesting me to change my training methods, but I would object if they're just trying to appease Simon Kholose and his family. I will change my methods, but the committee must demand Kholose stops his poaching activities. And tell me, if my team is prohibited from entering the parks, how will the committee make sure Kholose complies with that order?'

CHAPTER 35

A FTER the chat with Luke, Alan looked for June. He found her reading in the front room. 'June, I'm so sorry about Henry. He was a good friend, and I miss him. But you two were lifelong friends. It's devastating to lose a colleague, never mind a close friend. He was one of the best recruits and the most committed. That's why I took him with me that terrible evening. There's nothing I can do to bring him back, but I can't help blaming myself for what happened.'

'And so you should. Since you've been here, saving Mthwakazi, three recruits have died and at least fifteen other people. Do you think black lives don't matter? Is this a macho game to you? Poachers are also human beings. What about the families? Don't they count?'

'Yes, black lives matter. All lives matter, but those poachers were stealing the country's heritage, the future wealth of Mthwakazi, Zimbabwe, whatever. The poachers have killed only one member of the team.'

'For the poor, poaching may be a necessity. They poached because they were poor. The poachers have to feed their families somehow.'

'If they hunted for food, there wouldn't have been a firefight. None of those men hunted buck to feed their family. They poisoned waterholes to kill elephants for ivory and rhinos for the horns. We've lost three of the team but saved the lives of many others. Do you know how many national park rangers the poachers kill every year? With the training we've provided, the recruits may yet kill even more poachers and save the lives of more park rangers.'

'Well, I'm sorry. What you're doing isn't right.'

'I've already told your father there will be no more training of recruits in the national parks.'

'That's up to you, but I want no part in it. You can visit my father here, but I don't think we should see each other anymore.'

'June, I'm a soldier, here to train soldiers to defend the cause your father supports.'

'That's too bad. It may be his cause, but it's not mine. I can't support the cause anymore.'

Alan drove back to the apartment, depressed by the turn of events. What a day! First, discovering members of the MFF took part in the heinous poaching operations and now falling out with June. He liked her a lot, more than liked her, and couldn't fault the value she placed on human life. But June wasn't there; she didn't appreciate the danger they faced and the need to fight for their lives. They didn't intend to get into firefights. What did Samuel Johnson say? *Hell is paved with good intentions.* Yes, that's the expression, but it was them or us.

Alan walked to the refrigerator and grabbed a beer. Ironic that June said, her father's cause was not hers. Those exact words also applied to him before he witnessed the carnage in the national parks. Too late to change course now. The MFF and CMG depended on him to further the cause, and his team did too. He'd seen their enthusiasm and commitment. How could he betray their trust and pull out of the training programme now? It would also be a betrayal of Molly and her memory. He knew how much the cause had meant to her.

June's sudden changed attitude disturbed Alan more than anything else. Yes, he could understand her being upset, but she wouldn't listen to his attempts to explain his actions. June did not seem to appreciate he was just as upset as her about Henry's death. Should Henry's fate become a permanent barrier between them? June seemed very final about ending the relationship. Perhaps she would see things differently once she got over the news of Henry's death, but her steely resolve didn't give him any cause for optimism.

This was crazy. In the past, losing a woman never worried Alan. Friends accused him of being easy come easy go, but now .... When Mary Lou LeBauer's parents moved suburbs and put her in a different kindergarten to Alan, he was certain his world would end. But that was different. Mary Lou didn't want to leave him, and she cried her eyes out. That made Alan feel much better. But June said it was over between them, and she seemed impervious to his reasonings. Damn, damn, damn! Perhaps it really was the end of their relationship.

CHAPTER 36

Most of the time, George Drake based himself in Melbourne or Singapore, where he conducted the bulk of his business operations. His travels also took him on frequent visits to Johannesburg, London and New York. His employees found it difficult to keep up with his itinerary, which he changed on a whim. George liked it that way; it kept his managers guessing, never knowing when he might turn up unannounced. From time to time he caught out one of his managers taking advantage of his absence to work on their own private business at the company's expense.

Few people asked George what the Latin words printed under his company's stylised logo meant. *Homo non habeat fiduciam*, Trust No Man, was the motto George lived by, and it underpinned his success in building a business empire.

George Drake sat at a table in the corner of the cafe, reading a copy of *The Straits Times*, Singapore's leading English language newspaper. As he took a sip of coffee, he noticed a black man in deep conversation with a Chinese man, sitting at a table in the cafe across the lane. The Chinese man sat with his back to George, and his face was largely obscured.

George liked to chat with any African he met on his overseas travels. He was born in Rhodesia, and he was always interested in striking up conversations with blacks on the off chance they came from his homeland. Given the situation in Zimbabwe, that happened more and more often these days. The dictatorial Mugabe regime led to approximately twenty percent of the Zimbabwean population emigrating.

The Chinese man glanced to one side, and the movement pricked George's interest. There was something familiar about him. George returned to scanning the paper but kept on eye on the two men in the cafe over the road. A second cup of coffee would give him the excuse to linger a little longer.

The Chinese man stood to leave. Good God! It's Wong! George was surprised to see his office manager talking to someone of African appearance, possibly a Zimbabwean. Singapore was a cosmopolitan city, so it was a common occurrence for people of different races to socialise or meet for business. But coincidences always raised George's suspicions, and he did not become a business success without a healthy dose of the latter. His company motto was at work again.

For weeks, George puzzled over Andrew Dube and Tyson's disappearance. How was their kidnapping in Thailand's Islamic Songkhla Province arranged? Who knew they travelled on the Jungle Railway? Mr Wong did. George left the arrangements to him and told nobody else about their itinerary. Even he wasn't aware, until afterwards, Wong booked them on the train through the Jungle Railway.

After Wong left the cafe, George saw the black man finish his drink and pay the bill and walk out onto the pavement. George left his second cup of coffee untouched and hurried to pay for it and follow the black man along the pavement. At the end of the block, the black man crossed the road and walked into a hotel. He approached the reception desk and picked up his room key and walked into the empty lift.

George watched the man from a discreet distance, and when the lift doors closed, he stepped up to the lift and pressed the button, noting the lift light stopped on the third floor. He hurried to reception and spoke in an agitated voice to the person on duty. 'Excuse me! I've just missed Mr, er, er. You know the black man? He left his confidential papers on the table at the cafe down the road.'

'Oh, you must mean Mr Hilton Nyoka, Sir. He just went up in the lift. Would you like me to give him the papers?'

'Er, no, that's not the name. I must be mistaken. Do you have any other black guests?'

'No, Sir. Just Mr Nyoka.'

'My mistake. Sorry I troubled you.'

George left the hotel, pleased his little charade worked so well. Hmm, Hilton Nyoka? I'll ask Peter Nkala to find out about him.

Back in his office, Jenny, the receptionist greeted him. 'Mr Drake, you never told us you were coming. Mr Wong is out right now. He should be back soon.'

No sooner had George entered his own office when the phone rang. 'Sir, a gentleman, Mr Boonliang, is on the phone for you.'

'Drake.'

'Mr Drake, I'm Superintendent Boonliang of the Thai Border Patrol Police. I would like to visit you to discuss the disappearance you reported of a Mr Dube and his son.'

'Can we meet at my hotel? It's more private.'

'Yes, Sir, that will be fine.'

CHAPTER 37

THE next day in a quiet corner of the hotel lounge, George met Superintendent Boonliang for afternoon tea. Now six months since Andrew Dube and Tyson disappeared, George did not expect to find them alive.

'There were other black passengers on the train that day, Mr Drake. An African American couple and their son were also in Sungai Kolok wanting to go through Hat Yai to Bangkok. They said an Asian man held a board with the name Dube written on it. When the man saw the husband, he approached and tried to persuade him and his son to get into a car parked outside the station. The husband tried to explain their name was not Dube, but the Asian couldn't speak English and was most insistent. The Asian kept on repeating "Drake, Drake". Only when the American's wife returned from the toilet did the Asian seem to understand he'd got the wrong person and walked away. Later, the Americans noticed two black men talking to the Asian. They think they left in the Asian's car because they never saw them after that.'

'So, someone targeted them?'

'Yes, so we must ask ourselves, who knew their itinerary?'

'Only my Singapore office manager as far as I'm aware.'

'May I speak to him?'

'Yes, if he's in the office. It's only a five-minute walk from here.'

George and Superintendent Boonliang walked to the office.

'Jenny, ask Mr Wong to join us please,' George said to the receptionist.

Wong entered George's office, looking a little apprehensive. That was his usual manner, so nothing could be read into it.

'Mr Wong,' said the superintendent, 'who else knew Mr Dube would be on the Jungle Railway that day?'

'Oh, everyone in the office.'

'Anyone outside this office?'

'I dropped them at the station in Johor Bahru. Perhaps they met someone there and talked about their travel plans.'

'So, you didn't put them on the train?' said George.

'No Sir, I needed to get back to the office, so I left them there.'

Superintendent Boonliang appeared satisfied with the answers George and Wong gave him and put away his notes in a small carry bag.

'Are you returning to Thailand this evening, Superintendent, or can I take you for a delicious Singapore dinner?'

'Sadly, Mr Drake, duty calls, and I must urgently return to my base. This isn't the only case I'm working on at present.'

After the superintendent left, George spoke to Wong again. 'Did you show Mr Dube's itinerary to Hilton Nyoka?'

The colour drained from Wong's face. 'To whom, Sir?'

'Hilton Nyoka.'

'Who is that, Sir? I'm not familiar with that name.'

'Who was that African man you shared coffee with this morning?'

'It's the first time I've met him, Sir. The cafe was busy, and we shared a table.'

'I told you the visit was confidential. Now you're saying you told the whole office about it.'

'I'm sorry, Sir, I forgot.'

'Have a look at page two.' George handed Wong a thin newsletter. It was an old trick George often used when confronting someone he held at a disadvantage. He noticed the tremor in Wong's hands and the difficulty he had turning over the page. 'That's all for now, thank you, Wong. Tell me later what you think of that article.'

'Yes Sir.' Wong hurried out of George's office, keen to get away from the inquisition.

George picked up the phone and dialled a number. 'I have a job for you. Meet me at my hotel for a beer at six o'clock.'

* * *

The ambitious Mr Wong sat at his desk reviewing emails and going through his list of things to attend to the following day. Wong liked to be the last to leave the premises each evening and discouraged the others from working back late. He trusted no one, and in that regard, he fitted George Drake's company well. Working late gave him the opportunity to conduct his private affairs and the chance to check the desks and computers of other staff members to learn what they were up to when he was out of the office. Wong reasoned if he used the office for his personal purposes, the other staff members might do the same. He judged others by his own standards.

As often as not, Wong sat at his desk in the office when the cleaners arrived, so the sound of a key in the lock and the squeak of the front door as it swung open didn't perturb him. He looked at his watch and noted the cleaners were a little earlier than usual. Wong focussed on his computer screen and the new emails that arrived after the regular office hours and thought no more about it until he became conscious of someone standing in his doorway. Wong looked up to see two scruffy men with unwashed, matted hair and dirty, torn clothes. The tears in their jeans didn't come from an overpriced fashion boutique. Dark, rough skin and gnarled hands identified them as men who worked outdoors, probably Indonesian labourers or construction workers. Wong sensed trouble, and his skin crawled. He suspected these desperate looking men were on a mission, dirty men for dirty work.

'Mr Wong?'

'Yes, can I help you? How did you get in here? I locked the door myself after the receptionist left.'

The man smiled, displaying a row of rotting teeth.

CHAPTER 38

Hᴵᴸᵀᴼᴺ Nyoka hurried to Captain John's office. 'You wanted to see me, Sir?'

'Yes, Nyoka, take a seat. Your man in Singapore said Andrew Dube was on his way to Chiang Mai to meet with George Drake. Is that right?'

'Yes, Sir.'

'Khumalo tells me a white man named Alan Drake has turned up in Bulawayo. Apparently, he's Luke Ndlovu's security consultant. What does that suggest to you?'

'What, Sir?'

'Well, consider this; could there be a connection between George Drake and Alan Drake, or is it a coincidence they go by the same surname?'

'Yes, Sir.'

'Are you saying yes to the first part of my question or the second?'

'I'm not sure, Sir.'

Captain John rolled his eyes. 'Give me strength, Nyoka! Now, what about Luke Ndlovu?'

'He's a member of the MFF, Sir.'

'Yes, and?'

'And what, Sir?'

'What's the matter with you today, Nyoka? Did you have a late night?'

'No, Sir.'

'Luke Ndlovu is Don Nkomo's father-in-law. Don knows all about our poaching operation and all our contacts. Might the Ndlovu family be muscling in on our territory?'

'Sir, as much as I don't like Don Nkomo and his fancy ways, I find it hard to imagine he'd be silly enough to get involved in something like that. It must be a coincidence.'

'My gut tells me something is not right about all this, Nyoka. Our men mysteriously disappear. No, they must have joined another gang. Anyway, I will find out more about this Alan Drake. I'll give you one hundred to one he's related to George Drake, and we all know that man is trouble.'

'Why don't you ask Don Nkomo about it, Sir.'

'What a clever idea, Nyoka! I never would've thought of that if you hadn't suggested it. Here I am feeding you with information you were slow to pick up on, and now, you come back with this brilliant idea. What would I do without you?'

Nyoka grinned. 'I've no idea, Sir.'

CHAPTER 39

A LAN lay on his bed, looking at the ceiling. Twelve long months! Only three weeks ago, staying twelve months or more looked attractive, but now… Six months without a woman! Is that a world record? No, suppose not. So, where to from here? Stay put until the MFF committee decides what to do? But what to do in the meantime? Where did June hear how many poachers the team killed? I should have asked her while I had the chance. Too late to ask her now. Maybe she's just grieving over Henry. Once she's over it, a fresh start might be possible.

A knock on the door? No one knocks on the door except the guards delivering messages, but they've already been tonight. Alan jumped off the bed and padded to the front door. He picked up the Glock 22 which he always kept handy. Perhaps Simon Kholose's men were here to teach him a lesson?

Alan opened the door and caught his breath. 'Avril!' Alan couldn't hide his surprise and pleasure at the tall, slim figure who stood on the landing. Avril looked even more glamorous than he remembered. Her short hair hung in loose curls about her face, and her smooth brown skin set off her eyes that lit up like lanterns when she smiled.

'Hello Alan, I understand things have been a little rough recently. I thought you might like a little company and share a drink.'

'Would I ever! How nice to see you! Where's Don?'

'Don's at a high-powered meeting in Harare tonight.'

'Oh! When will he be back?'

'Tomorrow evening.'

'Sorry, but I've only got beer.'

'Beers fine, but I brought a bottle of Black Label, just in case.'

'The ice cubes are waiting in the fridge. I planned to buy a bottle of Scotch as soon as I got the chance.'

'What a nice spacious flat and beautiful big bed.'

'It's comfortable. The flat, I mean. But the bed's also comfortable. Would Don approve of you visiting me here?'

'Probably not.'

'Who's looking after the kids?'

'I don't have any kids.'

'Who were those three children you brought to Luke's house on Christmas Day?'

'My cousin's. We brought them along to keep Mae's children company. You know how boring it can be for kids when there's only two of them in a big group of adults.'

Avril poured the Scotch into two glasses and handed one to Alan.

'I'm glad you left room for the ice,' said Alan, looking at the half-full tumblers.

'Sip it. Don't gulp it.'

One large Scotch goes down as easily as a small one, and before long, Avril was pouring the second round. Alan relaxed as Avril settled on the three-seater sofa. His alcohol intake was much reduced in Zimbabwe, and his ability to hold his drink less than it once was. A beer or two with Daniel and Alexander and the occasional whisky with Luke was poor training for half a bottle of Scotch, but now, the alcohol emboldened Alan.

'May I ask you a personal question?'

'Sure.'

'What decided you to visit me here this evening? We've only met once before tonight.'

'Well, I weighed it up in my mind. I lined up all the reasons to visit you tonight. Then I considered all the reasons against it. The former outweighed the latter. I heard you weren't seeing June anymore. We were both alone, so it seemed a good idea to get together for a social drink.'

'Do you think June may change her mind about me?'

'Yes, I suppose so, though she can be stubborn when she wants.'

'June said, you were the family's femme fatale.'

'Whatever gave her that idea?'

'Are you here to tease me again?'

'Tease?'

'Yes, like on Christmas Day.'

'Didn't you enjoy it?'

'Yes, and you did too, but it was awkward with everyone standing around watching.'

'That's why I kept you close. You didn't imagine any other reason, did you?'

'There you go, teasing me again.'

'I'm sorry, I didn't mean to tease.'

'Liar.'

'But you must agree, the spectators made it extra delicious.'

'As I recall, I was the one who kept you close, and you didn't resist.'

'Have you ever known a lady to resist a compliment?'

'Is that how you saw it?'

'Yes. If you didn't find me desirable, you wouldn't react like that.'

Alan stared at Avril, studying her face as if seeing her for the first time; a slimmer version of June though lighter skinned with a higher forehead and less prominent cheekbones. It was obvious the two were sisters, but the subtle differences gave each their own unique beauty.

'Where's this going?' said Alan. 'I mean, what now?'

Avril smiled. 'That's up to you. I'm your guest, so I'm in your hands.'

'Literally or figuratively?'

'Figuratively, so far.'

'I wish you hadn't said that. You tempt me to break all my promises in one evening.'

'Oh yes, and to whom did you make those promises?'

'To myself.'

'So, no consequences in breaking them, then.'

'I'm not so sure about that.'

Alan promised himself not to mess with Luke's daughters. He respected Luke and worried he might view it as a betrayal. June was single and lived at home. Any move on her would be difficult and might affect his relationship with Luke, but that was academic now.

But Avril was an independent married woman. She knew what she was doing. What about Don? He'd only met him once, so there was no question of loyalty involved. Then, if he could screw Aunt Ruth at the Crowne Plaza hotel when Solly was away on business, why should he worry now about Don? Ruth made all the running when she accompanied him to his room. Who could blame him for responding? He planned to visit Joburg and Aunt Ruth again, but he'd been too busy to get away.

Now, here was Avril in his apartment with a bottle of Scotch. She would know where that might lead. Six months is a long time. Bugger it! You've only one life.

* * *

'My! You are full of surprises,' said Avril. 'I've never felt so desired in all my life. You exceeded my expectations.'

'Doesn't Don make you feel desired?'

'Business is Don's first love, and it keeps him distracted.'

'Then, I'm pleased I filled the void.'

'Oh, you filled the void all right.'

'I'm glad you came.'

'Do you mean that?'

'I haven't had a woman since I arrived in Zimbabwe.'

'I hope I didn't disappoint?'

'Are you kidding? I couldn't get enough of you.'

'You know, I can't come back?'

'Why not?'

'Because I'm afraid I will want what I can't have. I wouldn't have come if you and June were still together. I'm with Don, and that's the end of it.'

'You came here last night. What's changed since then?'

'Last night I came here for fun. If I came again, now I've tasted you, it would be for a different reason. I don't want to be hurt or hurt anyone else. I better go now.'

Avril slipped on her pencil skirt, white blouse and black high-heel shoes and picked up her car keys and handbag.

'Wait!' said Alan, 'Leave me your knickers as a souvenir of last night.'

'Do you ask all the women you sleep with for their knickers?'

'No, only the best.'

'OK, but if you get back with June, you must return them.'

'Yes, I promise.'

Avril slipped off her panties and tossed them to Alan and disappeared out the door. Alan put on his bathrobe and walked onto the balcony to watch Avril leave. Her parked car stood right in front of the apartment. She looked up and smiled. Alan waved goodbye with the frilly white lace he held. If that was a consolation prize, it was a darn good one.

CHAPTER 40

MARCH 2014

Don Nkomo bounced through the front entrance of the COU premises, waved to the security guard and stopped at the secretary's office door.

'You're looking ravishing as always, Melissa.'

'Really, Mr Nkomo? I'm sure you say that to all the girls.'

'No, only to my favourites.'

'How many favourites are there?'

'Not enough, but you're number one. How about dinner tonight?'

'I'd like that very much, but I never mix business with pleasure.'

'It's the same with me, Melissa. I only want to discuss business with you over dinner.'

'I can guess what business that is, Mr Nkomo.'

'You misjudge Melissa. Where did you get this wrong impression of me?'

'From the women who've worked here.'

'But you're not like the others. I'm serious about you.'

'Talking about serious, Captain John is waiting.'

* * *

Captain John sat at his desk, scowling. Hilton Nyoka sat in one of the two chairs facing his boss. The secretary knocked on the open door. 'Yes, Melissa?'

'Sir, Mr Nkomo is here.'

'Good, we're ready for him.'

Moments later the big, moustachioed, balding man appeared at the door. 'Good morning, Captain John.' He looked to the other occupied chair and nodded. 'Hilton,' he said in acknowledgment. Hilton Nyoka nodded unsmilingly while Captain John beamed. Don Nkomo's visits always seemed to cheer him. He liked the big, jovial man from Bulawayo. 'Come in Don. How good to see you!'

Nyoka was sensitive to the fact Captain John addressed him by his surname but called Don Nkomo by his first name. Captain John suspected this and exaggerated his familiarity with Don to irritate the ambitious Hilton Nyoka.

'Now,' said John, getting serious, 'we have important issues to discuss. Don, what news of Michael Duze?'

'There is no news, Sir. The men have checked out his house and all his usual haunts, but they've found nothing.'

'Uh-huh! What if I told you we've spoken to him, and he's sending us a written report of his suspicions about the way you run things in Bulawayo?'

Don Nkomo's jaw dropped. 'What! Where is he? Where has he been? When did he make contact?'

'Never mind all that. Duze claims you organised a gang to kill the poachers and steal the ivory and rhino horn. One of the gang leaders is a white man who is a member of your family or soon will be.'

'That's complete nonsense, Sir. My wife's younger sister has a white boyfriend who I've only met once at Christmas. He's a security contractor looking after my father-in-law's properties. There's no way he could lead any gang when he's only recently arrived in Zimbabwe and speaks none of the African languages.'

'No way, unless your father-in-law helped organise it. We've checked into the young man's background. Are you aware he was with the Australian special forces?'

'No, I wasn't.'

'This wouldn't be the first time a family got greedy and tried to take over someone else's business.'

'Captain John, if I knew anything about this, and if it were true, I would stop them. I wouldn't let anybody muscle in on your business. You of all people! With anyone else's business it might be different. But yours …. Never!'

'I'm inclined to believe you Don, but I didn't become a success by trusting people, no matter how much I liked them. I'm also wondering if you or your family had a hand in the Gonarezhou episode. If that's the case, we've lost seven men and eight contractors to this group. It's time to resolve the issue.'

'Captain John, before you do anything, please let me look into this. I will investigate and report back, but I'm sure it's a misunderstanding.'

'Can I trust you Don?'

'Yes, on my life!'

'All right, I'll give you one week, and if nothing changes my mind, you and your family will be sorry. Remember, I also want the money taken from Michael Duze together with the elephant tusks and rhino horn.'

'Yes, Sir. I'd better get back to Bulawayo and start the investigation.' Don Nkomo walked out of Captain John's office, his mind in turmoil. Back in the rented car, he phoned Avril.

'Honey, what do you know about your Dad and June's boyfriend involved in poaching in the national parks?'

'What are you talking about, Don? This is the first I've heard of it, and I don't believe it.'

'Some bad people here in Harare are telling me it's true, and they say the whole family will pay if we don't back off at once and stop poaching.'

Avril couldn't believe Don associated with such ruthless men. She also couldn't believe her sister and father, together with Alan Drake, were part of any takeover of the poaching operations in the national parks. 'I'll be on the next plane back to Bulawayo,' said Don. 'I need to speak to your father.'

With a few hours to kill before the flight, Don took out his cell phone and dialled the number burnt into his memory; the number that was too risky to set in his phone. He didn't want Avril chancing across it.

Back in the COU offices, Captain John spoke to Hilton Nyoka. 'Don's time here has ended. Deal with him as soon as you get the money and the tusks and rhino horn.'

'Didn't you give him a week's grace to clear himself?'

'What and let him concoct a story with his family? No, the week I gave him is the most he has left. It's a pity because I like Don. I'd rather see him than your boring face, but business comes first.'

'How do you want it done?'

'Live up to your name, Nyoka. When does any African snake warn how and when it will strike? But I want it done as soon as possible. The details are up to you.'

'Why did you tell Don that we'd spoken to Michael Duze and that he was sending us a written statement about the way Don ran things in Bulawayo? What if he called your bluff and asked to confront Duze about the accusations? Duze might be helping the lions fertilise the bush by now. There's no sign of him anywhere.'

'If Don asked to meet with Duze, to confront him, I'd suspect him less. But he didn't.'

'Perhaps he was rattled, and it never occurred to him.'

'Maybe.'

* * *

The young woman answered the knock on the apartment door.

'Tsitsi! Beautiful, as always.'

'I hoped you would come yesterday.'

'Business kept me in Bulawayo,' Don lied. What kept him away from Tsitsi the night before was the attractive woman he sat next to on the plane. His jovial charm often set him on a new adventure and a bed for the night. Don saw every woman he met as a new challenge, but Tsitsi was the exception. Don paid for her flat and visited her every time he was in Harare. She was less than half his age and an irresistible bundle of fun. In the year he'd known her, she'd become an essential part of his fitness regime and was more demanding than any gym workout.

'Will you stay the night? Are we eating out this evening?'

'Sorry, Tsitsi, but I must return to Bulawayo this evening to see to unexpected, urgent business.'

'When can we be together full-time? Why do you stay with that skinny wife of yours? You should get rid of her and marry me. She hasn't even given you any children. I can give you lots.'

'Patience, Tsitsi. My wife isn't skinny. She's what the whites refer to as slim. Lots of children are for poor people. I don't plan to be poor.'

'Humph! Whites wouldn't know about real beauty in a woman. You always said you liked my curves.'

'Yes, but there're new developments I can't ignore. Let me sort things out first, and then I'll try to visit more often.'

'Have you told your skinny wife about us?'

'All in good time, Tsitsi, but she's probably already guessed I have someone to entertain me when I'm on business in Harare.'

'When will you come again?'

'This time next week.'

'But what's so important you have to rush back to Bulawayo?'

'Shh! Enough now. We only have a short time before I must catch the plane.'

Wrapped in each other's arms, in bed with Tsitsi, was Don's idea of heavenly bliss.

'Tsitsi, if I died, now, here in bed with you, I'd be happy.'

'Don't say that. It can bring bad luck.'

CHAPTER 41

L UKE was in a sombre mood when Alan entered his home office. 'The first bit of bad news, Alan, is the MFF committee have decided against training in the national parks. But they neglected to make any statement requiring Simon Kholose to stop his poaching. I tried to make that point, as did Peter Nkala, but the influence of the Kholose family has scared a few members of the committee. They're adamant Simon will stop poaching as a gesture of his goodwill, and they say any specific statement about the poaching would just antagonise the Kholose's and be less likely to yield a positive outcome. Rumours are, Simon's father, Senior Kholose, and his supporters are planning a vote of no confidence in Peter Nkala's leadership.'

'Using the poachers for training was an idea that came out of the Chiang Mai meeting, and as I recall, Luke, the MFF committee enthused about it.'

'That's true, but at that first meeting you attended, the Kholose's weren't present. Given the sensitive nature of the discussions at MFF meetings we don't keep minutes, but Peter Nkala would have informed Senior Kholose of what the committee decided. The Kholoses raised no objection. Perhaps they didn't appreciate the implications. Also, they wouldn't want everybody to learn of their involvement in poaching. Now that your team has shot three of their men, they're upset.'

After Alan's first visit to the Hwange National Park where he saw first-hand the slaughter of the wildlife, he empathised with the MFF. It shook his commitment to the cause when he discovered certain leading MFF members enjoyed the proceeds of poaching. Now, with the committee's latest decision, Alan felt disillusioned. He didn't doubt the sincerity of several of the MFF leaders, but the personal ambitions of a few undermined their more noble goals.

* * *

'You said that was the first bit of bad news. What's the next bit?'

'There's a problem with Avril's husband, Don. She sounded anxious.' Alan tensed. Was it connected to his night with Avril? 'Don flew to Harare for a business meeting day before yesterday. This afternoon he phoned Avril with disturbing news. She's on her way here now to talk about it.'

'OK, I'll leave you to it, then.'

'Ah! There she is now,' said Luke. 'I can hear her car in the drive. Stay, Alan, you might have an interest in what she says.'

Alan turned and looked down the passageway to see the big Mercedes scrunch to a halt on the gravel drive. The door swung open and Avril stepped out, looking radiant in an orange summer dress. 'Perhaps she'd rather talk to you alone,' said Alan.

'No, no, stay. Whatever the problem is, it might need your input.'

Avril appeared in the doorway to Luke's study. 'Hello, Dad. Oh! Alan, hi.'

'Come in my dear,' said Luke. 'I've asked Alan to stay in case we need his help.'

'Well, that's OK,' said Avril, 'because it concerns both of you.'

'What is it my dear?'

'Don has told me a dangerous poaching gang thinks you and Alan are trying to take over their territory. They're also threatening him because they believe it involves our whole family. He says they are ruthless and will stop at nothing to get rid of their competitors.'

'How does Don know this?' Luke asked.

'They might have threatened him over the phone, but I suspect there's more to it than that. Perhaps he has business dealings with them. He always has plenty of money but tells me nothing about his work and says it's best I don't know. Lawyers can earn a lot of money, but how can anyone in Zimbabwe have access to so many US dollars?'

Luke frowned. 'If they think it's a family business, we may all be at risk, even you.'

'That's another thing that made me wonder if he had prior dealings with the gang. I asked him if I was in danger, and he said, they didn't go after the women unless they were part of the problem.'

Luke turned to Alan. 'Any ideas?'

'The whole family, including Don, could be at risk. If they're ruthless, like he said, they won't hesitate to act on their suspicions. What have they got to lose? Threats may not work or can backfire. If they've threatened Don, they'll be after us soon. You better warn Mae to tell her husband to make himself scarce.'

Luke rubbed his chin. 'How would the poaching gang find out about us and our operations?'

'Does the name Simon Kholose ring a bell,' said Alan, with a touch of sarcasm.

'What! He'd betray the whole Mthwakazi project just to continue his poaching?'

'Do you think he wouldn't? I don't trust that man one bit. And given the leeway the committee has allowed him, I'm not so sure about some of them either.'

'Alan, surely not!'

'Luke, you told me that Peter Nkala beat Kholose's father, Senior Kholose, in a close vote for the leadership of the MFF. What if there's a plot afoot to discredit Peter at all costs, and for Senior Kholose to take over the organisation? You said there were rumours of a no confidence motion. It wouldn't surprise me if Kholose is in with this gang of poachers and maybe even the government.'

'If he betrayed the project to the government, it would be the end of the MFF. There'd be no advantage for Kholose.'

'Yes, there could be. The leadership of the MFF is a lucrative position. Perhaps Kholose is working with the government. He could lead the MFF and make grand speeches about Mthwakazi and Ndebele rights while informing the government about the MFF's plans, strategies and alliances. The organisation would face strong headwinds and be neutralised. A win for Kholose and a win for the government. It wouldn't be the first time an Ndebele put personal gain over tribal loyalties.'

'Alan, what you are suggesting would be treason against Mthwakazi and the Ndebele nation. It's unbelievable that any Ndebele would do that.'

'I've never met the older Kholose, but remember that expression, *the acorn doesn't fall far from the tree.* If I were to judge from Simon Kholose, I would also be wary of his father. You often refer to that family as a unit, the Kholoses. That tells me you also see them as being much alike.'

Luke was thoughtful, contemplating Alan's words. 'One thing that's puzzled me is how the Kholoses made their money. They weren't wealthy in the past, but in the last ten years they've become rich. I wonder if they are deeper into poaching than any of us appreciate. Their wealth has bought them influence. If Senior Kholose became leader of the MFF, and if they are into poaching, I hate to imagine the consequences for our remaining wildlife.'

'There's one other thing, Luke. You've often spoken of Andrew Dube and his son, Tyson, who were abducted in the south of Thailand. My father, with all his connections in that part of the world, hasn't been able to find them. All he's discovered is a connection between his Singapore office manager, Mr Wong, and the mysterious Hilton Nyoka. He also found out an Asian man was looking for them at the station in Sungai Kolok in Southern Thailand. Andrew Dube was Peter Nkala's predecessor. It was Dube's disappearance that led to the election where Peter defeated Senior Kholose. Who do you think organised the abduction, or provided the information that enabled the abduction to succeed? Could it have been an ambitious Senior Kholose?'

'What you're suggesting would be a diabolical plot.'

'Yes, but it adds up, doesn't it?'

'It is possible. So, what do we do now?'

'I'll give you my two best men as a bodyguard. We'll also keep an eye on the family and your supermarket.'

'What about you?'

'I can look after myself.'

'Ah, the overconfidence of youth.'

'Avril, Don said they didn't go after the women unless they were part of the problem. But if they can't get to your dad or me, they might make an exception. Be careful. Perhaps you should move in with your parents for a time. The less dispersed our resources are, the stronger your protection will be.'

'We can't live like this forever,' Luke said.

'No, we'll take the fight to them once we find out who they are. These men are dangerous. You heard what happened to my father's office manager in Singapore. They found him at the back of his office building. He fell nine floors. The police say it was suicide because he was about to lose his job, but I've wondered if someone pushed him. Perhaps he knew too much and someone silenced him. Any news of Hilton Nyoka? When we last spoke, my father asked me if we'd made any progress in finding him.'

'No, not yet. Peter Nkala and the others are trying to find out, but he's a man of mystery. Do you suspect Nyoka was behind Andrew Dube's disappearance?'

'Possibly, but we can't be sure.'

CHAPTER 42

Two things nagged at Alan. First, was the role of Simon Kholose and the part he and his family might play in the poaching. What further damage could he do to the project and members of the MFF committee? Alan only had circumstantial evidence and a strong gut feeling Simon was up to his elbows in undermining the cause.

Second, was David's incompetence and dereliction of duty in allowing Michael Duze to escape in the Hwange National Park. After a promising start, David showed signs he was one of the least committed of the recruits Alan trained. He spent his time trying to avoid his share of the chores Alan allotted to the recruits. As a result, he became the least reliable of Alan's men. He was not a team player. Where did his loyalties lie? Alan's suspicions strengthened when Luke told him David's father was one of Senior Kholose's closest supporters.

'Somehow, we must confirm our suspicions or accept we have misjudged those two,' said Alan. 'These suspicions are eating away at me and probably eating away at the other recruits. One dissident in the team can wreck the whole project. Perhaps David is feeding Simon Kholose with information, and perhaps Simon is passing it on to the poachers or the government, or both.'

'What did you do with the rhino tusks and rhino horns you rescued from Michal Duze?' said Luke.

'I got the men to bury them.'

'Do you think they're still there?'

'Have the Kholoses heard about the committee's decision to stop my training programme in the national parks?'

'I'm not sure. The committee decided only an hour ago. A conflict of interest prevented Senior Kholose from attending the committee meeting. That's normal MFF procedure.'

Alan took out his cell phone and punched in the number. 'I'd like a dozen eggs please. Pronto.'

* * *

Alan drove back to his apartment and found Alexander and Daniel already waiting there. The *pronto* code word told them to go at once to Alan's apartment and expect to be away for an indefinite period. 'If we are going into the Hwange Park, Sah, what about our rifles?'

'Don't worry, before we left the park, Henry and I buried our rifles, plus Molly's rifle and all the ammunition. So we each have a rifle. We need to get there in a hurry, and if my hunch is correct, before too long someone will arrive at the spot you buried the tusks and rhino horn. There's too much money left lying in the ground, and someone won't be able to resist it. The question is, who will turn up to retrieve the buried treasure? I'll bring my camera and record who's involved in the poaching.'

The drive out to the Hwange National Park was uneventful. The police roadblocks were there as always, and the US one-dollar unofficial toll worked well. Michael Duze's handgun, hidden behind the dashboard of the old Land Rover, concerned Alan. When he and Henry drove to Bulawayo in the bakkie, it sat in the glove box beneath a pile of papers and the service book. Alan wasn't prepared to take that chance again.

On the edge of the park, Alan found the spot where he and Henry buried the rifles. Despite the rains and soggy ground, they were dry and in good order thanks to the thin plastic wrapping. Alan took a chance with the thin plastic, but heavier grade wrapping took up too much room in their back packs. The dash cam recorded the rest of their journey into the park. They drove as near as they dared to the spot where Alan's team buried the tusks and horns and found a suitable hiding place for the Land Rover. They unloaded enough supplies to last them through to the next evening and walked the rest of the way.

'We can come back tomorrow for more supplies,' said Alan. 'There's no point carrying it all if we are there for only one day.'

When they arrived at the spot where Daniel and Alexander buried the poached items, they examined the area carefully.

'The ground is as we left it,' said Alexander, 'though the rain makes it difficult to be sure.'

'Good,' said Alan. 'The trick now, is to find somewhere we can hide and video the poachers without them seeing us.'

'Should we dig up the tusks?' said Daniel.

'No,' said Alan, I want the poachers to dig them up, so we can record it on the video.

Alan found separate spots for his colleagues and himself. The scattered brush didn't give them as good cover as they would have liked, but the military skills of the trio meant it would suffice. They brushed the soft ground with branches, using the leaves to erase all signs of their footprints.

'It will be even better if it rains tonight,' said Alan. 'That will help mask our presence.' None of them relished the thought of a wet night on damp ground, but they were former soldiers and used to such conditions.

'Now remember you two, no shooting unless we have no choice. I don't know how long it will be, but I can't imagine them leaving the tusks to rot in the ground.'

'What if no one comes?' said Daniel.

'We'll wait for three days. If no one comes, our plan will have failed, and we'll go home.'

'What makes you think anyone will come, Sah,' said Alexander.

'It's a hunch, but if there's one thing I know, it's that greed is predictable. The committee has decided we will no longer train in the park. So, if anyone knows where you buried the tusks, they will feel it's safe to come and look for them. They won't expect us to be here. We told the committee we buried the tusks near the waterhole. If Simon Kholose is involved in the poaching, he may know which waterholes his men planned to poison.

'Let's look at the other possibilities. Could the cyanide man, who escaped, have seen where you buried the tusks? Michael Duze also escaped, and he saw where you buried the tusks. Then there's David, whose father is close to Senior Kholose. David helped you bury the tusks, so he will also know where to find them.'

The sudden flash of lightning in the inky blackness of the night gave the trio a start. An enormous clap of thunder assaulted their ears. Moments later, large drops of rain made craters in the dusty ground. Now, the lightning was more constant and the thunder deafening. Lightning flashes illuminated the sky and the earth, and the raindrops became a downpour. The three men, wrapped in their light raincoats, presented a dismal sight as they pulled down their bush hats to prevent the icy drops from running down the back of their necks.

'There's no chance they will come tonight,' said Alan. 'Let's go back to the Land Rover and sleep in there.'

They made their way in the darkness, punctuated by the flashes of lightning, back to the vehicle, being careful to keep off the road where their footprints might be visible if the rain eased. The Land Rover was well hidden, and they cast around to find it in the unhelpful conditions. At last they found it and hurried to get inside to escape the rain and the gusts of chilly wind.

'With this rain, there's no chance they'll find any sign of us in the earth around the area where we buried the tusks, said Alan.'

In the Land Rover the windows soon fogged up, and the musty smell of dampness pervaded the confined space in which the three struggled to find comfort and sleep.

CHAPTER 43

AFTER the freshness of the morning air, cleansed by the overnight downpour, the intensity of the blazing sun seemed incongruous. By late morning there was no sign it rained most of the previous night, and the ground was dry and rock hard once more. Alan and his two companions spent a long, hot, boring day, lying in wait. The hours passed at a glacial pace. It seemed like the day would never end, but at last, the hot afternoon gave way to the cooling early evening breezes. The buzzing flies that tormented them all afternoon seemed to have gone.

Alan noticed a series of bellows, grunts and deep mooing sounds in the distance. Cape buffalo, the killers of the bush, just as likely to take exception to a human presence as a rhino might. The sounds were getting closer, and Alan looked at the leaves to check which way the wind blew. The erratic movement of the leaves made it hard to tell, but he smelt the pungent odour of the herd now, so the buffalo were upwind. A blessing, for if it blew the other way, they could expect unwelcome attention.

With the buffalo only fifty yards away, Daniel and Alexander pressed themselves down into the soft earth. Alan followed their example. It seemed an age before they were able to relax. The buffalo looked to be on a mission, probably in search of water, and didn't stop to graze in the immediate vicinity. The incident reminded Alan the area was devoid of sizable trees. Any aggressive inspection by the buffalo would have presented them with a difficult situation in the scrubby bush.

As Alan's heartbeat slowed, he noticed a flash of light in the distance. Dusk was falling, and bit by bit the headlights of an approaching vehicle became visible. Alan willed them on, fearing his camera might not give a clear vision in the bad light. He double checked the settings and zoomed in on the vehicle. The number plate was clearer than he expected. Click! He took the photo. Alan moved the setting to video mode and waited for the vehicle to stop.

Three doors slammed, so, only three men. Alan started to video the scene. Hah! Just as I thought. Simon Kholose, David the traitor and that third man with a bush hat? Darn the light! It's disappearing too fast. We'll find what the big screen shows up when we get back to Luke's place.

Kholose threw a shovel towards David. 'Get digging!' The ground was soft after the rains, and David soon pulled out the first small bundle, containing one of the rhino horns. Then another two small bundles followed by the pair of elephant tusks. 'That's it,' said David. 'That's all they had.'

'Right, let's move,' said Kholose, 'Dr Chen is waiting at the surgery.'

As soon as Kholose and his companions left, Alan, Daniel and Alexander hurried back to the Land Rover and followed as fast as they dared. They stopped to bury the rifles in the same location as before and raced on to catch up to Kholose. The police roadblocks presented no hold-up, and Alan put his foot to the floor. The old Land Rover was sturdy but slow, and Kholose's vehicle was out of sight. Kholose nursed his new four-wheel drive over the deteriorating roads. He didn't want to risk his car's suspension over the potholes. Dr Chen could wait.

Back in Bulawayo, empty streets greeted Alan. He drove down Main Street and couldn't believe his luck when Kholose's vehicle turned into the street, a short distance ahead of them. Alan knew where Dr Chen's surgery was and suspected the transfer of the tusks would take place in the back alley behind the surgery.

Parking in the city centre at night was never difficult, but in the early hours of the morning it was a cinch. Alan parked in a space next to the alleyway across the road from the alley behind Dr Chen's surgery. He slipped into the dark shadows and set his camera on maximum zoom. As he waited to record the proceedings on the video setting, a light flicked on, and Dr Chen emerged from the building to speak to the men in the vehicle. 'Thanks for the light doctor,' Alan whispered. The three men got out of the vehicle and with Dr Chen's help carried the tusks and rhino horn towards the building. The group disappeared behind the courtyard wall of the neighbouring property. Alan needed to get closer.

He hurried across the road, and moving on the darker side of the alley, Dr Chen's side, he kept close to the wall as he edged towards the open courtyard at the back of the surgery. As Alan peered around the corner of the neighbouring building, Kholose, David and the third man came out the back door to return to their vehicle. It was too late for Alan to leave the alley unseen. He backed into the doorway of the neighbouring building, trying to make himself as flat as possible.

Kholose started the engine of his vehicle and switched on the lights. There was no prospect of Alan remaining unseen if he was caught in the full glare of the four-wheel drive's headlights. He breathed a sigh of relief when Kholose's vehicle moved forward. He was driving on through the alley to the next avenue. Then, Alan's heart skipped a beat as Kholose braked, put the vehicle into reverse and backed towards him. Alan suspected Kholose would be armed, while he only carried the camera with its incriminating evidence. He pressed up hard into the corner of the doorway when suddenly it opened. Alan fell through the doorway, landing in the courtyard at the feet of the startled butcher.

'I'm sorry, Sah. I didn't know you were leaning against the door.'

'Please don't worry. I've never been so happy to take a tumble.' Alan jumped up, brushed himself off and walked out into the alley as if nothing happened. Outside he bumped into Daniel and Alexander, who came to look for him when they saw Kholose drive out of the alley.

'I'm not sure whether the tusks are in the car or in the surgery,' said Alan.

'Not in the boot, Sah,' said Daniel. 'From my position in the Land Rover, I could just see the back of Dr Chen's car. The boot never opened, so the elephant tusks are in the surgery.'

'You have a prepaid SIM card in your cell phone, Alexander. Make an anonymous call to the police and tell them Dr Chen has poached elephant tusks and rhino horn in his surgery. Also tell them he parked his car at the back of the building, just off the alley. Say they should hurry because the president will be angry poachers have killed his elephants.'

CHAPTER 44

Alan and Luke sat back with their Scotches to look at the photos and videos on the big screen in Luke's home office. The pictures were a lot brighter and clearer than Alan feared with the limited light offered by the falling dusk. 'There's no mistaking Simon Kholose's four-wheel drive,' said Luke. 'He's very proud of his car, and everyone would recognise it at once.'

'And there's David,' said Alan. 'He helped bury the tusks, so it was easy for him to take Kholose to them.'

'Alan, that man in the bush hat, do you have a clear picture of his face?'

'No, he always had it well pulled down, so there's only occasional fleeting glimpses.'

Luke's wife, Enid, knocked on the door and entered the room. 'Luke, Don is here to see you.'

'Oh! I wasn't expecting him.'

'What is that video of Don you're watching? I haven't seen that one before now.'

'Don? You think that's Don?'

'Yes. You can't mistake his walk, and that's the jacket Avril bought him for Christmas.'

Luke and Alan looked at each other. Now that Enid pointed it out, Alan and Luke agreed there was a likeness to Don. 'Send him in, Enid.' As they waited for Don, Luke said, 'Leave the video running, Alan. I want to see his reaction.'

Alan's mind was elsewhere, and he missed Luke's comment. He again worried his night with Avril might be the topic for discussion. He stood to one side to avoid being the first thing Don saw when he entered.

Alan needn't have worried. Don entered Luke's office in his usual gregarious manner, shaking hands with Luke and slapping Alan on the back. 'Scotch for you, Don?' said Luke, standing with his back to the big screen.

'Yes, thanks Luke...' Don's eyes fell on the big screen behind Luke. 'Er, on second thoughts, I better not. Avril's expecting me early for dinner tonight. I only popped in to say hi to you and Enid and the girls.'

In a minute, Don was gone. 'Well, what do you think?' said Alan. 'There's no doubt he reacted to that video.'

'Didn't you want to question him?'

'First, I need to consider the implications. If we expose Simon Kholose and David, we'll also expose Don. What's Avril going to say?'

'OK, but the longer we leave it, the more opportunity they have to think up an excuse for why they were in the park, digging up those tusks and horns. Perhaps I should confront David tonight. He's the weakest link in that group and might blurt out everything.'

'Good idea, and tomorrow we'll decide what to do.'

* * *

Alan called Alexander and Daniel to bring David in for a chat.

David entered Alan's apartment like a condemned prisoner about to be sentenced. His shoulders were rounded, and he kept his hands folded in front of him. His eyes darted around the apartment as if looking for the hangman's noose. The Instructors didn't tell him the reason for the meeting, but he suspected he was in trouble. Alan motioned for him to sit in a chair at the dining table. Daniel and Alexander stood behind him, like guards in charge of a prisoner. It did nothing to ease David's apprehension. Guilt was written all over his face.

Alan pulled out a chair and sat opposite David at the dining table. 'David, do you remember the elephant tusks and rhino horn you helped bury in the park?'

'Yes, Sah.'

'They're no longer where we buried them.' Alan paused for David's reaction.

'Not there, Sah? How can that be?'

'I hoped you could tell us where they are now.'

'I don't know, Sah.'

Alan placed two photos on the table. David stared at it, and his eyes grew big and round as he recognised himself and the others digging up the elephant tusks and rhino horn. The second photo showed him holding a tusk while Simon Kholose examined it.

'Well, David, do you recognise those men?'

'Yes, Sah.' David trembled as he stuttered and stammered over his responses to Alan's questions.

'Who is the leader of your group?' Alan demanded.

'Mr Simon is my leader, Sah, and he deals with Mr Don.'

'And who is Mr Don's boss?'

'Someone in Harare, Sah. Mr Don sells the ivory and horns to the doctors, but the big boss is in Harare.'

'Dr Kim and Dr Chen?'

'Yes, Sah, the doctors from North Korea.'

'OK, thank you, David, you can go.'

Relief was etched on David's face when he realised nothing would happen to him, for now at least. 'Thank you, Sah, thank you.'

After David left, Alan counselled his two men. 'We better be on guard. David will tell Simon Kholose about this meeting, and that might draw out the poaching ringleaders. Simon Kholose might take matters into his own hands, or the bosses in Harare may send someone to deal with us. Now they will know we have proof of their poaching, and they may want to get rid of all the witnesses to their crime. So watch out for yourselves. You can't be too careful.'

CHAPTER 45

'DID you hear the news this morning, Alan?' Luke asked. 'The radio said the police arrested a third man linked to a poaching syndicate. This one is a local man connected to the two North Koreans they arrested yesterday.'

'Did they give the person's name?'

'No, but you can guess what I'm thinking.'

The phone rang and Luke picked up the handset. 'Yes, yes, Avril, my dear. Yes, try not to worry. I'll see what I can do and call you as soon as there's any news.' Luke looked at Alan. 'We have our answer. Avril says the police came to the house at six o'clock this morning and took Don away. She's been down at the police station since then, trying to see Don, but the police sent her away. I must talk to my lawyers to find out the next step.'

Later, in the evening, Luke brought Alan up to date on the events of the day. 'The two North Korean doctors have done a deal with the police and told them Don made the approach with an offer to supply ivory and rhino horn. The police and the North Koreans will make Don the scapegoat for the poaching charges.'

'Damn! If we hadn't phoned the police with that anonymous call about the tusks in the surgery, Don wouldn't have been caught.'

'Don't blame yourself, Alan. You didn't realise Don was the third man in the vehicle until Enid recognised him in the video on the big screen. Neither of us did.'

'I still feel bad about the whole thing, Luke, and I'm not sure the family will support your view on this mess.'

Alan was right. Enid and Avril didn't say much, but June didn't hold back. 'That man has caused us a lot of trouble. He has got several black people killed, including Henry. Now, he's destroying the family by getting Don arrested. I'll never forgive him.'

'But Alan didn't know Don was involved in the poaching,' said Luke, 'and neither did I.'

'This whole project stinks. How could you fall for the white men's scheme?'

'The MFF approved the project, and the committee asked the white expatriates for their help with the funding.'

'Why can't we solve our own problems? If we need help from the whites, we're not ready to take on the responsibility of the cause. Alan being my boyfriend was a stupid idea. It's embarrassing.'

'You didn't object at the beginning. You even liked him, and he liked you.'

'No, I never liked him. I was just going along with the silly charade.'

'You'll think differently when you've calmed down a little.'

'No, I won't. And Avril, how can you stay so calm?'

'I not calm, June, I'm stunned. First, I find out about Don's secret life of crime in poaching, and then I discover you all kept this charade of you and Alan a secret from me.'

'Avril, my dear,' said Luke, 'the fewer people who knew about the special arrangements we made for the project the better.'

'Well, that's the end,' said June. 'I'm finished with that man for good.'

CHAPTER 46

CAPTAIN John frowned. 'So, there's a problem with your man in Singapore. You said everything was nice and tight over there.'

'I thought so, Sir. It's odd. Everything was fine when I last saw him, but when I tried to contact Wong at home last night, his wife said he'd committed suicide. Apparently, he was about to lose his job. Asians take that seriously. It's all about losing face, and it looks like he resolved the situation by jumping out of the office building.'

'Why was he about to lose his job?'

'His wife wasn't sure, but she said Wong's boss asked him to look after two important visitors, but they went missing.'

'But how could they hold Wong responsible once he put them on the train? Might George Drake have found out about his connection to you?'

'No, I doubt that, Sir. Wong and I were very discreet. The last time, we met in a tiny cafe, tucked-away in a narrow side street.'

'We can't leave any of our contacts out there if they're compromised, Nyoka.'

'Well, Sir, if Wong was compromised, he did us all a favour.'

'Did he give you any more information about Dube and his son? The client has already paid us for that job. It would be an embarrassment if Dube and his son suddenly turned up back in Bulawayo.'

'There's no possibility of that happening, Sir. Mr Wong said, before they died, they admitted to being on their way to meet George Drake in Chiang Mai to discuss plans for Mthwakazi.'

'Hmm!'

'Should we pass that information on to our contacts in the government, Sir?'

'No, let's hold on to it until the timing suits us. Remember, Nyoka, we're a business. The COU doesn't take sides, and we don't go touting for business. If we did, the clients would try to negotiate on price. If someone wants the COU's services and can pay, we will work for them. Many Ndebele want to set up Mthwakazi as a separate state. That's no secret. Did that meeting in Chiang Mai go ahead? If so, what did they discuss?'

'There's no news about that, Sir, but Dube said Peter Nkala also planned to attend. Perhaps we could find out from him.'

'That's interesting, but one thing at a time, Nyoka. This new enquiry we've just received will be difficult to conclude without a contact in Singapore.'

'Don't worry, Sir, we'll soon get a replacement.'

'Let's hope so. This one is as big as it gets. I don't feel confident enough to ask for a deposit just yet. We'll be at a real disadvantage without someone local on the ground there.'

'Sir, if we don't go touting for business, how does anyone find out about us?'

'Word of mouth, Nyoka, is the most powerful form of advertising. The people who use the COU's services mix with other people of that ilk. If anyone needs our services, somebody will refer them to us.'

Hilton Nyoka's cell phone rang. 'Yes.' Hilton listened in silence for a minute before ending the call. 'That was Simon Kholose. He says the police picked up Dr Chen soon after they delivered the tusks to the surgery.'

'Don, Simon Kholose and the boy, David, were the only ones who knew about the plan to pick up the tusks. What does that tell you? Don must have leaked the information to his wife or father-in-law. He's like a leaking tap. We need to stop that leak, Nyoka. Get onto it. You know what to do.'

* * *

Nyoka returned to his office and closed the door. He punched a number into his cell phone and waited. 'Kholose, I'm coming down to Bulawayo. I have a job to do, and I may need your help. In the meantime, keep an eye on Don Nkomo.'

'Haven't you heard the news? The police have arrested Don Nkomo. They're questioning him now.'

'Damn! We don't want him talking to the police. If he talks, we'll be on the news next. I'll phone our friend and see if he can tell me anything.' Nyoka rang off and punched in another number. The important numbers were in his head; the ones too dangerous to save on his phone. 'Inspector?'

'Chief Inspector, if you don't mind.'

'Yes, yes, sorry about that. What's the situation with the poachers?'

'The North Koreans are claiming diplomatic immunity.'

'And the third one?'

'They're all being sent to Chikurubi on remand. They'll handle it on that side.'

'When are they leaving?'

'They've already gone. They're going by road.'

'When?'

'Two hours ago.'

'Thank you, Chief Inspector.' Nyoka had a broad smile on his face. How convenient! The police were bringing the target to him. It would be easier to settle things in Chikurubi.

CHAPTER 47

Max Sibiya, Luke's lawyer, responded quickly to his instruction to get bail for Don. They weren't too hopeful because of the seriousness of the charge. The family couldn't believe their luck when the judge granted the request. 'What do we do now?' Luke asked Max as they stood on the pavement outside the court.

'Now we start work on Don's defence. We must look at the evidence and take it apart bit by bit. Remember, they must prove him guilty. He doesn't have to prove he's innocent. The police only have the word of the North Korean doctors. The poached items were at their surgery, so it's hard for them to deny their involvement. If they don't have CCTV, video evidence or other witnesses or something else to corroborate their story, we'll say the doctors are trying to downplay their part in the crime by accusing others.'

'OK, I'll bring Don to your chambers this afternoon, and we can take it from there.'

Enid and June returned home while Luke and Avril accompanied Max to the police station to pick up Don.

'I'm sorry,' said the police sergeant on the front desk, 'by now they'd be halfway to Harare.'

'We must stop them,' said Max, 'the judge has granted bail to Mr Don Nkomo. We need to speak to the chief superintendent. Now!'

'The chief is away, but I'll check if the superintendent is free.'

The sergeant climbed the stairs to the first floor and after several minutes returned carrying a cup of tea. 'I'm sorry, the Superintendent says you must take up the issue on the Harare side. He isn't authorised to call them back.'

In front of the judge they got the same response. Frustration was etched on his face, but he declined to do anything about the police's pre-emptive action. 'Deal with it in the Harare jurisdiction. That's my advice.'

* * *

Back at the house, Luke defended his position on the poaching issue. 'But Alan, look at it from my point of view. Don is a family member. I can't just abandon him to Zimbabwe's fickle legal system.'

'I appreciate your point of view, Luke, and I sympathise, but you understand Simon Kholose will get away with his poaching if we keep our video secret?'

'There'll be other opportunities to catch him. Your job here, Alan, is to train our best people to train others who join the cause. You're not here to stop poaching.'

'Yes, but how can I train your best people when we suspect Simon Kholose and his family's motives? While they remain members of the MFF, we might be wasting our time.'

'There'll always be someone whose motives are suspect. We must carry on the best we can.'

'OK, Luke, I don't want to make things any more difficult for Don. Do whatever you want with the video.'

'Let's keep it as a fallback for now. We might need it one day.'

'OK.'

'Avril may have to move to Harare to take care of Don. You know, they often don't have food or water for the prisoners in Chikurubi. For many, being sentenced to prison in Chikurubi is equivalent to a death sentence. If you don't have a family to take care of you, you're in big trouble.'

'So, what now?'

'I'm going up to Harare with Avril and Max Sibiya. We'll apply for bail for Don. The earlier bail ruling should work in our favour. If we fail in our application, I'll find somewhere suitable for Avril to stay. I'll be back within a week. In the meantime, please keep an eye on the family.'

On his way out, Alan caught a fleeting glimpse of June, walking down the passage to the back of the house. She looked attractive as ever. Could things between them ever return to the way they were before Henry's death? They were never truly lovers, but that dinner at the Indaba Book Cafe held so much promise. It was only a few weeks ago, but June's coldness towards him made it seem so much longer.

* * *

Chikurubi Maximum Security Prison, sixteen kilometres from the Harare CBD. Don Nkomo looked at his surroundings in disbelief. The dusty courtyard and the twenty-foot concrete walls topped with barbed wire told Don he was not in a good space. Upon their arrival at Chikurubi, the guards separated Don from his North Korean companions, and that was the last Don saw of them. It disturbed him when the doctors talked of diplomatic immunity. Perhaps they'd get away with their part in the crime, and he'd be left to take the blame for the whole poaching operation.

The prison was crowded. So many people! A guard told Don to wait in the courtyard; someone would attend to him soon. He waited and waited. They must have forgotten about him. What was he supposed to do next? A siren sounded, and several prisoners disappeared into a building. Others seemed not to notice.

'You! What are doing here?' The guard shouted the question at him but didn't seem to want an answer. Each time Don tried to explain, the guard told him to be quiet. 'Come with me.' Don followed the guard with an increasing sense of foreboding. At the end of a dark corridor, the guard opened a cell door. 'Go in here.' Half a dozen prisoners occupying the cell barely seemed to notice his arrival.

Don sat down near the cell door and waited; waited for what? After several minutes a fellow prisoner sidled up to him. 'Man, I wouldn't stay near the door if I was you. If you need to pee at night, it's better to be near a bucket.'

Don noticed the two buckets in the back corners of the cell. 'But why do I need to sleep near a bucket?'

'Man, it gets crowded in here. When everyone comes in, you can't move. It's like a tin of sardines.'

'When do we get something to eat?' Up till then Don focussed on his predicament but now he felt famished.

'Maybe tomorrow morning or lunchtime.' The man noticed Don's portly figure. 'I tell you man, you come in here looking like an Africander bull, and you leave looking like a greyhound. That is if you don't starve to death first.' Don responded with a weak smile. 'Serious, Man, ask anyone. People starve to death in here. I've seen it many times.'

'You've been in here before now?'

'This is my third time. First time was robbery, next rape and the third time for murder.'

'So when will you get out?'

'The judge said eleven years, but many people here have finished their sentence and they forget to release them. Many prisoners lose track of time and they don't even know their release date.'

'You're kidding me?'

'No, serious man. Lots of people in here have finished their sentence, but if the government doesn't want you to leave, they just forget about you.'

Don put his head in his hands. This was a nightmare. He couldn't bear the prospect of a long sentence in Chikurubi. Don took his new companion's advice and moved next to one of the toilet buckets. Minutes later, others entered the cell, and soon the relative peace was overtaken by a chattering crowd of prisoners who all seemed to know each other. 'Lie down now,' his new companion advised. 'There may be no room to lie down if you wait till later.'

The uncertainty and fear twisted inside Don. Surrounded by murderers and thieves and packed in like sardines, Don's jovial personality evaporated in the crushing realisation that Chikurubi might be his world for a long time. It was a prospect too terrible to contemplate. Since the police picked him up early that morning, he'd focussed on his dire circumstances from the time of his arrest, the drive to Harare and his arrival at Chikurubi. Now, his thoughts turned to Avril and his comfortable home. Thinking about what he'd lost made matters worse.

After a sleepless, uncomfortable night, Don and the other prisoners were allowed out of their cell. Don needed food and could think of nothing else. As he passed a narrow lane between two buildings, he heard someone call his name.

'Don, come here, I have a message for you.'

Could it be a message from Luke? Don guessed his father-in-law would do his utmost to help him get out of the mess he created for himself. He walked across to the man, who was dressed in prison khaki shirt and shorts. 'What's the message? Who's it from?'

'It's from Hilton Nyoka. He asked me to give you this.'

* * *

Avril and Luke waited anxiously with Max Sibiya for the opportunity to see Don. It was Saturday, and nothing could be done about a bail application until Monday morning. Max spoke to a prison officer standing nearby. 'We're here for Mr Don Nkomo. He arrived at the prison yesterday. When can we see him?'

'Wait, I'll check.' The prison guard disappeared into the guard room.

Time passed and Avril and Luke were getting impatient. 'Don't worry, it's always like this,' said Max.

After almost half an hour, the guard reappeared. The trio looked up expectantly. 'The Superintendent will meet you soon.'

'Why must we meet the Superintendent?' Luke asked.

The guard shrugged.

'Perhaps they will say we must wait until after the bail hearing,' Max suggested.

Ten minutes later, the guard came back and asked the trio to follow him. They walked into the administration building and shown into an office with a large desk and four chairs for visitors. 'The Superintendent won't be long,' said the guard.

Within a few minutes, a serious looking man entered and sat behind the desk. 'You're here to see prisoner Don Nkomo, yes?'

'That is correct,' said Max.

'Mr Nkomo got into a fight with a fellow prisoner. I'm sorry to tell you, he died of his injuries.'

The news left the three visitors speechless as it swept away all other thoughts from their minds. The Superintendent continued. 'We are investigating the matter. All I can tell you is he was stabbed with a sharp implement, probably a knife. We have not found the murder weapon, and we do not know the identity of his attacker.'

A long silence followed the dreadful news.

'Can we view his body?' asked Luke.

'You can go through a formal identification on Monday. It is a police matter now, so they will take charge of the investigation. You can ask them when and where you can view the body.'

The trio left the prison in a state of shock. Avril was too stunned to react to the news, and Luke and Max remained silent.

The news only hit home with Avril when she and Luke identified Don's body on Monday morning. Don looked as if he was sleeping. Many times, she'd seen that look on his face. The morgue attendant said his peaceful countenance showed he died instantly from the stab wound to his heart. He wouldn't have suffered or known what hit him. It was an expert hit by a trained assassin or a chance blow.

Don was a ladies' man, but Avril loved him for his good nature and thoughtful ways. He was a happy-go-lucky rogue but a good provider. She would be sure to miss his good humour and enthusiastic personality. Don was good company when he was home, which was less and less often these days. If he wasn't travelling on business, he'd be at a meeting. One thing was consistent, the smell of alcohol on his breath and the faint fragrance of perfume on his clothes. Was Don's fate her punishment for her night with Alan? But she soon dismissed the idea, as Don himself often wandered.

CHAPTER 48

APRIL 2014

Back in Bulawayo, the family arranged Don's funeral. Alan attended along with all the family and several of Don's relatives and business associates. It was a sombre affair, like the funerals he attended with his father back in Melbourne. For Alan, it was an excruciating experience because he felt responsible for the circumstances that led to Don's imprisonment and subsequent murder.

After the wake, Luke voiced his thoughts to Alan. 'It's hard to imagine Don fought with a fellow prisoner.'

'Yes, someone silenced him before he could reveal who was behind the poaching operation. We still have that video of Simon Kholose. Maybe he knows who ordered Don's murder. Why don't we offer Kholose a deal? He tells us who's behind the murder and we forget about the video. Otherwise ...'

'What happens if he gives us the information? The police won't do anything.'

'Once we get the names, we'll decide what to do. Don't worry; we'll handle it.'

'We'll handle it! Who are we?'

'The training team will handle it.'

'Seriously? It's a balance between Don's reputation and avenging his murder. I must think about it.'

'C'mon Luke, we're wasting time. There's nothing to think about. Don said those men were dangerous, and his murder proved him right. The family and you could be at serious risk, and me too.'

'OK! OK! Let's talk to Kholose.'

*　*　*

Alan scanned the newspapers but found nothing about the two North Koreans or Don's murder. Luke arranged for Alan and himself to meet Simon Kholose at eleven o'clock in the bar at the Bulawayo Rainbow Hotel. The ultimatum was a gamble that could backfire, but it would force the poachers' hand. Giving Kholose an ultimatum might make it even more likely Don's killers would come after them or Luke's family.

'Once Simon Kholose finds out about the video recording,' said Alan, 'we'll all need to be extra careful with our security. David will have already reported back to Simon about the photos, but neither have any idea the video exists.'

'If David told Simon about the photos, why would the video make it more dangerous for us?'

'The photos have no audio. The three might have been collecting the tusks to return them to National Parks or the police. In the video, you can hear Kholose tell the other two to hurry because Dr Chen is waiting for them at his surgery.

'Don was murdered soon after he entered Chikurubi. It was probably the first opportunity the killers had to access him. They wanted to silence him in case he confessed and implicated others. So, if the killers plan to target us, it will be soon.'

Simon Kholose entered the bar with the look of a caged leopard, nervous and dangerous. He sat down at the table with no pretence of niceties. 'So, what do you want to discuss?'

Luke took the USB from his pocket and handed it to Simon. 'Your future.'

'What's this?'

'A video, showing your poaching activity. This USB shows you with Don Nkomo and David, digging up the elephant tusks and rhino horn in the Hwange National Park. Do you remember telling the others to hurry because Dr Chen is waiting at his surgery for the tusks? It's all on there. The video is crystal clear. You'll like it.'

'So, why are you giving me a copy?'

'We want you to see what we'll give the Bulawayo Chronicle and The Herald at three o'clock in the afternoon, day after tomorrow.'

Simon licked his lips. 'What do you want?'

'The names of the people responsible for killing Don Nkomo.'

'Don was our link to the poachers. How would I know who killed him?'

'But you know who ordered it. Simon, you wouldn't take part in something like this without knowing who's in charge.'

'And if I get you the names?'

'We'll forget this recording ever existed.'

'I can't promise anything, but I'll see what I can do.'

'Remember, we want the names by three o'clock, day after tomorrow, or...'

'I will try to find out who's responsible. Where can I find you to give you the names?'

'Mr Drake or I will phone you before the deadline. You can give us the names over the phone.'

Simon Kholose pushed his chair back and left the bar.

Luke turned to Alan. 'Let's get back to my place. The whole family will be there, so they won't be able to get to anyone. Are your men ready?'

'Daniel and Alexander are already there. Your house will be tight as a drum. No one can enter without your permission.'

'Let's hope so. It's a pity we needed to give Kholose so much time to respond.'

'Yes, but my bet is the killers will travel down from Harare, so extra time was essential.'

'That, I understand, but keeping my family confined together for so long is another matter. It's a shame you and June fell out. A united team is much better.'

* * *

Simon Kholose returned to his car and took out his cell phone.

'Hilton, it's Simon. Luke Ndlovu and Alan Drake know about the poaching operation.'

'How can they?'

'They took a video recording of Don, David and Me, digging up the tusks and rhino horn. They must have hidden somewhere in the bushes and recorded the whole thing.'

'Anything else?'

'No, but they're threatening to send USBs to the papers if I don't tell them who's responsible for Don's murder. They've given me until three o'clock day after tomorrow to give them the names. If I give them names, they'll forget about the recording.'

'Don't worry Simon, we'll take care of things from this end. OK?'

'Yeah, fine, but you better hurry. We don't want their next move enmeshing anyone else, do we?'

Simon rang off, and Hilton Nyoka went to Captain John's office to tell him about the call. 'Nyoka, I want you to handle this one personally. Take your two best men as backup. As Simon said, time is short. I want these loose ends dealt with fast.'

CHAPTER 49

AFTER their meeting with Simon Kholose, Luke and Alan returned to Luke's house where all the family assembled. Mae, Ted and their children were on holiday in South Africa, but Avril, June, Rita and their mother Enid anxiously waited in the front room.

Three of Alan's men patrolled the grounds. 'Is three enough?' said Luke.

'We're keeping a twenty-four-hour watch,' said Alan, 'and we need our men to be fresh and alert. That spreads us thin. But don't worry, I'll keep the night watch with the three men on guard.'

'When do you think they'll come?'

'If they come, it'll be when it's dark.'

'Be careful, Alan, remember, you and I are probably their main targets. If you're keeping watch at night, stay inside the house. Don't go wandering in the garden.'

Alan and Luke had no way of knowing whether the assassins were already in Bulawayo or on their way. The greatest danger continued until the three o'clock afternoon deadline they gave Simon Kholose. Alan couldn't imagine the poachers would allow the deadline to pass without an attempt to silence them. There were two nights before then.

June remained as cool as ever towards Alan. Avril grieved for her lost husband, and guilt about the night she strayed tugged at her. She tried to keep a balanced view of things, but when she spoke to Alan, he warned her that as he was a potential target, everyone should keep a safe distance from him. The same applied to her father. Enid would have none of it and stuck close to Luke despite the danger.

At one in the morning, a muffled cry in the garden. Had someone attacked one of his men? Alan slipped out the kitchen door to check on the three guards. In the front garden the guards were alert. Did they hear the cry? Neither could be sure. 'Maybe a bird, Sah.'

Alan moved on to the third guard. A dark moonless night made it hard to find him, but then Alan spotted him sitting on the ground. 'Gideon, what's up? What's the matter?'

'My leg, Sah. I cut it on a garden post. It's bleeding.'

'I told you to get familiar with the layout of the garden before dark. This is the reason.'

'Yes, Sah. Sorry, Sah.'

'OK, come into the house, and I'll have a look at your leg.'

Gideon turned pale when he saw the amount of blood soaking his trousers. Alan raised the loose trouser leg and washed the wound. He applied antiseptic and bound it with a pressure bandage. 'You need stitches in that leg, Gideon. Zachariah can drive you to the hospital. Zachariah, I need you back here as quick as possible. Here are my flat keys. After the hospital, drop him at my apartment and get back here ASAP. We'll take Gideon home in the morning. Jonah and I will guard the grounds until you get back.'

The remaining hours passed without incident. At six in the morning, the relief shift arrived. After organising the new guards, Alan ate breakfast and retired with a blanket and cushion to the comfy sofa in Luke's office to catch up on lost sleep. He was exhausted and needed rest, but although he soon fell asleep, he dreamt he was in action back in Afghanistan. Still, sleep was sleep, and he got a full seven hours. Alan felt drugged, but after a shower, clean clothes and an early dinner, he was ready for anything.

* * *

On the second night, Alan increased the guard to four. As the deadline neared, the likelihood of an attack increased. Alan suggested that the whole house be kept in darkness, but Luke insisted he had work to do. 'I've ignored my business long enough,' he protested, before going into his office and closing the door behind him.

Everyone else followed Alan's advice and turned in for an early night. Alan sat in the shadows of the front room, keeping an eye on the road for passing traffic that might drive by too slowly. It seemed like he was on duty back in Afghanistan, but his surroundings were much more comfortable than they'd been in the desert.

Time crawls on guard duty late at night. The trick was to stay alert and not let his mind drift back to that girl in the bar somewhere or to his complicated relationships with June and Avril.

What a mess! He knew this project wouldn't be easy, and he'd vowed to stay away from women while in the country, but June was an unexpected distraction. She was most attractive, and she'd given him signals a grand prize might await him in due course. He'd always kept his dealings with women under control. His military discipline, applied to his love life, made for a comfortable existence. Somehow, June gave that comfortable existence speed wobbles. Alan rationalised it as the natural desire for something unattainable. Now that June dumped him, he wanted her more than ever.

Alan couldn't be sure if Luke knew the true nature of his relationship with June. He doubted it because Luke often told Alan, June would come around in time. He imagined Luke viewed their relationship as a platonic convenience, assisting the MFF cause. Would Luke be so encouraging if he was aware of their intimate evenings in the front room? Perhaps he would view their passionate kisses on the couch as a betrayal? Those evenings ended only two months before, but to Alan it seemed an age.

Avril was an irresistible sexual force. She was a married woman, and somehow his night with her didn't seem like a betrayal of Luke's trust. It didn't even feel like a betrayal of Don, once he discovered Avril's husband liked to play away from home. Alan was more concerned about how his night with Avril might affect his damaged relationship with June, but he often found himself thinking about June's delicious older sister.

That bang? Was it a car backfiring or a gunshot? Alan would have no trouble distinguishing the difference under normal circumstances, but his mind was a million miles away, preoccupied with other thoughts. He saw his two guards in the front garden, alert and looking down the road. Alan slipped out of the house and hurried over to them. 'What's going on?'

'We don't know, Sah. A car passed, and then a bang. It might have backfired, or ....'

'You two get back to your positions.' Alan suddenly thought of Luke. He ran back into the house. A thin line of light glowed under the office door. Alan withdrew the handgun tucked into the waistband at the back of his trousers and reached for the door handle. He inhaled.

'Alan, what are you doing?'

Alan jumped at the voice of Luke, who stood behind him.

Luke smiled. 'I go to the bathroom for a minute and return to find you ready to burst into my office with a gun. You're not the assassin, are you? Perhaps you wanted to give me a fright.'

Alan laughed. 'No, but I heard a bang, so I thought I better check on you.'

'Hmm, you are jumpy tonight. I hope the family is safe with you waving that gun around.'

Alan tucked the handgun back into his waistband. 'Better safe than sorry, Luke. One always thinks it can't happen to them, until it does.'

Luke went back into his office and shut the door. Alan hesitated for a few moments in the passageway. June's bedroom door was only a few feet from where he stood. He half-hoped she'd emerge from her room to enquire about the noise. She didn't, and Alan reluctantly walked away down the passage to go check on the guard in the back garden.

CHAPTER 50

HILTON Nyoka felt buoyed. He loved these assignments. Everyone knew he was the COU's assassin par excellence. It still irked him he'd missed his attempt on the targets in Gaborone. It remained the only blot on his otherwise impeccable record, but as soon as Captain John gave him the green light, he'd remedy that. He picked out two of his most promising protégés, Jay and Ken, and booked the evening flight to Bulawayo.

At the airport, a limousine driver met the group. 'Good evening, Mr Nyoka. Welcome to Bulawayo. The bag you ordered is in the boot. Return it when I take you to the airport for your morning flight day after tomorrow.'

At the Bulawayo Rainbow Hotel, Hilton unzipped the bag the driver gave him and saw the glossy walnut stock of the rifle. He grunted with satisfaction as he recognised it as the one he'd used in an earlier hit. It was ideal for his current job. The driver told him the sights were not adjusted since he last used the rifle. That meant, Hilton could take a long shot if required.

'Tonight, we have fun, and tomorrow night we work,' said Hilton to his companions. It didn't take the three of them long to down a quick dinner and join the pulsating crowd in the nightclub next to the Bulawayo Rainbow. Hilton didn't conceal his presence or that of his colleagues. He maintained a contempt for the ability of the local police to connect him to the planned killings. Hilton's focus was on finding a suitable companion for the night.

At breakfast, Hilton was on a high. 'Any luck with the ladies,' asked Jay.

'Are you kidding? There were so many women wanting me, it was hard to choose. How about you?'

Jay gave a thumbs up, looking pleased with himself. Ken seemed disinterested. 'I'm not interested in those easy women.'

'You mean you couldn't get anyone to go with you,' said Jay. He and Hilton laughed as Ken focussed on his fried eggs and bacon.

'We came here to do a job,' said Ken. 'We're not here to screw women.'

'You're right,' said Hilton. 'Leave the women to Jay and me.' Again, he and Jay laughed as Ken ordered more tea from the waiter.

* * *

The car crawled down the dark, wooded avenue before rolling to a stop amongst thick bushes on the edge of the road. In the affluent outer suburbs, there were few street lights, and those that were in place boasted missing bulbs or dull, faded beams. The evening air smelt fresh from the afternoon rain. A beautiful Bulawayo night, with frogs keeping up a deafening chorus down at the nearby creek. The road was a dead-end with few properties, so there would be little chance of passing cars at eight o'clock on a weekday night.

'Ken, you stay with the car and keep watch for any trouble. Jay you come with me in case I need backup. Make sure your phones are on vibrate.'

Hilton and Jay got out of the car and closed the door with its reassuringly dull thud. They ducked to squeeze through the strands of a steel wire fence after checking it was not electrified. There was little ground cover, but the property was thickly planted with trees and bushes. Hilton cursed silently as every bush they brushed past showered them with cold drops of water from the earlier rain. The night was pitch black, and the cold water running down the back of their necks made it even more uncomfortable as they walked most of the three hundred yards to the house.

Though it was still summer, the late evening breezes carried a chill with them, and Hilton admonished himself for not wearing a hat and warmer jacket. At least, the damp, sandy soil allowed the pair to pad through the grounds, which would otherwise crackle with leaves and twigs in the dry winter season.

Hilton stopped at a point with a clear view of the house while maintaining a safe distance. The side of the house they faced stood in total darkness. A dog barked somewhere in the distance, on a neighbouring property. If they moved their position to view the other side of the house, the building would stand between them and their escape route. As Hilton considered his options, a light came on in the corner room nearest their hiding place. A figure entered the room and crossed the floor to a computer, sitting on a desk. He stood for a moment gazing at the computer screen before sitting down in front of it.

Confident their presence went undetected, the intruders crept nearer to the warm light that streamed from the window. 'We must make sure it's the right person,' Hilton whispered. 'Captain John is sensitive about collateral damage.'

As the men reached a suitable vantage point in the treed garden, the figure stood up and stared out of the window in their direction. 'That's him,' said Hilton. He carefully rested his rifle in the fork of a tree and took aim, lining up the cross hairs of the telescopic sights. The figure in the window returned to the computer screen and sat before it, unmoving. Hilton needed to make sure of a single successful hit. He decided on a head shot. He looked up and licked his lips and took aim again, breathed in and breathed out slowly and squeezed the trigger.

The figure in the window disappeared as if by magic. Loud voices and shouting in the house followed, and Hilton and Jay hurried back to the car. The motor was already running when they jumped in, breathless from excitement and their hasty retreat. The car U-turned and raced off down the road. 'One down, one to go,' said Hilton. He punched in a number into his cell phone. 'Where is he now? OK, thanks.' Hilton turned to his companions. 'Our contact says he's at home.'

CHAPTER 51

ALAN rang Simon Kholose's number, on schedule, at three in the afternoon. No reply. He tried five minutes later, but again, no answer. It was almost half-past three when Alan's cell phone rang. 'Hello Alan, Peter Nkala speaking. Senior Kholose called me a few minutes ago to tell me Simon was shot dead at his home last night.'

'Do they know who did it?'

'No witnesses and no leads, according to the police. He was working at his computer when there was a sudden bang. A single head shot, so he had no chance.'

'It sounds like a professional hit.'

'Something is going on here. We all need to be careful.'

As Alan put his phone down, Enid came into the lounge. 'Alan, one of your men is asking for you.'

Daniel stood at the front door with his hat in his hand. 'Yes, Daniel, what brings you here?'

'Sah, Alexander sent a message to say David is dead.'

'David?'

'Yes, Sah. Someone finished him.'

'How? Where?'

'At his house, Sah. They cut his throat.' Daniel passed his open hand across his throat to make his point.

'Is something wrong?' said Luke, walking up behind Alan, standing at the front door.

'We need to talk,' said Alan. 'I've a sneaking suspicion the danger may be over, though we won't take anything for granted just yet.'

'What do you mean?'

'Everyone involved with the poaching syndicate has been killed or disappeared. The cyanide carrier and Michael Duze were the only survivors from our firefights in the Hwange National Park. Since their escape, no one has heard from them. They were unarmed, so maybe predators killed and ate them. Even if the cyanide carrier escaped, do you think they would have told him who ran the operation? I doubt it. Michael Duze's house remains undisturbed, so it's likely he didn't survive.

'Don and the two others we videoed have been murdered. David probably wouldn't know who ran the operation, but I'm sure he's been silenced just in case Simon Kholose said something to him. With Simon and Don both gone, who can lead us to the poaching gang?'

'What about the two North Koreans, Dr Kim and Dr Chen?'

'I doubt they'd still be in Zimbabwe. If they were, they could also be a target. They might still operate somewhere in Africa, but where?'

'My old friend, Dr Enos Zondo. Perhaps he can trace them through his medical circle.'

* * *

Luke scratched his head. 'Enos Zondo says none of his medical connections have any news of the doctors Kim and Chen.'

'That's that then,' said Alan.

'No, old Enos doesn't give up so easily. He's scheduled a visit to Joburg next week, and while he's there, he plans to visit the North Korean embassy in Pretoria and pretend he wants to visit the country. In the process he'll make a casual enquiry about the two doctors. It should be a convincing story because he has met them before, so why wouldn't he ask after them?'

'Sounds like a good plan, but he better be careful. I wouldn't trifle with those North Koreans. If they suspect his motives, it could be dangerous for him.'

'Don't worry, he's a smart man. I'm sure he won't let anything slip.'

CHAPTER 52

Captain John picked up the phone on the third ring. 'Captain, are you familiar with a Dr Enos Zondo?'

'No, Jeung, why do you ask?'

'He phoned our embassy in Pretoria to make enquiries about a visa for North Korea. He says he met doctors Kim and Chen at a medical function in Zimbabwe, and as a result, he's interested in looking at the medical practices in our country. Given recent events, there might be another motive behind his call. Zondo is visiting the embassy at two o'clock next Tuesday afternoon.'

'OK, Jeung, thanks for letting us know. We'll find out if there's anything to worry about.' Captain John put the phone down and stroked his chin. 'Nyoka, come here, I have a job for you.'

* * *

The phone rang and rang. Irritated, Captain John picked up the phone. 'Yes!'

'Dr Zondo asked about Kim and Chen and how he could contact them.'

'Oh, Jeung, it's you.'

'They confirm they met him briefly at a function but say there was nothing in their discussion likely to stir any interest in North Korean medical practices.'

'OK, Jeung, thanks.'

Captain John rang off and at once dialled another number.

'Nyoka, from what I hear, the doctor is nosing around, asking questions about Kim and Chen.'

'Sources tell us that Dr Zondo is a friend of Luke Ndlovu.'

'Ah! That makes sense now. The doctor needs a little discouragement.'

'We followed him back to his hotel and know his room number, so we can do room service if you want.'

'Whatever, but remember, if you get caught doing something illegal in South Africa, no one will help you.'

'It won't be the first time I've done something illegal in South Africa, Sir.'

Hilton switched off his cell phone and put it back on the low table next to his deck chair by the hotel's indoor pool. He picked up his glass and took another sip of Scotch. 'Don't fall asleep over there, Jay. We've just received a request for room service this evening.'

Jay grunted from his reclined deck chair but showed no sign of stirring. Hilton got up and walked across to Jay and kicked his foot. 'Come on, you lazy bastard. Rest after we do the job. If you didn't spend all night chasing women, you wouldn't be so tired.'

'I didn't spend all night chasing women. I just had one woman and spent all night trying to stop her from getting away.'

'If you weren't so ugly, she wouldn't have been trying to get away. I had trouble getting my one to leave.'

'Hah! That's because she was so ugly, she had nowhere else to go.'

The two men laughed as they gathered up their things to go back to their rooms to get ready for their evening mission.

CHAPTER 53

EIGHT o'clock on a black, moonless night. Alan sat sipping a Scotch, chatting with Luke in his darkened lounge, when Luke's cell phone rang.

'Luke, it's me, Enos.'

'Yes, Enos, my old friend.'

'Tell your colleague the embassy claims they've returned to North Korea. The man I spoke to was very cagey, so I'm not sure if that's true. There was something in his manner that made me suspicious. He cross-examined me about why I wanted to know the doctors' whereabouts. The people in the embassy are probably aware the doctors had dealings with the poachers, and they might even have played a role in shipping the tusks and rhino horn overseas. Hang on, someone's knocking at my door. It must be my room service.'

'OK Enos, thanks for your help. When you get back, we'll talk more. Bye for now.' Luke turned to Alan. 'No luck with the North Koreans. The embassy says they've returned home to North Korea, but Enos has his doubts.'

'Ah well, it was worth a try. But why weren't they in Chikurubi with Don when they were all in the poaching business together?'

'If the embassy is telling the truth, they'd be out of our reach in North Korea. The only reason they wouldn't be in jail is if they travelled on diplomatic passports. We could ask our people to keep an eye out, but most of our members would never have met them. Now that Simon Kholose is gone, we can trust our members to keep quiet about what we are doing.'

'We have pictures of the doctors. When Henry visited their surgery, he brought back a brochure with pictures of their faces in it. Perhaps we can enlarge the pictures and print out copies. Do we have anyone in Joburg or Pretoria to keep a watch on the embassy to see if they turn up there?'

'Yes, but for how long? The area around the embassy doesn't make it an ideal spot for a stakeout. The doctors could also have moved to Tanzania and be beyond our reach.'

'One thing at a time, Luke. Let's focus on Zimbabwe and the Pretoria embassy, but my guess is they are no longer in this country.'

* * *

Luke looked shaken when he walked into the lounge room. 'Alan, this whole thing is bigger than we expected. I've just received word from Enos Zondo's wife. The poor woman says Enos was badly beaten in his hotel room in Pretoria. He's in hospital. The police say it was a robbery gone wrong. He ordered room service, but when they took the tray up to his room, they found him unconscious on the floor. When he called me yesterday, he ended by saying someone was knocking on his door and he thought it must be room service.'

'I wonder if the hotel has CCTV?'

'I'll ask our people down there to check.'

'Luke, the aim of this project was to train young Ndebele men to be soldiers to protect Mthwakazi if there was another attempted Guku-rahundi. It seems our training, utilising the poachers, has stirred up a hornet's nest that's not even connected to our main purpose. When I came here, I thought any risk we faced would be from the security forces, but we're in a battle with the poachers.'

'Yes, perhaps using the poachers for training our recruits was a mistake.'

'The question is, who's backing the poachers? Is it the security forces or someone even higher up the order? Independent poachers are also operating in the national parks, but I'm sure it's a bigger and more organised force working against us. And now, our purpose seems to be turning into an exercise of vengeance against the murderers of Don and those who assaulted Enos Zondo. I'm sure the same group committed all these crimes.'

'I agree.'

'We've got ten good, trained recruits, and two good leaders in Daniel and Alexander. The problem is the project is at a standstill thanks to these issues that sidetracked us. June was right. Your family is in danger and so many people killed, and we're not even at war.

'Once we're sure you and the family are not at risk, my involvement should end, at least for the time being. Daniel and Alexander can continue the training and build the numbers. My presence is in danger of drawing attention to your cause, and that's the last thing you need.'

'But Alan, I regard you as part of my family. I'd hate to see you go and so would the rest of the family.'

'That's not true, Luke. June has resented me ever since Henry was killed.'

'If you have patience, Alan, June will come around. Give her a little more time. I know my daughter, and I know she likes you a lot.'

'I doubt that, Luke, and now, I feel responsible for Avril losing her husband.'·

'Avril doesn't blame you for Don's death. He was dealing with ruthless men. It's the risk he took, and it caught up with him.'

'Maybe, Luke, but this phase of the project should end. Who knows, perhaps we can work together again, down the line.'

'So, what now?' Alan.

'First, we must make sure you and your family are safe. I'm not going anywhere until I'm confident of that.' Alan took out his phone and punched in a number. 'Hello, I need a delivery of a dozen eggs please. I'm expecting my dinner guests at seven o'clock.'

CHAPTER 54

MAY 2014

Seven pm, Alan heard the knock on his door. When he opened it, his two Instructors stood there beaming. They relished visiting Alan in his flat as he always offered them ice cold beers from his fridge. This occasion was no exception. Alan explained about the threat to him, Luke and Luke's family. Between them, they worked out a schedule for who would guard which location.

'There's something else fellas,' said Alan. 'This arrangement can't go on forever. You remember the two poachers who escaped from us at the waterhole in the Hwange National Park?

'Yes, Sah,' Daniel and Alexander responded in unison.

'One was the leader, Michael Duze. The other carried the container of cyanide.'

'Yes, Sah.'

'We need to know who's making the threats against Luke Ndlovu's family. Once we find out who they are, we can deal with them. We already know Michael Duze has not turned up in Bulawayo, so maybe we should search for him and the cyanide carrier in Hwange, Lupane and Victoria Falls. Get our local men in those areas to keep an eye out for them. With Don Nkomo, Simon Kholose and David all gone, if we can't trace those two men, I don't know how we will find out who's making the threats. As a last resort, we may have to use Luke or me as bait to lure the gang into the open, but I'm not crazy about the idea.'

'OK guys, let's get to it, pronto.'

Soon after Daniel and Alexander left, Alan noticed Daniel's packet of cigarettes on the coffee table. A knock on the door! Ah, Daniel, back for his cigarettes. Alan picked up the packet and walked to the door and opened it. 'I've got them here, Daniel. I knew you'd—'

'Mr Drake, what a pleasure to meet you.' The man put his foot against the door and pointed his handgun at Alan's face.

'Who the hell are you?'

'Who I am is not important, but you can call me Phineas. My boss sent me to discourage you and Luke Ndlovu from taking over our territory.'

'We're not trying to take over anyone's territory.'

'Ah, Mr Drake. I'd like to believe you, but your activities have gained notoriety. You bumped into our men in the Hwange National Park, no?'

'You mean the poachers?'

'We call them entrepreneurs.'

'Did you kill Don Nkomo?'

'No, I didn't. But I'm not the only talent in our organisation with such capabilities. Someone else got that job. Now come; we must hurry. We're taking you on a tour of our beautiful country.'

A second man with a handgun stepped into the light on the landing at the head of the flight of stairs leading to Alan's first-floor apartment.

Alan looked for any handy potential weapon. Damn! His handgun was well out of reach. He always took it to the front door with him, but on this occasion, he assumed it was Daniel who knocked.

'Don't try anything silly, Mr Drake. I can kill you here and now, but my superiors want to give you a sporting chance.' Phineas signalled with his handgun for Alan to move down the stairs. 'After you Mr Drake.'

Alan stepped onto the metal fire escape, which doubled as the stairway to his front door. He slowly descended the stairs, his mind racing, looking for any opportunity to escape. The second man, in front of him, descended the stairs backwards, keeping his handgun trained on Alan's chest with his other hand resting on the handrail. Alan was sure Phineas at the rear would keep him covered. Surprise would offer the best chance of escape. Alan went down each step, steadying himself on the handrails that bracketed the stairs.

Three steps from the bottom, the man in front glanced round to check where the stairs ended. In a flash, Alan lifted himself on his arms on the handrails and swung his legs, connecting the man flush on the chest. The man sprawled back, hitting the ground with a heavy thud. His handgun slid across the concrete surface of the courtyard towards a third man standing by a car. Alan was in a race to reach the handgun, but as he leapt off the step, brilliant stars of red, blue and white flashed in front of his eyes.

* * *

A relieved Luke took the phone call from Alexander, telling him the guards were on their way to the house. 'Alan has moved fast to get the bodyguards in place. We can all relax now,' said Luke, as he passed June in the corridor.

'We wouldn't need bodyguards if it wasn't for that stupid idea to train the recruits in the national parks. Alan has been a big disappointment.'

'It wasn't Alan's idea, June. The MFF committee approved the plan.'

'As a trained soldier, he should have discouraged you all from such a silly idea.'

'Listen, My Girl, changing the committee's collective mind is no easy task. Alan said from the beginning the project was a mad scheme. Neither our overseas backers nor the committee accepted that view.'

'With luck, he'll soon go back to Australia and let us resume our normal lives.'

'There's nothing normal about our lives under the present regime. If we're waiting for the president to die of old age, we'll all be long gone before then. Ah! Here they are. I'll say hello. Ask your mother to make them a flask of tea.'

Luke walked out to the car. 'Hello, Alexander, that was quick.'

The driver got out. 'Mr Luke Ndlovu?'

'Yes.'

The powerfully built driver pinned Luke's arms to his side and pushed him against the car. The rear door swung open, and from within, a pair of hands helped to drag Luke onto the back seat. He'd no opportunity to cry out for help, and in a few seconds, the car turned and sped down the road. It was an efficient and silent abduction, and when Alexander and his men arrived minutes later, none of the family were aware Luke was already several blocks down the road.

'Where are you taking me?' Luke asked.

'We're taking you and your friend, Mr Drake, for a pleasant drive.'

'Mr Drake? Will you pick him up now?'

'Your friend is troublesome. Look what he did to my companion. We had to subdue him.'

Luke looked at the silent man in the passenger seat and noticed his face and right hand, scraped and covered with blood. 'See this poor man?' said the driver. 'The concrete courtyard at the back of Mr Drake's apartment needs resurfacing and sealing. It's in a terrible condition, a disgrace. Many whites call us black men savages, but that Mr Drake is the real savage. With that damaged face, my friend has no future with women. We will now call him Scrape Face. Mr Drake is to blame for that.' The driver burst out laughing, and Scrape Face glowered at him.

'Where is Alan Drake?' said Luke.

'You'll soon find out,' said the driver.

* * *

Distant, muffled voices echoed in Alan's brain. A faint scuffling sound and a door slammed. More muffled voices, faint at first, gradually getting closer. Alan lay in that middle world, halfway between wakefulness and sleep. When would his dream end? He was torn between getting up and trying to sleep a little longer. His bed vibrated. It reminded him of the big air transport flights back in Afghanistan. Was he still there? He'd dreamt he was in Africa with people he didn't know. What strange places our minds visit when we sleep.

Sometime later, Alan again stirred. He couldn't tell how long he'd slept. The night was pitch black. He sat up and banged his head. Damn these army bunks! That's funny, I banged my forehead, but the back of my head is pounding. 'What the–' Alan's hands were bound behind him and his feet tied together. The vibration was no air transport. he was in the boot of a moving car. Everything came back to him. That bastard, descending the stairs behind me, hit me on the back of my head.

Something made a sloshing sound next to Alan. He turned his back to it and felt it with his bound hands. A jerry can. That accounted for the petrol smell in the confined space. Where were they taking him? How long was he unconscious or asleep? The three Africans proved a handful earlier, but now with his hands tied behind him, what chance did he have? He considered trying to open the jerry can but thought better of it. He had no matches, but even if he could start a fire, he'd be its first victim.

The car now bounced along the dirt road, throwing Alan around the boot. He almost hit the lid on one or two occasions. He pictured what his fate might be. They were driving into the bush. Perhaps they would shoot him and burn his body or bury him in a lonely grave to be dug up by animals who'd scatter his bones far and wide. Neither option was appealing. How could he escape this predicament? His father always said one day he'd get into one scrape too many. He never imagined his father would be the one to put him in it.

Alan tried his best to find out more about his dark, confined prison. Was there something he could use to cut his bonds? A knife or screw-driver. Anything sharp. It was almost impossible to check out the interior of the boot in the blackness with his hands bound behind him. He knew most car boots had an internal release, but did this car have one? If it did, where was it? If he could open the boot, he might escape when the car slowed for a bend or other obstacle. With hands and feet bound, there was a high risk of getting killed or injured, but it was his only chance. He'd not die at the hands of a criminal thug if he could help it.

Alan remembered seeing a dark BMW parked in the courtyard off the back alleyway behind his apartment. One of his abductors stood next to it as he descended the stairs. This must be the same car. Some of these models sported folding rear seats unlocked from within the boot. Alan was thinking, thinking. What use would it be to unlock one of the back seats if all it achieved was to get him into the cab full of the thugs who abducted him? Perhaps his best chance of escape would be when they opened the boot to take him out.

* * *

The car slowed, did a three-point turn, and stopped. 'This is the spot,' said the driver.

'Out old man!' said the thug, sitting next to Luke.

'No, wait!' said the driver. 'You two deal with Drake first, and then it'll be Mr Ndlovu's turn. Close the doors behind you.'

'How many times must I tell you?' said Luke. 'We're not trying to take over your territory. It's a misunderstanding.'

'A misunderstanding killed three of our best men.'

'Yes, a mistake.'

'Tell it to the judge,' said the driver, pointing to the roof.

Scraped Face, in the front passenger seat, and the thug next to Luke, got out of the car and walked to the boot. The driver sprung the boot open.

Scraped Face forced a twisted smile through his bloody split lip. 'Now, Mr Drake, it gives me great pleasure to give you a sporting chance and set you free, but soon you'll wish I hadn't.' The man held a flashlight and a box cutter. 'Feet first', said Scrape Face. As he leant into the boot to cut the cable tie, he turned the light into Alan's eyes, blinding him with the intense beam of the military grade torch. Now roll over onto your stomach and I'll free your hands. Alan obeyed, but his mind raced, alert to grasp any opportunity to escape. The relief of having his hands free was a momentary pleasure in an impossible situation.

Everyone jumped at the piercing scream. Then another scream. The two thugs standing at the boot hopped as if on fire. 'Help! Help us, Phineas. Hurry! Hurry, Phineas!'

'What the hell now? Can't you two idiots handle him?' Phineas shouted as he grabbed his handgun from the glove box and jumped out of the car.

Alan fumbled to find the rear seat release handle. It seemed to take too long, but his memory served him well. He found one of the two handles and flicked it and heard the reassuring sound of a rear seat unlock. Alan grabbed the box cutter the thug dropped in the car, pushed the seat forward, and wriggled through into the rear of the cab. A startled Luke jumped at Alan's sudden appearance beside him. Alan was even more surprised to find Luke sitting there. Quick Luke, lock the doors!

Luke, who'd sat in quiet contemplation during the long drive, leapt into action. He slipped through between the two front seats, pulled the driver's door closed, and pressed the button that locked all the doors.

Phineas gasped at the horrific scene in front of him and turned to jump back into the car. He pulled on the door handle, but it was locked. 'Open the door!' he screamed. 'For God's sake, open the door!'

'Drive Luke! I can't see. One of those bastards blinded me with his torch.' Luke switched on the engine and pulled away, leaving Phineas to his fate. The open boot of the car bounced gently up and down as Luke drove over the rough dirt road.

The torch rolled and bounced in the boot, casting flashes of light and dark shadows into the cab. Alan slammed the rear seat shut and used the box cutter to remove the remaining cable ties around his wrists and ankles. It was a delicate task as the car bounced and swayed. In his semi-blinded state, Alan did not see what happened, but their chances of survival looked a lot brighter than only half an hour earlier.

After a short distance, the road surface improved, and Luke slowed the car. 'We better close the boot. We can't drive onto the main road with it open. It will attract attention at the roadblocks.'

The car stopped, and Alan jumped out, falling over as his cramped legs gave way. He stood up stiffly and shuffled to the car boot, with his left hand on the car roof to steady himself.

As he reached out to shut the lid of the boot, Alan saw the muzzle of a handgun, and then another blinding flash dazzled him once more. His hands were already on the boot lid, and he slammed it down as hard as possible. A yell of pain rang out as Alan heard the dull thud of metal on flesh. But in an instant, a pair of hands grabbed Alan by the throat and squeezed. Alan instinctively pulled back as hard as possible and a figure tumbled out onto the ground.

Unarmed combat was Alan's thing. Semi-blinded or not, his aggression in a situation like this made him a formidable foe. Fists, knees and elbows rained down on the shadowy figure. A final roundhouse kick followed by a cry of pain told Alan he found his mark. Suddenly in the darkness there was silence. Where was his assailant? Alan slammed the boot shut and hurried back to the car and jumped into the passenger seat.

'Go Luke, go!' Alan's eyes watered and spots danced in front of his eyes. The effects of the torch's strong beam lingered, but Alan's stiff joints forgotten in all the excitement.

'Luke, I wasn't aware those bastards brought you along for disposal.'

'They picked me up after you. I didn't know you were in the boot until we arrived in the park, and the driver told the others to deal with you first.'

'What happened? I heard screams, but I couldn't see anything.'

'Same here. It was dark and everything happened so fast. My only concern was to escape, but I was not quick enough. It must have given Phineas enough time to jump into the boot as we pulled away.'

'Where are we?'

'We're in the Hwange Park, near to where you said you spent the night in the village hut.'

'I wouldn't like to be Phineas walking alone in this area. The villagers say the Devil's Children roam here at night.'

The drive back to Bulawayo was uneventful. Luke always carried one-dollar notes, which he now handed out at each roadblock. None of the policemen asked to search inside the boot or in the vehicle. At two or three roadblocks, the policemen seemed to recognise the car and waved it through without them having to stop.

'I know a great place to leave the car,' said Alan with a wry smile. Outside the Bulawayo police station, the pair searched inside the car and in the boot. 'Look what I've found,' said Alan, holding up the handgun Phineas dropped when Alan slammed the boot lid on his hand. 'I better hang on to this. It might come in useful sometime. We're building quite a big collection of firearms thanks to those poachers.'

* * *

Alan listened, fascinated, as old Bob Jones, a former park ranger, chatted with him in the bar of the Holiday Inn in Bulawayo. It was a chance meeting, but when Alan discovered the old man's former profession, he asked him about hyenas. Luke didn't see what happened to Phineas and his henchmen, but he mentioned to Alan that there were a lot of hyenas in the area where their abductors stopped the car. Could they have attacked the three men?

'Packs of hyenas often follow lions because it's an opportunity to get food. Many people regard hyenas as cowardly scavengers, but that is not so,' said Jones. 'Some hyenas fit the stereotype, but others are different. The behaviour of spotted hyenas differs from region to region and pack to pack. Many are scavengers, while others are savage hunters. Spotted hyenas can drive lions off their kill and bring down a lone cape buffalo. The sounds of the African bush at night isn't the lion's roar but rather the cackle and hoot of hyenas on the hunt. Their calls keep the pack together and attract help from others of their kind.

'Hyenas are intelligent animals and learn fast. It is possible that a pack may learn through experience that being vocal attracts more hyenas or other predators and scavengers. They may have discovered that silence helps avoid unnecessary competition for food. I've seen hyenas approach and attack prey without making a sound.'

'How can you tell if hyenas killed a person?' Alan asked.

'Perhaps the paw prints will show if hyenas are active in an area, but unlike lions who often leave the bony parts of a victim, such as the head and hands, hyenas take everything. But in either case, other scavengers are likely to clean up any bits and pieces that remain.'

A stab pierced Alan's heart when he thought of Molly. Were hyenas the Devil's Children that the hospitable Nancy spoke of when Molly disappeared?

Alan told Bob Jones about the missing villagers and Molly. 'Well, it could be hyenas,' Jones said, 'but it's more likely a leopard was the culprit. When you searched for your missing tracker, did you check the trees? Leopards often store their kill up in the trees to keep it safe from other predators.'

'No, I didn't. Perhaps the villagers checked the trees, but there were a lot of trees in the area. It wouldn't be an easy task.'

'And don't discount lions. Leopards often attack children, but if adults are taken, it probably was lions. If a lion becomes a man-eater, other members of the pride may share the meal and then the young ones also learn to eat human flesh. The whole pride can end up as man-eaters.'

'So, the culprits might be lions, a leopard or hyenas? Anything else?'

'Lions usually eat on the spot where they made their kill. If lions killed your tracker, you probably would have found signs such as a patch of bloody ground or flattened, blood-flecked grass. It's likely any hyena tracks in the area would be from hyenas moving in after the lions finished eating. Also, hyenas and jackals often carry off any remnants from a lion kill. Leopards, on the other hand, usually move their kill to a safe place to eat at their leisure away from any scavengers. If you want my opinion, my money would be on a leopard.'

Later, Alan pondered Bob Jones' comments. Luke told him Phineas looked for a specific location in the park, and when he saw it, he said, 'This is the spot.' Phineas and his two colleagues may have delivered other unfortunate victims to the area. With each delivery of a miserable, live human, the predators would lose their fear of people and recognise a vehicle at night meant food. Why wait for the delivery van to offload one person when two healthy specimens were already standing out in the open? Ironically, with each of their horrendous crimes, Phineas and his men might have sealed their own fate by unwittingly training the predators to become man-eaters.

CHAPTER 55

HILTON Nyoka frowned. He needed to face Captain John with unwelcome news. Four months earlier, a three-man COU team disappeared without a trace. They were on a mission to buy ivory and rhino horn from poachers in the Hwange National Park. No one had seen them or the money since then. Now, a second team, assigned to deal with a troublesome rival gang, also vanished.

Hilton dawdled along the corridor, imagining the longer he took to reach Captain John's office, the better the chance he'd not be there. He knew this was a forlorn hope. Captain John never went home early, and he never left the premises without notifying him of the fact. Hilton arrived at his boss' open door and tapped softly on the door frame.

'What is it Nyoka? Bad news again?'

'What makes you say it's bad news, Sir?'

'Because, whenever you slither around my door frame, I know it will be bad news.'

'A problem with team A, Sir. Phineas and his men.'

'You needn't explain what team A is Nyoka. Do you imagine I've forgotten who makes up that team? Get on with it, man. Did they complete their mission?'

'There's no news from them, Sir.'

'Weren't they supposed to phone you as soon as they completed the job?'

'Yes, Sir, but they haven't called. I expected them to report in last night or this morning at the latest.'

'Well, perhaps they're out of cell phone range or their car broke down in a remote location.'

'That's what I thought, Sir, but there's a problem.'

'A problem? What problem?'

'Phineas and his men picked up Drake and Ndlovu last night, but our man in Bulawayo saw Drake this morning.'

'Are you sure it was Drake? All white men look alike. Perhaps your sources are wrong. Maybe it was another white man who looks like Drake. What about Ndlovu?'

'I have someone checking out his home and his office. I'm expecting them to call me soon.'

'Well then, wait until we know more. It would be impossible for Drake and Ndlovu to escape from Phineas and his team.'

'Yes Sir, but Phineas should have called us by now. Something must have happened to them.'

'Enough! Enough of this negative talk. Come back when you've got definite news. Don't waste my time until then.'

'Yes Sir.' Hilton walked back to his office, focussed on the wooden strip flooring and dragging his feet. He sat down heavily in the chair behind his desk and tapped his fingers on the ink blotter in front of him. A Scotch would go down well now. Captain John never shared his Scotch with anyone. Although Hilton was the captain's second in command, the boss never once offered him a tot from the bottle he kept locked in his desk cabinet. Perhaps he should keep a bottle of Scotch in his own desk cabinet. Johnnie Walker Red Label might not be up to the captain's high tastes, but it was better than nothing. Black Label was the least the captain would accept, but Hilton also glimpsed a bottle of Blue Label from time to time.

The phone rang.

'Yes.'

'Nyoka, is that you?'

'Yes, you idiot. Who else would answer my phone? How many times have I told you not to use my name over the phone?'

'Sorry, Nyoka. I mean, sorry Sir.'

'Get on with it, idiot. What news.'

'Ndlovu is in his office at the supermarket. I was on the pavement in front of the shop when he walked right past me.'

'And Drake? Are you sure it was him you saw this morning?'

'I'm sure. I'd stake my life on it.'

'You better be right. I will not take the blame for any false information you give me.'

Hilton walked back to Captain John's office. His boss was on the phone, so Hilton waited patiently at his door. Captain John noticed but didn't signal Nyoka to take a seat opposite him. This was the captain at his finest, showing his authority. The leader of the pack, the alpha male, was happy to leave Hilton hanging at his door. He deliberately took his time over the phone call, questioning minor details and pondering over the answers on the other side of the phone.

When John put down the phone, he called out to Hilton with an exaggerated impatience. 'Yes, Nyoka, what now?'

Hilton stepped into Captain John's office with trepidation. 'Bad news, Sir.'

'Well, come on man, out with it. Sit and let me hear the news.'

'My Bulawayo source says Ndlovu walked right past him and into the supermarket this morning. He also swears the white man he saw earlier this morning was Drake.'

Captain John sat in silence for a long time, looking at Hilton, who shuffled his feet, trying to think what he should say next. Then he spoke in a slow, patient voice. 'Well, there's only one thing for it, Nyoka. You must get rid of them yourself. I couldn't trust any of the remaining idiots here to do the job. If Phineas and his men failed, there's only you left.'

'Yes Sir.'

'Make sure it looks like an accident. If it looks suspicious, there will be a big fuss, and it might affect what little tourist industry we have left, and then the government may investigate. That's the last thing we want.'

'Any preference for how it's done, Sir?'

'You decide. I'm sick of making every decision for you all.'

'Just one thing, Sir.'

'Yes?'

'My source tells me Drake is the problem. He doesn't think Ndlovu would cause us any trouble if he was on his own.'

'So, you're suggesting we deal with Drake and leave Ndlovu for the time being?'

'Yes, Sir, if you think so.'

'OK, fine, but be it on your head if Ndlovu is still a problem when he's on his own.'

'Yes Sir. Thank you, Sir.'

CHAPTER 56

'Make sure it looks like an accident.' That's what Captain John said. It's easy for him to say, but how the hell do I do that? A car accident would look like an accident, for sure, but it was a hit-or-miss method and so many targets survived car accidents these days. Sure, it can mess them up or slow them down a little, but the client won't pay if the target is still walking and talking. Also, you need a third party to drive the other vehicle, a potential loose end which wouldn't please the captain.

Poison, hmm! That's a woman's method of disposing of a nuisance problem, but how would it look like an accident? Drug overdose or electrocution? Difficult to set up either. Fall from a building? Too many practical problems when you think about it. A robbery gone wrong? That's a possibility, especially if I do it on my own. No witnesses, no loose ends. Yes, perhaps that's the best way.

Hilton thought back to the time he dealt with his former school principal. That was easy, but dealing with Drake wouldn't be that simple. He'd be wary of a knock on the door after the abduction incident, so he'd be on guard. Also, Drake was young and fit and aggressive.

A panga would be the best weapon to use on Drake. Its long blade would keep him at arm's length. To succeed, it would have to be a surprise attack. To look like a robbery gone wrong, it needed to take place in his apartment. Drake was a professional, always on guard in public places, but the apartment was a different matter.

Hilton checked the records for Alan Drake's residential address. 'Eunice, book me on the afternoon flight to Bulawayo please.'

'Yes, Hilton. Anything else?'

'The Bulawayo Rainbow, book me into the Bulawayo Rainbow for the next three nights.'

'Three nights! Has Captain John approved that?'

'Don't worry about it. I'll sort it out with him.'

Hilton returned to his office and phoned Khumalo to arrange the things he needed for his visit. He walked down the corridor to tell Captain John of his plans but stopped short of the captain's door as he heard Eunice's voice. 'He spends a lot of money on these trips, Sir. Is it necessary for him to go for three nights?'

'I'm sure he'll have his reasons, Eunice. No one would be silly enough to take advantage of the COU's finances.'

'Well, maybe I'll book him into a standard room, Sir. That way it won't be so expensive.'

'Yes, Eunice, that's a good idea.'

Hilton stepped forward and knocked on the captain's door frame. He forced a pained smile at Eunice as she picked up a file on the desk and left the room.

'Nyoka, I don't want to know the details. Just do it.'

'Yes Sir, I have a plan.'

'Good and don't disappear on me like the others.'

'No Sir.'

'You know I will find you if you join a rival gang.'

'I would never do that, Sir.'

'Eunice says you are costing us too much money, so watch your spending on this trip.'

'Yes Sir.'

'Your last trip cost us a fortune.'

'We were a team of three on that trip, Sir.'

* * *

Hilton Nyoka walked across the tarmac to the terminal. He always enjoyed his visits to Bulawayo.

Khumalo waited at the airport to meet him. Hilton travelled light with only hand luggage, so they soon left the terminal building for the car park. 'This is the car I've hired for you. I hope it's to your liking, said Khumalo.'

'It'll do.'

'Everything you need is in the boot.'

'Good.'

Khumalo parked the Mercedes at the side of the hotel, next to his own car. 'Good luck with the mission. When you check out of the hotel, leave the car keys at reception and catch a taxi to the airport. I'll fix up the car hire from this end.'

'Do you know about my mission here?'

'Nothing, other that the items you requested.' Khumalo put his car into reverse and backed out of the parking spot and drove off into the darkness.

Hilton opened the boot of the Mercedes. It was empty except for a folded blanket. He turned up the corner of the blanket and saw the shiny silver blade of a sharpened panga. He grunted with satisfaction.

The receptionist gave Hilton an enthusiastic welcome. 'Back so soon Mr Nyoka?' Hilton smiled. If he couldn't find anything better, he might try his luck with her. On his last visit, he picked up a young woman who was more than satisfactory, but Hilton fancied variety and kept an eye out for new talent. The receptionist wasn't as glamorous, but there were compensating factors. The last young woman displayed a professional touch, but Hilton preferred an enthusiastic amateur. They tried harder and appreciated his sexual prowess. But that was for later; first, he had a job to do.

A bitter taste burned at the back of Hilton's throat when he opened the door to his hotel room. It wasn't anything like the deluxe double room he enjoyed on his last visit. The views, the room size and the proximity to the noisy nightclub combined to make for a lesser experience, an insult. That bloody bitch, Eunice! His mind returned to her overheard conversation with Captain John. She'd said something about booking a standard room, but he never thought she meant it.

Hilton picked up the phone and spoke to reception to upgrade him.

'I'm sorry, Sir, but when your secretary made this reservation, she specified a standard room. She said if you wanted an upgrade, you would have to pay the difference yourself. Do you want me to check if a deluxe room is available?'

'No, no, it's all right thanks. This room is fine.' Hilton put down the receiver. His knuckles were white and his jaw clenched. If he ever took charge of the COU, he'd give that bitch her marching orders. Three nights in a standard room! The room was fine, but it dented Hilton's pride. He'd never mention it to anyone. How could he live down this challenge to his status? It pained him to think that bitch, Eunice, down-graded him and persuaded Captain John to go along with it. What right did she have? He, second in command of the COU, and she, only the secretary.

When Eunice first came to the COU, Hilton made tentative advances, but she remained aloof and spurned him. Eunice eyed the big prize, Captain John. The boss was showing his age while Hilton was a good ten years younger. How could Eunice choose the captain over him and his undoubtedly superior performance in the areas that mattered most to the attractive young women he dated?

After a cooling beer at the bar downstairs, Hilton ate a light dinner in the hotel and focussed on the job at hand.

Outside, the streets were quiet. Even the noisy nightclub was subdued at the relatively early hour. Hilton's walk took him three blocks west down 10th Avenue and left into Fife Street, not too far from Alan Drake's apartment. He crossed the street for a better view of the apartment from over the road.

As he neared the building, he saw the apartment was in darkness. Suddenly, a voice called from the shadows. 'Are you looking for me, Sah?'

Hilton jumped at the sudden intrusion of the voice. He was embarrassed and irritated by his own involuntary reaction. 'Why would I be looking for you?'

'Something tells me you're a man of taste who'd only accept the best life has to offer.'

'And you think an ugly whore like you is the best life has to offer?'

Only then, Hilton noticed a mumbling in the shadows. Aside from the woman who spoke to him, several other women stood there. 'A rude man like you is not worthy of our attention,' one of them shouted.

Hilton stepped over to the woman and slapped her face. The woman screamed and clawed at him with her nails. He slapped her again. The women descended on Hilton like hyenas on a buck. He punched and kicked against the determined attack. The effort needed to fight them off was a lot greater than he expected.

'Hey you! Leave those women alone!'

It was Alan Drake, shouting from his balcony. It was a momentary distraction, and he ran, but not before one woman tripped him up, causing him to fall flat on his face on the pavement. He leapt up and raced down the road with the women in pursuit, shouting insults and laughing.

At the end of the block, a flushed and panting Hilton stopped and looked back. In the distance, a white man spoke to the women. Drake had raced down the steps and come to the women's aid, but they'd done well enough without him. Hilton, all too conscious of his ignominious retreat, now turned the focus of his anger from Eunice to Alan and the prostitutes. His right knee was sore from the fall.

Once a safe period passed, Hilton limped down the alley behind Alan Drake's apartment to view it from the rear. He saw the narrow fire escape leading to the landing at the apartment door. The small windows on the rear of the building, probably the bathroom and kitchen, were not within easy reach.

The balcony at the front of the building overlooked the street. Although in public view, it was the only way into the apartment. But how would he get up there? The concrete, shop-front awning over the pavement was high off the ground. If he could get onto that, it would be an easy step over the apartment's balcony wall. The prostitutes over the road were a problem as he didn't want any witnesses.

Hilton returned to the hotel to clean up after his altercation with the prostitutes. He looked in the bathroom mirror and groaned at the sight of the deep scratches on his face. His right knee throbbed. Those bloody whores are dangerous. I don't want to run into them again.

Half-past ten. Hilton set his radio alarm for one-thirty in the morning and flopped into bed. He figured the whores would have all gone home by two o'clock, and he could inspect the front of Alan Drake's apartment, undisturbed. The fight with the whores exhausted him.

When the alarm sounded, it seemed like he'd slept for three minutes, not three hours. He felt refreshed, so he must have slept well despite the noisy nightclub. Hilton hopped out of bed, forgetting about his injured right knee which collapsed under him, shooting a sharp pain through his entire leg. Perhaps if he exercised his leg, it might recover faster.

Hilton stepped out into the cool night air and limped to Fife Street where he turned left and headed to Alan Drake's apartment. This time he did not cross the road, and he approached the area with more care. From a discreet vantage point he peered into the dark shadows. He was sure no one stood there, but he waited to let his eyes grow accustomed to the dim lighting. No, no one there. The whores were gone.

Now, Hilton could examine the front of the building. There was no obvious access to the first-floor apartment. The columns, supporting the concrete, shop-front awning, were too far from the edge to be of any help in climbing onto the awning. A gutter ran around the edge of the awning and along the front of the neighbouring buildings that didn't have one. It appeared too flimsy to hold his weight, so a grappling hook wasn't the answer. Besides, a grappling hook on a concrete surface might make too much noise and alert Alan Drake to his presence.

As far as he could tell from across the road, it looked like the balcony door of Drake's apartment stood open. If he could get onto the concrete, shop-front awning, the rest would be easy. But how? He'd worry about that tomorrow. Back at the hotel by a quarter past three in the morning, Hilton placed a Do Not Disturb sign on his door.

* * *

The day dawned sunny, but soon dark rain clouds built up, threatening a heavy downpour. Hilton hoped the walk to Alan Drake's apartment in the early hours would have helped ease the pain in his right knee, but now, it seemed swollen and throbbed.

After a late breakfast, Hilton called Khumalo from his pre-paid cell phone. 'Khumalo, I want you to hire a self-drive truck with a twenty-foot container loaded on the back. A ten-foot container might also be fine. We'll need it for tonight and tomorrow night. Keep it at your place until I call you. I will tell you then what to do, but you must deliver it within half an hour of my call. Oh, and another thing. We may need the services of your friend, Hector. I've hurt my knee, and he may have to do the job for me. Warn him to be ready at short notice, day or night.'

So far, this trip provided no opportunity for play, and Hilton was more than a little irritated. Now, he had the whole day to rectify that situation, but there wasn't much in the way of entertainment in Bulawayo, during daylight hours on a weekday, and his right knee throbbed.

The day dragged, so Hilton caught up on sleep. Around six in the evening he caught the lift downstairs to the bar. He couldn't afford to drink much more because he needed his wits about him if he did the job tonight. An early dinner and early to bed. When bored, he always felt tired. Again, he put the Do Not Disturb sign on the hotel room door and set his alarm for one-thirty in the morning.

This time he found it hard to sleep. Perhaps he'd rested too much during the day, and the thump, thump of the bass music in the nightclub didn't help. Hilton snatched a little sleep, but he was already awake when the alarm sounded. He dressed, and this time he got into his car and drove slowly down towards Alan Drake's apartment.

Damn! Those women still hanging around at this hour of the morning. Hilton drove on past, under the watchful eye of the ladies, looking for one last client in the early hours. It was almost two a.m. A few blocks down the road, Hilton stopped and parked He put the driver's seat into a reclining position and closed his eyes.

Suddenly, he was awake. He checked his watch: three-thirty, no time to lose. Hilton reversed the car out of the parking and drove back towards the apartment. Even from a distance, he could make out the form of Alan Drake leaning on the balcony wall chatting with two women standing in the road. They moved aside as Hilton drove past, doing his best not to glance in their direction, in case they recognised him.

Tonight, wouldn't work. Maybe this time tomorrow. Another boring day, sleeping and waiting for the hours to pass. Damn! If I can't do it then, I'll need to extend my stay. Captain John and that bitch, Eunice, won't be happy.

* * *

At half-past one, the alarm's jarring buzzer sounded. The odd hours were taking their toll on Hilton. Tired, he forced himself from the bed. This was his last chance. If he didn't do it tonight, he'd have explaining to do. Captain John was bad enough, but with that bitch, Eunice, on his case, he felt at a disadvantage. Bugger her! She was only the secretary, and he was the second in command. Why should he worry about her? He'd seen the way Captain John watched her each time she entered or left his office. Hilton suspected that damned woman might have more influence than her position warranted.

Once again, Hilton drove towards Alan Drake's apartment. The pain in his knee didn't make driving too easy. He approached with caution and drove past slowly, straining his eyes to see if anyone stood in the shadows across the street. No one! The whores were off duty or busy elsewhere. Now was the time to act. Hilton drove his car around the corner and parked in the deep shade between two large trees. He took out his cell phone and dialled.

'Khumalo?'

'Yes.'

'I need the truck.'

'At this time of night?'

Hilton didn't answer.

'OK, OK, I'll bring it now.'

'And bring Hector with you.'

'Yes Sah.'

'You must drive to Drake's apartment and park the truck as near to the kerb as possible. The rear corner of the shipping container must be next to the corner of the awning above the pavement. Try to do it in one go so it doesn't look suspicious. Make sure the damned whores aren't standing in the shadows, over the road. Then open the trucks bonnet and stick a sign on the windscreen to let people know it's broken down or out of petrol. That should satisfy any nosey policeman, and no one will try to steal it.'

'How do you want me to disable the truck?'

'I don't know! You're the motor mechanic. Disconnect a lead or something. Make sure you can fix it and drive off after I tell you. Now hurry!'

Thirty minutes later, Khumalo startled Hilton when he tapped on the driver's side window of the car with the truck keys. 'That was quick. Have you done what I told you?'

'All done.'

'Anyone across the street?'

'No.'

'Good. Now listen, I've hurt my knee and can't climb onto the awning. Hector must stand in for me.' A wild looking man stood behind Khumalo. He had bloodshot eyes and rotting teeth, exposed by his mindless, permanent smile.

'What must he do?'

'Climb up into Drake's apartment and finish him with the panga.'

'And then?'

'Get out of there. Then you can reconnect the truck and drive it home.'

'No need. I didn't hire the truck, I stole it. We can just leave it there.'

'OK, when Hector returns, you can give me a lift back to the hotel and take the car. Even putting my foot on the accelerator is painful.'

Hilton opened the car boot, took out the panga and handed it to Hector.

'I'm glad you didn't ask me. I've never killed anybody,' said Khumalo.

'It's easy. It's no different to cutting a goat's throat.'

Hector walked to the corner of the block, made sure no one stood deep in the shadows opposite, and hurried to the truck. Just then, he noticed the approaching headlights of a police car coming down the opposite side of the street. Hector ducked behind the truck's cab. He heard the police car stop and the doors open. The voices carried in the quiet of the early hours. 'It's OK, it looks like it's broken down or run out of petrol. It will probably be gone by morning.' The policemen laughed and got back in the police car and drove off at speed.

Reaching for the handle, Hector opened the passenger door of the truck and wound down the window. He placed the panga on the roof of the cab, and with the aid of the truck door and the passenger seat he hauled himself up beside it. He then placed the panga on top of the shipping container and climbed up after it. The top of the shipping container lay almost level with the shop-front awning, and it was a simple matter for him to jump over to it. He walked across the concrete awning and peered onto Alan Drake's balcony. The door was open. Hector smiled and pulled himself up and over the balcony wall.

Hector's eyes took a minute to adjust to the darkened room. He saw the sleeping form lying in the bed and stepped towards it. The edge of his shoe caught the leg of a small coffee table hidden in the shadow below the window. The slight scraping noise on the parquet floor was enough to wake Alan. He half sat up, trying to focus his eyes. 'Who is it?'

The figure, shrouded in darkness, said nothing. Alan saw the glint of the panga's blade.

'Who are you? What do you want?'

'My name is Hector. Hilton Nyoka is my friend. He wants me to kill you.'

'Hilton Nyoka? The person who arranged Andrew Dube's abduction?'

'I know nothing about that.'

'Who's Hilton Nyoka's boss?'

'We both work for the COU.'

'What's that?'

'Did you say your prayers tonight, Mr Drake? I hope so because you don't have time for them now.'

Hector took another step towards Alan.

'Where can I find Hilton Nyoka?'

Hector didn't respond. His eyes widened, and his mouth opened, and he groaned. He stood as if in a trance, then dropped the panga and sank to the floor.

'What the hell!' said Alan.

'It's OK, Sah,' said a woman's voice. 'It's me, Joice.'

Alan snapped on the bedside lamp. A woman stood there. He recognised her as one of the women who often stood across the street. 'Quick, help me get him into the bath before he bleeds all over the floor,' said Alan. The two of them carried Hector's body, face down and placed him in the bathtub. The woman withdrew her knife from his back and rinsed it under a tap.

'Thank you,' said Alan. 'You saved my life.'

'We all watch out for you, Sah. All of us girls.'

'How did you get in here?'

Joice explained how the police sometimes fined the woman but at other times demanded favours. The two policemen demanded favours this evening, and when they finished with her, they dropped her back at her usual spot. Joice looked up at Alan's balcony to see if he was there, but then she saw Hector with his panga, standing on the top of the shipping container. Joice, young, fit and athletic, had no trouble following Hector's path into Alan's apartment. She and several of the others carried knives for self-protection, and tonight, it came in handy. Alan didn't have the heart to tell her that under the bedclothes he held his handgun while Hector was talking. Still, not having to use the handgun saved him from a lot of awkward questions from the police.

Alan did what he often did in the circumstances. He called his Instructors, Daniel and Alexander. 'I might have found you new recruits.' Alan's call at three in the morning puzzled the Instructors. 'Get here fast, there's rubbish I need removed before dawn.'

As far as Alan could tell, the bedroom was free of blood. Moving Hector to the bathroom in quick time was a good move. Daniel and Alexander arrived after what seemed like a long delay though in reality it was only thirty minutes. The Instructors took in the scene with the help of a hurried explanation from Alan. Daniel made a call, and within ten minutes a white van pulled into the back courtyard. Painted on the side, the proud sign, Prestige Butchery. Daniel and Alexander wrapped Hector's body in a large length of plastic sheeting they got from the butcher's van and struggled down the steps with the dead weight. The driver opened the back door, and they shoved Hector's body into the van. The Instructors jumped into the front seat of the van, next to the driver, and off they drove. Alan rinsed out the bathtub and everything looked back to normal. The truck that Hector and Joice used to climb up onto the shop-front awning was still there. Now, four in the morning, Alan was too keyed up to sleep. He shared a beer with Joice before she left, and then he locked his balcony door and flopped back on the bed, lying there, thinking about what might happen next.

Joice assured Alan that the evening would be their secret. In part, she honoured the undertaking. As time passed, an embellished version of her story leaked out. The other women listened in fascination as Joice related how the well-endowed white man invited her up to his apartment for an evening of drunken abandon and passionate lovemaking. With each telling, the story grew. Alan often wondered about the reverence and awe the women held him in, and what contributed to it.

CHAPTER 57

HILTON knocked on Captain John's door frame. Usually, it was a loud rat-a-tat-tat, but on this occasion, there was something tentative about it. The knock signalled to Captain John he wouldn't be pleased with the news.

'Come in Nyoka. Tell me about your trip.'

Hilton hobbled into Captain John's office. 'I injured my knee, Sir.'

'Did Drake do that to you?'

'No, Sir. I tripped on the pavement and fell on my knee.'

'And what about Drake? Is the job done?'

'I'm not sure, Sir. Because of my knee, I passed the job to Hector.'

'That crazy idiot!'

'He took the panga to go to Drake's apartment, and I watched him walk around the corner of the block. After fifteen minutes, he still hadn't returned, so we left.'

'Have you spoken to Khumalo since then?'

'Yes, Sir, there's no word from Hector.'

'This is serious, Nyoka. Hector could tell Drake all about us.'

'It won't be a problem, Sir. Hector only knows Khumalo and me. We never told him anything about you or the COU.'

'You can't be sure of that. You don't know what Khumalo may have said. What if Hector leads Drake to Khumalo?'

'He doesn't know where Khumalo lives, Sir. Khumalo always finds him when we need his services.'

'You must not use that drug crazed bastard again. He's unreliable and dangerous and could make trouble for us. Tell Khumalo to inform us as soon as he finds him, and then you can get rid of Hector. How many times must I tell you Nyoka, no loose ends? In this business you cannot risk dropping your guard.'

'Yes Sir.'

'Now go to the doctor and get your injured knee fixed. I need you fit and operational.'

Hilton returned to his office, reflecting on Captain John's questions. In particular, the questions relating to Khumalo were a concern. Hilton liked the man, and he worried Captain John may see Khumalo as a loose end and also order his disposal.

The lack of follow-up instructions for dealing with Alan Drake also troubled Hilton. Normally, his boss would instruct him to get out there and deal with the problem himself. This time, nothing. Perhaps the captain thought he needed time for his injured knee to settle down, but if that was the case why didn't he say so?

Something else worried Hilton. It nagged at him even when his focus was elsewhere. Was it one of those things he might laugh about when he realised how trivial it was? But no, this was different. What was it again? Oh, yes, that bitch Eunice.

Every time Hilton went to Captain John's office she seemed to be there, about to leave. That bitch was getting in the captain's ear. He didn't seem to confide in Hilton as much as he once did. These days, the captain always seemed keen to get him out of his office as fast as possible. Sometimes, Hilton needed to go back to check on an important detail the captain forgot to tell him. The woman was clouding the boss' judgement and threatening the effective operation of the COU. The next time Hilton found him in a receptive mood, he resolved he'd talk to him about her.

An idea came to Hilton. The captain instructed him to get rid of Hector. That meant a trip to Bulawayo, but it also gave him an opportunity for a second crack at Alan Drake. He wouldn't say anything to Captain John, but if his plan worked, it would redeem him in the captain's eyes.

Then, he'd talk to his boss about that bitch secretary. And if he failed in his second go at Alan Drake, no one would be any the wiser.

The vibration of the cell phone in his pocket interrupted Hilton's thoughts.

CHAPTER 58

JUNE 2014

Luke worried about the intruder at Alan's apartment. Would someone else come after them? They still didn't know who led the poaching syndicate and the threat they might present. Alan's team continued their guard duty outside Luke's house and business premises. Since Don's death, Avril moved back in with her parents so as not to stretch Alan's security resources too thin.

What did Daniel and Alexander do with Hector's body? All they'd say was no one would find him.

'So, you buried him in the bush?' said Alan.

'No, Sah.'

'What then?'

'Hector has been eaten, Sah.'

'You left him in the bush for wild animals to eat?'

'No, Sah.'

'No?'

'People won't find him, Sah. He is scattered everywhere.'

'So, you cut him into little pieces?'

'No, Sah, the butcher put him through the machine.'

'What machine?'

'For mince, Sah. The butcher has sold him.'

'What! He's selling Hector as mince?'

'Yes, Sah, for dogs.'

'Are you sure he won't sell him for people to eat?'

Daniel and Alexander exchanged glances as if for confirmation. 'Sure, Sah. The butcher can't sell him for people to eat.'

'Dear God, I hope you're right.'

'Perhaps, Sah, it's better if you don't buy mince for a while.'

Alan took a deep breath. Hell! what next?

* * *

The weeks passed, and Alan sensed June was once again warming to him. Nothing happened between them, but she seemed less distant and didn't make herself scarce when he visited. Perhaps she now understood the dangers that Alan faced. Maybe she reconciled to his role with her father's cause and was just being polite. But something, something about her manner gave him hope they could resume their budding, interrupted romance.

Luke still worried about the family's safety as regards the poachers. He was all too aware of the threat posed to his daughters. Everyone knew Luke's daughters were the best way to get at him. Alan was not surprised when Luke spoke of the arrangements for Rita. 'It's one of the best private schools in Johannesburg with an excellent academic record, and it will prepare her for university. Rita has always wanted to follow in June's footsteps and go to Wits after she finishes school.'

Alan nodded in agreement, but the next bit of news disturbed him.

'June has applied for a two-year, postgraduate, business administration course in New York. The girls will be out of harm's way until the trouble blows over and we're safe again.'

'That's good Luke,' said Alan, trying not to show his disappointment. Just when June's attitude towards him seemed to thaw, a new obstacle threatened their relationship. 'When will she go?'

'The semester starts in August. Not so long now. June will stay with my sister, her aunt. I'd like her to leave as soon as possible to settle in before the semester. It's just a matter of waiting for final confirmation from the university that they have a place for her.'

Luke's news put Alan in a bind. There was little time to further improve his relationship with June. A two-year separation would challenge them both. With the uncertainty surrounding their relationship, Alan pondered what to do. They needed a frank discussion on where things lay between them. A schism in any relationship was hard to mend, especially in one as new as theirs.

* * *

Far sooner than Alan hoped, confirmation arrived of June's successful application for a place at the university in New York. Preparations for her departure moved forward at a pace. In the meantime, Luke's business had to carry on as normal. 'Alan, June must attend a quarterly meeting with one of our suppliers in Harare. I have an important business meeting on Monday afternoon. Would you mind taking June to the airport and seeing her off safely?'

No, Alan didn't mind. He wanted time alone with June. 'Luke, is it wise for June to go to Harare, given the situation with the poachers.'

'Oh, yes. It's a private meeting with the supplier. June has done this often. She won't leave the hotel at night, and on Tuesday morning she'll go straight to the meeting. In the afternoon she'll go direct from the supplier to the airport and catch the early evening flight back to Bulawayo.'

* * *

On Monday afternoon, Alan drove to Luke's house to find June waiting at the front door. 'I'm not late, am I?'

'No, I'm early.'

Alan picked up her overnight case and put it on the back seat of the old Land Rover. With a hoot and a wave to Enid, they drove out onto Park Avenue and were on their way. With plenty of time before the early evening flight to Harare, Alan drove slowly through the city blocks before turning right into Fife Street and past his apartment.

They sat in silence until they emerged from the matrix of the city streets. Alan spoke first. 'I will miss you when you go to New York. I know I disappointed you. It's the last thing I wanted, and I'm sorry that things got so mixed up between us.'

'No, I'm sorry that I acted like such a fool. I see everything more clearly now. I'm sorry that I wasted so much of our time together.'

'Could we start over again, from square one?'

'Yes, we could try.'

'Your father is doing what's best for your safety. I also want you to be safe. Bulawayo is a dangerous place for you girls right now. And just imagine, you'll come back with all that new business knowledge to help your father in his business.'

'Will you be here when I return from New York?'

'If you want me, I'll be waiting here at the airport to meet you when you come back.'

'Yes, I do! I want you here, waiting for me.'

'Can I pick you up tomorrow evening?'

'Yes, just tell my Dad you'll meet me.'

Alan's stomach tightened as they turned into the short road leading to the airport. Already there, so soon, the drive was short and much left unsaid.

After parking the Land Rover in front of the terminal building Alan carried June's overnight bag to the check-in counter. Something about airports, even small airports, made everything seem rushed. Even worse, it was hard to remember all the important last-minute words he wanted to say. The time had come. They hugged. June kissed Alan on the lips and said, 'When I go to New York, you will write to me, won't you?'

'Yes, but will you reply?' The smile Alan got in response to his question was all the answer he needed.

June walked out of the departure gate, over the tarmac and up the stairs to the plane. She turned and waved before disappearing through the dark entrance. Alan couldn't see her after that. Perhaps her seat was on the far side of the plane.

Alan watched the plane take-off and stood there seeing it get smaller and smaller in the distance until the tiny spot disappeared altogether. He drove back to town with mixed feelings. It thrilled him their relationship promised a fresh start. In New York she'd be beyond the reach of the poachers, but already he missed her. June was going overnight to Harare, but then they'd have only a few, short weeks before a much longer separation. Alan wasn't at all sure how he'd deal with that.

CHAPTER 59

HILTON answered the call on his cell phone. He was relieved to hear Khumalo's voice, the one man he could rely on and trust. Friends in the COU were becoming harder to come by these days.

'Khumalo, have you caught up with Hector?'

'No, Sah. I've tried to contact him to find out what happened in Drake's apartment. So far, there's no reply. Drake may have done him in.'

'OK, but if you find him, we've got another job for him.'

Hilton hoped Hector was still alive. He needed him for the excuse to visit Bulawayo for a second go at Drake.

'I've got more news, Sir.'

'Yes, what?'

'This afternoon at the airport, I saw Drake saying goodbye to an African woman, catching the plane to Harare.'

'Are you sure it was Drake?'

'Yes, I'm certain.'

'Rumours are, Drake is going out with one of Luke Ndlovu's daughters.'

'That must be the one then. He kissed her goodbye.'

'Is she pretty?'

'She's beautiful.'

'What a waste! Wasted on a white man.'

'She's dressed in a black business suit and carried a red travel bag.'

'That is interesting, Khumalo. Thanks for letting me know, but you must understand there's nothing we can do about her. Captain John does not like us using family members to achieve his goals. Some say it's his only weakness.'

Hilton ended the call and looked at his wristwatch. The Bulawayo flight would land in Harare in about half an hour.

CHAPTER 60

CAPTAIN John raged. 'Dammit, Eunice, what the hell is happening in Matabeleland? Phineas and his men disappear without a word or any trace, and now, Hector has also gone.'

'Khumalo's people in Bulawayo found Phineas' car parked in front of the police station, Sir.'

'Isn't that where they found Michael Duze's car?'

'Yes, Sir. Perhaps the police are behind all this.'

'It wouldn't surprise me. I've never trusted them. They're criminals in uniform.'

'Not all, Sir.'

'Why do we bother with police contacts if they don't tell us what's happening down there?'

'Well, we've asked them, but so far there's no news.'

'Any news of Drake and Ndlovu?'

'Yes, Sir, I spoke with Khumalo, and he says they've seen Luke Ndlovu and Alan Drake going about their business as normal. Phineas and his men had gone missing without completing their task, and now, Nyoka has also failed in his mission. Khumalo says he and Nyoka waited in the car for Hector, but he never came back. When they drove past Drake's apartment, the lights were on, so Khumalo suspects something must have gone wrong. He drove Nyoka back to the hotel and then returned home.'

Captain John dropped his head and exhaled. 'They must have all gone over to Ndlovu and Drake's gang.'

'Perhaps not, Sir. All our buyers are complaining about the reduced supply of ivory. If our men joined Ndlovu's gang, wouldn't they sell to our buyers? Khumalo says there's no evidence that Ndlovu and Drake are poaching. His men can't find any store of ivory, and no one has approached the buyers to fill the gap. Don Nkomo sold most of our Hwange harvest to the Korean doctors, so if the remaining buyers are complaining of a shortage of ivory, there must be a significant drop in supply.'

'OK, Eunice, perhaps we should wait to see what develops. If Ndlovu and Drake are not poaching, our men may be with another gang or are working for themselves.'

'Yes, Sir, or perhaps they've been arrested or killed by park rangers or rival poachers.'

'We would have heard if they'd been arrested, Eunice.'

'If they've joined another gang, it might be one with a base here in Harare and who use different buyers.'

'This is our worst attrition rate since the business that ended the first COU.'

'You must tell me about it one day, Sir. I understand you hate the people responsible, but why? What happened?'

'Two former operatives turned against the COU. They weren't only a threat to us, but potentially, an embarrassment to the government. I wanted to hunt them down and eliminate them, but I was ordered "to let sleeping dogs lie". The COU was a quasi-government operation then. They seconded me from the army to run the COU, so I followed orders. After COU operations were suspended, they transferred me back to a boring role in the army supply stores. Then, I came into money and resigned my commission. Now the COU is my private business, and I'm no longer beholden to government or anyone else.'

'Was it ever a government operation, Sir?'

'I thought it was, but I never found out where my orders originated. An anonymous voice on the phone gave me my instructions. The targets were dissidents or critics of the government, so I presumed the orders came from state security. Given the status of some targets, I expect the word came down from on high. They covered all our expenses in cash and always paid our fees on time.'

Captain John's pretty secretary sat opposite him on the other side of the desk. She crossed her legs, giving John a flash of lace underwear. Eunice knew how to cheer up her boss.

'That Nyoka, he is too ambitious, always rushing in when he should first consider the situation. You're the only one I can rely on, Eunice. Can I pour you a glass of Scotch, My Dear?'

Eunice smiled. Captain John loved his Scotch and never offered it to anyone. This was an exception. She appreciated the Scotch wouldn't come free, and she'd have to give something in return. But then, she was happy to oblige. Bit by bit, she gained John's trust. Eunice studied for an arts degree at the University of Zimbabwe. Quick on the uptake, smart and alert, she prided herself on being a step ahead of the men in the office, including Captain John and Hilton Nyoka. Her pay and conditions improved faster than any man in the COU. Eunice liked to think it reflected her value to the organisation, but she was not naïve. She had something the men didn't, and she was prepared to use it.

'I'll just make sure everyone has left and lock up the office, Sir. The men are so unreliable about locking the windows and doors before going home.' Eunice did not have a high regard for the other operatives in the office and disliked Hilton Nyoka in particular. As his star faded, her confidence grew. She was determined no one else in the COU would have Captain John's ear before her. The boss didn't know it yet, but she aimed to be his number two, and she'd make sure it stayed that way. But first, she needed to get rid of Hilton. The possibilities amused her, but she could wait. No hurry. Eunice was in her early twenties and time was on her side. From listening to Captain John speak, she deduced over-ambitious subordinates did not impress her boss.

John poured the Scotch into two crystal glasses. One for Eunice and one for himself. He cleared everything off his leather-topped desk except for the two glasses of Scotch. The young woman appeared to understand him better than anyone else. John would now test how deep that understanding went.

Moments later, Eunice walked into the room, saw the cleared desk and stopped. 'What's happened to your desk, Sir? Would you like me to polish it?'

'Yes, Eunice. Something like that.'

Eunice at once understood why John cleared his desk. His intentions were transparent, and she'd long known this moment would come. Up till now, she played the demure innocent secretary. Surrendering herself to her egotistical boss would bring high dividends, especially if he thought he was in control.

'Eunice, it's time we talked about your future. You could go far in this business.'

CHAPTER 61

Early evening, the next day, Alan waited at the airport for June's flight from Harare. He'd arrived well before the plane's scheduled arrival and could hardly wait for her to emerge from the dark entrance into which she disappeared the previous day. At last, suddenly and unannounced, the plane dropped out of the sky. A nice smooth touchdown, the slow taxiing to the terminal, and the usual frustrating wait for the plane door to open and the passengers to stream out.

Alan focussed on every person who walked down the steps from the plane. No, not that one, or that one. Any minute now.

The passengers emerging through the plane doors slowed to a trickle, and then after a longish gap, the air hostesses emerged. Alan walked to the information desk to enquire about June.

'I'm sorry, Sir, we can't give out that information.'

'I'm supposed to pick up a passenger, but I didn't see her get off the plane.'

'If you didn't see them get off the plane, Sir, you can assume they weren't on it.'

Alan tapped the number into his cell phone. 'Luke, June didn't arrive on the flight. Did she miss it?'

'Hang on, I'll check with Enid. Perhaps she phoned and left a message.'

Alan waited, watching the arrivals gate, in case June was late getting off the plane.

'Alan, June hasn't called home. I've tried to call her on her cell phone, but there's no reply. I'll phone my contact at the supplier. Maybe he can tell me something. I'll call you as soon as I find out anything. In the meantime, why don't you come to the house and wait with us for news?'

The drive to Luke's house seemed to take forever. Alan drove as fast as he dared. Aside from the condition of the road, he didn't want to risk attracting the police who always looked for an excuse to fine motorists.

Alan arrived at the house to find an anxious looking Enid standing by the front door. 'Luke's on the phone talking to his supplier. Have you heard anything?'

'No, nothing.' Alan's temples throbbed and seemed to be constricting. He was conscious he squinted with the strain.

Luke came out of his office, his face drawn. 'He says they held their usual meeting with June this morning, followed by lunch. They booked a taxi for three o'clock to take June to the airport to catch her flight. Johnson always takes her to the airport, but today he had another meeting to attend. I phoned the airline. They're looking into it and will phone me back.'

A moment later the phone rang, and Luke hurried back to his office to answer it. Enid and Alan followed and stood by the door as Luke listened on the phone in silence.

'What does the airline say?' asked Alan.

'They say June was a no-show. If they find out anything more, they will call me.'

'Perhaps she caught another plane with a different airline?'

'There are few alternatives, but I'll phone the airport and check if any other plane left for Bulawayo.'

'If she changed her plans she would have phoned,' said Enid. 'Luke, phone the hotel and see if she checked out.'

Several phone calls later, the family's options ran out. Luke, Enid and Alan looked at each other in stunned silence, each with their own thoughts and fears. The worst part was their collective feeling of frustration and helplessness. What to do?

'Tomorrow, I'll go to Harare and speak to the suppliers June met with this morning,' said Luke. 'Johnson might have overlooked some detail that can help us. Alan, you stay here and look after things in Bulawayo.'

'Perhaps June missed the flight and stayed in Harare for a second night at a different hotel?' said Alan.

'Never,' said Enid, 'she would have phoned us straight away. She's very responsible.'

The airport confirmed there were no other flights from Harare that evening. Alan returned to the apartment, but trying to relax or sleep was beyond him. Luke needed rest before heading off to Harare the next day, and the family went to bed, sick with worry. Alan paced around the apartment with a sense of helplessness. What to do and where to start? If anyone could locate June, it would be Luke, with his connections in that city.

Alan sat in an armchair, but that wouldn't help find June. He stood up again and paced around like a caged lion. His dark thoughts settled on killing anyone involved in harming June. But who, and how to find them? He walked out onto the balcony, and the women across the road greeted him, but Alan was not in the mood for small talk or banter. Back inside the apartment Alan called Daniel and Alexander to come in for a confab.

No news from Luke or the family, and Alan was desperate. It was getting late when the knock on the door signalled Daniel and Alexander's arrival. It seemed like ages since Alan called them, but only twenty minutes had passed.

'Is there anything we can do?' Alan asked.

'Sah, we are Ndebele,' said Daniel. 'Harare is not our town.'

'I have a cousin who lives in Harare,' said Alexander. 'Perhaps he can do something. The problem is, he works for a bank and doesn't move amongst those people involved in criminal activity. He is a straight fellow. Not much fun. Doesn't drink or smoke cigarettes or go with women. His wife is very strong. He wouldn't risk making her angry. But I can ask him if he knows anyone who can help.'

'Thank you, Alexander. Any little piece of information might help,' said Alan as he opened another round of beers for his two friends.

* * *

The next morning Alan phoned Luke, but there was no news. Like Alan, the family spent a sleepless night, worrying and wondering.

'If I find June, I'll phone you straight away,' said Luke. 'If not, I'll call you tonight and tell you what's happening. Alan, please keep an eye on the family. We're all beside ourselves with worry.'

Luke had no news to give that evening, or the next. Alan heard the weariness creeping into Luke's voice as he lost hope of finding June. A cold, heavy sensation settled in Alan's core, and an icy hand seemed to twist at his heart.

Alexander's cousin was little help, though he made enquiries with every Ndebele he knew in Harare. A few suggestions came back from Alexander's cousin, but Luke had already tried them. Alan suggested making enquiries with Shona contacts, but either these were limited, or Alexander's cousin's associates were reluctant to go down that path. Luke's Shona contacts also came up with nothing.

Sleepless nights, frustration, helplessness and hoping for a miracle, day after day, wore down Alan and the family. They were all exhausted, their emotions ragged. Alan even put the word out on the street, through the women who stood opposite his apartment every night. They spoke to others and even spoke to the police. No one knew anything. June, June, where are you, the voice in Alan's head screamed. The situation was beyond bearing. Each member of the family suffered in their own way. None of them expected anything like this. It can't be happening; it can't be true! Every morning was a new coming to terms with the dreadful reality of the situation.

Luke spoke to the prostitutes he saw loitering in the Avenues in Harare. Many were reluctant to speak to the Ndebele visitor from Bulawayo, while others talked of bad men who'd do anything for money.

None of the information Luke uncovered provided any lead to June or her abductors.

The days of the week dragged, with no news of June and not a single lead to follow. The family and Alan were frantic, paralysed with worry. What was the next step? The police in Bulawayo referred the matter to the police in Harare. No one seemed interested in following up on June's disappearance. Luke showed June's photo to everyone who worked at the airport in Harare. Nobody, it seemed, saw or recognised her. The taxi company claimed there was no sign of June when the taxi arrived to pick her up from Luke's supplier's premises. Johnson said, if it were not for his other meeting, he would have waited on the pavement with her or taken her to the airport as usual.

A second week passed. Luke advertised in Harare and Bulawayo and put up posters with June's photograph on lamp posts. In no time, vandals defaced them or tore them down, scattering them on the ground. Apart from family and friends, it seemed no one cared. After two weeks or exhaustive searching, Luke returned to Bulawayo, defeated.

It pained Daniel and Alexander they couldn't help Alan in the search. The strain left the family shattered, and Alan, sick and empty. All his hopes dashed. He concluded he was a curse on the people who meant anything to him. Molly's death was bad enough, and he'd only had a working relationship with her. But this was too much to bear. His relationship with June was so much deeper. After their farewell at Bulawayo airport, all Alan's waking thoughts focussed on their rekindled romance. Now, he tried to resist dwelling on what might have been, but that proved impossible. It only made his loss harder to endure.

Alan's feelings for June differed from anything he'd ever experienced The world seemed brighter when all was well between them, and he bubbled with energy and enthusiasm. When they were at odds, he felt lonely and apathetic. But now, with the renewed promise of their romance so cruelly snatched away, Alan burned with a hollow bitterness. He raged at the unknown enemy he imagined responsible. He alternated between promises to himself he'd make them suffer and the debilitating awareness he didn't have a clue as to their identity.

Then, one name sprang to mind; the name that might lead to finding out what happened to June. His father, George, told him about Hilton Nyoka, the mysterious African man he thought responsible for Andrew Dube and Tyson's disappearance. Peter Nkala and Luke tried once before to find Hilton Nyoka. They'd come up with nothing, just like Luke's unsuccessful search for June. No one recognised his name. It seemed as if he didn't exist.

June's disappearance ate away at Alan like a cancer. Losing June drove him mad with rage. What unimaginable agony must her family be suffering? As the weeks passed, Alan could stand it no longer. The city he'd grown to love now seemed dead to him. He couldn't focus on his work or enjoy the banter with the prostitutes across the street from his apartment. He still liked to visit Luke and the family, but they'd gone through the same grieving process as him. The memories of June hung heavy over Luke's house, making light-hearted conversation impossible. Dinner at Luke's was a silent affair, a time for reflection.

Slowly, Alan's mind turned to going home to Melbourne. First, he had a duty to perform. He needed to keep the promise he made to Nancy at the village on the edge of the Hwange National Park.

CHAPTER 62

OCTOBER 2014

Alan and Luke drove down the Victoria Falls Road with the music playing and the car windows open. Luke was ready with a wad of US one-dollar notes, so they expected no trouble at the roadblocks. Alan was relaxed, more so than in a long time. They chatted about everything bar the project. When they passed through Kenmaur, one hundred and forty-five kilometres from Bulawayo, Luke remarked, 'Only thirty to go.'

Before leaving Bulawayo, Luke checked the MFF records for the address Alan needed. Soon they drove into Lupane. 'I remember this area in the old days, said Luke. With people moving to the country and all the development that's gone on, it's not as wooded as it used to be. It once was quiet and rural, but now it has grown into a town.'

Helpful locals gave them directions to their destination. Luke's Mercedes rolled to a graceful stop in front of the neat little house. It was nothing special but looked loved.

Two young girls and a boy came to the front door, curious about the visitors in the big car. Then, behind them appeared the figure of a mature African woman. 'Mrs Sibanda?' said Alan.

'Yes, I am Mary Sibanda.'

Luke and Alan introduced themselves, and Mary invited them into the house and asked her older daughter to put the kettle on for tea.

'You have a nice home, Mrs Sibanda,' said Alan accepting the cup of tea Mary handed him.

'Yes, it's small but cosy. For the first two years after my husband left for Johannesburg, we lived with my family in our traditional village. But the children needed to go to school, and my parents helped me get this place.'

Alan took out Dr Sibanda's passport from his pocket and gave it to Mary. She looked at it, and tears came to her eyes. Alan explained where the passport was found and related his and Luke's experience in the car in the same area. 'Perhaps your husband travelled in the same car as the one used in our abduction. It might be a comfort for you to know he didn't die far away in Johannesburg, but close by here, on his way to see you. This is the gift he planned to give you.' Alan handed Mary the gold bracelet found with the passport and given him by Nancy in the village bordering the Hwange National Park. 'I'm sure he also brought gifts for the children, but this was all the villagers found.'

Mary was overcome with the news, and grateful Alan and Luke had taken the trouble to find her and tell her what happened to her husband. 'Now I can rest,' said Mary. 'I have waited in hope my beloved husband would walk through the door one day, but in my heart, I knew he never would. Bless you two for coming so far to find me. My husband's spirit can now also rest.'

Alan and Luke waved goodbye to Mary and the children as they drove away. 'I'm so glad we took the time to come here,' said Alan, a lump rising in his throat. 'Imagine, that poor woman, waiting, wondering what happened to her husband, knowing the MFF leadership wrote him off as dead.' The irony of the situation had not escaped Alan, for he and the family were in the same situation regarding June.

* * *

June's disappearance hung over the family like a heavy, dulling presence. For Alan, it was no different. He hadn't disclosed his last conversation with June to any family member. As a result, he bore a deep wound as he grieved alone. Alan was torn between a need to flee the memories, and the feeling that leaving Bulawayo would be a betrayal of June and her family.

The winter days since her disappearance were grey with cold, blustery winds. The dust blew into Alan's eyes, making them feel gravelly, and his lips, fanned by Bulawayo's bone-dry winter air, cracked into crazy paving patterns. Alan lay on his bed in the apartment on Saturday and Sunday afternoons. He needed to be alone. It was a far cry from the fun afternoons he'd spent at Luke's house when he and June first kindled their relationship.

Alan avoided Avril as he struggled to combat his guilt about Don's imprisonment and murder. He could rationalise he wasn't responsible but for the nagging thought his activities contributed to it. He would understand if Avril blamed him. Now, she was inscrutable, and Alan couldn't read her mind. At first, the events following their illicit night together buried the guilty secret they shared. But now, Don's death, followed by June's disappearance, seemed to twist a knife in Alan's conscience.

Three months passed since the attempted abduction of Luke and Alan. They both considered the danger to their personal safety no longer existed.

Luke tried to persuade Alan to give it more time. 'I still need security guards for my business. Especially now the economy is deteriorating again.'

'You built your business without me, Luke. I'm sure you'll manage well with Avril working by your side.'

'I'm sorry things soured between you and June. For a moment I imagined...'

'What did you imagine, Luke?'

'Luke smiled. It doesn't matter now. How does that old saying go? There're many pebbles on the beach. I'm sure there'll be other suitable sons-in-law waiting for me somewhere. Avril may get married again at some point, and then, there's Rita.'

The two men laughed. Their relationship developed over time from colleagues in a conspiracy to one of an easy friendship.

'If it's any consolation, Luke, when I took June to the airport that Monday, she and I agreed to start over again.'

'I'm pleased to hear that, Alan. Before you, June wasn't interested in men. All her focus was on work. She must have seen something special in you. Just like I have.'

When the time came for Alan's departure, Enid cooked a farewell dinner of roast beef, roast potatoes, green peas, carrots, onions and gravy with minced horseradish on the side. The family toasted Alan with a bottle of Cabernet Sauvignon from Luke's stock.

What did the family members think about him and his departure? Alan knew Luke's view, and Enid had been nothing but gracious towards him. Did Avril resent him? Not only had she lost her husband but also her favourite sister. If he hadn't come to Zimbabwe, they might still be alive. Don may have walked a dangerous line, but June would still be there. Alan couldn't shake the thought he was running out on the family. But Bulawayo without June was unbearable for him.

Luke, Enid and Avril took Alan to the airport the next morning.

'You will write?' said Luke.

'Well, I might send an occasional text or email a line or two. Soldiers aren't good at corresponding, except for the night before the final battle. That's when what's really important comes to the fore.'

Enid kissed Alan on the cheek and Avril gave him a big hug and a kiss. Luke shook Alan's hand and then also gave Alan a hug. 'Remember, you are always welcome in my home.'

Alan and the other passengers walked out onto the tarmac to the steps leading up to the plane. He sat in the window seat and waved to the distant trio who seemed to be the only ones seeing off the plane. The engines started, and the plane taxied to the end of the runway before it turned, ready for take-off. The engines increased their pitch to a scream, and the plane shook, and then the pilot released the brakes. Alan waved to the distant figures in the airport building, and in a moment, he was gone.

This time Alan didn't stop in Johannesburg. Ruth and Solly were in Cape Town, so he caught a connecting flight to Perth and then on to Melbourne. The miles flew by; had he made a mistake? As the distance between Alan and the family grew, a creeping suspicion washed over him that one cannot run and hide from one's memories.

What was there for him in Melbourne other than his dominating father who would try to drag him into his business? Yes, it would provide him with money, but Alan understood it wouldn't be a free ride. His father fought and clawed his way to the top, and he'd expect Alan to do the same. It was not Alan's idea of how he wanted to spend the rest of his life.

CHAPTER 63

OCTOBER 2015

Alan sat at the bar counter, nursing his beer. Back in Melbourne for almost a year, he was bored. Ten to twelve hours a day in his father's business was no pleasure, and the longer he worked there, the more he realised that way of life was not for him. The manner in which Alan's stint in Matabeleland ended displeased George Drake. 'I told you to get in there and train up the locals, not start a bloody war with the poachers and God knows who else.'

George understood Alan had little choice but to leave Zimbabwe when he did. The project was at risk of exposure and premature termination. George resented the need to defer the plans for Mthwakazi he made with Andrew Dube.

'Where's this strategic mind your officer training course was supposed to give you? Was your effort the best the Australian special forces could produce?'

'What's the point of sending me on a hair-brained scheme when criminals and supporters of the other side have infiltrated the people I'm supposed to be training. And don't forget, the Chiang Mai Group, not me, suggested using the poachers for training the recruits.'

'Only one of your men worked with the poachers.'

'Yes, but they infiltrated the MFF committee, and they received copies of all my reports. The project was doomed from the start when Andrew Dube and his son Tyson went missing.'

'That was unfortunate. Mr Wong, my Singapore office manager, appeared trustworthy. I don't know how he got tied up with Hilton Nyoka and his abduction plot. Anyway, that greedy little Chinese bastard paid the price.'

'What do you mean?'

'Well, we couldn't risk having him around once he betrayed us.'

'You mean, you organised his—'

'Wong jumped, someone pushed him, I organised it, Hilton Nyoka organised it, what difference does it make?'

'This whole business is getting more and more smelly.'

'Well, next time, make sure you involve yourself only in low-key basic training. No more heroics.'

'I doubt there'll be a next time. And as for heroics, make sure your contacts in Zimbabwe understand why I'm there. They seemed to think I'd lead them into battle.'

'So, you will go back if we clarify your role?'

'No, never, not in the foreseeable future.'

'Well, decide! Which one is it?'

Alan snorted in disgust, picked up his jacket and retreated to the bar of The Elephant and Wheelbarrow Hotel in Fitzroy Street in St Kilda.

Since leaving the army, Alan lost touch with his army buddies and made no new friends in civvy street. He'd spent his time drinking and chasing girls for one-night stands. His only clear direction since leaving the army was the spell in Zimbabwe. Alan also missed Luke and his two Instructors, Daniel and Alexander, and it occurred to him they were his only real friends.

Alan regretted the way things ended with June. So much time wasted in their short relationship. Their last goodbye at Bulawayo airport held so much promise, and for the first time in his life he'd entertained serious thoughts of the future. Would she have laughed at him, doubting his serious intent?

June briefly resented Alan for the death of Henry, her childhood friend. It might just as easily have been him who was killed instead of

Henry. Only after Alan's narrow escape from the intruder in his apartment, did June seem to understand the risks that came with his job. But what the hell! His father didn't seem to appreciate the risks either.

Then there was Avril whom he avoided after Don's death. He felt bad about her situation and would understand if she resented him. But Alan often relived that wonderful night with Avril. For a brief period, he'd been closer to her than he ever was with June. He thought about both sisters often.

Since his return to Melbourne, Alan reverted to the social life he led before his Zimbabwe escapade, but it no longer satisfied him. One evening in a wine bar, across the room, he saw Gail, the attractive young woman he'd taken back to his apartment the night before he left for South Africa. She chatted to an attentive young man, no doubt raising his hopes with her flirtatious manner. Alan didn't even bother to approach her and say hello. Instead, he left before she noticed him. He realised one can never go back. Even his luxurious apartment seemed dull and uninteresting. Life moves on, and the experiences one goes through changes them. Chasing women for the pleasure of the hunt led to one-night stands. Alan no longer enjoyed the process or the result. Each of his successes seemed empty, and instead of boosting his ego, they somehow diminished him. And worse still, he drank too much.

Alan emptied the beer glass and waved to the bartender. As he took his first sip from the new glass, he heard a beep on his cell phone. A text message from Luke!

Government of Zimbabwe advertising for hunters to eradicate one or more man-eating leopards, terrorising villages on the edge of the Hwange National Park. Thought you might like to know. Regards, Luke.

CHAPTER 64

JOHANNESBURG's O.R. Tambo International Airport was as bustling as ever when Alan's South African Airways flight from Australia landed in the early evening. As usual, he was travelling light, so all he needed to do was grab his carry-on bag and head for immigration and customs. Once out of the terminal building, he walked across the road and into the Intercontinental Johannesburg O.R. Tambo Airport Hotel. Alan booked on the early morning flight to Bulawayo, and the Intercontinental was the most convenient. He didn't contact the Bernstein's, and he'd not even told his father he was heading to Zimbabwe; that was something to worry about later.

* * *

The plane banked to its right and aimed for the runway. Alan saw the skyline of Bulawayo in the distance. It seemed like he was coming home. As he descended the steps of the plane, he breathed in the cool, early morning breeze that often preceded a blistering hot day. The long yellow grass, that covered the undulating open country adjoining the airport swayed gently in the breeze, looking somewhat like a low swell on the ocean.

Ever since he received Luke's text message, a fire burned within him He couldn't wait to get back into the Hwange National Park and dea with the Devil's Children. Alan recalled poor Molly, who asked little o. life, and life obliged. Every time Alan thought back to that fateful nigh his anger grew. The last time he was in Zimbabwe events overtook him and he never even considered the possibility of eliminating the awful presence that terrorised the villagers on the boundary of the national park.

Immigration and customs were slower than ever, but Alan didn't mind. He was relaxed and free from the yoke of time. Luke waited in the terminal, beaming from ear to ear, impatient to see Alan once again. 'Welcome back my friend. For me, the sun shines brighter this morning.' The two men hugged each other. 'I have missed you, as have the others.'

'So, Daniel and Alexander and the MFF committee also missed me, did they?'

Luke smiled and opened the car boot with his key. 'Well, I'm sure Daniel and Alexander did. The committee must speak for itself.'

Alan put his bag into the car boot and slammed it shut. Luke got into the Mercedes and Alan opened the passenger door and jumped in beside him.

'Enid is preparing your favourite meal for dinner tonight.'

'If Enid is cooking, I know it will be delicious.'

The drive from the airport cleared Alan's head and his lungs. The air smelled fresh after the overnight rain. Alan sat back in the plush leather seat and lapped up the familiar surroundings and sites and every kilometre of the drive to Luke's house. It reminded him of his drive back from the airport that evening when June didn't emerge from the Harare flight. It tugged at his heart. The Devil's Children first, and then he'd deal with whoever was responsible for June's disappearance. Alan often fantasised about avenging June, but he knew it would never happen if he remained in Melbourne and might not even happen in Zimbabwe.

Preoccupied with his thoughts, Alan struggled to respond to the barrage of questions from Luke. This did not detract from the pure pleasure of his return though it made it difficult for Alan to concentrate on Luke's inquisition.

The big Mercedes turned into Luke's driveway, and Alan heard the familiar scrunch of the large tyres on the gravel. He jumped out and lifted his bag from the open boot of the car. As they came to the front door, it flew open and a pair of arms flung themselves around Alan and hugged him tightly.

'Avril!' Alan caught his breath. She looked wonderful: beautiful, slender, and...

'Guess what we're having for dinner tonight.'

'I don't have to guess; I already know. Your dad told me.'

'Mum's in the kitchen. Come and say hello.'

'Your mum always forbade me to enter the kitchen.'

'Well, times have changed.'

* * *

After all the greetings were over, Enid showed Alan to his room. They walked down the familiar passage with Luke's home office on the left. They passed Rita's room on the right and stopped at the second door. 'We've put you in here,' said Enid.

Alan stepped through the doorway he'd often dreamed of entering. His throat constricted, causing a choking sensation as he whispered, 'June's room.' Alan was conflicted. For the first time he saw what her room looked like, her views into the garden, the faint scent of her favourite perfume and the bed she slept in each night. The room was welcoming, but it brought back the terrible memories and the sense of helplessness he suffered when he was last in Bulawayo.

'Avril is next door to you,' said Enid, cutting into Alan's thoughts, 'and Luke and I are at the end of the passage.'

The afternoon flew by as Alan and the family caught up with each other's news. Enid and Avril joined them for a time before leaving the two men alone. Luke handed Alan a Scotch on the rocks and they chatted as they watched the evening rain come down, pockmarking the garden bed outside the window. 'So, you'll be spending time in the Hwange National Park, chasing The Devil's Children?'

'Yes, I needed to come and help them with that problem. While I'm there, I'll look up Nancy, the hospitable woman who sheltered us that night on the edge of Hwange Park. I'll give her two or three camp beds and new blankets.'

Alan remembered how closely Luke's youngest daughter, Rita, resembled June. He was almost afraid of seeing her again because of the memories it would bring back, but he had to ask. 'Luke, where is Rita?'

'She's at school in Johannesburg. We won't see her again until the Christmas holidays.'

'And the MFF? What news there?'

'We put the project on hold. When Simon Kholose was shot at his house, his father, Senior Kholose, at first blamed your team and threatened to tell the authorities about the MFF and our plans. I think he eventually accepted we weren't responsible, but there's always that niggling suspicion he might act on his threats. Then, with your departure, a few of us in the inner circle decided we needed to rethink our strategy.

'Senior Kholose is not a well man, and it's rumoured he may die any day now. The inner circle thinks we should wait until that happens, as the risk of exposure is too great. The other thing we decided is we'll not include anybody who shows signs of strong political ambition. Peter Nkala is our president, but he would be happy to hand over the leadership if the committee preferred someone else. We want an independent, prosperous and peaceful Mthwakazi. Individuals set on power and personal gain will lead us to another version of Zimbabwe.'

'What about those members of the committee who voted for Senior Kholose?'

'That group has melted away. Everybody now recognises the danger of a controlling, over-zealous leader. We all want democracy, not a dictatorship.'

'What happened to our Instructors, Daniel and Alexander, and the recruits we trained?'

'They're still going strong, and together with your first group of trainees, they're now training new recruits. The approach has changed from when you first started. We paid attention to your report where you said the recruits were city boys, blundering around in the bush. The emphasis is now on bushcraft and survival rather than military skills, so now it's more like a scouting movement. The committee believes bush-survival training would make it easier to adapt their skills to a military footing if it became necessary.'

'That makes sense. The government can't accuse you of treason or conspiracy for teaching young people scouting skills or running Outward Bound courses.'

'Yes, we always lived with the fear of exposure of our activities. If they discovered us, we could have been jailed or even executed. Mind you, a long period in Chikurubi, or any other Zimbabwe prison, has been an effective death sentence for many inmates.'

* * *

Enid and Avril busied themselves in the kitchen, putting the finishing touches to the dinner. The smells from the cooking teased Alan's hunger pangs. He'd forgotten all about food, but now, he was starving.

After a delicious dinner of roast beef, roast potatoes, green peas, carrots and onions served with hot English mustard, the family retired to the lounge for coffee. They chatted away with more questions for Alan about what he'd been up to over the past twelve months. Luke discreetly avoided raising any matters concerning the MFF.

Alan felt very much at home and couldn't help reflecting on his awkward first dinner and Christmas Day at Luke's house. Then, he'd felt out of place. What a difference compared to now!

Enid whispered to the maid and, a moment later a young African woman came in carrying an infant on her back. Avril jumped up and took the baby as the young women undid the tiny knot on the towel that held the baby in place. 'Alan, meet Donna.'

Alan stared open-mouthed at the tiny infant. 'Is this the maid's baby?'

'No, she's my baby, and Don's. If she was a boy, we'd have called him Don, but Donna was the best we could do for a girl.'

'Gosh! She's a pretty, little thing. She looks…'

'Light-skinned?'

'Er, yes.'

'You know Don's great-grandfather was white?'

'Yes, June told me.'

'That makes her six-and-a-quarter-percent white.'

'She looks a lot lighter than that.'

'Yes, the genes can show themselves many generations down the line. She's a throwback to her great-grandfather.'

'How old is she?'

'She'll be one in December.' The last time Alan caught that look in Avril's eyes was the first Christmas when they danced together in Luke's lounge with the whole family watching.

CHAPTER 65

Luke showed Alan the newspaper advertisement about hunting the man-eaters terrorising villages on the edge of the Hwange National Park. 'It's a tiny advert,' said Alan. 'It's almost as if they don't want too many people to notice it. Did you see this advertised anywhere else?'

'No. As far as I'm aware, that was it.'

'The advertisement suggests it's on behalf of the government, but there's only a phone number to call. I'll try it.'

Alan called the number on his cell phone.

'Hello.' A woman's voice.

'Er, hello. I'm phoning about the man-eating leopards terrorising villages near Hwange National Park.'

'Yes?'

'Well, I'm interested.'

'One moment, please.' Alan could hear voices in the background.

'Can you come to the Bulawayo Rainbow Hotel tomorrow morning at eleven o'clock?'

'Yes.'

'Ask for Jonas at the reception desk.'

'OK. Is that it?'

'Yes.' The person ended the call.

That was strange. It was not the communication he expected with a representative of a government department.

* * *

The next morning, Alan dressed for his meeting with the government official. Something about the curious, informal discussion on the phone didn't seem right.

Alan drove to the hotel and parked in Josiah Tongogara Street. He walked into the lobby and over to the reception desk.

'Good morning. I'm here to meet Jonas.'

'Mr Drake.' A woman's voice behind him. Alan turned to see a trim, short woman in a navy-blue business suit. 'I'm Miriam. The minister will see you now. Please follow me.'

Alan followed Miriam to the lift. She pressed the button for the fifth floor. 'Was it you I spoke to yesterday on the phone?' said Alan, trying to make conversation.

'The minister has several staff members.' The curt response made it clear to Alan, Miriam was not up for any conversation.

Miriam led Alan to a door where she knocked. A dapper man in a dark suit opened the door. 'Come in Mr Drake, I'm Jonas. Please sit. Can I get you tea?'

Jonas ordered Miriam to get a black tea, no sugar for Alan, and a white tea with two sugar for himself. 'Well, Mr Drake, let's get straight down to business. What price did you have in mind?'

'No price, I'm willing to do it for nothing.'

Jonas smiled, giving Alan a quizzical look. 'No, no Mr Drake, you misunderstand me. What I mean is, how much are you willing to pay to hunt leopards in the national park? Do you know, an official licence and other charges for one leopard can cost you over ten thousand dollars? I can give you unfettered access to hunt leopards in the park on a per head basis for half the price.'

'Is that legal?'

'Yes, if I give you the authority to hunt man-eaters terrorising the villages on the edge of the park. How about five thousand dollars per head?'

'How many man-eaters are there?'

'As many as you want Mr Drake. The leopard you shoot might not be the man-eater. It's a trial-and-error situation. Once the man-eating stops, I will need to withdraw the licence to shoot leopards in the park, so perhaps it's a good idea to first shoot them in areas away from the trouble spots.'

'What if it's not a leopard?'

'Even better. That means you can shoot leopards for as long as the man-eating continues. But I'm sure the man-eater is a leopard. Only leopards are so silent and cunning that people can disappear with no one noticing.'

'I don't want to shoot leopards, only man-eaters.'

'I'm only authorised to issue a licence to hunt man-eating leopards. The advertisement specified leopards, Mr Drake. Tell me, if you are not a trophy hunter, why did you respond to the advertisement?'

'A close friend of mine disappeared from a village on the edge of the park. Others also disappeared from the same area. The locals talk about the Devil's Children. I thought the advertisement related to that area.'

'I can't promise you any particular area because another hunter may have already taken it. You must take any area I allocate to you.'

'What's the point of allocating me an area other than one where people are living in fear of man-eaters?'

'Ah, so you're on a mission, Mr Drake.'

'Yes, perhaps.'

'Men on a mission are dangerous, Mr Drake. If I gave you a licence, you would try to shoot the man-eaters and would likely succeed. Where then, could I get five thousand dollars for each leopard shot.'

'It seems we're on different paths, Minister. May I ask, what department do you control?'

'That is not important, Mr Drake. Please leave your phone number with Miriam. If we need to shoot the man-eaters, we'll call you. Miriam please see Mr Drake out.'

* * *

Alan's meeting with the minister preyed on his mind. 'I ask you, Luke, what chance does the wildlife have with people like Jonas running the show?'

'Let's look up his name and find which department employs him.'

Luke and Alan searched the list of government ministers, assistant ministers and senior civil servants. Nowhere could they find anyone named Jonas. 'He didn't want to tell me his surname or what department he ran or represented.'

'Yes, Jonas must be a cover. I wonder how authentic his hunting licence would be?'

'He was so brazen about his money-making venture. I'm not surprised we can't find anything about him.'

'Don't worry, Alan, I still need a head of security for my shops. You can do that if you wish. You will stay on, for a while at least, won't you?'

'Yes, Luke,' said Alan with an exasperated sigh, 'I will. But the high-level corruption in Zimbabwe really gets me. How can you live with it?'

'What choice do we have, Alan?'

'Yes, hence the MFF and Mthwakazi, but you know my opinion of a few of the MFF leaders.'

'There's corruption on all sides in Zimbabwe and in other countries. It's the nature of humans to take advantage where they can.'

* * *

Alan forgot about Jonas, but one evening, a month after meeting the minister, Alan's cell phone rang. It was soon after the security guards' inspection parade before they went on night duty.

'Mr Drake, this is Jonas speaking. We are planning a new job, and I believe it can accommodate your mission to avenge your close friend who disappeared near the national park. Can you meet me at my hotel tonight?'

'Yes. Can you tell me more?'

'It's confidential. I can't talk on the phone, but I can say you will be most interested.'

'OK, where do we meet and when?'

'Now, at my hotel. Same room. Don't bother waiting in the lobby for Miriam. Come straight up to my suite when you get here.'

Alan was curious but cautious. What does the corrupt bastard want now? Alan hopped into the old Land Rover and drove the short distance to the hotel. As usual, parking in Josiah Tongogara Street was easy. Before he got out of the Land Rover, he slipped his handgun into the back of his trouser waistband and put on his jacket. He wasn't taking any chances that this might be a trap.

He walked through the reception area to the lift and pressed the button for the fifth floor. On the way up, Alan checked his handgun was secure. He knocked on the door and Jonas opened it, beaming. He shook Alan's hand enthusiastically. 'Come in, come in Mr Drake.'

A quick glance around told Alan no one else was in the hotel suite, but to be sure, he stood, facing the bathroom door.

'Alan, may I call you Alan?'

'Yes, Minister.'

'Call me Jonas. Miriam's not here, so I can offer you a real drink this time. She watches my alcohol intake like a hawk. Will a Scotch do?'

Alan watched Jonas pour the drinks. Scotch and soda. It seemed straight forward enough. 'Good health and good business,' said Jonas, raising his glass. 'May our partnership be long and fruitful.' Alan waited for Jonas to take the first sip before he tried his.

'And what partnership is that, Jonas?'

'You want to kill the man-eater that ate your close friend? I've got a licence for you at no charge. It covers any creature that may be a man-eater, lion, leopard, whatever.'

'What's behind the change of heart? Last time it was all about shooting leopards for five thousand dollars per head.'

'Ah, yes. There's a little problem, you see. The man-eating has not reduced, and the people upstairs are getting impatient and asking questions. In Zimbabwe, impatience always leads to dire consequences for somebody. I don't want to be that somebody, so I now give you my blessing to shoot the man-eaters.'

'And what about your little leopard shooting venture?'

'That has to finish. It was profitable enough while it lasted, but it's over for now. You can shoot whatever you want, but the man-eating must stop.'

'Why did you call me? Can't any of your trophy hunters do the job?'

'I called you because I trust you. I waited to see if you would try to report my dealings. You didn't. So, you've done me a favour by staying silent, and I now grant you a favour by letting you go after the creature that killed your close friend.'

'OK, I accept the task. I need to take my two guides with me on this job.'

'Yes, fine, fine. Now, let's have another Scotch. First, let's shake on the deal. And remember, you must do this job soon.'

'Will the park rangers and the authorities know I have permission to hunt in the park?'

'Of course.'

'Also, I need to work at night. That's when any self-respecting man-eater operates.'

'No problem. Just deal with the man-eaters before the locals start a riot and the government blames me. If this works out, we may put other deals together.'

'Jonas, you old crook, I don't want to get dragged into anything illegal.'

Jonas laughed at Alan's switch to informality. 'Don't worry my friend, I need a squeaky-clean associate to keep my reputation unsullied. You fit that description perfectly.'

'I'd be amazed if your reputation was unsullied, and I want none of your real reputation rubbing off onto me.'

'You really are an innocent, Alan. My reputation is second to none You wouldn't believe what others get up to when nobody is watching. I may have made over one hundred thousand dollars through the leopard hunting scheme, but I've had no one killed or maimed.'

'So, tell me Jonas, what position do you hold in the government?'

'A privileged position, my friend. Let's leave it at that. I'm thinking of your welfare when I say it's better for you not to know. You are in no danger from me, but like everyone in any senior position in Zimbabwe I have enemies. It is my enemies who might threaten you if we got too close. They might try to get at me by getting at you.'

'OK, Jonas, enough said.'

CHAPTER 66

A LAN received the hunting licence within two days of meeting Jonas. Both he and Luke examined it and concluded it looked genuine. Alan remained wary of Jonas and didn't want to risk taking anything on face value. The licence met all of Alan's requests and gave him permission to hunt in the national park. The accompanying letter invited him to pick up a rifle and ammunition from the police station. It concerned Alan, the signatures on the letter and the licence were not decipherable, and there was no printed name or position of the signatory. But the inspector at the police station expected him, and everything seemed official.

Daniel and Alexander were thrilled to go with Alan on another visit to the Hwange National Park. The licence allowed Alan two guides or helpers, but there were no rifles for them. It didn't matter as Alan planned to dig up their buried rifles and use them for the task if needed.

'We're not going in the Land Rover this time,' said Alan. 'We need to hire a three-ton tip truck with three seats in the front.' Luke made a few calls on his cell phone, and it turned out that a suitable truck stood available for them in Hwange, so they would travel in the old Land Rover at least that far. Alan arranged for gloves, masks, goggles and protective clothing for himself and his Instructors. He also arranged ration packs for five days. 'That should be more than enough. If we've any left over, we can give it to Nancy and the villagers.'

Armed with the licence and several one-dollar notes, Alan and his two Instructors set off on their trip. The licence and official letter helped them through the police roadblocks but did not save them from the standard one-dollar fee. The group arrived in Hwange at lunch time and headed straight for Luke's contact to pick up the three-ton truck.

'Remember, when we bring the truck back, you must wash it well. Wear protective clothing, hats, masks, gloves and goggles!'

'Don't worry, Sah, we know what to do.'

Alan and his men transferred all their supplies to the truck, including the pick and two shovels he always carried in the Land Rover. 'We'll leave the Land Rover in your compound until we return your truck,' said Alan.

After a lunch of fish and chips, Alan and his two companions jumped into the truck and drove to the park. The park gate would test what influence the licence and letter might have. It turned out they had a lot of influence. The rangers waved the truck though after a most cursory inspection of the documents.

The trio first stopped at the overgrown track to recover the buried rifles and ammunition. They'd been underground for well over a year, but when they unwrapped them from their plastic sheets, they looked in fine condition. Before burying the rifles, Alan and his men cleaned and oiled them and wrapped them in the plastic sheets. For good measure, they also sprayed the outer side of the sheets with insect repellent. Now they feared that termites might have attacked the wooden stocks, but this was not the case.

Alan drove the truck to the area where Phineas and his men took him and Luke, the night they were abducted; the spot where Phineas' colleagues were attacked. It was close to Nancy's village. If the Devil's Children took Molly, they probably also took Phineas and his men. It was early evening when the truck pulled up at the village. There was much merriment and excited greetings when Alan and his companions jumped out onto the hard ground in front of the huts. Nancy squealed with delight at Alan's return and soon arranged for a hut to be at his disposal.

'We'll stay here tonight,' said Alan, 'but first there's work to do.' The area was on the boundary, just outside the national park, and Alan planned to shoot buck for the village and for their own needs. Poaching and hunting had depleted the game in the area, but despite this, Alan and his men soon shot three fat buck, which the villagers helped carry back to the huts. 'Cook one for dinner, and put two in our hut,' said Alan. 'Tomorrow morning, we will need to shoot another two or three.'

'Why so many, Sah,' asked Daniel.

'You will find out tomorrow, my friend.'

Alexander smiled. He guessed the reason.

That night the village celebrated. Big fires and the beating of drums kept away any predator tempted to inspect the immediate surrounds. There was no threat from the Devil's Children while they all stayed together. But as the evening's celebrations ended, everyone disappeared into their huts without delay. Even Alan's two seasoned companions wasted no time in following him into the hut.

* * *

The next morning, Alan and his men rose early. They needed to shoot more buck. The villagers were also quick to rise, and several accompanied the men on the hunt. By mid-morning, Alan had three more buck, plus one for the village pot. 'Are you two sure you remember where you buried the cyanide,' said Alan, enjoying a cup of tea with Daniel and Alexander.

'Yes, Sah. No problem, Sah.'

Late morning, the trio drove out to the spot where they ran into Michael Duze and his gang. Between them, Daniel and Alexander soon discovered the spot where the cyanide lay buried. They dug with care to avoid damaging the container holding the cyanide. It took time to find it. 'Are you certain you buried it here,' said Alan.

'Yes, Sah. You told us to bury it deep.'

At last the plastic wrapping appeared through the earth like a long-buried treasure. The men had taken great care to follow Alan's instructions. The well-wrapped container stood upright with the lid secured in place. 'Now we'll see what this can do,' said Alan. 'We'll fight fire with fire.'

Back at the village, Alan told Nancy the villagers needed to go about their business as normal and retire early, as was their custom. 'If we finish the Devil's Children tonight, we can celebrate with the second buck tomorrow night.' After an early dinner, Alan and his men retired to their hut with their ration packs.

It was a pitch-black moonless night when the three men emerged from their hut, but soon the full moon peeped over the horizon. 'Thank God for that,' said Alan. 'At least we'll be able to see what we're doing.' The men dressed in their protective clothing before loading the four buck carcasses into the back of the lorry. Alan drove a little distance from the village and stopped the truck. He and his men set about making several incisions in the carcasses. Alan opened the container and sprinkled a liberal amount of cyanide into the cuts and over the dead animals.

Daniel and Alexander remained in the back of the truck with their rifles, and Alan drove slowly down the road towards the spot Phineas stopped the car over a year ago. *I hope these guys are as intelligent as people claim.* He didn't know whether anyone else was dropped off there, late at night, since his and Luke's visit. But if not, would the Devil's Children remember a vehicle's headlights signalled a free late-night meal for all?

* * *

She saw the approaching vehicle and at once recognised its significance. There was a long gap between their fresh meat deliveries, but recently they'd recommenced. The vehicle approached at a painfully slow rate and the eager family salivated at the prospect of another delicious meal. And then the vehicle stopped at the spot it always stopped. It did the usual three-point turn and waited.

The family rushed forward as a heavy buck thumped onto the ground. They all rushed to be there first. The truck advanced a few metres, and another plump buck hit the ground. Two more followed, and soon the family members gorged themselves on the carcasses.

But something was wrong. This was not the delivery they expected. Still, it was a free meal. Those thoughts flashed across her mind just before the stab of pain hit. She stood and swayed before sitting down and then lay down in agony.

* * *

Alan grabbed his rifle and climbed from the cab onto the back of the truck. He waited until the group at the fourth carcass stumbled and swayed, and then, one by one, he and his men put the clan members out of their misery. 'Now, for the hard part,' said Alan. 'We must load the remains of the four buck and every dead hyena onto the truck. We can't risk any other animal stumbling across these carcasses and enjoying a free meal of poisoned meat.' The partially eaten buck were now much lighter, but the hyenas weighed up to almost seventy kilos.

Some members of the clan tried to crawl back to their burrows or other resting places, but few made it. By the time they were all loaded and piled high in the back of the truck, Alan counted nineteen dead hyenas. If these were the Devil's Children, as Alan suspected, they'd decimated the clan. He'd keep his fingers crossed and wait to see if the man-eating ceased. It struck Alan no other predators or scavengers appeared on the scene. That was fortunate, given his controversial method of eliminating the man-eaters. It seemed the unusual hyena pack must have driven off all competition for food in the area.

Alan drove slowly back to the village with the gruesome cargo. The three returned exhausted from loading the dead carcasses onto the truck. Alan knocked on Nancy's door and asked her to warn all the villagers not to go near the vehicle because of the poison.

* * *

The morning dawned bright. After breakfast, Alan and his men donned their protective clothing. The villagers dug a large open pit near the spot where they discovered Molly's green bandanna. Other villagers cut dried

branches and pieces of wood they found in the surrounding area and li
a massive bonfire. Alan and his men threw the remains of the four buc
and nineteen hyenas into the flames. The near-empty cyanide containe
and its plastic wrapping followed.

All day the fire burned. It was like a cleansing of the village and sur
rounding area. In the late afternoon, heavy storm clouds gathered. Ala
took out Molly's green bandanna from his breast pocket and tossed i
into the flames. It burned with the ferocity of a match head and wa
gone in an instant. 'Molly's spirit can now rest,' said Alan, and all the
village murmured something he didn't understand.

The downpour began, but the villagers continued to fill in the hug
pit they dug earlier that day. Later, as the evening sun slanted acros
the village and the rain-washed air sweetened their lungs, the villager
started a fire to prepare their second buck for the celebratory feast.

Once they'd all eaten and were enjoying their African home-brewe
beer, Alan made a short speech. 'I cannot guarantee we have defeated the
Devil's Children. We must wait to find the answer. But if they return
we'll come back to fight them again.'

Everyone clapped and called out, their happy faces relieved and hope
ful. Later, back in their hut, Alan asked Daniel and Alexander what the
people were calling out after his speech. The two men laughed. Some
women were saying they wanted to marry you, Sah. You can have you
pick. This time, Alan joined in the laughter.

Over the next three nights, Alan, Daniel and Alexander went out i
the truck and shot any stray hyenas they found wandering in the area
but it was slim pickings. On the fourth evening there was no sign o
hyenas.

* * *

While Daniel and Alexander readied the truck for their departure, Ala
shot another buck for the villagers to eat after they'd gone. Nancy, who'
become the village spokesperson, made her own short speech, invitin,

Alan and his men to come back again and not forget them. She also took the opportunity, amid much laughter, to announce the names of the women who offered themselves in marriage.

'I don't think their husbands would be too pleased,' said Alan.

'If our husbands can take more than one wife,' Nancy replied, 'why can't we women take more than one husband?'

CHAPTER 67

'THE job is done, Jonas, so you should be off the hook with you friends in Harare. I hope they will be as pleased with the resul as I am.'

'But Alan, how can that be? You stayed in the national park for onl four days.'

'That's right.'

'Where's the leopard skin?'

'I burned it.'

'What! Have you any idea how much a leopard skin is worth?'

'Never mind that, Jonas. Let's wait and see if the job is complete. I the attacks stop, that's it, but if they continue, I will have to look again

'Well, I'm not reporting the job complete until we're sure. They'll as how I resolved the matter so fast after they threatened consequences They might imagine I dragged my feet before this.'

'Well, you did.'

'Yes, but they needn't know.'

Alan smiled when he switched off his phone. Did Jonas have n shame? He was an out-and-out crook, but he had charisma, and Ala quite liked him. Jonas should have been in jail, but his open and naïv admission of his corruption put an air of innocence about him.

* * *

Weeks passed, with no reports of attacks in the area. Daniel and Alex ander brought news that village life had returned to normal, and peopl ventured out in the evenings once more. Then came news of a curious incident.

One night, long after the villagers had gone to bed, a loud banging on a hut door woke them. When the villagers emerged from their huts, they saw a man in a crumpled suit standing there. The man claimed he was abducted and taken to a spot where his abductors left him after almost blinding him with a brilliant flashlight. It took ages for his eyes to grow accustomed to the dark. He walked along the road for about half an hour before he saw the village in the moonlight. The people in the village called him the Midnight Man.

The man said he worked in Harare for and an organisation called the COU, run by a man known as Captain John. He'd fallen into disfavour and targeted for disposal.

'Aha!' said Alan. 'That proves the Devil's Children are no more. No one could walk near the village after dark if they were still active. Luke, we need to find that man. He may lead us to the people who took June.'

Alan put Daniel and Alexander on the case. Soon they reported back, saying the villagers told them the police turned up the following day and took the Midnight Man away in a police car. Alan visited the police station in Bulawayo to enquire about the incident and the whereabouts of the man. The police knew nothing about the incident. 'Try the Lupane police,' said the inspector. 'Perhaps they can help you.' The Lupane police referred Alan on to the Hwange police who referred him to the Victoria Falls police.

'Nothing, absolutely nothing,' said Alan, referring to his lack of progress. 'The Midnight Man has vanished.'

'At least we have the name of the organisation and the person who runs it,' said Luke.

When they tried to look up the organisation in the various directories and registers, they found no record. 'Under normal circumstances, I'd say the Midnight Man was drunk or delusional. But the same thing happened to us, so we know it's true,' said Alan.

'We must keep our eyes and ears open,' said Luke, 'and little by little we might uncover this secret organisation and its mysterious leader.'

* * *

On a lazy, sunny Saturday afternoon, the maid told Alan a man at the front door asked for him. It was strange; few people knew he stayed at Luke's house. The visitor had a nervous manner, looking about him as if to check no one was watching.

'You wanted me?' said Alan.

'Yes, Sah, I heard you looked for me. I am the man who walked to the village near the national park at midnight.'

'The Hwange National Park?'

'Yes, Sah. Bad men, they drop me in the park, so the animals would kill me.'

'So, you're the Midnight Man?'

'Yes, Sah,' said the man, smiling, proud of his new nickname.

'Come, sit with me on the garden bench, and tell me about it.'

The man spoke at length about his experience, and the people who planned his death. In particular, he mentioned Hilton Nyoka and Captain John and the organisation known as the COU. 'I can show you where Hilton Nyoka lives, Sah. Once, I drove with another operative to his house to deliver files. No one knows where Captain John lives, but I can show you where the COU offices are.'

'OK, Midnight, on Monday, you and I are driving to Harare. We have work to do. Can you meet me here on Monday morning at nine o'clock?'

'Yes, Sah.'

After the man left, Luke approached Alan.

'What did that man want?'

'That was the Midnight Man. He says he can lead me to the source of our troubles.'

'Can you trust him?'

'Can you trust anyone? I will be careful.'

'So, what are you going to do?'

'I'll confront Hilton Nyoka. That evil bastard has caused so much harm. I'm sure he's responsible for June going missing. Perhaps I'll find out what happened to her and where she is.'

'Stop torturing yourself, Alan. We all believe she is dead. Otherwise, he would have contacted us long ago.'

'Well, I have to find out. I will never rest if I don't at least try.'

* * *

On Monday morning, Alan rose early and waited, restless and keen to be underway. He armed himself with a supply of one-dollar notes and bottles of cool drinks. He'd learnt from his experience on the Victoria Falls Road that politeness went a long way towards a speedy passage through the police roadblocks. The Midnight Man arrived early, so they were on their way by eight o'clock.

Along the way, Alan discovered that Midnight was an operative in the COU but had fallen foul of the leaders when he refused to join an assassination team sent against a friend of his family. As a result, they labelled him a loose end, earmarked for elimination. Captain John charged Hilton Nyoka with overseeing the process, and Hilton settled on one of his favourite methods of elimination; a live delivery to the national park for the predators to remove all trace of the victim. The horrific thought hit Alan. June may have suffered such a fate. Losing Molly that way was bad enough, but June...

Early in the afternoon, Alan and Midnight arrived in Harare. First stop was the COU office on the eastern edge of the CBD. Midnight feared the prospect of passing the office and risking recognition. He sank low into the seat of the Land Rover as Alan drove slowly past the nondescript building. Midnight's face was a picture of fear as beads of sweat trickled down his temples.

Next, Alan drove to the west side of the CBD where he booked rooms for himself and Midnight at a small private hotel. They ate a late lunch of hamburger and chips and counted down the hours for Alan's showdown with Hilton Nyoka. Midnight made it clear he would show Alan where Hilton lived, but under no circumstances would he go with him onto the premises.

'What about Captain John,' said Alan. 'Do you think we could get to him?'

'Sah, he has strong security like the president. His car is bullet proof. It would be too dangerous to tackle him. His nickname is The Leopard. Remember, Sah, a cornered leopard is the most dangerous. It is best not to be greedy. Hilton Nyoka should be enough. Perhaps another day, Sah.'

It was clear to Alan, if he went after Captain John, he would be on his own.

At seven o'clock, Alan parked the Land Rover a discreet distance from Hilton Nyoka's house in the leafy suburb of Borrowdale. It was a good spot where he and Midnight could keep Hilton's house in view without being observed. Half an hour later a car came down the road and turned through the open gate and stopped on the gravel drive in front of the house. A tall, athletic-looking man jumped out and slammed the car door and closed the garden gate before striding to the left of the building.

'That's him,' Midnight whispered. 'That's Hilton Nyoka.'

The house was an attractive single storey with the frontage parallel to the road and a wing on the right-hand side swept back at an angle of thirty degrees. It was a boomerang shape. A passion fruit hedge covered the diamond mesh perimeter fence. The garden was all lawn.

After waiting twenty minutes, Alan took his handgun from its hiding place behind the dashboard and tucked it into the back of his trousers. He nodded to the fearful looking Midnight and walked to the front gate and opened it. After three noisy steps on the gravel, Alan stepped onto the lawn. No lights were on inside, and Alan hurried to the left of the house where he earlier noticed a door in a wall about four metres high. There was a thick tangle of creepers hanging over the wall from the inside and Alan guessed it must be a courtyard through which Hilton entered

he house a little earlier. He hadn't gone through the front door when
e got home.

The sound of loud music playing drifted over the wall. Alan took a
deep breath and exhaled. He tried the door handle and pushed. It was
ocked. Alan searched for a way to enter the courtyard but found none.
Then he looked at the creepers which hung about three metres above
he ground. If he could gather several ends, they might hold his weight.
Alan considered jumping to reach the creepers, but if he missed getting
a grip, the noisy gravel border against the wall might warn Hilton of his
presence.

Standing on the tips of his toes, Alan could just reach three ends, and
f he was quick and pulled himself up on them before they broke, he
might grab another few. It all depended on how anchored the creepers
were behind the wall. If they grew in the ground, they might be fine, but
f they were in pots…

In his left hand, Alan gathered the ends he could reach and focussed
his attention on the ends he would try to grab with his right. He tested
the strength of the creepers by pulling them taut. They felt strong
nough, but pulling himself up with his left hand, to grab more ends
with his right would have to be a lightning quick, one-two move. Alan
braced himself, then leapt into action.

For a few seconds, Alan dangled on the ends of the creepers, both
hands stinging from the stems holding his weight. So far, so good. With
his biceps aching and cursing under his breath, he gathered the creeper
tems into a single, strong rope and dragged himself up the wall. Once
on top, he rested for a moment to recover from the exertion, which was
more likely to have resulted from nervous tension rather than physical
ffort. He turned his back to the dark courtyard, and hanging onto the
wall, he lowered himself on his arms before dropping to the ground in a
ilent, cat-like motion.

A rippling swimming pool lay in front of him with change rooms or
ervant's quarters to the left.

As Alan's eye's adjusted to the dim lighting, he noticed a man lying in a hot tub set between the house and the pool. With his eyes closed the music blaring, and the bubbling of the water, the man was unaware of Alan's presence. To the left of the hot tub stood a low side table with a bottle of wine and a half-full wine glass upon it. To the right, a dim mood lamp threw transitioning shades of red, purple, green and blue. It was plugged into a wall socket to one side of the French doors, leading into the house. The filtration system stood against the wall behind the hot tub. Set into a timber facade next to it was a row of power points.

Alan took a step forward. 'Hilton Nyoka?'

The man in the hot tub looked startled but quickly regained his composure.

'Mr Drake, I presume. What a pleasant surprise. How did you discover where I lived? If you told me you were coming, I'd have prepared a welcome for you.'

'I'm sure you would have. Now I'm here, I'd like a few answers from you.'

'Such as what?'

'Such as, where is Andrew Dube and his son?'

'Yes, I heard they disappeared. I imagine they're lying in the jungle somewhere in southern Thailand. Eaten by ants and maggots by now I'd say.'

'So, you admit your part in their murder; your part in the crime?'

'Don't be so melodramatic Mr Drake. You and I are the same kind.'

'I don't think so.'

'Oh, no? Do you know what happened to Mr Wong, your father's office manager in Singapore? He didn't jump out of his office building. He wasn't that brave. Your father had him pushed, murdered. So, your father isn't that different from my boss. Neither carry out the dirty work themselves anymore. They use people like us to act on their behalf. Other than giving the nod, they stay free from any blame.'

'What happened to June Ndlovu? Where is she?'

'What's it to you Mr Drake? She's only another black woman, crowding out this country.'

'Like you, Nyoka, only another black man, crowding out this country.'

'So, she's the daughter of your poaching partner, Luke Ndlovu. Why isn't he here to seek revenge? Why is it you? Don't tell me! She was special to you. Is that it?'

'Just tell me where she is!'

'My boss wouldn't let anyone harm his competitors' family members, particularly the women and children. If she didn't involve herself in the poaching, she'd be safe.'

'Do you always follow your boss's instructions? I doubt it. Where is June Ndlovu?'

'While we're on that subject, Mr Drake, where is my man, Hector?'

'Is he the one you sent to my apartment to kill me?'

'Yes, where is he? What have you done with him?'

'I've no idea where he is. Perhaps he made other enemies, and they dealt with him.'

'So, Mr Drake, you and I are the same. We are both the go-to killers for our masters, but often we pass the task on to someone else. I don't know where your June Ndlovu is, any more than you know where my Hector is.'

'We're nothing alike, Nyoka. Now is your last chance to tell me where June Ndlovu is.'

'Mr Drake, you're getting tiresome, breaking into my private property and making demands.'

'You arranged for her disappearance, right?'

Hilton Nyoka looked to reach for the wine glass but came up with the handgun that lay hidden in the shadow cast by the side of the hot tub. 'Goodnight, Mr Drake.'

Alan threw himself to the right as a searing flash of orange scorched his left cheek. Almost in a single movement, he grabbed the mood lamp and hurled it into the tub. The lead was too short, and the plug pulled out of the wall socket, killing the colourful display. In a flash, Alan rolled behind the hot tub so that Hilton's back was to him. He reached for the handgun tucked into the back of his waistband. It wasn't there. It must have fallen out when he lunged to avoid Hilton's shot.

In the confusion, Hilton wasn't sure where Alan was. He sat up, to see if Alan lay dead or wounded on the deck.

Alan remembered the outdoor power points near the filtration system behind the hot tub. He cast around for the mood lamp's lead, but in the darkness, he trod on its wall plug. A sharp bolt of pain shot through the thin sole of his shoe. Alan gasped and Hilton swung around to face him. 'Before, it was goodnight, Mr Drake, but this time it's goodbye.' He raised the handgun just as Alan plugged in the mood lamp and flicked the switch. Simultaneous flashes of orange, from the handgun and the mood lamp, lit up the courtyard. The whole area plunged into total darkness.

CHAPTER 68

THE end of the working day, and Captain John was in a bad mood. 'Blast it, Eunice! I was relying on that idiot, and now, he's killed himself. How stupid to place an electric lamp so close to a hot tub! Wouldn't it be obvious to anyone the damn thing might fall into the water?'

'To make matters worse, he was drinking and firing off his gun. Everyone knows you shouldn't drink when you go near water. And why fire off his gun? This isn't South America where they fire off guns at will. Imagine, wasting our bullets like that. At least, we don't have to fork out his last pay.'

'Sir, Nyoka's behaviour was becoming more and more erratic. Perhaps it's a blessing he's no longer with us. Who knows what he might have done next? He could have become an embarrassment to the COU.'

'Yes, Eunice, maybe you're right, but he used to be such a good operator. He showed initiative, and he was the person I could go to when I needed a job done properly. None of the fools working here could fill his shoes. Who can I go to now?'

'Don't worry, Sir, I'll help you rebuild the team. And if you need a job done well why not try me?'

'You? Yes, perhaps you're right, Eunice. The COU needs a new angle, woman's touch. Women can be so much more cunning and ruthless when the mood takes them. Take my wife, for example.'

'Yes, Sir, you've told me all about her.'

'Then you know what I mean.'

'I do, Sir.'

'We'll make a good team, Eunice. Yes, a good team.'

'May I suggest something else, Sir?'

'Go ahead.'

'We wait for clients to contact us when they want a job done. When things are quiet on the political front, we must rely on our poaching to keep us going.'

'Hmm, yes.'

'We understand the political lie of the land.'

'Uh-huh.'

'Well, when there's spare capacity, why don't we approach a few big wigs and suggest jobs that might interest them? That way, we'd keep our core business at a more constant level. We're all aware of the rumour that many of the high-ups have an interest in poaching. They might even be our direct competition, and if we're not careful, we may step on some very big toes. Perhaps our poaching activities are taking our focus away from our core business where there's less likelihood of us falling foul of the high-ups.'

'Eunice, if I approached any bigwig, it would compromise my anonymity. You know how much I value secrecy in this business.'

'That, Sir, is where I can help. Outside the COU, no one knows I'm involved with this organisation. I can approach the bigwigs as an independent agent and suggest the jobs and then tell them I'll sub-contract it to any one of several suitable operators. They needn't know they're dealing with the COU and not knowing who completes the job puts more distance between them and the hit.'

'Eunice, that might be a good idea. You understand, if you fall foul of the clients, I will deny all knowledge of you?'

'Yes, Sir, that's how we play this game.'

'Where would you start with your approach to bigwigs?'

'There are dissidents outside the country working against the interests of the government. If we lured them back to Zimbabwe, we could deal with them here and avoid the need to answer embarrassing questions from a foreign police force or government. That way, we'd provide our government or the CIO, or whoever, with two different services. First, we lure dissidents back to Zimbabwe, and second, we make them disappear without a trace. We can charge for each service separately. It will mean we can charge the client twice as much as we do now. We should start with the dissidents in our neighbouring countries and then move on to the UK and the US.'

'I like the way you think, Eunice. Yes, we'll make a great team.'

'It's just a question of fresh blood for fresh ideas, Sir. But we need to tell the rest of the operatives I'm your official second in command.'

'Hilton Nyoka was angling for that position, but now he's checked out, it's over to you, Eunice. I'll tell the team tomorrow.'

'Would you like me to close up the office, Sir, while you pour the Scotches?'

'An excellent idea, Eunice, we'll toast your promotion.'

When she returned five minutes later, Eunice saw Captain John had cleared his desk of everything bar the two crystal glasses of Scotch on the rocks. These days, Captain John liked his desk polished regularly.

'One other thing, Sir. Given the high attrition rate we've suffered, do you think it might be wise to forget about the Ndlovu and Drake gang for now?'

'You're right, Eunice, let's put a hold on that. If there's no evidence of them poaching, why waste our resources on them?'

'Up to now, Sir, my duties included answering the phone, making routine calls, running errands and doing many odd jobs for you around the office. I notice you always do your own filing. Can't I help you with that?'

'No, Eunice, those files are for my use only. The bottom drawer of the cabinet is for completed jobs. Those files are to protect us in case of any disputes. They show who requested a job and how much they paid. That makes it difficult for any disaffected client to make an official complaint against us. The top drawer is for jobs that are still outstanding. They include all the jobs we will carry out in due course.'

'And the two middle drawers, Sir.'

'The second drawer is for potential jobs. Those include targets who made themselves unpopular with someone who can afford our fees. You would select the bigwigs you want to approach from that draw. The third drawer is for job orders we decline. Either, because they are too difficult or the potential client was unwilling to meet our price.'

'Sir, those files are a rich resource for blackmail.'

'Blackmail is a dangerous path to go down, Eunice. No, those files are strictly for our protection. People bring us their business because they trust us. If we used their enquiries or job orders to blackmail them, we'd soon lose our good reputation.'

'Yes, Sir, you're right.'

'Business will pick up soon, Eunice. With ZANU-PF divided, we can expect more enquiries. The Lacoste group wants Mnangagwa, The Crocodile, as the next president, but the G40 group are backing Grace Mugabe. There's bound to be fireworks down the line, and that's good for us.'

'You're right, Sir.' As she turned away from John to sit on the edge of the desk, Eunice smiled to herself. Skinning The Leopard might be a lot easier than she expected.

CHAPTER 69

DECEMBER 2015

Once the painting and refurbishment was complete, Alan planned to move back into his old apartment in Fife Street. When he first returned to Bulawayo, the apartment was occupied, so he boarded with Luke and the family. One evening, when Luke returned from the supermarket, he mentioned the tenant was leaving. That's when Alan discovered Luke bought the apartment. 'It's a good investment,' Luke said. 'You can stay here with us as long as you like, Alan, but maybe you'd prefer your own place. Perhaps you would like to sleep there during the week and stay with us on weekends. It's up to you.'

'Luke, you treat me like part of the family.'

'The family all regard you as one of us, Alan.'

Alan felt more at home and part of a family than at any time since his mother's death. The conversation turned to Luke's family history and his children.

'We're all lucky to be here,' said Luke. 'My great-grandfather died towards the end of the 1896-97 Matabele Rebellion, six months before my grandfather's birth. If he died any earlier, me and my daughters would never have existed.'

'You're lucky to have such fine daughters, Luke.'

'Yes. Avril has stayed close to us, but Mae has gravitated towards Ted's family. June also remained close to us, and we will have to wait to see which way Rita goes.'

'Why did Avril and Don wait so long to start a family? They were married almost eight years, I believe?'

'There was talk of Don being unable to have children, so it surprised us when Avril fell pregnant. Like my great-grandfather, Don managed it just in time. Which reminds me, when Enid visits her sister next Wednesday afternoon, I'd like Avril to help me pick out a present for Enid for Christmas. Can you take care of Donna while we're out? Avril said she'd speak to you about it. The nanny's mother is sick, so she's gone to her village in Plumtree to care for her.'

* * *

This was the first occasion Donna would spend time alone with Alan. When Avril handed her over, Donna laughed and gurgled and held out her arms to him. 'Dada, Dada,' she said, and everyone laughed.

'Well, Alan,' said Avril, 'it doesn't look like you'll have any trouble from her.'

Alan gave an awkward smile. Donna was the youngest child he'd ever held. Young children and babies did not feature in his father's sterile business world, and Alan had little experience of them. The late afternoon and early evening passed quicker than Alan expected. Donna kept him entertained until the family returned. She sat on the sofa with her head resting against his arm.

'Donna didn't give you any trouble?' Avril asked.

'No, none. She's cute, really cute.'

The first sign of distress came when Avril picked her up, saying, 'Bed time my girl.' Donna whinged and wriggled, holding her arms out to Alan in an appeal for his help to save her from having to leave him.

'Well, you made a hit with her, Alan,' said Luke.

December was a busy month for the family. Enid and Avril helped Luke in the supermarket, and Alan looked after Donna more often. To his surprise, he enjoyed the role.

* * *

The plain brown paper envelope arrived at Alan's apartment. He opened it and read the instructions. They were simple enough. He filled in the form and put it in the envelope.

New shipments arrived at the supermarket, and Luke needed Enid and Avril to help him unpack cartons and stack the shelves. Alan would babysit Donna once again. He showered and dressed in fresh clothes. Alan loved the summer and the start of the rainy season which signalled Christmas was close. He revelled in the balmy atmosphere. The yellow, slanting rays of the evening sun poked through the gathering storm clouds. Alan walked down his apartment steps and jumped into the Land Rover, when he remembered he'd left the envelope on the kitchen counter. He ran up the steps to fetch it.

When Alan arrived at Luke's house, Rita answered the door. Back from Johannesburg for the Christmas holidays, she spent most of her time with her old Bulawayo school friend. She would come home late to sleep and would join the family at mealtimes, but she was out more often than not. Luke often commented they saw more of Alan than her. Tonight, she was home as her friend was suffering from a summer cold.

Rita was almost seventeen, and Alan couldn't help noticing, as time passed, she looked more and more like June. She still had a little puppy fat but was growing into a real beauty. Soon after the family left for the supermarket, Rita disappeared into her bedroom to do whatever girls her age did in the era of the internet.

Luke and the two women returned just after ten o'clock. Donna was long in bed, and Alan sat reading one of Luke's business magazines. 'Time for a quick Scotch before bed,' said Luke.

Avril went through to check on Donna, and Enid added, 'Yes and time for a quick cup of tea.' Alan accepted both offers.

On the way home to his apartment, Alan remembered the envelope in his pocket and drove to the post office in Main Street and dropped it in the post box.

* * *

The prostitutes across the road were delighted to see Alan back in his apartment.

'We didn't like the man who lived in your flat,' said Joice, standing in the road, looking up at Alan on the balcony. 'He kept telling us to go away from here, and he even phoned the police, but they did nothing. When the police come, they only want free time with the girls or give us fines. If we go away from here, the police won't be happy. They told that man to stop wasting their time. We are just waiting here. We have not committed a crime.'

'Well, I won't complain about you,' said Alan. 'I like you being there. When you're there, I know I'm safe.'

'A woman came to visit you two nights ago. You were out, so she left.'

'Can you describe her?'

'Very fancy lady. Beautiful for you.'

'Is that your best description?'

'It was dark. Not easy to see.'

'If it was dark, how do you know she was beautiful?'

Joice laughed. 'Would you have an ugly woman visit you?'

Alan loved the African sense of humour, which he found sharp and perceptive.

'Did she have a car?'

'I don't know. She walked around the corner.'

'Was she a white lady?'

'No, dark like me.'

Daniel and Alexander often sent female recruits with messages or security-guard reports for Alan. They joked they would find him a wife. The next time he saw them, they'd make a point of asking him what he thought of the last messenger. The topic led to much hilarity. Alan discovered his Instructors had a wager, a week's pay for the first one to find him a girlfriend. He suspected the female recruits took part in the joke as several were flirtatious.

* * *

Christmas was close now. Alan expected he would be in Bulawayo for Christmas, and this time he'd brought presents from Australia.

The time of the year, the weather, the buzz of Christmas, the family atmosphere at Luke's house, and Enid's traditional Christmas cooking all built a level of excitement for Alan he'd not experienced since early childhood. He couldn't wait for Christmas Day to arrive. He looked forward to staying with the family from Christmas Day through New Year. To him it felt like going home for Christmas. A real thrill.

Soon, Christmas Eve arrived. The shops would close within two hours. Alan walked downstairs to check the mailbox. Two items! One he recognised as a Christmas card from his father's company. He knew the annual message by heart; We wish all our customers, employees and associates a Merry Christmas and Happy New Year. The other item was a plain brown envelope.

Alan climbed the stairs to the apartment and took out a Zambezi beer from the fridge and sat down at the dining table. He opened the Christmas card and stood it up on the kitchen dresser. Then, he carefully opened the brown envelope and read the lines, skipping over the usual gobbledygook. His eyes settled on the bold print. He caught his breath. It read, 99.9% match. Alan took a big swig of his beer.

An hour later, with the sun setting, Alan still sat at the table with his first beer. His thoughts whirled in his head, never advancing beyond a certain point. A loud knock on the door brought Alan back to earth. He jumped up to open it. 'Avril!'

CHAPTER 70

ALAN woke to see Avril sitting at the dining table in one of his T
shirts, examining the letter in front of her. He'd left it on the table
and forgotten to put it away, distracted by Avril's unexpected arrival.
Alan slipped on a pair of rugby shorts and walked across the room and
kissed Avril on the neck. 'Merry Christmas!' Without another word, he
walked to the kitchen sink and filled the kettle with water. He switched
on the kettle and gave a satisfied grunt to find the electricity working.

'When did you guess?' said Avril.

'When were you going to tell me?'

'Never.'

'Why not?'

'I didn't want it to look like I was trying to back you into a corner.'

'When you told me Donna's age, I counted back to the night you
visited me here in the apartment. It was easy to calculate. I never believed
Don's white ancestry was responsible for her colouring.'

'Are you angry?'

'No, I knew Donna was too cute to be anyone else's.'

'So?'

'I'm her father. I'm not going anywhere.'

'So, you're staying in Zimbabwe?'

'I guess so. I'm happy here, but if ever I wanted to leave, I wouldn't go
without you and Donna.'

'That's why I didn't tell you. I didn't want you to feel trapped.'

'Well, now I know, but I don't feel trapped.'

'Are you sure it's what you want? I overheard Don tell you he'd give you tips if you joined the family, but he never got around to it, did he?'

'That true, so now, you must help me find my way through the maze of Ndlovu family matters. What did your Mum and Dad say?'

'Do you imagine I'd tell my parents I slept with one of their employees while I was still married to Don?'

* * *

Alan was nervous to approach Luke about Donna and Avril. When he considered all the things he'd done and the mischief he'd created, why on earth would he be so nervous now? He respected Luke as a person and didn't want to lose the older man's respect or friendship. Also, Alan would hate to disappoint Enid. So gracious and kind, she filled the role of his missing mother, not that he needed much mothering at his age.

It was different with his own father. Yes, he respected him, but his father's authoritarian manner invited Alan to rebel, and Alan always obliged. To a degree, this rebelliousness extended to all his father's associates. It started when Alan was a teenager, and it was a habit that proved hard to break. Perhaps the night with Ruth at the hotel in Joburg was one example of this.

Alan struggled to pluck up the courage to raise the issue with Luke, and each time Avril saw him leave Luke's home office she'd raise a questioning eyebrow at Alan. His attempts at pretending he hadn't noticed that look didn't fool her for one second. 'When are you going to talk to him, Alan? You haven't changed your mind, have you?'

'No!'

'Well then?'

'Soon, I'll talk to him soon.'

It was almost two weeks before Alan saw the opportunity for a serious discussion with Luke. Avril and Enid were working at the supermarket, and the nanny looked after Donna. Luke sat at the big desk in his home office.

'Er, Luke, can I have a word with you if you're not too busy?'

'That sounds rather formal, Alan.'

'Well, It's awkward.'

'What is, Alan? What's awkward?'

'Avril and I get on well.'

'Oh good, so you're not still worried she holds you responsible for Don's death.'

'No, but there's something else.'

'Oh?'

'I mean, we get on really well.'

'I never expected I'd ever hear myself saying this, Alan, but speak up What's the problem?'

'Not really a problem, Luke. It's just that, er, well.'

'Hang on Alan, can I pour you a Scotch?'

'Yes, that might be a good idea. And one for yourself.'

Luke rose from his chair and went to the bar fridge and took two crystal glasses and poured a tot over ice in each. He handed one to Alan and sat down at his desk. 'Sit down, Alan, you're making me nervous.'

'Yes, OK.'

'Now let's hear it, Alan. Come on, I've never seen you so nervous You're not like this when you go into battle, are you?'

'No! It's just that… I want to marry Avril.'

Luke spilt his Scotch over his leather-topped desk. He jumped up to get the tea cloth lying on top of the bar fridge and mopped up the spill After pouring himself another tot, he sat down again and stared at Alan

'And Avril has said yes?'

'Not exactly. I haven't asked her yet, but she knows I planned to talk to you.'

'To get my approval for your marriage?'

'Er, no.'

'Well, what then?'

'Luke, I'm Donna's father.'

Alan expected Luke to react. Outrage perhaps or a lecture on culture or protocol. Instead, Luke stayed calm. After a long silence, he said, 'Well, I'm not surprised. I found it hard to believe Don fathered such a light-skinned child. That, and a sudden pregnancy after almost eight years of marriage, gave me my doubts. I've noticed for a time how fond of you Avril is. Tell me, is this wish to marry based on love? Has she said she loves you? Do you love her?'

'Yes, I love her, Luke, but we've never discussed it. Nothing could drag me into a marriage with a woman I didn't love.'

'Shouldn't you two clarify that point first? Having an illegitimate child is not the basis for a good marriage.'

'OK, Luke, I'll talk to Avril. Can you please tell Enid about our discussion?'

'No, Alan, that's your job. You owe Enid an explanation.'

* * *

Avril returned with Enid in the mid-afternoon. After tea, Enid disappeared into the kitchen to organise the evening meal with the cook. Avril put Donna down for her afternoon nap, and Luke went back into his home office. When Avril returned to the lounge, Alan took her hand. 'Let's go into the garden,'

As they walked under the large shady trees, Avril became conscious of Alan's thoughtful silence. 'Have you spoken to Dad about Donna?'

'Yes, I have.'

'What did he say?'

'He wasn't surprised to hear she was not Don's child. He's held those suspicions for a long time. Your dad was calm about it.'

'Will I get a lecture?'

'No, I got the lecture.'

'Oh, sorry about that.'

'There's something else, Avril. You know I loved June, but fate removed her from the scene, and I've only had eighteen months to get over her disappearance; we all have. But coming back to Bulawayo and seeing you again and finding out about Donna seems to have sped up time. It's like events have compressed a three-year process into a year and a half.'

'What do you mean?'

'The MFF partnered June with me for the Mthwakazi business, and things developed from there. You were with Don. What I'm trying to say is, in other circumstances, it could have been you and me. June and I wasted so much of our precious time together. I won't make that same mistake with you. Now, I've found you again, I'd like us to be together.'

'Alan, you know how much I care for you. I've loved you almost from the first time we met, but I don't want you obligated just because we share a child.'

'Avril, I thought about you a lot during my time in Australia. When I received your dad's text message, the prospect of seeing you again played a big part in my decision to return.'

'But you avoided me before you left for Australia, and you haven't paid me much attention since you returned. If I didn't visit your flat the other night, we wouldn't be talking like this now.'

'Yes, that's true. I felt guilty about what happened to Don, and wouldn't have blamed you if you hated me. But I need you to know, I love you, Avril. That doesn't lessen my memory and love for June, but I do love you and want us to be together. I want to marry you.'

'Oh Alan! I never blamed you for what happened to Don. Yes, I will marry you, but you must get my father's blessing first.'

'I've already spoken to him, and he said marriage must be for the right reasons. We've just established we have the right reasons.'

*　*　*

In the evening, Enid was her usual pleasant self, talking on her favourite topic, the various dishes and how she prepared them. Luke often commented how much the meals improved after Alan turned up on the scene.

But in Alan's opinion, the meals were always delicious, and Enid basked in his praise.

'You must show me more of your cooking secrets, Mum,' said Avril.

'My dear, what's brought on this sudden interest? You and Don always had your dinners catered or cooked by the servants.'

'Well, it's time I learnt about good home cooking.'

Rita was once again at a friend's house, so there were only the four of them seated at the dinner table. Alan sensed an air of expectation in the room. Avril was aglow, and Luke gave Alan several meaningful looks while Enid chatted away about how she prepared the caramelised pears.

Luke took the opportunity presented by a brief gap in Enid's chatter to change the conversation. 'Enid, Alan wants to tell you something.'

Enid turned to Alan. 'Yes, dear, I hope you're not planning to leave us again, so soon?'

The sudden switch caught Alan off guard, but he soon recovered. He took a deep breath. 'I never want to leave, Enid. I want to stay here and marry Avril.'

If Luke's interjection was not enough to silence Enid's chatter, Alan's announcement was. Enid raised her eyebrows and sat for a few moments in silence. Alan worried she might not approve. Perhaps he should have broached the news in a more subtle manner and not something akin to jumping with big boots into the middle of a puddle. Was his big news too sudden?

But Enid's reaction was just as sudden. She squealed and jumped up from her chair and ran around the table to give Alan a kiss and a big hug. 'What wonderful news! I'm so happy for the two of you and for us as a family. Luke hates it when you're not here.'

'Alan has more news, Enid,' said Luke.

Enid looked at Alan waiting for his next utterance.

'Well,' Alan cleared his throat, 'I'm Donna's father.'

'Goodness, Alan,' said Enid, laughing, 'I've always known that.'

'You have?'

'Yes, I've never been taken in by that nonsense about poor Don being twelve-and-a-half percent white. And I can also count the months. Besides, a mother always knows. Luke laughed when I told him what suspected, but I knew I was right.'

'Yes,' said Avril, 'and we'd like a second.'

Now it was Alan's turn to be surprised. It took a moment for him to absorb Avril's words. 'Oh! Christmas Eve? I never thought...' Alan cut short his blurted response and blushed with embarrassment.

'Enough of this chatter,' said Luke, 'I've got a bottle of my best Champagne cooling in the fridge.'

Only then, Alan noticed the Champagne glasses at each place setting.

* * *

Christmas Day dawned with the usual passing clouds, but for Alan, it sparkled. It would be a fine day.

The year before, Alan moped about in Melbourne. He grieved for June, and nothing could cheer him. He remembered how he celebrated with June and her family, the most enjoyable Christmas. The prospect of Christmas lunch with his father and his associates did nothing to lift Alan's gloom.

But that was then. This year he would celebrate with his fiancé and daughter and their family. The rush of unplanned events confounded everyone, including Alan. He'd not even bought an engagement ring for Avril. The traditional Christmas dinner was like the one, two years earlier, when the family was all together. After lunch, Alan took it upon himself to toast June's memory. 'To June, forever in our hearts.' It was sad moment in an otherwise perfect day.

At four o'clock, Peter Nkala and his wife Rosie arrived. The servant gave cool drinks to the children and served Champagne to the adults including themselves. 'And now,' said Luke, 'I have exciting news for you all. I'm delighted to announce my oldest daughter Avril and my dear friend Alan Drake are engaged to be married.' The announcement ame as a huge surprise to everyone. A stunned silence turned to excited hatter and laughter as Luke led the toast. Aside from those at the dinner able on the night of Alan's revelations, the engagement was a closely uarded secret. Even Mae and Ted were gracious in congratulating Alan nd welcoming him to the family. The staid Ted amused everyone by eferring to Alan as the latest Ndlovu in the clan.

Later that evening, when everyone had left, Alan, Avril, Luke and nid sat in the lounge sipping coffee and Luke's special vintage port. Llan was finally home and part of a family, something he'd unknowingly onged for all his life.

CHAPTER 71

DECEMBER 2016
'Well Dad, it's up to you. If you can attend that would be grea'
but I can't change the wedding date just because of your crowded, ever
changing business calendar. If I tried to accommodate your meeting
and other appointments, I'd never get married.'

'Who is this girl, Alan? Is she from a good family? You haven't tol
me anything about them.'

'Yes, Dad, a good family. Her father is a well-off businessman. No
in your league, of course.'

'How did you meet? Was she a tourist?'

'Enough of the inquisition, Dad! You'll get all the answers if you com
to my wedding.'

'Is it one of the Davis-Jones girls? They're one of the few wealth
families still based in Bulawayo.'

'Patience, Dad! Surprises are fun.'

'Damn, Alan, I hope it's worth my while coming all that way for
wedding.'

'What do you mean? You visit Joburg all the time. And it's not ju
for a wedding, it's for my wedding.'

'Well, it's still damn inconvenient, but I'll do what I can. No promise
though.'

* * *

Alan waited at the airport to meet his father on the early morning flight from Johannesburg. The old bugger found a gap in his busy schedule. Curiosity got the better of him, and he'd try to assess the new in-laws or any business opportunities.

As George Drake came through customs, Alan could tell something was wrong. His father looked even grumpier than usual.

'Hi Dad, over here.'

'Damn stupid hour to catch a plane,' George grumbled. 'Getting up in the early hours to catch a flight is crazy. The scheduling is pathetic.'

'I suppose, Bulawayo isn't a high priority on Johannesburg's international flight schedules.'

'That Davis-Jones is an odd fellow. I bumped into him in the boarding lounge. When I mentioned our families might work more closely together soon, he turned on his heels and walked off to the other side of the room. Arrogant twit. Perhaps he's forgotten about the wedding.'

'Dad, he's got nothing to do with the wedding.'

'I thought you said—'

'You don't listen, Dad. I never said I was marrying one of the Davis-Jones girls. I've never even met them.'

'Who the devil are you marrying then?'

'Grandpa, Grandpa.' The little girl tugged at George Drake's trouser leg.

'Shoo, go away, little girl. Where's your Mummy and Daddy? Go find your parents.'

'Dad, meet Donna. She's mine.'

'What! This little urchin? You've adopted a coloured child?'

'Not exactly. She's all my own work, and you're her grandfather.'

'What does your fiancé say about this?'

'My fiancé is her mother.' Alan's words silenced George Drake. 'One day Dad, this little girl might run your business empire. Remember, you said the organisation needed another Drake. Look, she's got the Drake family nose. Business acumen may have passed me by, but the girls in this family have heaps.'

George was stunned. 'I have a granddaughter?'

'Two granddaughters. June's not here, she's only three months old.'

'And what the hell's happened to your face? I don't remember you having a scar on your left cheek the last time I saw you.'

'It's a long story, Dad.'

Epilogue

They were all there, in the meeting room of the boutique hotel in Soi Four, waiting for George Drake.

'Well gentlemen,' said Noel with a wink, 'welcome to another meeting of the Bulawayo Boys' Club.'

'I'm not sure we should allow an outsider from *Bamba Zonke* (Harare) into our meetings,' said Kevin. 'You're not qualified to be here, Noel.'

'I think you'll find my money qualifies me, Kevin. Since when, did Bulawayo ever turn down financial support from us Bamba Zonkes?'

Everyone laughed at the banter between Noel from Hong Kong and Kevin from London. Noel, the only one not from Bulawayo, was born in Salisbury (Harare).

After Rhodesia became Zimbabwe, most of the white citizens, and many blacks, scattered to the four ends of the earth, like dust in the wind. Bulawayo was fortunate to have kept its original African name and was one of the few centres to escape renaming after the Mugabe regime took power. As a result, the people of Bulawayo kept a close ongoing fellowship irrespective of where in the world they resettled.

Also present at the gathering were Solly Bernstein from Johannesburg, Peter Nkala from Bulawayo, Mike from New York and Barry from Cape Town. 'Where is Vince?' asked Mike.

'Vince is with George, on their way here from Kuala Lumpur,' said Solly.

'What were they doing in KL?'

'George will fill us in when they arrive.'

Mike poured everyone a Scotch, except for Peter Nkala who passed in favour of a soda water. Before Mike even took a sip of his Scotch, the door opened and George Drake entered, followed by Vince. Amid the greetings and back-slapping, Mike jumped up to pour Scotches for the new arrivals. As always, the room sprang to life with George Drake's arrival. There was no disputing his popularity and leadership of the group.

'We were just discussing if Noel should be a member of the Bulawayo Boys' Club as he has christened it,' said Barry.

'He's paid his ten-million-dollar entrance fee,' said George.

'That's what I said,' said Noel.

'Is that enough?' said Kevin. 'He's from Bamba Zonke.' Everyone chuckled. 'And what about you, Peter? When are you going to cough up your ten million?'

'A Matabele leader has automatic admission,' Peter replied. 'We qualify for membership by coughing up the manpower.' More laughter.

'OK, guys. Down to business. We can have fun later,' said Solly. 'What's the latest, George?'

'Well, the situation is most promising. The bad news is, we had to suspend the project in its original format as we seem to have inadvertently disturbed a beehive and got into an undeclared war with a poaching syndicate.

'The good news is the project is continuing under the guise of a scouting or outward-bound movement which we can soon militarise if needed. My son, Alan, has based himself in Zimbabwe and stands by ready to help when we need him.

'The achievements of phase one is we have twelve first class Ndebele trainers to lead the recruits. We disrupted the poaching syndicates operations in the Hwange National Park from both the supply and buying sides. In addition, we took out the second in command of the poaching syndicate, and we have the name and location of the leader. The second in command was the person responsible for Andrew Dube and his son Tyson's abduction. In due course we will also take out the leader of the syndicate.'

'This is exciting news,' said Kevin. 'We didn't realise we were making uch good progress.'

'Well, there's more. Vince has his base in Zurich, which gives him the pportunity to make some interesting contacts. One of those contacts ut us in touch with the Russians. As we all know, the Mugabe regime as close ties with China, but Russia is also interested in this part of he world. Vince and I were in Kuala Lumpur meeting two high level Russians to gauge their interest in Mthwakazi.'

'Hell! What was their reaction?' said Barry.

'Well, they were non-committal but interested. They were well in-ormed about our natural resources, including coal, gold and tungsten nd were interested in exploring for other minerals. They also expressed n interest in oil and gas exploration.'

'What's in it for Mthwakazi?' said Mike.

'No promises, but there's the possibility of arms and other military upport and technical help with maintenance and training. You remem-er, in the Rhodesian Bush War the Russians supported ZIPRA which as Ndebele based. Mthwakazi comes out of the same tribal group. It as always irked the Russians they backed the wrong horse in Zimbabwe. hey didn't understand tribalism. It was inevitable the larger tribe would in the post-colonial elections. More surprising though is the Ndebele aders didn't recognise that sooner.'

'Bloody hell!' said Mike.

'The other news is,' said George, 'Noel is in low level talks with Com-unist Party officials in China. It's too early to comment on this devel-pment, but if Mugabe antagonises the Chinese and the Russians don't me through, it might be another avenue for investigation down the ne.'

'Jeez, George!' said Kevin. 'You don't mess around, do you?'

'Remember the words of the famous American architect, Daniel urnham, "Make no little plans; they have no magic to stir men's blood ."'

'It could lead to all-out war,' said Barry. If the last time we inadver tently disturbed a beehive, this time we might knock down a hornets nest.

'Other Mthwakazi groups are trying to follow a peaceful route of ne gotiation and diplomacy. If that works, we will support it. No one want war and suffering. The blacks in Zimbabwe didn't win control of th country through negotiation and diplomacy. Their guerrilla war didn' win them control either, but it won them world opinion, and that's wha took them to power. What makes you think it will be any different fo Mthwakazi? Thanks to the Mugabe regime, many countries view Zim babwe as a pariah state. We need to use that to our advantage.'

'What if the Russians or Chinese report back to the Mugabe regim about your discussions?' said Kevin.

'We've made no mention of the MFF, and we spoke hypotheticall They wouldn't have any idea who we represented. Vince took the lead and I didn't use my real name.'

Everyone in the room could see the rationale of George's argumen The assembled group supported the motion to continue using low-ke methods to build an effective defence force for Mthwakazi.

'Who knows,' said George, 'if a democratically elected, non-trib government replaces the Mugabe regime, Mthwakazi might even op to stay a part of a United States of Zimbabwe. Now, I believe one c two of you have been thinking about putting your ten million dollars t better use elsewhere. I understand your reasoning on this issue, and pro vided you keep the money in an available liquid form, there's no problei with you taking your money out of our Mthwakazi account. The mai thing is to make sure, if we need your money urgently, you can compl If anyone wants to withdraw their money on that basis, let me know.'

'I'm happy to leave my money in the fund,' said Barry.

'Me too,' said Vince.

'And me,' said Solly, Mike, Kevin and Noel.

No one wanted their money out of the fund. Once again, Georg Drake controlled the decision's and direction of the Bulawayo Boy's Clul

With no dissenters, and no one wanting to be excluded from a George Drake venture, the meeting reached a natural conclusion.

'Have you boys looked around Chiang Mai?' said George. 'The last time we were here we all left in a hurry, following the no-show of poor old Andrew Dube and Tyson. You should stay a few days and see the sights. It's a lovely little city.'

With the formalities over, Mike poured another round of Scotch for everyone, and this time included Peter Nkala, who accepted the drink with a little trepidation.

After everyone returned to their rooms to freshen up for the evening dinner, George and Solly sat chatting, nursing their last pre-dinner Scotch.

'How is Alan doing?' Solly enquired. 'Has that boy of yours finally settled down, or is he still running wild?'

George didn't answer, instead raising his eyebrows, looking at Solly over the rim of his glass of Scotch.

GLOSSARY

L IST of frequently used words and terms, and people and organisa tions relevant to Zimbabwe.

Abel Muzorewa *Prime Minister of Zimbabwe Rhodesia: 1st June – 11 December 1979*
    Bakkie *Ute or pick-up*
    Baas *African pronunciation of Boss*
    Braai or Braaivleis *Barbecue*
    Chibuku *African beer brewed from sorghum, maize or millet. Due to i heavy sediment content it is also known as shake-shake*
    CIO *Central Intelligence Organisation*
    COU *Covert Operations Unit*
    GFC *Global Financial Crisis*
    Generation 40 *The political group of younger politicians known as Gener ation 40 that support Grace Mugabe to succeed her husband, Robert Mugab*
    Gukurahundi *Shona word meaning 'the early rain which washes awe the chaff before the spring rains'*
    Ian Smith *Prime Minister of Rhodesia: 13th April 1964 – 1st June 197 Leader of Opposition in Zimbabwe: 18th April 1980 – May 1987*
    Jambanja *Shona word for state-sponsored lawlessness – white farm invc sions*
    Joshua Nkomo Founder and *leader of ZAPU and Vice President of Zin babwe: 1987-1999*
    Knobkerrie *African carved wooden club with a knob at the end*
    Kraal *Small African village or cluster of huts*

Lacoste *A political group supporting Emmerson Mnangagwa to replace Robert Mugabe. The Lacoste logo relates to Mnangagwa's nickname, The Crocodile*

Lobola *Bride price, traditionally paid in cattle to the bride's family*

Madala *Zulu word for old man*

Marula *Tree bearing fruit similar to lychees*

Mealies *Maize plants or corn on the cob*

MDC *Movement for Democratic Change*

Morgan Tsvangirai *Leader of the MDC opposition in Zimbabwe*

Mthwakazi *Area including Matabeleland and eastern edge of Midlands, ruled by King Lobengula before white settlement*

Murambatsvina *Shona word meaning 'drive out the rubbish'*

Murungu *Shona word meaning white person of European origin, or urban-youth slang for blacks with money or power*

Panga *Machete approximately forty to forty-five centimetres long*

Robert Mugabe *Prime Minister of Zimbabwe from 4th March 1980, and President from 22nd December 1987*

Rondavel *Round African pole and dagga hut with a thatched roof*

UDI *Unilateral Declaration of Independence*

Varungu *Plural of Murungu*

Veldskoens *Suede bush shoes; usually grey or brown*

ZANLA *Zimbabwe African National Liberation Army – ZANU's military wing*

ZANU *Zimbabwe African National Union*

ZANU-PF *Zimbabwe African National Union - Patriotic Front –the merger of ZANU and ZAPU in December 1987*

ZAPU *Zimbabwe African People's Union*

ZIPRA *Zimbabwe People's Revolutionary Army – ZAPU's military wing*

MAP OF ZIMBABWE

S HOWING towns, roads, railway lines and national parks.

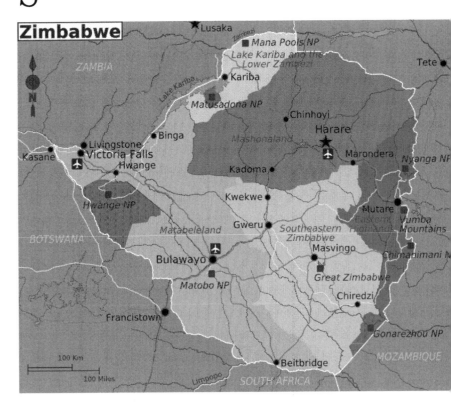

he precise area of Mthwakazi is disputed. At a minimum, it includes Matabeleland (shaded in light green), the Hwange National Park south f Hwange, and the part of the Midlands that runs along the eastern dge of the orange shaded area described as South-eastern Zimbabwe.)ther maps show a larger Mthwakazi, incorporating most of the orange naded area and the Gonarezhou National Park.

Author's Note

The story is set in the period from mid-2013 to late 2016.

The Covert Operations Unit (COU) is a fictitious organisation but it sits comfortably with the factual Central Intelligence Organisation (CIO) and other shadowy branches of the security services. Similarly The Matabeleland Freedom Front (MFF) is fictitious, but groups with similar goals exist.

The borders of Mthwakazi are not clearly demarcated, and almost every map shows differences ranging from subtle to substantial. Broadly the constituent parts of Mthwakazi are Matabeleland North, Matabeleland South, Bulawayo, and the eastern edge of the Midlands.

ZANU-PF has since independence in 1980 tried to impose a single Shona identity in Zimbabwe, even as far as naming streets in Bulawayo after Shona figures.

Support for Mthwakazi grew following the Gukurahundi when an estimated twenty thousand Ndebele civilians were murdered by the North Korean trained, Shona 5th Brigade between 1983 and 1987.

L.T. Kay
Find out more at my website https://ltkay.com

ABOUT THE AUTHOR

Bulawayo was my home town. That's where I grew up and got my first job. Anyone who has lived in Africa, even for a short time, will confirm you can never really leave it. No matter how far you travel, like the grass seeds that stick to your socks, Africa goes with you.

I lived and worked in Zimbabwe/Rhodesia and South Africa for over thirty years, alternating between Bulawayo, Salisbury (Harare) and Jo hannesburg.

The Bush War got serious while I was living in Hong Kong, and o my return to Rhodesia, I was called up for military service in the army.

Professional qualifications in accounting and marketing helped me se cure senior management positions with companies in diverse fields, in cluding engineering, textiles, clothing and cosmetics manufacture, an service industries.

Today, I live in Melbourne with my wife Maggie and write fiction se in Southern Africa, principally Zimbabwe. Since the turn of the centur that country has led a dark, surreal existence that keeps many peopl shaking their heads in disbelief. It would be funny if it wasn't so sad.

L. T. Kay

Find out more at my website https://ltkay.com

OTHER BOOKS BY THE AUTHOR

THE Leopard Series is a trilogy of novels set in the troubled years of Robert Mugabe's dictatorship in Zimbabwe. The first two books in the series are published and the third is a work in progress. *The Bulawayo Boys' Club* is book 2 in the series.

Feeding the Leopard - Book 1 in The Leopard Series

It is 2008, and the global financial crisis sees Ian Sanders out of a job in Melbourne. He flies to Africa, the land of his birth, to follow his dream to write a novel set in the wilds of Zimbabwe.

In his twenty-year absence, much has changed. The country is in turmoil. A new power-sharing government is imminent, but the political situation remains volatile. People fear the police, and violent crime goes unpunished. Supermarket shelves are empty, and essential goods are scarce. Cholera rages and the Zimbabwean dollar is in free fall.

Ian plans to focus on his novel and stay out of trouble, but slowly he is drawn into a web of conspiracy and fear that pervades the lives of so many of the country's people. He is in peril, but who should he most fear: the police, the secretive COU, the wildlife or the enigmatic Sarah?

He and those around him find their values, beliefs and prejudices challenged in their fight for survival. Nearly thirty years after independence, many Zimbabweans still wait for their promised freedom.

L. T. Kay

Find out more at my website https://ltkay.com

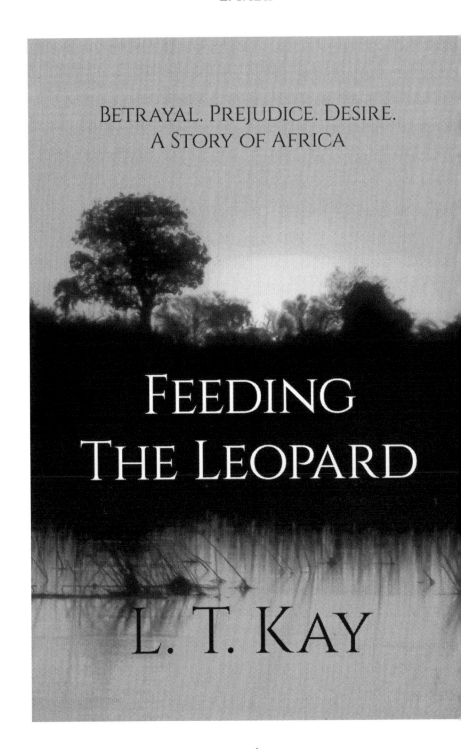

BETRAYAL. PREJUDICE. DESIRE.
A STORY OF AFRICA

FEEDING
THE LEOPARD

L. T. KAY

Printed in Great Britain
by Amazon